COUNTER CULTURE

JL MERROW

*To the original Archie, faithful familiar and
most excellent of octopodes.*

Steampunk is an eclectic world of cogs and rivets. It is airships, goggles, and steam. It is romance. It is traveling on clouds and diving beneath rugged waves. — Aether Emporium

Steampunk is what happens when Goths discover brown.
— Unknown.

TABLE OF
CONTENTS

CHAPTER

I t had been a bright, sunny autumn day, the perfect weather for a walk in the park to admire the rich colours of the trees and crunch through fallen leaves. At least, Robin assumed it had been. All he'd seen of it were tantalising glimpses through the store windows, and the cheery smiles and reddened noses of scarf-muffled shoppers coming in from the cold. A new staff hire hadn't turned up today, meaning he'd had to work through lunch. To add insult to injury, as it was a Thursday and therefore late-night shopping evening at Willoughbys Department Store, he hadn't been able to clock off until after nine.

Even Sheppy's Mum, who kipped down with her dog in a doorway near to Willoughbys and probably wouldn't know *well rested* if it jumped up in front of her and did a hula dance on the pavement, had told him he looked tired when he stopped to say good night in passing.

The sun was just a distant memory by the time Robin made his weary way home from the bus stop, and the only fallen leaves on his street were mixed with discarded crisp packets and no doubt hid the sort of litter you really wouldn't want to be crunching through. Or, as it might be, squelching.

A few deflated Halloween pumpkins stood sentry at doorways, but others, it appeared, had already gone to their ultimate destiny: makeshift footballs for groups of lads or ladettes. One or two buildings still showed signs of having been egged, which was a terrible waste of food in Robin's current opinion.

If he hadn't moved out of his parents' house, an inner voice that sounded a lot like Mum insisted on pointing out, Robin would have had a much nicer street to walk down. And he'd have been home by now, tucking into a plate of cottage pie or ham and eggs, rather than racking his tired brain to think of something appetising he could whip up before he fell asleep from exhaustion. Available ingredients, from memory: a shrivelled, sprouty onion, a packet of instant noodles and the bottle of gravy browning Mum had shoved into his hands when he'd moved into the new flat.

There was always the chippie. But it was two streets out of his way, which might as well have been two continents. And the woman who worked there scared him, with her partly shaven hair, weirdly retro vibes, and belligerent manner, like the fifties pinup love child of Tank Girl and Rosie the Riveter.

Halfway home, Robin faltered mid-trudge and stopped to stare at the strange scene by the side of the road, illuminated by a flickering streetlamp.

There was a pair of legs sticking out from behind a fridge.

Robin felt very strongly that fridges didn't belong at the side of the road in a well-ordered world. Oh, he was willing to concede that sometimes they had to occupy that position for a night or so while waiting for the council to pick them up and take them to their final resting place or, as was more likely these days, nightmare dystopian recycling plant. But what he *wasn't* prepared to accept was any situation in which they should require human occupancy.

Maybe the man was homeless? From what he could see—battered combat boots, and a pair of tweedy trousers that might have belonged to someone's not-overly-particular great-grandad—that could very well be the case. Robin reminded himself he was all for having consideration for the less fortunate members of society. And anyone who couldn't find anything more comfortable to snuggle up to than chucked-out old white goods probably needed all the consideration they could get.

Should he suggest a local hostel? Point out that it was a reasonably clement night for the time of year and that the local park was only a hop, skip, and a jump away, at least for those unencumbered by obsolete kitchen appliances?

Just as he was thinking that it was probably best to leave well alone, there came a triumphant cry of "Got you, you rascal!" and the rest of the man emerged with a grin. He was tall, about Robin's height or maybe a smidge over, and his broad shoulders were nicely showcased by a rather dapper-looking waistcoat over a striped, grandad-collar shirt. There was an actual pocket watch chain draped casually across the waistcoat front.

Robin blinked. "Did I somehow stumble into an episode of *Doctor Who*? Because I've always wanted to travel in time, but a bit of advance warning might have been nice." He darted a mildly panicked glance at the houses beside them, and had never been so glad to see a satellite dish in his life.

"Ah . . . No? I'm pretty sure this is the twenty-first century. I think more would have changed if it wasn't. We'd probably have noticed." The grin had faded and its owner now wore an expression of concern. He had a neatly trimmed beard, and a moustache with curly, waxed ends, like a Victorian dandy or cartoon villain. Robin was suddenly thankful that the nearest railway track was miles away. Tattoos bordered the man's neck, spelling out some word or phrase that was partially hidden by his shirt.

He was strange. And hot. And did Robin mention *strange*?

Robin tried desperately not to stare. Or to think about the fact that he'd been babbling on about time travel to a perfect stranger. "Fine. Sorry. I just— Sorry." As he turned to go, oddly mortified, something the man was holding glinted rose gold in the lamplight, like one of those Ted Baker water bottles Robin had his eye on in the sports department. Words burst out without him consciously willing it. "What the hell is that?"

The wicked grin returned as the man held up a thick, loose coil of copper wire with strange, silvery bits on the ends. His strong forearms were bared by rolled-up sleeves. Why wasn't he shivering? Maybe his planet had a colder climate . . .

"That, I'd say, is an aetheric field generator." There was a strangely compelling gleam in his eye. "Or possibly a miasma detector. Haven't decided yet. What do you reckon?"

Robin wasn't at all sure what he reckoned. Apart from that the whole *Doctor Who* thing was looking increasingly likely. "Uh . . . do they often put those in fridges?"

"Pretty much all the time, yeah. I mean, they *call* them thermocouples, but you and I know better, don't we?" The (tall, fit, and possibly villainous) man tapped his nose significantly, and the ends of his moustache quivered.

Robin might have quivered too. He hoped the strange (and hot, and delusional) man/alien hadn't noticed. Very slowly, he raised a hand, and tapped his own nose in reply as if exchanging a secret Masonic sign. Oh God. Perhaps that was it, and he'd just claimed membership in some bizarre organisation that partook in ritual fridge disembowelment.

Dark eyes widened. "Right, got to run. Left the horseless carriage on a double yellow. Rest of her's all yours. See you around!" And with that, Robin was alone. Staring at a violated fridge. Having apparently been invited to make himself likewise free of its innards.

He averted his eyes, shook himself, and walked briskly home.

CHAPTER 2

T he next day did not begin well. Robin slept through his alarm and struggled out of bed groggily, his head fogged with vague yet enticing dreams of mad men in boxes.

By dint of missing breakfast and sprinting to the bus stop, he managed to just catch his bus. Only to realise five minutes into the route that it was the *wrong* bus, which had lulled him into a false sense of security by heading towards the town centre before veering off in the direction of villages unknown.

Miraculously, he made it into work only twenty minutes late. Unfortunately, as Robin slunk into the menswear department, trying to blend in with the Ben Sherman shirts and Timberland jackets, his manager, Gail, caught his eye from over by Gifts and Accessories. Fixing him with a stern glare, she marched over to him, heels *click-clack*ing on the tiled floor, and folded her arms. "Well?"

The expression on her thin, perpetually frowning face said (a) his excuse for his tardiness had better be good and (b) she wouldn't believe it anyway.

Robin did *not* cringe. "Sorry. I'll set two alarms tomorrow."

"This isn't good enough, Robin. You're supposed to be setting an example to the junior staff. And I'm sure you're well aware this is the most important time of the year for Willoughbys."

She said that all year round, but Robin was guiltily aware it was actually true this time. "Sorry," he said again.

"Now, don't just stand there. Get to work. I've got more important things to do than cover for staff who can't be bothered to get up in the morning."

She *click-clack*ed away. Robin glared at her suit-clad back, stuck up a surreptitious but heartfelt middle finger in her direction, then scurried behind the counter to become a picture of professionalism and customer service.

An elderly lady doddered up to the sales point. "I'll take these handkerchiefs," she said in the overly loud voice of the hard of hearing. "And a bag, although it still seems a nonsense that we have to pay for them. Back in my day, it was all part of the service."

Robin rang up the sale and bagged the hankies. "I'm afraid it's a legal requirement, madam. But it all goes towards the environment."

"Not that I'll live to see the benefit," she complained loud enough that they probably heard her upstairs in Furnishings. "Still, I suppose it was worth an extra 5p to see you making rude gestures at that hoity-toity young madam of a manager."

As the old lady shuffled away, Robin cast a mortified glance around, hoping against hope no other customers had been in earshot.

And looked straight into Gail's furious eyes.

Robin offered her a weak, apologetic smile that fizzled and died in the burn of her glare, and scuttled off to rearrange the socks.

At lunchtime, he had his best friend, Azrah, crying on his shoulder about her latest breakup.

Since it was Azrah, there wasn't any *actual* crying involved. More along the lines of cursing and swearing eternal vengeance. But still, it wasn't the most relaxing of mealtimes.

They'd gone to their favourite café in the town centre, the one near the church. The in-store café wasn't the place for emotional conversations. Walls had ears. So did the accounts department, who tended to eat en masse around now. Generous to a fault with any and all gossip that came their way, they weren't just hooked in to the workplace grapevine, they *were* the workplace grapevine.

Robin had known Azrah since they were at primary school together. They'd been friends ever since he'd naively asked her one playtime why Jayden Simpson had called her a Paki and she *hadn't* stabbed him with her newly sharpened colouring pencil (Jayden Simpson hadn't been so lucky). They'd spent the next seven years with Robin's mum persistently referring to Azrah as "your little girlfriend" despite their increasingly loud denials, until he'd come out at age fourteen mostly to get her to stop.

It'd worked only too well—Mum had barely spoken to him at all for the next week and a half. Not only that, but she'd seemed on the verge of tears every time she even looked at him. Still, a decade on, she seemed to have mostly come to terms with it.

Mostly.

One of the reasons—all right, the main reason—Robin had moved out of his parents' house was so he could bring a boyfriend home once in a while. Mum had never gone so far as to *say* she didn't like him bringing men home . . . but then, she didn't have to, not with the whole awkward-politeness-and-unhappy-looks thing she'd had going on every time he'd tried.

They picked up their lunch from the counter and headed for their usual table at the back of the café. After a full morning on the shop floor at the beck and call of customers, neither of them fancied being on display in the front window like a couple of off-duty mannequins.

"So what happened?" Robin prompted Azrah when she only stared moodily into her cappuccino.

She flicked her long black hair angrily away from her face. "That bastard. He actually had the nerve to give me the whole 'It's not you, it's me' bollocks."

Robin snorted into his tuna salad. "And you're complaining? I'd kill for an 'It's not you, it's me' breakup. All I get is 'We haven't got enough in common' or worse, 'I thought you were more interesting when I met you.'" He shuddered at the still-painful memory.

"Be fair. It was only Ethan who called you boring." Azrah took a savage bite out of her chicken and pesto baguette. "And he was a tosser," she added with her mouth full.

"You think all of my exes are tossers."

Azrah swallowed. "And what does that tell you?"

"You have impossible standards?"

"Think again, white boy. Think again. Come on, Ethan's idea of *interesting* was someone who preferred clubbing to conversation, knew where to get him the good drugs, and didn't mind watching him get off with other blokes."

Robin sighed. "Yeah, but he was hot." Warmth tingled through him for a moment, turning to a shiver when he ruthlessly replaced the memory of Ethan-in-bed with one of Ethan-being-disparaging.

Azrah huffed. "Now you sound as shallow as him."

"I don't know." Robin's shoulders slumped, and he chased a bit of cucumber around his plate half-heartedly. "Maybe I am shallow? I mean, really, what is there to me?"

Azrah put down her baguette and studied him, her head on one side.

For a long time. Robin began to wish he hadn't asked. "Is it honestly that hard a question?"

"Uh . . . You're not bad looking, in a sort of twinkish way."

"I am not a twink! Twinks are . . . blonder. And musclier. And brainlesser."

"That's twinkist, that is. *And* I'm almost certain only one of those is actually a word."

"They might be words. Or potential words. Shakespeare made stuff up all the time. I was asking about deeper things, anyway. My inner qualities."

"If they're inner, how am I supposed to know about them?" She grinned. "Face it, it's not like I'm ever getting inside you, is it?"

"Ew."

"Yeah, well, likewise, I'm sure." She took another bite of her baguette in what Robin felt was an unnecessarily pointed fashion. "You're not boring, okay? You're funny—when you're not moping, at any rate—and you're shit-hot on fashion. Like, to a fault, actually, Mr. I-can't-go-out-in-a-belt-that-doesn't-go-with-my-shoes."

"No, the issue was that it *did* go, too well. You can't go around being all matchy-matchy. It shows a lack of imagination. I'd have looked like I'd been interior designed. And hang on, aren't you supposed to be building me up here?"

"Uh . . ." Azrah's pause once again went on quite a bit longer than was flattering. "Um, you're really focussed on your career?"

"Thank you so much. When it comes to dating prospects, that's just a sub-heading under *boring*." And it wasn't even true, not exactly. It was more that he didn't want to spend his entire working life being told what to do, and you had to get ahead to, well, get ahead.

Azrah sat up straight and all but bounced in her chair. "Ooh, I know one. A good one. You play three musical instruments. *That's* not boring."

"My mum says ukulele doesn't count." She was a bit on the fence about the guitar too, to be honest.

"Your mum says a lot of things." Azrah's tone was dark.

"Has she been hassling you about Islam again?" The pep talk having contained a lot less pep than Robin had hoped for—in fact, it'd pretty much been a pep-zero talk—he was keen to change the subject. And Mum never seemed to get that although Azrah's family were nominally Muslim, it didn't mean they were the world authorities on Sharia law or even went to the mosque, like, *ever*. Which was ironic, considering Mum would proudly announce herself to be Church of England despite not having set foot in a church for as long as Robin had been alive, leaving aside the traditional ceremonies to mark hatching, matching, and dispatching.

"Yeah. She came in for a new nonstick saucepan"—Azrah worked in the kitchenware department—"and to secretly check you're not dead yet from living on your own for two weeks already, and she was going on at me about the rights of women and dress codes and all that. I mean, look at me. I wear Western clothes all the time, and have you ever seen me in a hijab? Seriously, the last time I wore a headscarf was when I was a shepherd in the primary school nativity play." She snorted. "My dad had a right go at the school for that, I can tell you."

"Religious insensitivity?"

"Nah, he's just really anti people's beliefs being shoved in kids' faces. Anyway, I keep telling your mum, I'm not the person she should be asking about that stuff. But you know her. It's like she listens, but she doesn't *hear* you, right?"

"Yeah. Sorry."

"Why? She produced you, not the other way around. Mind you, she did say one other thing. Something about ungrateful sons who never visit, and how she was sure that never happened in Muslim families. Hey, do you think she's planning to convert?"

"Maybe we should warn the local imam. Got his number?"

"I know one digit of it." Azrah held up her middle finger and Robin grinned.

"Anyway," she went on, "why are we even talking about your mum? We're supposed to be talking about *me*."

Robin put down his fork and leaned towards her with an earnest expression on his face. "Go on, I'm listening."

"Fuck you." She shook her head. "Oh, what is there to say? It's always the same bloody thing, isn't it? Men. They're all the same. Present company excepted, obvs."

"Is that supposed to be a compliment? Anyway, you're wrong there. I met a bloke last night who was definitely different."

Azrah's eyes lit up. "Tell me more."

Robin gazed at the wall, lost in memory. "He was a bit like one of the old Doctor Whos. You know, the blokes."

"Yeah, which one, though? Christopher Eccleston or David Tennant? Either one of them would do for me, but I'm not sold on the rest of them."

"It wasn't like that. I mean, he didn't look like one of the actors. He just dressed a bit eccentrically and spouted strange science-y stuff at me. And then he ran off."

"So did you follow him? Ooh, is this going to turn into an alien-abduction story?" Azrah cackled. "Did he get out his probes?"

Robin couldn't help picturing the thick copper wire with silver . . . things on the ends the strange man had been so excited about. "Well, he *said* it was a thermocouple."

Her eyes widened to roughly the size of Robin's plate. "Do I even want to hear the rest of this story? And in case you're wondering, the answer is yes, yes, I do."

"Nothing happened! But he was definitely different."

"So are you seeing him again?"

"It wasn't that kind of meeting." Robin slumped. "I suppose I might bump into him again. If he's local."

"Local to Hitchworth, or local to that council estate no-go area where you live?" Azrah glanced around as if hoping a hot Doctor might saunter past at any moment.

Robin glared at her. "It's still Hitchworth, you know. There's some quite nice streets nearby. And there's nothing wrong with council estates."

"Or no-go areas?"

"Shut up. You're just a snob. Anyway, I met him on my street, but he might only have been there for the fridge."

"The . . . Tell you what, don't explain it. Leave it part of Mystery Bloke's essential mysteriosity."

"You mean 'mystique'?"

"You know, I always wondered why you spent three years at uni. It was so you could flounce around being all superior and correcting people's grammar, wasn't it?"

"Uh, I think you mean vocabulary."

"I think I mean *fuck you*. So what did he look like, your mystery man?"

Robin couldn't have held back the eye roll if his life had depended on it. "I thought you wanted to keep him mysterious? Fine. Tall, dark, and fit."

"Marathon runner fit or"—her voice went all low and husky—"hundred meters?"

"Sort of somewhere in between."

"Okay, that works. Dark skin or dark hair?"

"Hair. And, uh, beard." Robin shied away from mentioning the curly moustache. He had an instinct she might not treat it with the dignity it deserved.

"Hmm . . . beards can *look* good, but if I wanted to floss my teeth it's not his face I'd be kissing."

"Do you talk like that in front of your mum and dad?"

"Hah. What do you think? Just cos they're not into religion doesn't mean they're *totally* untraditional." She rolled her eyes. "They're not as bad as your mum and dad, mind. *Your* mum still thinks good girls should cover up like nuns and save themselves for marriage. Last time I bumped into her on date night she was going on at me how I ought to be careful about how I dress, in case the bloke thinks I'm up for a shag."

"She did not say 'up for a shag.'" Robin might not have been there, but he knew his mum.

"Well, she might have used the words, 'Offering something you're not ready to give.' But she definitely meant shagging."

"She's never said anything like that to me."

"Yeah, but that's cos you dress with taste and style. Not to look slutty." She shrugged. "What? Sometimes a girl just wants to let her inner slut out to play. You should try it sometime."

Robin sighed. "That's pretty much what Ethan used to say."

CHAPTER 3

After his shift ended, when he ought to have been heading home, free at long, long last to do stuff *he* wanted to—like, say, hang around the streets in case a certain moustachioed alien fridge-fiddler turned up—Robin had to stay behind for a staff meeting.

Everyone crowded into Gail's little office. There was only one chair for visitors, which by longstanding agreement belonged to Mary-from-Haberdashery on account of her varicose veins, so the rest of them had to stand around after being on their feet all day. Gail, of course, sat behind her desk like a queen receiving her courtiers.

"Now, as you know, we're holding a Black Friday sale this year to compete with online retailers. Profits this quarter . . ."

With the best will in the world, Robin couldn't stop his tired brain from zoning out as she recited a list of numbers in excruciating detail. He started to nod off on his feet, waking up with a jerk when Gail slapped a file down on her desk.

"Any questions?"

Azrah raised her hand. "Yeah, I got one. Why are we even having a Black Friday sale? It's an American thing—nothing to do with us."

Gail gave her a look like she'd just announced that she had ideological objections to selling stuff. "*Coca-Cola* is an American thing, Azrah, but you didn't seem to have any problem with keeping a can behind the counter in blatant violation of store policy. Don't think I didn't see you drinking from it when you were supposed to be working."

Oops. Robin would have let the ground swallow him up at that point, but it was illicit fizzy drinks off a duck's back for Azrah. "Yeah, but it's all to do with Thanksgiving over there. It's a public holiday, innit? Day one, enforced turkey dinner with the family. Like Christmas, but with no presents to open. Day two, they get let out to go shopping. Like Boxing Day, but with no presents to take back to the shops and change for what you really wanted. Here, it's just another day in November."

Gail's expression became, if anything, even more sour. "And how are we supposed to compete with online retailers if we don't discount our goods like they do?"

"That's like arguments for foot-binding, that is."

Every pair of eyes in the room turned to stare at Azrah from beneath identical baffled frowns.

She tutted. "They said, like, men won't want to marry a girl if her feet are bigger than other girls'. So everyone bound their feet and then they were back in the same position they were before. Only in pain and crippled."

The frowns deepened.

"I fail to see what this has to do with the retail industry." Gail's voice could have been used to build a snowman.

"If everyone discounts, everyone *has* to discount. If nobody discounted, though, then we could all sell at full price up until Christmas, and have our sales after that like God intended."

Robin, who unlike Azrah had been sent to Sunday School as a lad and therefore didn't *totally* reject the possibility of there being a God, wasn't sure this was what He originally had in mind for the celebration of the Saviour's birth.

Heath, the tall gangly redhead who worked in the electronics department and occasionally tagged along on trips to the pub, cackled. "And lo, an angel of the Lord appeared and said, 'Rejoice, for I bring glad tidings of great joy. Unto us a Sale is given.'"

"Thank you, Heath," Gail snapped.

"'The heavenly deals ye there shall find—'"

"*Thank* you."

Heath's voice dropped to a low mutter. In a room that size, he might as well have been shouting. "'Lying in a bargain bin—'"

"*Heath*!" Gail looked dangerously close to rupturing something. Possibly something Heath would find extremely painful.

There was an ominous silence. Gail let it settle for a moment before carrying on severely. "We all need to pull together on this. The Black Friday sale is an important boost to our turnover this quarter, and a kick-starter for Christmas shoppers. We can't afford to miss any opportunity to persuade shoppers to shut down their computers and come out to shop in a real store. I don't like to mention the word 'redundancies' in the run-up to Christmas, but . . ."

But she had. Robin's mood slumped, along with the shoulders of a number of his colleagues. Most of them were probably already calculating which of them was last in and therefore potentially first out. Robin had been working for the store practically since uni, so he ought to be okay—unless Gail was really peed off about the rude gesture this morning? He swallowed and crossed the offending finger over its neighbour. Anyway, what about Azrah? She was a lot newer. She'd been working in one of the local discount stores until that closed down, and Robin had put in a good word for her at Willoughbys. And Gail didn't like her much.

"Black Friday needs to be An Event this year." You could almost smell the capitalisation as Gail went on. "Hitchworth's Biggest Christmas Shopping Event. We don't want people idling in to see what we've got on offer."

"We don't?" Robin blurted. Wasn't that what it was all about?

"No! We want US-style scenes of people sleeping on the street so they don't lose their place in the queue. We want people booking time off work specifically to come to our Event from miles around. We want—"

"Fisticuffs in the furniture department, and wholesale riots in Haberdashery?" Heath had the gleam of the fanatic in his eye.

"Well, I hope not!" Mary-from-Haberdashery shifted in her chair, which squeaked in protest. "It's bad enough when we sell out of black embroidery thread. I blame people panic-buying and stockpiling the stuff."

"The situation could get ugly," Heath went on with enthusiasm while Robin was still trying to get his head around the idea of panic-buying needlecraft supplies. "I can see the headlines now: 'Shopper stabbed with knitting needle in dispute over discount yarn'; 'Bargain hunter bludgeoned with bolt of broderie anglaise'—"

"*Heath*!" Gail practically had smoke coming out of her nostrils. She cleared her throat. "I expect all of you to come up with initiatives to make this happen. We may be a small, independent department store, but we need to show Hitchworth—and the whole of Hertfordshire, for that matter—that we can punch well above our weight. Robin?"

Robin started, having only been half listening. "Yes?"

"I'm expecting great things from you."

She was? Why?

"As our only university-educated member of staff—"

"Hey, I did physics at Brighton," Heath interrupted.

Azrah snorted. "Yeah, for like two weeks."

"They were a very intensive two weeks. I learned a lot."

"Yeah, like where the bar was, and who sold the best weed."

Gail banged on her desk, probably because it was in easier reach than either Heath's or Azrah's head. "*As I was saying*, as our only *graduate* member of staff, I'm sure Robin will be keen to be involved in the planning process for our Event."

Everyone looked at Robin. He had an uneasy feeling he was blushing as red as his namesake. "Er, you do know my degree's in music, right?"

"Music and mathematics are supposed to be very close, but I can't say I've ever seen it," put in Mary-from-Haberdashery.

There was a moment's silence. Then Gail spoke up again briskly. "It doesn't matter what your degree's *in*, Robin. It's more that you've learned to think. I'm expecting you to come up with publicity initiatives that are relatable both to our core customer base, and more importantly, to those who don't currently shop here. Perhaps with a touch of humour—after all, you seemed to be using that to *extremely* good effect with your customers this morning."

Oops. Robin had been hoping she'd forgotten about the rude-gestures incident, seeing as she hadn't hauled him over the coals about it already. Apparently she'd been saving it up to guilt him into other stuff.

"Er, yeah. I'll get right on it."

She gave a tight smile. "Good. You should be asking yourself: How do we attract new customers to the store?"

"Free drinks!"

"*Thank* you, Heath."

"No, seriously. Mulled wine and mince pies. Everyone loves that stuff when they're Christmas shopping. Waitrose did it last year and I stopped going to Tesco altogether while it lasted."

Everyone goggled at Heath, probably as surprised as Robin was to hear what wasn't actually a bad idea coming from his lips. But then again . . . "No," Robin found himself saying. He frowned at his shoes. "I mean, yes, it's a nice idea, but can you imagine it in a Black Friday sale situation? If we get a crowd of new customers in, the kitchens would be overwhelmed. And there'd be crumbs and spilled wine all over the stock. That sort of thing's better for, say, a special Christmas shopping evening for loyalty card holders."

Robin glanced up to see everyone staring at him again, Gail in particular with a worryingly misty look in her eye. "That's perfect! I knew I could rely on you, Robin. Everyone, I'll expect you to give Robin your fullest cooperation as he's organising our Loyal Customers' Christmas Shopping Evening."

Robin groaned inwardly. The Christmas Shopping Evening had achieved audible capitalisation. There was no way he'd be able to get out of it now.

CHAPTER  4

By the time they were finally let go for the night, Robin was desperately in need of alcohol. It was probably too early to bump into Fridge Bloke, anyway. "Quick drink down the Millstone? It's Friday night."

Azrah made a face. "Aren't you working tomorrow? Cos I know I am."

"Yeah, but it's not like you're going to have a hangover." She didn't drink. Robin put it down less to her Muslim heritage than the fact that her mum and dad's house was *the* place to go if you wanted a lecture on how alcohol fucked up your life choices while giving you wrinkles. They seemed to have a knack of timing it for when you were terminally hungover and wanted to die quietly, but maybe that was just Robin. "I'll buy you some chips."

She let out a martyred sigh. "Go on, then."

"Yeah, cheers, mate." Heath—who Robin hadn't even noticed was still looming behind them—clapped Robin on the shoulder. "You're a good 'un." He leaned down to whisper in Robin's ear. "I think Gail *likes* you."

Robin jumped a foot away from him and nearly fell into a wall. "What? No she doesn't."

Azrah sniggered. "Yeah, we all noticed you're teacher's pet now."

"If she asks you to get into a cage," Heath said solemnly, "just say no. And remember, safewords are there for a reason."

"Gail does not *like* me. She's old enough to be my mother." Actually, Robin wasn't sure how old she was, but he was betting twenty-four was a distant memory for her. "And she's *a woman*."

"I wouldn't kick her out of bed. I like a strong woman." Heath sighed. "But she's only got eyes for Rockin' Robin here."

Robin shuddered. "Don't call me that."

Heath grinned. "The Boy Wonder?"

"Do you want these chips or not?" They'd reached the pub. As he glared at Heath, Robin's eye was caught by a tall figure on the other side of the street, striding away from them. The man was wearing a long overcoat, which wasn't that unusual this time of year—and a top hat, which definitely was. His heart leapt into his throat. Could it be Fridge Bloke?

Could it, logically speaking, be anyone else? "Wait a minute." Robin took a step down the road towards him, only to be yanked back by Azrah's hand on his arm.

"Hey, you promised us chips. You can't sneak off now."

"I thought I saw—"

He tried to pull away, but was thwarted when Heath took his other arm. "Not cool, man. If you don't deliver on your promises, that makes you no better than a Tory politician."

Azrah tightened her grip. "Yeah, you don't see me running out on my mates to ogle some random bloke's arse."

"He wasn't random!" Robin craned his neck to gaze after the retreating top hat as they dragged him bodily into the pub.

Damn it. But on the other hand, this was good, right? It meant Fridge Bloke probably worked in town. Or possibly just liked to parade through the streets attracting double takes. Either way, it meant there was more chance of Robin bumping into him again. Hopefully without frenemies like Azrah and Heath in tow.

If it'd been him. For all Robin knew, there might be a whole tribe or religious sect of men in Hitchworth who liked to party like it was 1899.

"Okay, you can let go of me now. He'll be gone anyway." Robin shook off Azrah's and Heath's loosened holds. "Right. Drinks and chips." Alcohol and comfort food, that was what he needed. Or better friends.

The Millstone was an old sixteenth-century coaching inn—or more accurately, it was around a third of an old coaching inn. The rest of it had been callously knocked down in the early twentieth century by a certain Mr. Willoughby to make room for his brand-new department store. There was still enough of the original structure to look impressively Ye Olde, with its steep gables and black timbers on white, and the arch the coaches used to drive through. It must have been quite something before the wrecking ball hit it.

Robin marched up to the bar. "Three bowls of chips, please, a rum and Coke, a Diet Coke without rum, and—" He glanced over his shoulder. "What are you drinking, Heath?"

"Pint of Old Peculier, ta."

"Why am I not surprised?" Robin got out his wallet to pay for the drinks and food, then blinked at the tenner Heath had thrust under his nose. "Don't worry about it."

"Nah, that ain't right, you buying us dinner and all."

"Heath, it was *literally* as cheap as chips. Get me a sandwich at work sometime if you're that bothered." Robin looked around for Azrah and spotted her in the corner, where she'd somehow managed to commandeer a table. He turned back to the barmaid and paid up. "We'll be sitting over there, thanks."

They took the drinks over, Heath sipping his en route and somehow managing not to spill it even when a gaggle of office girls in tight skirts and heels burst in with raucous laughter. He did give himself a froth moustache, though.

Robin couldn't help thinking of a different type of moustache. And its owner. Might he be on his way to molest white goods again tonight? Were there any left on Robin's street to be molested?

Should he consider putting out something as a lure? He didn't use the microwave *that* often . . .

"Oi, Earth to Robin. Are you going to hand me that Diet Coke or just stand there till it evaporates?"

Robin started, and quickly gave Azrah her drink. "Sorry. Long day."

"Too bloody right." She took a long swig of her Diet Coke. "Ah, that's better."

"I don't get how that works when there isn't any alcohol in it. How can that relax you? It's made of caffeine, artificial additives, and fizz." Robin sat down and took a sip from his clearly superior rum and Coke.

She shrugged. "It's the placebo effect. I think it's relaxing, so it is."

"Doesn't that only work if you don't know it's a placebo?"

"Yeah. So cheers for making me think about it and ruining the whole thing."

Robin raised his glass in a salute. "Anytime."

Heath, who'd somehow managed to sink half his pint already, put his glass down. "So who was this non-random bloke you were ogling?"

Robin froze. "Nobody."

Azrah gave a sly smile. "Was it Doctor Who again? Robin met him last night," she added to Heath.

"Maybe. I didn't get the chance to have a good look, did I? Thanks to you two." Robin glared at her. "Anyway, I said he reminded me of Doctor Who. Not that he *was* Doctor Who. Who doesn't exist, by the way. And is also a woman right now."

Heath stared dreamily into the middle distance. "Ah, she's another strong woman, that one. Knows what she's doing with a welding torch."

"Okay, I'm going to have nightmares about your sex life tonight." Robin took a thoughtful sip of his rum and Coke. He wouldn't mind betting that Fridge Bloke knew his way around a welding torch. That image probably shouldn't be as—heh—hot as it was.

"I bet your fridge guy knows what he's doing with a welding torch," Azrah said, making Robin choke on his drink and panic briefly that she'd read his mind.

"Fridge guy?" Heath asked. "He doesn't keep dismembered bodies in there, does he? Cos that could be a warning sign if you're planning to date him."

"The man I met last night, who *wasn't* Doctor Who *or* any kind of souvenir-keeping serial killer—"

"As far as you know," Azrah put in. Heath nodded solemnly.

"—was taking parts out of an abandoned fridge. *Fridge* parts, not human parts." Robin braced himself for a barrage of warnings to stay away from weirdoes, or alternatively a sad comment on the state of mental health care in the community.

"Oh. Cool." Heath glugged down the other half of his pint in one go. "Hey, looks like our chips are here."

"He said it was going to be a . . ." Actually, Robin couldn't remember exactly what arcane words Fridge Bloke had used. "Flux capacitor?"

The barmaid-slash-waitress, a short, slender girl with a pierced nose and a T-shirt reading, *Nobody cares I'm a lesbian*, placed three stodge-stacked bowls on the table.

"Awesome. You got any ketchup?" Heath gave her a winning smile and she grabbed him the sauce from the bar instead of telling him to get it himself.

Robin felt obscurely deflated.

"I'm not convinced he's real," Azrah said with her mouth full. "Fridge Guy. Maybe he's a ghost, like that plague doctor people keep seeing around after dark."

Robin snorted. "Oh, please. The plague doctor's just an urban myth."

"Is not." Heath sounded definite. "I've seen him loads of times."

Robin and Azrah stared at him.

He shrugged. "What? Perfectly natural supernatural phenomenon. And everyone knows Hitchworth was knee-deep in plague pits back in the day. This place was built right on top of one."

"Ugh. That means Willoughbys is too." Azrah frowned. "So how come we never see him haunting the shop? Where *have* you seen him?"

"Other side of town, over by the Brick and Bottle. Saw him having a drink in there too."

"A ghost having a drink?" Robin wasn't sure how that would work.

"Why not? It was hard, harrowing work them doctors did. You can't begrudge him a pint or two to take the edge off." Heath sent him a disappointed look.

"I'm not— Oh, never mind. I really don't think Fridge Bloke is a ghost. He was too technically minded for anyone from, like, a hundred years ago. Um. When were fridges invented?"

"Around 1750, the first ones," Heath said airily.

Robin glared at him. "He wasn't a ghost, all right?"

Azrah rolled her eyes. "Maybe he was a hallucination. Brought on by overwork and alcohol."

"Hey, I hadn't been drinking last night. Or before we got in here, either."

"So? It stays in your system for seventy-two hours."

"Says who?"

"My mum and dad, that's who."

Robin rallied. "None of you even drink, so how would you know for sure?"

Heath waved a chip at Robin. "Fact. Not just alcohol, neither. There's people who took LSD in the sixties who are still tripping."

"In the sixties." Azrah's tone said clearly that she wasn't entirely grateful for Heath's backup. "They'd be, like, a hundred now. That's not tripping. That's dementia."

"Yep. Caused by LSD."

The argument kind of degenerated after that. Robin munched his chips and let it wash over him. If he left now, what were the chances he might bump into Fridge Bloke again? Or would it be too late already? He ate a little faster. Did the man even have a set time for acts of white-goods vandalism, or did he simply head out, tools in hand, whenever the whim took him?

Robin was chafing with impatience by the time Azrah swallowed her last chip, stood up and groaned. "Why is it sitting down always makes your feet hurt worse when you get up? I'll see you tomorrow, Robin. You working, Heath?"

Heath shook his head. "Nah, I got a thing. I'll see you next week." He stood up too.

Robin got up so fast he knocked his stool over. "Oops. Okay, take care, you two."

"And you. Watch out for your Imaginary Fridge Friend!" Azrah was out the door before Robin could protest.

"Yeah, go easy on the weed, man," Heath threw over his shoulder as he loped off after her. "Who knows what they've cut that shit with?"

"I don't . . ." Robin was talking to himself. He rolled his eyes and followed them out, his heart beating a little faster at the thought of maybe seeing Fridge Bloke again.

Halfway to the door, the barmaid handed him a card with a drugs helpline on it.

Walking back from the bus stop, Robin's steps quickened as he approached the house where he'd met Fridge Bloke. The ransacked fridge had now been joined by a metal bedstead, its springs on wanton display for all to see. If copper coils were a . . . a thing, then wouldn't bedsprings work too?

There was, however, no sign of Fridge Bloke. Or anyone else, most people being apparently far too sensible to linger on freezing-cold streets after dark. There *was* a strangely bulky figure just visible in the glow from a far street lamp, but all Robin could make out from the distant, not-quite-human silhouette was that it was either an advance guard for the alien invasion, or someone carrying stuff. It *could* have been Fridge Bloke . . . but chasing him down the street in the dark to find out probably wouldn't go down well.

Robin hung around a bit, trying to look casual and not at all as though he were lying in wait for any deluded, handsome men who might stop by or turn around and come back for something they'd forgotten. All that happened was his toes went numb and people in three separate houses started giving him suspicious twitches of their net curtains.

Sighing, he trudged towards home.

CHAPTER 5

Archie whistled an old music-hall tune as he wandered down the street, a battered wooden chair on each arm. You never knew what you were going to find chucked out like old tin cans. These beauties were going to look a treat in the kitchen, once he'd stripped off the remains of the puke-green paint job some taste-deficient ne'er-do-well had inflicted on the poor things, and given them a nice coat of new varnish. They'd been lying forlornly in a skip, and the homeowner had been only too happy to let Archie have them. He'd seemed a bit bemused, though—kept asking Archie if he was sure he didn't want any money for taking them away.

Maybe he should have asked for a tenner, at that—Christ knew the homeless shelter on Queen Street needed all the donations it could get.

The only trouble was, Archie had actually been planning to pop back to the place where he'd found the fridge. It'd seemed to be an ongoing clearance, so there was a fair chance more stuff would've been put out. But these chairs were good and solid, and he didn't fancy dragging them all the way there and back. Ah, well. If he got there tomorrow and found the place picked clean, that was just the luck of the draw, wasn't it?

Of course, the *other* reason for going back would have been the, admittedly pathetically small, hope of bumping into the *Doctor Who* fan from last night again. Archie had been kicking himself ever since their little ships-that-pass-in-the-night encounter. Well, with appropriate breaks for eating, sleeping, and horrifying school parties with grim tales of strict rules, starvation rations, and oakum-picking in a Victorian workhouse. So, objectively speaking, he'd only been kicking himself for a total of an hour or so. Still, it had been enough to raise a painful metaphorical bruise.

He'd been cute, that lad, with his sharply styled blond hair flopping a bit in that rough-around-the-edges, end-of-day fashion, and those wide, blue eyes that had only got wider and wider as Archie had babbled on about aetheric bollocks to someone who clearly hadn't had a clue what he was on about and had been desperately trying to play along.

Archie hadn't *meant* to come over all full-on steampunk mad inventor on the poor guy. He was quite good at talking to normal people as a rule. It'd been a bit of a shock, that was all, to emerge from a fiddly bit of junk sourcing to find he was being stared at by someone who could have walked straight off the pages of *GQ*. Well, if you ignored the googly eyes, which probably weren't permanent anyway. And then it was as if a valve had blown in Archie's brain, and all the sensible, everyday vocabulary he used to navigate the real world flew straight out of his head in a puff of smoke.

And the lad had just run with it, doing his best to act like it was a big secret they both shared while underneath he had obviously been wondering what the hell was going on. You had to like someone who went to those sorts of lengths to make a stranger feel at ease. Archie had been *this* close to asking the guy to come up and see his racing teapot, which was why he'd had to run away, very fast, before the whole situation mushroomed into a repeat of the Gavin situation. Or the Kelsey situation. Or the . . .

Actually, now he came to think about it, maybe Archie *wasn't* so good at talking to normal people. At least, not ones he fancied. Fellow steampunks were so much easier. There was always something to talk about, like their newest outfit or gadget, favourite colour of Rub 'n Buff, or the age-old question of what made music steampunk (Archie could argue for hours on how it was ukuleles that did it). And there was never any difficulty about seeing them again, because it was pretty much guaranteed they'd turn up at a gig or a convivial soon enough.

Then again, that was how it'd been with Bridge, and while Archie wouldn't change a thing about the time they'd been together, it hadn't lasted, had it? They'd been comfortable with each other, yeah, and they'd taken some wicked cool photos, him in his top hat with the custom goggles and her in her corsets and petticoats, but that was all it had been, really. All they'd had in common was steampunk and an equal-opportunities approach to choosing a lover.

And an insufficient amount of due care and attention paid to contraception, as it had turned out. But hey, Archie wasn't going to complain about the little slip-up that'd given them Jerrick. Best mistake he'd ever made, Jerrick was, and Archie was pretty sure Bridge felt the same. Well, he hoped she did. On days after the kid had slept through the night, at any rate. Seeing as Jerrick lived with her and her parents, Bridge was the one who'd pulled the short straw and had to get up for night feeds and stuff.

Technically speaking, Archie was minding him right now, but Lyddie was on a fairly even keel at the mo and had been more than willing to do grandma duty. Archie had reckoned he'd be okay to go scavenging for half an hour or so, but it was probably time to get back now. Didn't want to push his luck.

When he got home, he found his mum sitting on the rug in front of the telly, which was showing *Strictly Come Dancing* on iPlayer with the sound turned right down. Jerrick was fast asleep in his little car seat next to her. Lyddie had every bit of silver she owned laid out on the rug, and was working away furiously at the tarnish on a tiny heart-shaped photo frame Archie had never seen before. Her face was hidden by long locks of brown hair that'd escaped from her messy updo and now bobbed to and fro as she rubbed.

Archie gave her a fond smile. "All right there? Got you some chairs." He held up one of them to show her.

Lyddie glanced up, blinking. "Chairs? What are they for?"

"Sitting on. Sorry, thought you knew, or I'd have said something about the sofa. Save you wearing out the carpet like that." Archie left the chairs by the door and crouched down by Jerrick's car seat to be reassured by the rise and fall of his little blanket.

Lyddie grinned. "Oh, screw you. Like I was going to risk losing my earrings down the back of the cushions. They're antique, some of these are. Least, that was what the bloke said when he gave them me, though between you, me, and the kitchen sink, I'm not sure he knew his antiques from his arse. So where are you going to put those chairs, then? Are they for Jerrick's room?"

Jerrick's room was more of a concept than an actual thing at the moment, seeing as he was still too young to care about wallpaper and there were other problems that needed seeing to first. Like the leak in the roof, and the Victorian plumbing. The house had been left to Lyddie by one of her old artist mates when he'd popped his clogs nearly a year back. While Archie wasn't one to ask a gift horse for its dental records, he couldn't help wishing someone had looked this one in its damp-ridden rafters before it'd got so bad. Still, he couldn't complain. The house was big enough to give them both a bit of space, and it'd stopped Lyddie fretting about how he needed a place of his own.

"Nah, kitchen. Thought we could have a table in there. Like a breakfast nook." Archie stood and picked his way back through the silver to the sofa.

"Ooh, posh. Or do I mean trendy? Yeah, trendy—posh would be a breakfast *room*, wouldn't it? Have you been looking in estate agents' windows again? I hope you're planning to repaint them first. That colour would put me right off my cornflakes." She mimed chucking up, and laughed.

"Yep, total wash and brush up, the works. I'll make a start on them tomorrow."

"What, no events to go to? Have all the steampunks gone into hibernation for the winter?"

Archie shrugged. "There's something on in Leeds this weekend, but it's too far for a day trip. And there's this lunch with Bridge's parents on Sunday, which, by the way, are you sure you don't want to go to?"

Lyddie made a face. "They don't like me."

"That's not true!"

"Is. You should see her dad's face when he sees me. Like I just asked him if he could spare some change for a cup of gin. And her mum's no better. *She* keeps making comments about how women ought to dress their age. Last time I saw her she offered to take me shopping. At bloody *Willoughbys*. I told her I'd rather walk around stark naked than spend a single penny in that place."

Archie winced. "She doesn't know—"

"I think I'll offer to take *her* shopping. Been a while since I've been to Camden Market. I'll show her *dressing my age*."

"Look, if you change your mind, just come along. Even if it's last minute. They won't mind." Hopefully.

There was a soft knock at the front door. Archie went to answer it, and gave Bridge a smile. "Good shift?"

She shrugged, but it turned into a roll of her shoulders and a hefty yawn. "Average. No drunks, but a few kids out way past their bedtimes. I don't know what some parents are thinking of. God, I'm turning into my mum. She'd have a fit if she could hear me now."

Archie grinned. "It's mature, responsible attitudes gone mad. Come on in. Jerrick's in the living room with his Nanna Lyddie."

She walked past him, bringing a strong waft of eau de chip shop with her. Archie gave an appreciative sniff. "Mm, your smell's making me hungry."

Bridge held up a middle finger. "I bet you say that to all the girls and guys. Which is why you'll never be getting laid again, ever. Although if you're very lucky, you might get arrested. Hiya, Lyds," she added as she swept into the living room.

"Oh, hello, Bridge. Are you off already? It can't be nearly midnight, can it?" Lyddie looked all round the room. "Archie, we need a clock in here. Why haven't we got a clock?"

"Cos he's a steampunk, Lyds. If he ever gets his hands on a clock, he takes it to bits for the cogs and stuff." Bridge tiptoed through the obstacle course on the rug to crouch down by Jerrick's side. "How's he been?"

"Like a little angel, bless him. You know, you could leave him overnight. Save you having to get him settled all over again. I wouldn't mind. Be glad to have him. I could give him breakfast, take him to the park in the morning—or maybe the zoo? Kids like zoos. Archie, love, is there a zoo around here?"

Bridge sent Archie a sympathetic look and answered for him. Again. "That's so sweet of you, but I'd miss him. Maybe do the zoo when he's older? I don't think he knows what animals are yet."

"Don't you believe it. They're like little sponges, kids are, learning all the time." Lyddie smiled, her eyes misting as she glanced at Archie. "If he's anything like his dad, he'll be picking up all sorts."

"Sounds like we'd better start minding our language around him, then." Archie could still remember the shocked silence when he'd innocently come out with a four-letter word on his first day at primary school.

"It's just words," Lyddie said vaguely.

Archie gave her a hard stare that probably veered off on a flight path several thousand feet over her head. "Yeah, and some of them cause actions."

Bridge perched her bum on the arm of the sofa. "What was Archie like when he was little?"

"Bright as a button. Daft saying, though. There's more dull buttons than shiny ones around, aren't there? He used to love buttons too—he'd spend ages sorting them into piles, like which were the shiniest and the biggest. And don't give me that look. I only let him play with the ones that were too big to choke him."

Archie's mood softened. "Yeah, you always took care of me. Any scrapes I got into were all my own work."

"Yeah, I can just imagine that and all." Bridge laughed, and then turned back to Lyddie. "But what was it like having a baby so young? Didn't you feel you were missing out on stuff?"

Archie frowned. "You know I can have Jerrick if you want a night out."

"*Duh*. Talking about your mum, not me. I've done my partying—I'm twenty-seven, not seventeen. Makes a big difference, that decade."

Lyddie shrugged. "Oh, I'd done plenty of partying by the time Archie came along. And if I wanted to go out, I took him with me. He was good as gold, most times. If he cried, there was always someone happy to hold him for me. He was like a canary. Or a . . . what's it called? That bit of paper that might go red or it might go blue."

Bridge and Archie exchanged blank looks.

Lyddie rolled her eyes. "*You* know. If they were good to Archie, I knew they were decent blokes."

Archie huffed under his breath. He was fairly sure he could remember quite a few exceptions to that rule. Being nice to kiddies apparently involved a very different skill set to being a decent boyfriend, even when your girlfriend was barely more than a kid herself.

"Archie's great with little Jerrick, aren't you, love?" Lyddie went on. "Such a good dad. You two were a lovely couple."

"Yeah, he's got good genes." Bridge stood up and rolled her shoulders. "Right, I'd better take him home so I can get my beauty sleep. Hah. Cheers for having him, Lyds."

"Anytime. You know I mean that, don't you? He's a darling. Like having my Archie back little again. Only better, cos I've got grown-up Archie too." She smiled mistily.

"I'll see you out," Archie said quickly.

"What, like I don't know the way?" Bridge gave him a look that said, clear as day, *She's your mum; deal with it.* "See you on Sunday."

"See you then. And the HISS pub night on Monday is still on, right?"

"Yep. Which you'd know if you were on social media instead of being a total Luddite."

"Hey, not everyone wants their whole lives trackable online. And you can't call me a Luddite. I don't go around wrecking machinery." Archie frowned. "Uh, so long as you don't count that fridge the other night."

Bridge laughed, hefted Jerrick's car seat and left, managing not to step on any bits of jewellery Lyddie had strewn around. The front door opened and closed quietly.

"She's a good girl," Lyddie said to the silver photo frame, which was now a lot shinier. "Are you sure you and her—"

"I'm sure. We were never meant to be together long-term."

"It's my fault, isn't it?" Lyddie gave him a moist-eyed look, twisting the polishing cloth in her hands. "You never had a proper dad, and . . . and I wasn't always there."

Archie knelt down beside her and put an arm around her shoulders. "It's not your fault. It's nobody's fault. It's not even a bad thing. Jerrick's got two parents who love him, and he's got you, and Bridge's mum and dad. He's got everything he needs."

"You never had any grandparents neither. That was—"

"And I grew up fine, didn't I? Come on. Leave the silver for now, and I'll make you a cup of hot chocolate." He steered her over to the sofa, and went to put the kettle on.

Archie wondered what Lyddie would think about that cute lad from last night. She'd like him, he was pretty sure. Maybe they'd bump into each other again another night? Archie gave himself a mental eye roll. He could hardly keep hanging around the streets after dark on the off chance. And anyway, when was he ever going to get time to date anyone? He spent his days at work, his evenings with Jerrick, and the odd weekend at steampunk events. The rest of his time was his mum's, and that was only fair. She'd given him everything while he was little. It was his turn to look after her now.

CHAPTER 6

Robin headed into work on Saturday with renewed optimism. The sun was shining, there had been plenty of seats on the bus, and moreover, his manager expected great things of him. Which meant he *definitely* wasn't on Gail's redundancy Christmas card list. He'd been thinking matters over, in the shower and while he shovelled down his breakfast, and he'd come up with a plan to hopefully save Azrah's job as well.

Firstly, he needed the Loyal Customers' Christmas Shopping Evening to be a roaring success. And secondly, he needed to make Azrah an integral part of it. That'd show Gail how indispensable she was. Maybe he should include Heath too. Heath wasn't exactly Gail's favourite person, either.

Yes. That was it. Robin would save the day for *both* of them.

He didn't get a chance to reveal his cunning plan to Azrah until lunchtime, when he found her in the store café, hiding in a corner with her Pasta of the Day (which, seeing as the Day was Saturday, was macaroni cheese. Wednesdays were also macaroni cheese; Tuesdays and Fridays were tomato sauce; Mondays and Thursdays were creamy mushroom. Robin was seriously thinking of buying the chef an Italian cookbook for Christmas). Heath sat opposite her with half the patisserie counter on his plate.

Robin pulled out a free chair and sat down with his salad. "I thought you weren't working today, Heath?"

"'M not," Heath said around a bite of jam doughnut.

Azrah drew away from him with a disgusted look. "Ew. Did you just spray sugar all over my pasta?"

"Would I?" Heath said, spraying some more.

Azrah moved the menu card to act as a shield. "That's so gross. If I come down with something horrible, I'm blaming you."

"Exposure to germs is good for you. Builds up your immunity. You'll be thanking me when there's an outbreak of Ebola and you're the only one who survives." Heath finished the doughnut and grabbed a custard slice.

"So what are you doing here?" Robin did his best to wrench the conversation bodily back on track.

Heath gave him a pitying look. "See, round about midday, most people like to have a bite to eat. It's called lunch, unless you're Northern, when it might be dinner, and then your dinner's your supper. Obviously. Unless it's your tea."

"I do know what lunch is, thank you very much. You might have noticed I'm a bit of a fan of the concept." Robin gestured pointedly at his plate.

Heath eyed Robin's salad with a frankly dubious expression. "You do know food is supposed to have actual calories, right?"

"Been telling him that for years," Azrah butted in with *her* mouth full. "One of these days he'll turn sideways unexpectedly while crossing the road and we'll lose him down a grating."

"Hey, I had chips last night. I'm just trying to have a balanced diet here."

"Oi, we all had chips last night." She narrowed her eyes and turned to Heath. "Did you hear that? He's trying to food-shame us."

Heath shook his head. "Not cool, mate. Not cool. Fat's a feminist issue."

"You're a bloke!" Robin spluttered.

"Hey, men need feminism too, you know. Keep your toxins away from my masculinity." Heath wagged what was left of the custard slice in Robin's direction. And then stuffed it in his mouth.

"Hah, that told you." Azrah snickered into her macaroni.

Robin thought about flicking a tomato at her, but his stomach rumbled and he decided his need was greater. Maybe he *had* underestimated the role calories played in keeping a man going through the day.

Then again, if he ate like the annoyingly skinny Heath, Robin would be the shape of a Christmas pudding before they'd even reached

Advent. And speaking of Heath . . . "You still haven't said why you've come in on your day off. I'd have thought you'd be snoring in bed at this time of day."

"Came in to see Gail. Had some ideas to run by her." Heath picked up his apple turnover.

"Ideas? What about?" *Robin* was supposed to be Gail's ideas man, not Heath.

Heath smiled and tapped the side of his nose with one irritating finger, leaving a flake of pastry there. Robin decided not to tell him about it. It'd only embarrass him. "Ah ah ah. Not saying a word until they're a go. But I think you're gonna like them."

Robin had mixed feelings. Part of him couldn't help being a bit miffed that, instead of waiting for Robin to save his job for him, Heath had had to go and be all proactive about it. The rest of him was just glad Heath was finally taking his career seriously and getting in well with the boss.

Okay. Maybe that part of him wasn't *really* all that glad. But it knew it ought to be, which was what counted, right?

"Got the idea from what we were talking about yesterday," Heath went on with a distinctly smug air of mystery.

Azrah threw her fork down. "Oh, come on. Give us a hint or bugger off."

Heath crammed the last of his apple turnover into his mouth and stood up. "I'll take door number two. See you later, worker drones. I've got things to see and people to do." He swept off.

Azrah made a disgusted face. "Did he just wink at me?"

"I think it was a general wink. Addressed to anyone who's not in on the secret so, like, everyone who's not him and Gail. But I could be wrong. With Heath, who knows? Are you going to eat the rest of that?"

She circled her plate with both arms. "Hands off. If you want some actual food with your lunch, you can get your own."

Robin cast a wistful glance over at the pastry counter. "No point going up for pudding. Heath's eaten it all."

"Should have thought of that, shouldn't you? So anyway, did you see your imaginary friend again last night?"

Robin choked on a cherry tomato. "No," he spluttered, eyes watering. "Why would I? It's not like he hangs around on the street waiting for me to walk past."

Azrah fixed him with a knowing look. "Or *does* he?"

"No. He doesn't. I'll probably never bump into him again." Great. Now he was hungry *and* depressed.

"You could try local car boot sales."

"What?"

"Duh. He likes junk, doesn't he? So you need to go to the places where junk goes."

Robin gave her suggestion the withering sarcasm it deserved. "Yeah, great idea. I'll just spend my days off hanging around the tip, shall I?" Come to think of it, he *did* have some boxes to get rid of from the move. Maybe he could get Azrah to give him a lift there in her mum's car . . . Except no, because he'd *literally* die of embarrassment if she found out he'd given that idea serious consideration.

"See if I try to help you get laid ever again. Pub tonight?"

"Yeah, why not? It's your turn to buy the chips."

"What happened to the balanced diet? No, don't answer that. I'll only end up feeling food-shamed again."

It being Saturday, the Millstone was pretty busy when Robin and Azrah finally finished work and trudged through its doors on aching feet. Mercifully, they got in just as a small group was leaving, and Robin zipped over to secure the table while Azrah elbowed her way to the bar.

"I ordered you sweet potato fries," she announced when she came back with their drinks. "So as not to unbalance you."

Robin pouted. "But you know I'm not keen on them."

"Which means they'll be even better for you, because you'll leave half of them. For me." She smirked.

"I thought you were worried about me not getting enough calories?"

"Nah, that was lunchtime. Now I'm only worried about *me* not getting enough calories."

"Cheers, Az. You're a mate." Robin raised a sarcastic glass to her.

"Hey, you don't want any excess pounds if you're going to be running after your fridge bloke. It'd only slow you down." She sipped her Coke. "Ah, that's better."

Robin took a swig of his vastly superior (i.e. rum-containing) drink, and couldn't help agreeing. "Hey, any guesses what Heath's big idea was?"

"Nope. I'm totally without insight into how Heath's mind works, and I'm happy to keep it that way."

"He said I was going to love it."

Azrah grinned. "Worried?"

"Bloody terrified. And how am I supposed to plan this event if Heath's already planned half of it without me?"

The barmaid with the piercings came over at that point, weaving her way expertly through the crush at the bar to plonk down a plate of chips in front of Robin, and a bowl of sweet potato fries in front of Azrah.

Robin beamed, relieved. "Aw, I knew you wouldn't really get me fake chips."

"Guess again." Azrah deftly switched the plates around and squeezed several sachets of mayonnaise on her chips. "And shame on her for gender stereotyping," she added, nodding at the barmaid's retreating back.

Robin slumped and moodily munched a sweet potato fry. "It could have been racial stereotyping. You know, I'm white, so all I'll eat is traditional English chips, not these exotic fries from . . . where do sweet potatoes come from?"

"Sainsbury's." Azrah shrugged. "What am I, some kind of expert on the ethnic migration of root vegetables?"

"Maybe she was feeling sorry for me with the food police around." Robin jabbed a fry pointedly in Azrah's direction. "Although probably not, given what she's wearing. Which, by the way, why would anyone buy a T-shirt that just says *Vegetarian*? I don't think people should just shove their political agenda in your face like that. And if you've *got* to brag about your holier-than-thou eating habits, at least come up with, I dunno, something a bit wittier."

"Robin—"

"You know, like *Give Peas a Chance*, or *Eat Beans Not Beings*."

"*Robin*. That second letter? That's not an *e*."

Robin squinted. "So what does that even mean? *Vaget*— Oh." He flushed. The barmaid turned at that moment, caught his widened eye, and winked. Azrah cackled.

Why were pub tables never big enough to hide under? Robin spent the next few minutes shaking salt onto his fries with possibly a little more care and attention than was really warranted. And on no account looking at the bar.

He perked up a bit when Azrah shoved a chip in his bowl of fries. But only a bit. It had mayonnaise on it.

"Cheer up," she told him. "Tomorrow's Sunday. A whole day to do whatever we want to. Stay in bed all day. Watch rubbish telly. Drink Coke without worrying Mrs. Bossyknickers is going to come along and confiscate it."

Robin nodded, cheering up as ordered. Then he remembered what he was *actually* going to be spending his Sunday doing, and his briefly raised spirits plunged back down into his boots and made themselves comfortable once more. Sod it. He couldn't face this alone. "Azrah?"

"Mm?"

"Can you do me a favour?"

"No."

"Pleeease?"

She rolled her eyes. "All right, what is it? But no promises, mind."

"How would you like a free Sunday lunch?"

"A free . . . *No*. No way. I've had enough of your mum's soggy Yorkshire pudding to last me a lifetime."

"It won't be round at Mum and Dad's. I've got a table booked at a restaurant."

"Yeah, but they're going too, aren't they? I mean, I can *believe* you're too sad to cook your own roast dinners now you're living on your own, but you're not telling me you've actually booked to go out for lunch by yourself."

"You do it sometimes. You've told me."

"Yeah, but that's cos I don't care what people think and I hate everyone anyway. Present company not excluded at this precise moment. *You'd* sit there paranoid everyone was staring at you and thinking you were a total saddo with no mates. Admit it. It's Sunday lunch with the 'rents."

"All right, yes. But please come, yeah? Mum *likes* you."

"No, she doesn't. Your mum doesn't like anyone."

"So? Just means you've got something in common! *Pleeease*? I haven't seen her for nearly a fortnight. I can't face all that saved-up guilt-tripping alone."

She heaved a put-upon sigh. "Proper Sunday lunch, yeah? And you're paying?"

"Absolutely. Pudding and everything. I'll even buy you a coffee after." Robin crossed his toes inside his shoes.

"Where are you eating? It's not the Ploughman, is it?"

"Um . . ."

Azrah groaned. "You know I hate it there. It's like they took all the worst bits of a pub, and all the worst bits of a restaurant, and mashed them together to make the world's least inspired dining experience. It's like a gastropub. Only without the gastro. Or the pub."

"But there's a carvery on Sundays, so you know the food isn't frozen stuff they've shoved in the microwave. And I'll owe you a favour," Robin added desperately. "Anything you like."

"You are going to owe me the world's biggest favour . . . Fine. I'll come." She folded her arms grumpily.

Robin fought the urge to lean across the table and hug her. "You're a mate. My best mate. I could kiss you right now."

"Ew."

"But I won't, because like you said, ew." He tossed back the rest of his drink in celebration. "Oh—it's your round. Make mine a double; I'm celebrating. And a packet of dry roast peanuts, please?" he called to her back as she marched towards the bar.

She'd probably throw them at him, but that was all right. Robin had got pretty good at ducking, over the years.

On his way home from the pub, his wallet lighter and his liver enjoying a gentle workout, Robin passed by the Fridge House. The bedstead was still there. But it was missing a number of springs.

Damn it. Fridge Bloke must have been here while Robin was at work. Or on the bus. Or at the Millstone. Why hadn't he come straight home?

More to the point, why was he obsessing so much over a bloke he'd met once for roughly thirty seconds? Standing there on the street, cocooned in the warm glow of a few too many rum and Cokes, Robin attempted to think about it objectively.

Well, the man was fit, no question. And different from anyone Robin had met before. Like, *ever.* And demonstrably knew his way around the back of a fridge, which . . . Robin tried, and failed, to think of any way that could be an advantage in his life. Okay, leave out the fridge. There was just something about him. The beard, maybe? Robin had always liked facial hair. On men, obviously. Not that he didn't think women should wear facial hair if they wanted to. It just didn't do anything for him. Because of, well, the *woman.*

Was it the tattoo? The possibility of other tattoos, in areas not usually seen in public? Robin took a deep, steadying breath and conceded that yes, that might very well have a little to do with it. But it wasn't just that. He'd simply seemed more *alive* than anyone Robin had met before. Also, yes, slightly manic, but Robin was prepared to take the rough with the smooth. He was *different.* He had style. Who waxed their moustache in this day and age? Robin doubted he'd ever have the nerve to do it, in the unlikely event he managed to cultivate anything beyond a sad, spindly caterpillar on his top lip. This bloke waxed his moustache to go fiddle with a fridge.

And Robin had had one chance to get to know him, to find out who he was, and where he lived, and he'd blown it.

The breeze picked up, cold fingers slipping inside Robin's jacket to tickle his neck with their icy touch. The glow from the alcohol had dissipated, leaving only a thick head and a desperate need to pee. Shivering, Robin set off once more for home.

Face it. He was never going to see the guy again.

When he finally got back to his flat, Robin picked up his ukulele to try to cheer himself up. It helped a bit at first, but then someone in the downstairs flat banged on the ceiling to complain and he realised he was playing "Mr. Lonely" for the third time in succession, so he put it down with a sigh and trudged to bed.

CHAPTER  7

Archie hunched into his jacket and quickened his steps. The sooner he got home, the better, and not just because he was walking down one of the rougher streets in the area on a peak drinking night. He'd dressed for a day of shifting donated goods at the homeless shelter, in an old shirt and no waistcoat, but he was missing the extra layer now. The temperatures had fallen with the night and the wind was bitter. Maybe he should have taken Dave up on his offer for a lift to his door, but he hadn't liked to take the bloke too far out of his way.

An unexpected sound wafted on the breeze. Archie frowned and slowed. Was that ukulele music? Despite the chill, he paused to listen, captivated by this chance encounter of a musical kind. The simple, haunting tune was coming from one of the flats nearby. Archie couldn't hear anyone singing along. The tune finished, then as Archie was about to move on, started up again at a slightly slower tempo.

There was a haunting familiarity about the song, but Archie couldn't place it. It tugged at his heartstrings, made him long for home and company, and he wondered if that was how the musician felt too. Were they alone right now? Archie made up his mind to applaud at the end of the song, just so the player knew someone was listening—but then there was a loud banging, a muffled shout, and the music stopped abruptly.

The spell broke. Archie winced on the musician's behalf and headed on home, his toes numb and icy in his boots, with the nagging sense of a connection severed before it could properly form.

CHAPTER 8

Sunday dawned bright and clear. At any rate, according to the previous night's weather forecast, it had been supposed to. Robin had been quite happy to let it dawn without him. He rolled out of bed sometime after eleven, had a yawn and a scratch, and reluctantly decided it was too late for breakfast. Even though his Sunday lunch date with Mum and Dad was at a restaurant rather than at home, Mum wouldn't be impressed if he picked at his food.

Not that she was ever that impressed. Not by anything Robin did at any rate.

At least Azrah would be coming along. Okay, Robin had had to bribe her with that most ominous of promises, A Favour to be Named at a Later Date, but it would probably be worth it. There was no point looking on the dark side all the time.

After all, he might walk under a bus tomorrow and never have to repay her.

Coffee on an empty stomach made him jittery, but looking on the bright side, it also made him marginally more awake. It was always wise to have his wits about him when seeing his mum. Otherwise he'd only find himself trapped in another labyrinthine guilt trip and end up agreeing to go to some excruciating social event hosted by one of Mum's friends. Where he'd be introduced to an earnest young lady who was "Just your age, Robin, and she's a lovely girl. Does volunteer work for the Salvation Army."

Mum had grudgingly accepted that he liked men *now*. She just hadn't given up hope of browbeating him into liking women too at some future date.

Robin stared at his wardrobe indecisively. On the one hand, dressing in what his mum would call "a nice pair of trousers and a smart jacket" would mean she had one less thing to moan about. On the other, it'd mean she had more time to focus in on the important stuff.

He grabbed a pair of jeans and, in a stroke of genius, a sweater she'd given him last Christmas. It wasn't too hideous—okay, it made him look about twelve, but Mum seemed to think he'd never exceeded that age anyway—and the combination of objectionable trousers and above-criticism sweater might even confuse her enough that she'd forget to start on his questionable "lifestyle choices" altogether.

And if all else failed, there was the Pride T-shirt he'd put on underneath. That was guaranteed to send her on a rant ("In my day, having sexual relations with people you weren't married to wasn't anything to be *proud* about") but it was a comfortable, familiar rant. Robin had long since perfected tuning that one out.

The table was booked for one o'clock, so Robin left the house at twelve. Buses weren't so frequent on a Sunday, and in any case he'd agreed to meet Azrah in the Millstone for a drop of courage first.

He strolled down the street, faintly regretting not having worn a jacket—there was a stiffer breeze than he'd expected, and more importantly it would have covered the sweater—and turned a corner into Verne Avenue.

The houses on this road were what Robin liked to think of as the distressed gentlefolk of the architectural world. Unlike Robin's street of depressing, blocky council buildings, mostly inhabited by depressing, blocky people, these houses had clearly once been posh. Now, most of them seemed to have been divided into flats, and the front gardens had been concreted over to give the occupants somewhere to park their cars, but one or two still sat coyly behind ancient shrubs and looming trees. They were the kind of solid, century-old homes in which you might, if you were lucky, find a wardrobe with a shortcut to Narnia.

It was out of the gate of one of these houses that a man stepped, just as Robin drew level. Robin stopped dead in his tracks, and only partly to avoid bumping into him.

It was Fridge Bloke. With a baby in his arms, nattily dressed in a onesie printed with a cartoon monocle and a moustache as dapper as his dad's.

Robin's spirits plunged into his boots, where they made a valiant effort to seep through the soles and sink into the pavement to poison the ground for years to come with their desolate, withering touch.

Fridge Bloke was taken. Or worse, *straight*. Which, granted, had always been, statistically speaking, very much on the cards, but then the man hadn't exactly *looked* like your stereotypical straight bloke, had he?

Robin had been lulled into a false sense of security by a twirly moustache. It was still twirly, with the faint gleam of a touch of wax. The jauntiness of it, together with the seductively dapper appearance of the man, was like a kick in the teeth to Robin's hopes and dreams. Fridge Bloke was today spruce as a Norwegian Christmas tree decked in Willoughbys' finest glass baubles. He wore a checked waistcoat, well-fitting trousers, tweed jacket and a pair of brogues that might have been lovingly polished only this morning by his own personal Jeeves. With his slicked-back dark hair, the glint in his eye, and his pointed beard, the image he brought to mind was something like the devil on his way to corrupt the vicar over the Sunday roast.

If the devil had a baby son. Or was possibly bringing one along as an amuse-bouche.

The only false note was his pocket square, which was overlarge and crumpled and, Robin realised belatedly, not actually a pocket square at all, but one of those cloths people gave babies to dribble on.

There was only so long you could stare at a man before he noticed the weight of your gaze. Fridge Bloke (perhaps in the light of his current attire, Robin should rename him Refrigerator Gentleman?) glanced up and raised a quizzical eyebrow.

Robin swallowed. "Oh, er, hi. Uh, we met before? A few nights ago? I'm Robin. I just moved in around here." Why the hell had he worn Mum's sweater? Far from being glad of its warmth, he was starting to worry about spontaneous combustion.

Fridge Gent's expression was, appropriately enough, frozen. Then it cleared. "Of course. The aetheric field generator. Good find, that. And good to see you again. I'm Archie, and this fine young gentleman is the cogling."

Robin could feel himself making a *This is the what now?* face. Hopefully the expression went with the fine shade of crimson he was probably sporting. "Uh . . ."

"Jerrick. Made him myself. Well, his mum helped, obviously. You might even say she did most of the heavy lifting. Say hi, Jerrick." Archie picked up Jerrick's little hand and waved it frantically at Robin.

Robin waved back. There didn't seem to be anything else to do. "Hi, Jerrick."

Concern flashed across Archie's face, to be succeeded by a somewhat manic grin. "Splendid to meet you. Again. Well, must fly—left the airship double parked."

Neither of them moved.

A house door slammed, and a woman with a voluptuous figure sashayed down the short garden path hefting a nappy bag in one hand and a kiddie car seat in the other. She was dressed in a fifties-style full skirt over a just-visible floofy petticoat and sheer tights that showed off her tattoos. Her hair—the non-shaven bit—was tied up in a headscarf with skulls on it. Beneath the heavy, black eyeliner and pillar-box red lipstick, Robin could clearly make out the features of the scary woman from the chip shop.

Robin stared. And then he fled.

CHAPTER

Bridge sniffed as she joined Archie on the pavement. "He wasn't very friendly. Mate of yours?"

Archie groaned. "No. And never will be."

"Why? What did he do? Get fag ash on your favourite waistcoat? Beat you to the last reel of copper wire at the junk shop?"

"*He* hasn't done anything. It's me. I can't seem to stop acting like a blithering idiot every time I see him." If he literally kicked himself, Archie wondered, would the physical pain detract from the metaphorical lead weight that had just materialised in his stomach? More likely he'd end up on his arse on the pavement with a bruised shin and a terminal case of embarrassment. With passers-by filming the whole thing to hold him up to public ridicule on YouTube.

Bridge gave him a sidelong look. "Fancy him, do you?"

Uh-oh. There was something in her tone that advised caution. It also hinted that admitting to his recent ex and the mother of his young child that he fancied another bloke might not be the most tactful move ever. Archie took a step back. Jerrick wailed in protest and reached for his mum, so Archie reversed his move, feeling like he was in some strangely sedate dance. The toddler two-step? "Uh, no?"

"You asking me or telling me?"

"Telling you. Definitely." All right, so it wasn't technically true, but it was effectively true. Archie had no intention of asking the bloke out, which was the same as not fancying him really, wasn't it?

"Okay."

"Okay?"

"Like I said, okay. I mean, it's no skin off my arse either way, is it?"

"You wouldn't mind if I did?"

"No. Course not. Why should it bother me? Come on, we're going to be late." She opened the door of her VW Beetle and slung in the nappy bag.

"It bothers you."

"Read my lips. Am I bovvered? No." Bridge busied herself setting up Jerrick's car seat.

"Then why's there this deep frown line between your eyes?"

"Cheers, Arch. Way to make a girl feel special by pointing out her wrinkles."

"It's not a wrinkle, and you know you look great. It's a frown line, caused by being bothered. Now tell me what's bothering you. And don't say *nothing*." Jerrick let out a not-quite-grizzle. "See? Even Jerrick's picked up on it."

"Maybe you're holding him wrong." Bridge thrust out her arms, and Jerrick leaned into them. "Come to Mama, baby boy. Is Daddy being an arse-wipe? Yes, he *is*."

"Good luck explaining to your mum why his first word is a four-letter one."

Bridge strapped Jerrick into his seat with a deft hand. "I'll just tell her *your* mum taught him it."

"Hey, that's not fair." Archie folded his arms.

Bridge emerged from the car to roll her eyes at him. "Sense of humour failure, much? I'm not actually in the habit of lying to my mother. Look, I don't have a problem with you seeing someone. If you think I'm nursing secret dreams of us getting back together, don't flatter yourself. It's just . . . I don't get it, all right? I mean, Jerrick's *everything* to me. I don't need anyone else. You thinking about someone else like that, it's like you're saying he's not enough for you."

Jerrick gave a wordless cry, as if in outraged agreement.

Thinking about someone else like that . . . Was he really that obvious? Archie replayed his few minutes of blither in his head and realised that yes, he probably was. Sod it. "Bridge, of course I'm not saying that. It's . . . just a thing, all right? A reaction. To a fit bloke. Who I'm *not* planning on asking out. Here you go, mate, here's your muzzy." He pulled the crumpled muslin cloth from his breast pocket. Jerrick seized it with eager hands and began to chew on it happily.

Bridge looked away. "This is how it starts, isn't it? You moving on, finding someone else. You'll be busy nights seeing whats-his-arse, so I'll start leaving Jerrick with Mum and Dad while I'm working. First it'll be odd nights, then it'll get to be a regular thing. You'll stop seeing him every day, and it'll be just once or twice a week. Then every other week. By the time he's in school you'll be down to Christmas and birthdays. If he's lucky."

"Thanks for giving me a say in how I live the next six years of my life. Bridge, listen. It's not gonna be like that. Jerrick's my son, and I'm his dad. I'm going to be there for him. Do . . . whatever dads do." Archie tried to smile through the old panic—what the hell did he know about what dads did, anyhow? There had to be more to it than kicking a ball around in the park or teaching the kid to ride a bike, but that was all he could remember wishing he had a dad for when he was a boy, and then only because he'd seen other kids with their dads.

Well. Until his mum had had to go away. He'd wished, then, he'd had a dad, or rather another parent of any variety, so he wouldn't have had to go . . . elsewhere. And maybe if there had been a dad around, he'd have looked after Lyddie, and she might not have got so bad. But when she had been there, his mum had been everything. Maybe Archie hadn't had ironed shirts for school or a lot of help with his homework, but he'd had fun.

Okay. It hadn't been fun all the time. But Lyddie had done her best.

"I'm not moving on, and I'm not asking anyone out, all right?"

Bridge deflated. "Sorry. Didn't mean to get all heavy on you." She dredged up a smile. "That kid was way too young for you anyhow."

She most likely wasn't wrong. Seeing him in daylight, in a sweater that had to have been bought by his mum, Archie had revised his estimate of the lad's age downwards to a depressing degree. He slung a not-entirely-altruistic arm around Bridge. "Doesn't matter how old he is, does it? Since I'm not going to ask him out. And don't worry. I may not have a clue what I'm doing, but I'm going to be there for Jerrick all the way. Think I'm gonna miss out on embarrassing him when he's in his teens?" Hopefully it wouldn't be by dating boys who were still in their teens themselves.

She gave a weak smile. "Think it'll take until then?"

"Probably not. What age are they capable of being embarrassed?"

"Weirdly, *not* actually one of the milestones in that baby book my nan got me. I'd guess primary school age, though. So you've got five years to work on being really mortifying. You know, learn some dad jokes, practice your dad dancing—"

"Work on the dad bod." Archie nodded, patting his stomach. "Hey, I could start on that this lunchtime."

"Wish you would." Bridge frowned down at her own figure. "He's six months old and I'm still the size of a bloody whale. Think it'd look weird if I wore a corset every day?"

"You're asking *me*? But yeah, probably. I'm guessing most of the mums down at the toddler group are a bit more casually dressed."

"Yeah, and it'd be a bitch getting the puke stains out. Sod it. Bring on the next Steampunk event. I want my figure back, even if it takes the whole flippin' family and a forklift truck to lace me up. And don't tell me I look great again. My skirts don't lie."

"All right, I won't say it. I'll just think it. While I'm wondering how exactly a forklift truck's gonna help lace anyone into a corset. Come on, your mum and dad will have started without us." Archie cast a final glance back at the house. He'd hoped Lyddie would relent and come with them. It didn't feel right, leaving her a cling-wrapped plate of sandwiches with a note saying *EAT ME* on the top.

"She'll be fine," Bridge said, reading his mind.

Archie's face twisted in an unhappy grimace. "I don't like her spending so much time on her own."

"You can't be there for her 24/7. And it's her choice. You have to respect that. Come on, get in the car, or I'm driving off without you."

Archie, Bridge, and Jerrick got to the Ploughman just as her mum and dad were getting out of their car. Bridge tooted her horn, and they all met up at the door of the pub. There was a hug for Archie from Bridge's mum, despite her only having seen him a couple of days ago.

"Aren't you looking splendid today? And as for my little angel . . . he'll be breaking hearts all over, won't he? Come to Nanna, darling." She held out her arms for Jerrick, who leaned into them happily.

As Bridge passed him over, Archie was left to return her dad's nod. Pat didn't do hugs—at least, not with other men. "All right, Pat? Shall we go in?"

"Well, I wasn't planning on standing out here in the cold any longer." Pat held the door open for the ladies.

Usually, when Archie saw him, Bridge's dad was sunk deep in his favourite armchair watching the telly, or sitting on the floor playing with his grandson. He worked long hours as a mechanic in a local garage, and when he was home he liked to put his feet up.

It always somehow came as a surprise to Archie just how big Pat was when he was standing up. Intimidating, even. There wasn't much difference in their heights, but Pat had a solid bulk to him, the softness of middle-aged spread not doing much to disguise the muscle underneath. They'd never got on as well as Archie had hoped they might, despite how much Bridge took after him personality-wise, and the breakup hadn't exactly helped. Archie always got a guilty feeling he ought to apologise to Pat for making Bridge a single mother, despite the fact that Bridge herself would tear a right strip off anyone who dared to suggest she hadn't chosen that route herself.

It must be a dad thing. Archie had never experienced parental opposition to anyone he'd been dating—Lyddie always seemed to fall in love with anyone he went out with, for as long as it lasted—but there were loads of jokes, and even TV shows, about dads disapproving of their daughters' boyfriends, so there had to be a kernel of truth in it, didn't there? Pat never actually *said* anything like that, obviously. He just had a dour, unsmiling way of looking at Archie that seemed to come with its own subtitles.

Or maybe I simply don't understand the dad dynamic, he mused as he made up the rear of their little procession through the Ploughman and over to their table at the back of the restaurant.

Janet, Bridge's mum, settled into the chair Pat pulled out for her, still holding Jerrick. She'd dolled herself up for the occasion as much as Bridge had, in a fashionable top and her biggest, dangliest earrings, which Jerrick was currently making a determined effort to yank out of her ears. Archie gave her a smile as he sat opposite. "Is that a new top, Mrs. M.? It looks great."

Her face creased into a happy map of smile lines. "Ooh, thank you. I only got it this week. Quite a bargain it was too. See, *some* people notice these things," she added, digging her husband in the ribs.

Pat leaned back in the chair next to her, sweater straining over his belly. "*Some* people have more important things to think about than clothes."

"Like what Liverpool's new manager thinks he's playing at, and whether they're going to win the cup this year?" Bridge shot back.

Pat found a smile easily enough for his daughter. "It's important stuff, football is."

"Just a bunch of overgrown boys kicking a ball around a muddy field," Janet sniffed. "What's so important about a flippin' ball?"

"Ah, but it's not a ball, is it?" Pat jabbed a finger at her. "It's a symbol of community and working-class pride."

"Working class? Have you seen how much those footballers get paid? Ridiculous. Ow! Don't pull Nanny's earrings, love. Bridget, can you take him?"

"I'll have him," Archie offered, but Pat already had his arms out.

"Come to your gramps, lad. That's better. Now, young man, when are you going to start walking? Can't kick a ball around until you're on two feet."

Jerrick listened gravely, while Bridge and Janet stifled giggles.

They weren't *trying* to make Archie feel like a spare part. He knew that. It just worked out that way sometimes, that was all.

"Right, has everyone chosen?" Bridge asked. "They'll be coming over to take the order soon. I'm starving."

There was a general opening of previously ignored menus.

"Anyone going for the carvery?" Archie asked.

Pat snorted. "I don't come to a restaurant to go fetch my own dinner. I'll have the curry."

"Vegan?" Bridge asked with a twinkle.

"As if. I'll have the lamb. What about you, lad?"

Archie, who'd had his head down in his menu after Pat's last remark, startled. "Same, I think." He hoped it wouldn't seem like he was trying to—hah—curry favour by following Pat's lead.

Bridge grinned. "His mum went veggie again last week, so he's missing his meat."

"How's she doing, your mother?" Janet asked in that careful and ever-so-slightly sympathetic tone she always used when speaking of Lyddie.

"Noticed she's not here with us." Pat jiggled Jerrick on his knee.

"She's fine. Just busy." Archie probably ought to say she'd sent her apologies, but he didn't reckon they'd be deceived for an instant.

Their waiter arrived, notepad at the ready, which was all to the good. After they'd given their food choices, Pat ordered beers for himself and Archie and a bottle of rosé "for the ladies."

"We are capable of speaking for ourselves," Bridge said without much heat.

"Oh, hush, love." Janet put a hand on her arm. "If your father wants to treat us, then why not let him?"

Archie made a mental note to insist on paying half the bill.

The conversation over lunch turned to work. Pat always had a few stories to tell about idiot drivers who didn't have a clue how their cars worked. Janet worked at Sainsbury's, and regaled them with the latest about the state of her colleagues' marriages, and which alcoholic customers had fallen off the wagon again. Bridge, who'd been yawning a bit while her mum retold stories she'd clearly heard before, then had them in fits about the late-night drunks who'd come into the chippie. Archie, feeling a proper part of the conversation at last, got a few laughs for the daft questions he'd been asked by recent visitors to the museum, such as did workhouse inmates get wi-fi, and why didn't they just claim benefits and carry on living at home?

He was the one to finish his meal first, so he hoiked Jerrick out of his high chair before he could get bolshie, and sat him on his knee. There was a suspicious fullness about the lad's rear end. "Think he's going to want a change soon." He sent Bridge an apologetic look.

"I'll do it," Janet said, putting down her fork.

"Mum, finish your meal," Bridge said with a touch of impatience. "He's not about to explode."

Pat huffed. "Why can't his dad do it? It's not like I never changed your nappies, young lady. I thought you young folk were all for sharing the burden."

"There's no changing table in the gents' here, and they're funny about blokes going into the ladies.'" Archie was starting to feel a bit got at again.

Janet stood up. "I can't manage any more of this anyway. They put far too much on my plate. Come on, hand over that changing bag."

"Sit down, Mum. I'm doing it." Bridge stared her mum into submission before heading off with bag and baby.

Janet picked up her fork again with a sulky air, while Pat grumbled something unintelligible yet somehow clearly disgruntled.

Archie would honestly have preferred to have been facing the nappy right now. Even if it'd been a cauliflower or broccoli one.

CHAPTER

Robin got to the bus stop just in time to watch the bus rumble away without him. He slumped in despair on the narrow, sloping bench seat, clearly designed to deter rough sleepers. The next bus, as it was Sunday, was due in half an hour.

And it was late. A furious text conversation en route established that no, Azrah couldn't be persuaded to head over to the Ploughman without him and let Mum and Dad know he was running late. Literally, as he legged it from the bus stop in the centre to the Millstone, grabbed a surly-looking Azrah, and hurried her across town to the Ploughman.

He got there a sweaty, dishevelled mess, wishing he dared take off his sweater but knowing he'd need all the brownie points he could get with Mum. The place was packed out, mostly with families of the grown-up-kids-and-wrinkly-parents variety, although there were also a fair few high chairs in evidence. Their occupants variously smeared food on themselves, shouted incoherently or banged crayons on the tray. Some of them were doing all three at once. There was a strong smell of gravy in the air, and Robin's stomach rumbled. He cast the bar a yearning look, but Azrah got a pincer grip on his arm and dragged him off through the restaurant to where Mum was waving impatiently from a table by the window.

"Robin! There you are. We were beginning to think you weren't coming."

"It's only two minutes past twelve!"

"Late is late, Robin. And I see you've brought your little friend." Mum's voice flattened noticeably at the end. Generally, she liked Azrah—as much as she liked anyone—but last-minute changes to plans never found favour.

"Hi, Mrs. Christopher," Azrah said in an aggressively chirpy voice.

Mum's lips remained resolutely turned-down at the corners. "I do hope the restaurant will be able to accommodate you. We only booked for three."

Robin's face ached as he tried to jolly her along. "Mum, you're sitting at a table with four chairs. In what world would they not be able to accommodate her? Hi, Dad."

Azrah courageously took the seat next to Mum, so Robin slid into the seat beside his father. Dad glanced up with a brief, sardonic grunt from the menu he was studying. Robin wasn't sure why he bothered. He always, without fail in all of the twenty-four years Robin had known him, went for the carvery anyway. "Glad to see you finally made it. Still working in that shop?"

"You make it sound like I'm stacking the shelves in some cut-price convenience store." Robin could hear the whine in his voice and cleared his throat. "Yes, I'm still pursuing a retail career."

Mum sniffed. "We warned you a music degree wouldn't lead to a proper profession, but you *would* have things your own way."

"Mum, did you even listen to what I just said?"

Azrah leaned forward. "Our manager is expecting big things from him," she said pointedly.

Dad snorted and returned to his menu.

Mum's daggerlike look was completely wasted on Dad, so she gave it up and turned to Robin with a forced smile. "I'm sure that's lovely, dear. And of course, you must get to meet a lot of nice young ladies there."

"Like me, you mean?" Azrah's tone was so arch you could use it to hold up a cathedral roof.

"I'm afraid we've long given up hope on that score. Still, perhaps it's for the best. Mixed-religion marriages can be terribly difficult."

Robin chipped in quick before Azrah could recover the power of speech. "Mum, you know I'm not religious. And neither's Azrah. Not that we've got any intention of getting married," he added hastily.

"Too right," Azrah muttered. "To anyone. Ever."

It was enough to draw Mum's fire. "You'll want children one day, and then what will you do?"

Azrah gave a tight-lipped smile. "I'm not planning on having kids."

"You'll change your mind. I was never very keen on children, but I gave in to it in the end." Mum sent Robin a glare that seemed to say, *I didn't make* that *mistake twice.*

The morning's coffee churned in Robin's stomach like an alien parasite about to make an explosive exit through his abdomen. Robin half wished it would. At least it'd put that godawful sweater out of his misery. Apart from its unfortunate looks, Robin was way too hot in it and the label appeared to have been made out of barbed wire. He rubbed his neck, trying to soothe it.

"Robin! Stop scratching at the table. It's so uncouth."

"Are you ready to order?" The arrival of the waitress, a pretty young blonde woman, was a lifeline Robin grabbed with both hands.

"Yes— I think so? Azrah, are you ready?"

"Yeah, I'm having the carvery. Gotta love that meat-feast."

Mum's eyes narrowed. "Make sure you get plenty of vegetables too. A young girl like you shouldn't be looking so peaky."

"I'll go for the carvery too," Robin said quickly, seeing Azrah bristle. "Dad?"

Dad made them all wait several minutes while he scoured the menu one last time before throwing it down on the table. "Carvery."

Mum smiled, order restored. "Four carveries, then. You don't need to tell us how it works. We've been here before. And we'd like some bread rolls, and a jug of water for the table."

The waitress assured them it was no problem and left.

Wishing she hadn't abandoned them so soon, Robin opened his mouth to say something innocuous about the weather. Mum beat him to the punch, though, as she turned to Azrah. "Are you quite sure it's all right for you to eat Sunday lunch, dear?"

Azrah gave a sugary smile. "Why, do you think I've put on weight, Mrs. Christopher?"

Mum gave her a slow, considering once-over. "No, I don't think you need to be worried *yet*. Although perhaps the Yorkshire pudding might not be the best idea. You're still a little too young to be losing your figure. I was speaking culturally. After all, it's really a *Christian* tradition, and I wouldn't want you to get into trouble at home."

Azrah gave Mum a serious side-eye, although to be fair, since she was sitting next to her a direct look might have given her a crick in the neck. "I've had Sunday lunch round your house loads of times!"

"Yes, but this is in *public*. People can see you."

"And yet, no one seems to care. Trust me. Even if I was a practising Muslim, who's gonna have a problem with me eating lunch? Sunday or any other day?"

Dad gave a loud, fake cough that sounded a lot like *Ramadan*. Then went back to peering at the wine list, although now with a faint smirk.

Robin sent Azrah an apologetic smile across the table. She glared, and mouthed back, *You are going to owe me your* soul *for this.*

"Mum, what did I literally just say five seconds ago about Azrah not being religious? And it's not polite to keep going on about that sort of stuff anyway."

Mum's face got all pinched. "Well, pardon me for taking an interest, I'm sure."

They sat in stony silence as the waitress distributed the bread rolls with a pair of tongs and an uneasy smile, as if she'd picked up on the atmosphere.

"Do you fast for *your* religion, Mrs. Christopher?" Azrah asked brightly once the waitress had gone, tearing her bread roll into tiny pieces.

"Don't be silly, dear. Would you pass the butter, please, Robin?" Mum sawed her own bread roll precisely in half and spread it with an even smear of butter before taking a dainty bite.

"You want to be careful with that." Azrah simpered. "Cholesterol's bad for older people."

"Mum, do you and Dad want to go up first to the carvery?" Robin said desperately. "Me and Azrah don't mind waiting."

"Azrah and I," Mum corrected, almost drowning out Azrah's muttered, *Speak for yourself.* "And yes. Come along, Peter."

Dad grumbled, but followed her up to the carvery, where a white-hatted chef, or at least some kind of pseudo-chef, waited to slice them off a few choice cuts.

"Your soul, *and* your firstborn," Azrah said darkly. "And I've been meaning to ask, what the hell are you wearing? That sweater makes you look too young to drive."

"Mum gave it to me. I thought it might put her in a good mood to see me wearing it."

"If that hideous thing's got any mood-enhancing powers, they're not working on me."

"*You* can talk," Robin said hollowly.

"What, it's worse for you because she's your mum? You don't even live with her anymore."

"It's not that." Robin waited for the concerned enquiry as to what it actually was. Then he remembered this was Azrah. "I bumped into him on the way out."

"Who? Talk sense, will you? I hate stupid guessing games when I'm hungry."

"*Him.* Fridge Bloke."

"What was he doing in your flat?"

"Not in my flat. On the street. Coming out of his house." Robin heaved a despairing sigh. "With his *wife*. And their *baby*."

"Fuck." Azrah's tone was heartfelt.

Robin nodded sadly, as a lady on the next table turned round to give Azrah a filthy look.

"Or rather, *no* fuck, to be brutally accurate." Azrah smirked, but Robin was almost positive there was a glimmer of sympathy in her eye. Either that or it was a reflection from the lights.

Robin heaved a sigh. "I don't know why I'm so depressed about it. I mean, what were the chances anyhow? Even if he'd turned out to be gay, he'd never have been interested in me. I'm too boring and ordinary. My life sucks."

"Yep. But hey, at least your mum and dad are coming back so we can *finally* get some food."

"Don't get the lamb." Mum plonked her laden plate down and started fussing with her napkin. "It's dreadfully undercooked."

"Probably means it's not actually turned to shoe leather," Robin muttered to Azrah as they wound their way through the tables to the carvery. "Yep, there you go—nice and pink in the middle."

He got the chef to give him two thick slices as an act of rebellion, while Azrah stood there for a long while, considering.

"Come on, it's not that hard a choice," he chivvied her along. "My food's getting cold."

"Yeah, but I was going to have the turkey, but that just reminds me of Black Friday and work, now. Then I thought, pork, but your mum'll start going on about me publicly betraying my culture again."

"So have the beef."

"I don't feel like beef. Sod it. I'll have the lamb."

Halfway back to their table, Chip Shop Girl and the Cogling crossed their path like a couple of ill-omened black cats in human form.

Robin nearly dropped his plate. He stared after Fridge Bloke's family and clutched at Azrah's arm.

She yelped. "Oi! You made me drip gravy on my top, you git."

"It's *her*," Robin hissed. "I mean *his* her. I mean *them*."

"Who? This is ten percent silk, you know. Says 'handwash only' on the label."

"You've never handwashed anything in your life. And it's *him*. Fridge Bloke."

"Where?" Azrah swung her head wildly, spilling more gravy.

"Over at the back, where the woman with the baby is just sitting down. But don't loo—" Robin winced as she craned her neck past him.

"The bloke in the suit, right? You didn't tell me he was a posh git. And she's all in rockabilly." Azrah pursed her lips. "Oh, she's pretty. Could be a bit of a cow, mind. Stylish but hard. Do you think that's his parents they're with, or hers?"

"Stop staring at them!"

"Why? Nobody's looking back— Well, they *weren't*."

Robin cringed as Chip Shop Girl sent a hard stare in their general direction. "Come on. Let's sit down and eat."

He strode off back to their table. Dad glanced up as he sat down. "Forget the way, did you?"

"It was Robin," Azrah said. "He's so indecisive."

"We always used to hope he'd grow out of it." Mum pursed her lips as she peered at Robin's plate. "Are you sure you really need that much meat, dear? It's not as though you're particularly large or muscular."

"Chance'd be a fine thing," Dad muttered, frowning at the roast parsnip he was dissecting.

"Maybe he's still growing?" Azrah suggested.

"I'm *twenty-four*. I'm not still growing."

"Nah, you're right. You've reached your peak." She snickered. "Well, your foothill, anyway."

Robin narrowed his eyes at her. "You're still pi— I mean, miffed about that gravy on your top, aren't you?"

Mum tsked. "Oh, you'll never get that out, dear. It's the rag basket for that one. A good thing it wasn't one of your best. Robin, do you know those people sitting at the back?"

Robin made a valiant attempt to inhale a carrot. "No! I mean, what people?"

"The family staring at us. And don't eat so quickly. You'll give yourself indigestion."

Robin kept his head down, his face so hot he was surprised his meal didn't start to char.

Azrah glanced over. "Oh, yeah, they are, aren't they? That's a bit rude. No idea what's brought that on."

"Some people have no manners." Mum sent a death glare over in Archie's family's direction.

Robin thought longingly of sliding under the table, never to be seen again.

CHAPTER  11

When she got back from changing Jerrick, Bridge had a face on her for a mo like a wet Whitby weekend—then she sat down and plastered her smile back on.

Archie wasn't fooled. "What's up?" he said in a low voice.

"Nothing."

He gave her a look.

She rolled her eyes. "Fine. Is that bloke stalking you or something?"

Luckily Pat and Janet were busy cooing over Jerrick, or the mood at table might have gone right downhill. "What bloke?"

"Your not-mate from earlier. Kid in the sweater. He's over there, just coming back from the carvery." Bridge jerked her head.

Archie shot a glance over to where she'd indicated, and yes, Robin was there. He seemed to be having a quiet yet intense argument with a petite, dark-skinned girl. Was that his girlfriend? Not that it was any of Archie's business, obviously.

Was this lunch ever going to end? Suddenly exhausted, Archie just wanted to go home. To check that Lyddie was all right, not for . . . any other reason.

Bridge looked like she was expecting an answer, so Archie roused himself. "It's a free country. Lots of people come here for Sunday lunch."

"Actually, I'm pretty sure I've seen him around before today," Bridge went on.

"Oh, who's this, love?" Janet piped up.

"No one," Archie said quickly. "Someone I've seen a few times, that's all."

"A few times, eh?" Pat's tone had a sour note to it.

"Now, dear." Janet patted her husband's arm with the hand not holding Jerrick on her knee. "Archie can see who he wants. You know that. He and Bridge aren't beholden to one another."

Archie choked on his beer. "I've just seen him, that's all. I'm not *seeing* him. We've barely spoken." He couldn't help glancing back over. Robin and the girl were now sitting down at a table with a sour-faced middle-aged white couple.

"That red-faced startled rabbit in the woolly jumper?" Pat huffed. "Looks closer to Jerrick's age than yours."

"Ooh, he does look young." Janet was frowning.

"I'm not seeing him!" Archie nearly shouted it.

"He's with a girl, Dad," Bridge broke in. "*And* his parents—Well, I'm guessing they're not hers."

"And they'd probably like to eat their lunch in peace, so maybe we should all stop staring at them?" Archie was getting desperate.

"I don't know why everyone's so interested in him," Bridge said shortly. "Haven't we got better things to talk about—like my son, for instance?"

Everyone stared at Jerrick, who up until then had been happily sitting on Janet's lap chewing on a button of her cardi. His little face crumpled under the unexpected adult pressure.

Archie stood up before Jerrick could kick into wail mode. "Hand him over—I'll take him for a wander. He could do with some fresh air. Bridge, can you give me his little jacket? I'll have whatever you're having for dessert."

As they were in town, there wasn't a handy playground at the back of the Ploughman, only a lobster-trap of a car park. Archie took Jerrick out the front instead and played aeroplanes with him until a nearby busker started giving them dagger looks and Archie realised he'd picked up an audience. Apparently a giggling tot re-enacting a First World War dogfight with his dad, complete with moustache-twiddling and exclamations of *Curse you, Red Baron!* had been judged more entertaining than another rendition of "Wonderwall" by Hitchworth's Sunday shoppers.

In the interest of community relations, Archie sidled over and suggested a joint effort of a dance number. It turned out the busker's repertoire didn't include all that many waltzes, and Archie found himself and Jerrick bopping along to "Walking on Sunshine," but at least the audience had sidled with them and started bopping too. It ended with honour intact, a healthy addition to the busker's finances, and smiles on all sides.

Archie mopped his brow with Jerrick's muzzy as he walked back into the Ploughman, the overheated indoor air hitting him like a slap with a blanket fresh from the dryer. He hoped his moustache wasn't about to wilt. The atmosphere at the table, too, appeared to have thawed—Janet greeted his return with a smile, and even Pat unbent enough to mutter, "Eat your apple pie before it gets cold, lad."

All right, it was hardly a public vote of confidence in Archie, but he'd take what he could get. He handed Jerrick back to Bridge with a smile, and tucked into his pud.

"You've gone a bit droopy," Bridge said after he'd finished, just as their coffees arrived.

Pat barked out a laugh. "Now, now. Shouldn't go casting aspersions on the lad's manhood."

Janet giggled. She and Bridge had finished the bottle of wine while Archie was outside with Jerrick, and Bridge never drank more than a glass when she was driving.

"Is that what they're calling moustaches these days?" Archie stood up. "I'd better go and, er, re-wax my manhood, then." He tried not to wince at Janet's shriek of laughter. Good thing he was used to people looking at him anyway. Patting his pocket—yep, tin of moustache wax present and correct—he strolled over in the direction of the gents'.

CHAPTER  12

Robin had done his best to choke down his roast lamb and all the trimmings. It could have been so much soggy cardboard for all he tasted.

He was going to die alone, he prophesied gloomily. And not be discovered for weeks. On the bright side, he wouldn't be eaten by his pets, because he loved animals far too much to condemn them to a life with a total loser like him.

"Was everything all right with your meals?" the waitress asked brightly when she came to clear the plates.

Mum gave her a hard look. "It would have been too late now if it hadn't."

The waitress's smile dimmed. She could probably hear the *chink* of pound coins as her tip tumbled down the drain. "Oh . . . I'm sorry about that. Was everything all right?"

"It was really good, thanks," Robin said quickly if not precisely honestly.

"Would you like to see the dessert menu?"

"Yes, please," said Azrah before anyone else could speak.

Robin had to admire her dedication to getting all she could out of this penance of a meal.

Menus passed around, they all stared at the choices, which were the usual sugar-and-cream–laden confections. "Why is there never anything like a fruit salad?" Robin wondered aloud, and glanced up to see three identical expressions doubting his sanity. "Um, nothing for me. I'll just have a coffee."

Dad humphed, muttered something that definitely included the words *girlish figure*, and announced his intention of having the triple chocolate fudge cake. His tone strongly suggested that real men ate puddings and liked them, although it was possible that Robin was being paranoid. Mum went for the apple pie and custard, probably so she could complain that it wasn't as good as hers.

"Cheesecake for me, please." Azrah said, rising. "And you'll have to excuse me. Need a trip to the ladies'."

Robin jumped up from his seat, desperate not to be left alone with his parents in their current mood. "Me too! Um, the gents', I mean. Not the ladies'."

Dad muttered something that sounded like, *Are you sure?*

Robin's wince was totally not visible to the human eye.

Azrah sent him a sympathetic glance, but he'd long suspected she wasn't entirely human. She linked her arm in his as they headed off towards the facilities. "Come on, we can touch up each other's makeup."

"You're not wearing any makeup."

"What, and you are?"

"No, but . . ." Robin shook his head and dropped her arm. "Never mind. See you in a bit."

He pushed through the double doors to the gents', and nearly had a heart attack.

Fridge Gent was there, his back to Robin. It was the first time Robin had had a good look at him from behind, and with his jacket off. It was an arresting view, his tailored clothing emphasising his trim waist and hips, set off by those impossibly broad shoulders. If they stuck him in the window of Willoughbys, waistcoat sales would quadruple overnight. He was standing in front of the mirror waxing his moustache, and why did that sound like a euphemism in Robin's head?

Play it cool. He strode confidently into the room, slipped on a rogue piece of loo roll, and only saved himself by flinging out a hand to the wall of the nearest cubicle. It hit with a sound like a clap of thunder, swiftly followed by an almighty *Oi* from the bloke inside.

"S-sorry," Robin stuttered. "Slipped."

As if drawn by magnets, his eyes rose to the mirror, where the reflection of Fridge Gent—Archie—was staring back at him in surprise, his eyebrows arching—hah!—in perfect counterpoint to that natty moustache. And yes, the monstrous, sweaty, anguished beetroot looming behind him was indeed Robin's face.

Maybe the ladies' would have been a better choice, after all.

Archie turned to stare straight at him, which didn't improve Robin's composure one bit. "Are you all right?"

"F-fine. Sorry." Robin turned to escape, realised that he did, actually, need to pee quite desperately, and spun back round again, almost tripping over his own feet as he did so.

Perhaps unsurprisingly, Archie was still giving him concerned looks. "Do you want me to get anyone? Treacherous things, tiled floors. You might have turned an ankle. Hit your head on the wall— *Did* you hit your head on the wall? You could have a concussion—" He stepped forward, a hand held up as if to feel Robin's brow for a fever.

"No! Really, I'm fine." To prove it, Robin marched up to the urinal—watching carefully where he put his feet this time—unzipped his flies, and waited for the blessed relief of an emptying bladder.

And waited. There was no sound of retreating footsteps behind him. Mortified, Robin flung an angry glare over his shoulder. "I can't go with you standing there!"

Was there a hint of a blush on Archie's cheeks? "Sorry. Just wasn't sure you were, er . . . I'll see you around, all right?" He turned and left.

Robin resisted the urge to bang his head against the tiles above the urinal. It probably wouldn't be very hygienic.

A toilet flushed, and a large middle-aged man lumbered out of the cubicle to cast Robin a morose glance. "Well, that's my digestion ruined for the day, thank you *so* much. You come in here for a bit of peace and quiet . . ." He stomped out, still grumbling.

Robin decided that anyone who didn't wash their hands after using the loos didn't deserve his sympathy, and *finally* managed to pee.

He got back to the table to find Azrah was already there, as were their desserts.

"Get lost again, did you?" Dad muttered.

Mum looked up from her dish. "You *were* a long time. Is everything all right? I did tell you not to have the lamb. He's always had a delicate tummy," she added to Azrah.

"I have not!"

Azrah sniggered into her cheesecake.

"You should have seen his nappies when he was a baby."

Dad threw down his spoon with a humph of disgust.

Hah. That'd teach him to be all superior about his chocolate fudge cake. Robin stirred cream into his coffee and tried not to glance over at Archie's table. Where he was with his family, including his wife-or-girlfriend and his *kid*. And for some reason, gazing over at Robin . . . Oops.

Fighting a hot flush to rival one of Mary-from-Haberdashery's, and hers were *legendary*, Robin tried a bit harder not to look at Archie.

"Robin? Robin!" Mum's strident tones were almost a relief, giving him something else to think about. "I've been talking to you for the last five minutes. Are you sure you're all right?"

"Sorry. Um, what was it?"

"Oh, never mind. I can't be bothered to repeat myself."

"I think he's just really into that coffee," Azrah said. "At least, *something's* got him all hot and bothered."

"It'll be the caffeine," Mum said decidedly. "I've told you before it's bad for you, Robin. Perhaps you ought to leave the rest."

"I'm *fine*, Mum."

"Well, if you can't sleep tonight, don't come crying to *me*."

As if. She'd broken him of that habit at a *very* early age.

"Really not sure about this bloke of yours," Azrah said once they'd finally waved goodbye to Robin's mum and dad and were sitting at an outside table, hunched against the cold but nonetheless glad of the fresh air. "Wearing a suit on a Sunday? Are you sure he's not a Jehovah's Witness?"

Robin put down his rum and Coke. He'd felt in need of a stiff drink after the ordeal, and even Azrah had gazed longingly at the alcohol before opting for a hot chocolate. "I don't know! I don't know a single thing about him. Except that he's got a wife and kid. Which means he's not my bloke. So can we talk about something else, please?"

Archie and his family had left the Ploughman a while before Robin's parents had. Not that Robin had been hyperaware of Archie's movements, or anything.

"Nah, Jehovah's Witnesses never have such cool moustaches," Azrah went on as though he hadn't spoken. "Or girlfriends who look like she did. Wives. Whatever. Actually, are they the ones that have lots of them?"

"Lots of what?"

"Wives. You could be his number two." She sniggered. "Sounds like a bit of a shit job to me."

"Har har. And yeah, that'd work so well, what with me being a *man*. It's Mormons who have all the wives, anyway. Do we even have any of those in Britain?"

Azrah shrugged. "You're asking me about stuff to do with religion? That's like asking Jesus how long you have to sit under a Bo tree to get enlightenment."

"I think you just undermined your own point, there."

"Whatevs."

"I know, maybe he's a Satanist?"

Azrah narrowed her eyes. "Have you been reading the *Daily Mail* again? I told you, they make all those stories up."

"Hey, Satanists get a lot of bad press, but I knew one at uni and he was the nicest guy around."

"Invite you over for barbecued goat every Sabbat, did he?" Azrah frowned "How come the Sabbath is a holy day, but a Sabbat is supposed to be evil? What's even the difference?"

"An *h*. And sabbats aren't evil. That's just medieval Christian propaganda. Like saying pagans always worship sky-clad."

"*What* clad?"

"Sky-clad. It means in the nuddie."

"'In the nuddie'? Is that how you talk to your blokes? 'Ooh, I want to get in the nuddie with you'?" She cackled.

"Shut up. I was being polite." Mum's company tended to have a regrettable ongoing effect.

"And anyway, you seem to know a lot about all this stuff. Are you sure you're not a Satanist?" Azrah gave an evil grin. "If I chuck some holy water on you, will you go up in a puff of smoke?"

Robin took a dignified sip of rum and Coke before he answered. "That's vampires. And no, I'm not a Satanist. You can tell by the general lack of occult symbols about my person."

"Hey, for all I know you've had a pentagram tattooed on your unmentionables."

"Mum would disown me if I ever got a tattoo." Robin brightened. "Hey, there's a thought."

"I bet your fridge bloke likes tattoos," Azrah said with a leer. "Especially on your unmentionables."

"He does. He's got like Latin around his neck? It's so hot." Robin deflated. "But every time I see him I make a complete arse of myself. Even if he wasn't married with a kid, there's no chance he'd ever want to see my—"

"Actual arse?"

"I was going to say *tattoo*, but yeah, that as well." Robin sighed.

He'd have been better off developing a crush on one of the Willoughbys Menswear mannequins. Then again, with his luck, the object of his affections would no doubt end up in a bridal display with a hot little model from Ladies' Fashions.

Later, feeling particularly masochistic, Robin found himself looking up the name *Archie* on social media. After all, how common could it be? Less common than *Robin*, probably, and he was pretty sure that anyone trying to look *him* up wouldn't have to wade through umpteen pages of false hits before they got to the right Robin. So he was expecting to find *his* Archie—no, *not* his Archie—fairly easily.

There was an American comic books company. There was a vocal quartet. There was even a member of the Royal Family, and Robin wondered if Archie's mum had seen *that* coming when she named him. But Fridge Bloke, there was not.

Robin gave fervent thanks that he hadn't been able to attempt this little bit of internet stalking before Azrah had seen the man. Otherwise he might have been seriously worried he'd hallucinated him. But *why* wasn't he on social media? How did he, like, talk to people, or find out what his mates were doing?

Then again, Archie *did* have a definite retro vibe going on. Maybe the internet was the sort of new-fangled rubbish he didn't hold with.

Robin sighed and gave up. After all, it wasn't as though finding endless photos online of Archie smiling happily at his wife and child would have made him feel any *better*.

CHAPTER  13

Lyddie was in the kitchen, clearing out a cupboard she'd cleared out only last week, when Archie got home from the Ploughman. "How was your posh Sunday roast with the in-laws?" she asked, putting a tin of tomatoes on top of the cooker.

Archie, who'd been lost in thought, blinked at her fake smile and answered it with one that was equally forced. "Yeah, good."

She gave him a look that said she not only wasn't buying it, but she wouldn't take it as a gift even if it was all wrapped up with a bow on top.

Archie sighed. "Oh, her dad's still a bit . . ." He made a helpless gesture.

"Thinks you seduced and abandoned his little girl?"

"Kind of. And then there was Bridge . . ." Archie shook his head. "It's nothing, and it's not even true, but it hurts that she'd think it, you know?"

"Think what? Archie, love, what did she say to you?" Lyddie put her hands on her hips, looking ready to march off on her bare feet and confront Bridge this minute.

"She's worried I'll forget about Jerrick if I meet someone else. Stop being a dad to him." His chest ached thinking about it.

"That's bollocks, and I've a good mind to go straight round and tell her so. You, abandon your own kid? My Archie? Who does she think she is, throwing accusations like that?" Her narrowed eyes widened again, and she cocked her head to gaze at him. "*Have* you met someone else? How come you didn't tell me? You know you can tell me anything. Who is it? Do they like you back?"

Archie groaned. "Maybe? I don't know."

"Which? You maybe met someone? Wouldn't you know? Unless you were on drugs. Archie, love, you'd tell me if you were on drugs, wouldn't you?"

He had to laugh. "No, I'm not on drugs. Cross my heart. No, I just keep bumping into this guy—"

"Oh, well, it's fate, then, isn't it? You and him. Meant to be."

"Doubt it. I'm pretty sure he's got a girlfriend. And he thinks I'm weird and probably scary." Archie cringed, remembering how spooked Robin had been in the gents'. "And he's almost certainly too young for me."

"Who wants someone who's the same as every other bloke? And if he likes you, this girlfriend can't be serious, can she?"

"I don't even know if he *does* like me." Sometimes he thought there was something there . . . but since most of their interactions had mainly consisted of Archie babbling inanely while Robin stared at him like he'd grown an extra head or three, there most likely wasn't. Archie's heart sank.

"Course he likes you. How could anyone not? So go on, tell me about him. Is he cute?" Lyddie's smile was sunshine-bright.

"Yeah, he's cute. Nice eyes. Sort of dark-blond hair, a bit fluffy? But he's probably still in his teens."

"Oh, age is all relative," Lyddie said vaguely. "I never worried about it."

And yeah, that had been half the problem, hadn't it?

CHAPTER 14

Robin's Monday started with a summons to Gail's office. Heath, who'd delivered the message, tapped one overlarge foot while Robin made sure the till was covered, checked he hadn't buttoned up anything the wrong way this morning, and headed off. Apparently not trusting him to find the way himself, Heath fell into step beside him. "It's like being back at school and getting sent to see the headmistress," Robin muttered, mentally casting Heath as a jobsworth prefect in that scenario.

Heath smiled mistily. "Innit just? And they say you can't go back."

Gail was, if possible, looking even more harassed than usual. "Come in, both of you, and shut the door."

Robin did as she asked, by which time Heath had co-opted the only visitor chair, spun it around, and plonked himself on it backwards, his chin in his hands and his elbows on the back of it as if trying to re-create that sixties photo of Christine Keeler naked. They'd reprinted it in the *Telegraph* Sunday Supplement one week, and Mum had been so outraged she'd switched to the *Observer* for a month.

On the whole, Robin was quite happy to be standing. At least no one was looming over him.

"Right," Gail was saying. "I've decided on the date for the Loyal Customers' Christmas Shopping Evening."

"Or *Customas*, as we're now calling it," Heath put in. "Celebrating our customers, see?"

"It's going to be on the third Thursday of November," Gail continued.

Robin frowned. "Wouldn't Tuesday or Wednesday be better? It'd make it more special. We always stay open late on Thursday."

"Which *means* we already have staff rostered in for that evening." Gail's tone was impatient.

"Or later in the month? You know, nearer Christmas?" Robin persisted.

"It can't be the following Thursday, as that's Thanksgiving," Gail said sharply.

"But we don't celebrate that. Nobody in Hitchworth's going to be sitting at home in a turkey and pumpkin pie coma."

"Speak for yourself, mate." Heath grinned. "Some of us just go where the party is."

"The point is," Gail said impatiently, "there's no sense having it the day before Black Friday. The customers will be confused and we'll be too busy."

"What about the Wednesday that week? Although I suppose that's still a bit close as the crow flies." Robin frowned. Had he actually said that? He had, hadn't he? Hopefully no one had noticed. He went on hastily, "Or even earlier, like the week before?"

"It *can't* be earlier than the third Thursday," Gail said with the force of a deity handing down the commandments, "as the town's Christmas lights don't go on until the day before. We can't have a Loyal Customers' Christmas Shopping Evening—"

"Or Customas," Heath interrupted helpfully. She seethed at him.

"—if lights-up hasn't happened yet. The atmosphere wouldn't be the same. We want people in a festive mood, ready and willing to spend their money on their loved ones."

Robin knew when he was beaten. "Okay, Thursday the third. I mean, the third Thursday. So we need to sort out publicity, catering... um, how many mince pies do you think we'll need? And what about mulled wine? Do we want to water it down a lot so they won't have to worry about driving home, or do we keep it strong so they'll spend more? And—"

"Heath will be handling the catering."

"He will?" Robin had mixed feelings about this. On one hand, it was nice to not be responsible for *everything*. On the other... wasn't this supposed to be *his* baby?

On the third hand, hadn't he wanted to get Heath involved and seen as indispensable?

Heath beamed. "I got all the figures."

"How?"

Heath tapped his nose. "That, my friend, would be telling."

Gail huffed. "There's no need to be mysterious about it."

Heath sent her a pointed look. "Or *is* there?"

She blinked, then visibly decided she wasn't being paid enough to worry about it just now. "In any case, Robin, you can leave that to Heath. I want you to handle publicity."

"Azrah would be good at that," Robin said quickly, remembering his plan.

Gail frowned, then shook her head. "If you think she'd be better for the job, then I suppose I have no objections. I'll call a general staff meeting to brief everyone on the plans, and ensure Heath and Azrah get every assistance they require."

Wait, what? "So I'll be, uh . . ."

"Don't you worry, mate," Heath said. "I've got a pivotal role planned for you."

"Which is?"

Gail opened her mouth but Heath beat her to the punch. "All in due course. Gotta set a few more plates spinning first, lob a few more balls in the air, but you'll be the first to know on the night."

"And I'm sure *you'll* give Heath your fullest cooperation, Robin." Gail's gimlet glare managed somehow to convey subtle disappointment. "Now, if you could send Azrah to see me?"

Robin walked out of Gail's office in a daze. He'd gone in—or so he'd thought—as an up-and-coming star of the retail industry, with a key sales event to plan and execute.

He'd come out as Heath's dogsbody—pivotal role his arse. And Azrah's messenger boy.

"So how did it go?" Robin asked Azrah morosely some hours later when she popped into Menswear on her way back from her break. "I mean, with Gail, about the event thing." He was *not* going to call it Customas.

"Really well." Azrah appeared to be taller, somehow. Was she wearing heels? Robin snuck a glance. No, that wasn't it. Maybe she was just standing straighter. "She's not as bad as you think, is she?"

"Isn't she?" Robin sighed. "Maybe it's just that *I'm* not as good as she thinks I am."

"Or *does* she?" Azrah gave a creditable impersonation of Heath at his most gnomic.

"That was not the part of my statement that I wanted you to cast doubt on, you know."

"Or *w*—" Azrah caught herself, possibly on seeing Robin's glare. "Gotta go. See ya! Don't forget your sleeping bag tomorrow!"

Robin didn't find out what she was on about until he was closing up the till, and Gail stopped by to fix him with a stern look. "Don't forget tomorrow is Bring Your Sleeping Bag to Work Day."

Robin blinked. "Uh, what?"

She tutted. "Really, Robin, do *try* to keep up. I thought Azrah had passed on the message? All staff are bringing in sleeping bags tomorrow."

Robin stared. "Are they servicing the boiler or something? Wouldn't big coats be better? I mean, you can't really move around much in a sleeping bag—"

"You won't *be* moving around. It's for the photographer." She tutted again. Apparently Robin's face was doing a bang-up job of showing his confusion. "For the advert. For the sale? You *do* remember we're having a Black Friday sale, I hope?"

"Oh—yes. Sorry. So, this advert—we're going to be the queue? Sleeping on the streets to keep our places?"

"Obviously."

"Right. Um. Anything else we need to bring?"

She raised an eyebrow. "Such as?"

"I don't know—pyjamas, teddy bear . . ."

Gail clapped her hands together. "Excellent idea. Do that."

The problem was, now he was living on his own and free of parental censure, Robin didn't actually wear pyjamas in bed. Or anywhere else. He'd never quite got over Azrah turning up unexpectedly at his mum and dad's during his short-lived teenage phase of experimenting with the Noel Coward PJs-and-smoking-jacket look, and laughing her arse off.

When he'd moved out of his mum and dad's house, all the nightwear his mum had bought him had been furtively donated to a local charity shop, so the only pyjamas he had left to his name were the set he'd left at Mum's. They were a size too large, because apparently Mum thought he was still growing, and they had Rudolf the Red-Nosed Reindeer on them.

Maybe he could somehow get hold of a less objectionable set of jammies by tomorrow morning? Say, from Willoughbys? Could the gossip about what he might be trying to hide about his normal nightwear be any more embarrassing than exposing his *actual* nightwear to his colleagues?

Yes, yes, it could. Heath in particular could usually be relied on to come up with some inventive ideas.

Damn it. Rudolf jammies it was. Now all he had to do was get them back from Mum and Dad's. Robin sighed. He was going to have to make a detour on the way home tonight.

It felt strange, pushing open the wrought-iron gate and walking up the garden path of his childhood home as a visitor, rather than a resident. As if he'd moved out far longer ago than a couple of months. The house even loomed slightly smaller than it did in his memory.

Although he still had his key, Robin felt oddly as though he should ring the doorbell. Fortunately, he remembered in time just how much Mum disliked going to open the door to unexpected callers— "*If I'd wanted to be put out, I'd have invited them.*"

He opened the door and stepped inside, calling, "Hello? Mum? Dad?"

Nobody answered, but he could see his mum through the open door to the kitchen. She was standing by the worktop, glaring at a pile of potatoes as though they might start to peel themselves out of sheer embarrassment.

"Hi, Mum," Robin said as he walked into the kitchen.

"Oh, Robin." Mum's voice was flat. "I'm in the middle of cooking dinner. If you'd *said* you were coming over, I'd have made sure I bought enough for you. As it is, I'm afraid it really won't stretch. And in any case, you were the one who was so keen to move out and get your independence. I'm not at all sure how independent you're being if you think you can come here for a meal at any time of the day or night—"

"I'm just here to pick up some stuff, Mum," Robin said quickly, although he couldn't help thinking that if there was any time of day or night when he might reasonably have had some hope of getting a meal, it was *dinnertime*.

She brightened. "You're taking your Doctor Who toys at last, are you? I must say, I won't be sorry to see the back of them. They take up a great deal of space in the second spare room—"

"The second . . . Oh, you mean my bedroom? And they're figures, not toys."

"Don't interrupt. It's rude. And of course there's all the dusting. I knocked three of them off the shelf when I went in the other day, and— Robin? Robin! I hadn't finished speaking to you."

Robin took the stairs two at a time. He should have known his collection wouldn't be safe without him to care for it. What if she'd chipped the paint? Or worse, actually broken any of them?

He pushed the door to his room open. The little china plaque that had proclaimed it to be "Robin's Room" for as long as he could remember was gone, leaving only a faint darker patch in the paint to show it had ever been there. Inside, too, there had been some changes made. A table with Mum's sewing machine now took up most of the floor space. She seemed to be in the middle of making something from a vast quantity of spectacularly vile floral material in garish shades of pink and orange. Robin shuddered, crossed his fingers it wouldn't turn out to be curtains for his new flat, and trod carefully round it to his bookshelf.

Most of his books having moved on to either the new flat or the Oxfam bookshop, he'd left the shelves looking rather bare. They were bare no longer. A comprehensive collection of Mills and Boon classics now graced the top shelves, which was the first shock—Mum read romance? Surely they weren't *Dad's*?—swiftly followed by the second shock, which was the sight of his prized collectibles shoved roughly into a corner on the bottom shelf. Half of them weren't even standing up.

And they were dusty.

Robin mentally apologised to each precious figure as he took it from the geek ghetto and carefully inspected it for damage. All were intact, thank God—but there was no way he was leaving them here a moment longer. If current trends continued, they'd be in the bin by New Year. Maybe he shouldn't have downplayed to Mum about just how much they'd cost?

On the other hand, that might have led to her listing them on eBay.

Robin suppressed the urge to march downstairs and demand to know why Mum hadn't taken more care of his stuff. He'd had urges like that before, and they never ended well. Instead, he dived under the bed to find a storage box and dumped out its contents, a collection of cotton reels and embroidery threads, on the bed. He regarded the resultant tangle with great satisfaction and a hefty dollop of guilt, which he manfully pushed down into a corner of his soul he did his best to ignore. It was getting a bit overfilled these days.

Now, how to pack them to be safe on the bus? Sadly the original boxes weren't an option— Mum had had most of those in the bin seconds after he'd opened them and taken out the figures, and on one memorable occasion, *before*. Inspiration hit, and he pulled open his bottom drawer. Yep, still full of the lifetime's supply of socks Mum had made it her mission to provide him with over the last twenty-four Christmases. He carefully socked up each figure, then padded the box out with his pyjamas.

By now the smell of cooking meat and onions had started to drift up the stairs, and Robin's stomach gurgled loudly as he tried to decide firstly, if he had the makings of a meal at home, and secondly, if he'd be able to make it back there without keeling over with hunger. Maybe he could grab something from the kitchen while Mum's back was turned?

When he got downstairs, though, he found Dad waiting for him.

"Funny how all the strays turn up at meal times." Dad huffed. "I suppose I'll have to ask your mother to put some more veg on."

"No, it's—"

"I've already spoken to him," Mum yelled out from the kitchen over the sound of sizzling. "I've told him he can't stay. It's for his own good."

Dad rolled his eyes. "First she worries about you not eating enough, now she thinks starvation is good for you."

"I'll be fine, Dad. I'll get some chips on the way back or something. I'd better go—don't want to disturb your dinner. Er, nice seeing you."

Dad huffed again and wandered back towards the living room. Robin clutched his storage box tighter to his grumbling stomach, and headed out into the dark, autumnal street.

He got lucky with the buses, catching one with only minutes to spare, which gave a much-needed boost to his spirits. With a whole seat to himself, he got out the Doctor and Rose to check they'd survived the journey so far. Yes, they were looking good. Robin gave them a smile and a little pat, and wrapped them up again carefully in their socks. When he glanced up, a short-haired teen in a man's overcoat gave him a smile and a thumbs-up, but Robin's stop was coming up so he could only give his fellow fan a nod in passing.

All in all, he was in much better spirits by the time he stepped off the bus and feeling *totally* equal to a short detour to the chip shop where the scary probably-Mrs.-Archie worked. He prided himself on serving difficult customers with a smile, so he shouldn't be scared of anyone on the other end of the service transaction. It would be good for him too—stop his ridiculous pining after someone who was already taken. His stomach growled in agreement. Robin squared his shoulders, hefted his storage box high, and marched through the streets to the chippie.

There was a cluster of customers milling around waiting for their food to be cooked, so it wasn't until Robin had excuse-me'd his way into the shop that he saw him.

Archie, his back to Robin and his baby in his arms, talking to Scary Chip Shop Girl, who had a big smile on her face as she cooed at her kid. Robin stalled, and whether it was his sudden stillness or his constant Robin-ness, he didn't know, but something made her glance up. Their eyes met, and her smile became a quizzical frown.

Archie turned, one eyebrow raised. "Robin?"

Robin shifted the box in his arms. "Uh, yeah. I mean, hi. Again." He dried up.

Archie coughed. "I brought Jerrick in to see his mum at her job."

"That's good. Um, it's never too early to instil a good work ethic." Robin swallowed.

Mrs. Archie's frown lost its quizzical quality, which upped her Scary quotient quite a bit. "Are you going to order something? Only there's people behind you."

Robin whirled. Yep. There they were. People. "Um, sorry." He turned back, reluctantly. His appetite had fled. Clearly it had more sense than the rest of him. "Er, small chips, please?"

"One pound sixty. Salt and vinegar?" She was viciously shovelling up chips as she spoke.

Robin rested his box against the counter and fumbled for the right money, eyeing the growing pile of fried food with misgiving. "Yes, please. And, uh, that was a *small* chips." He glanced at Archie for support, and found him giving the proceedings an equally worried eye.

"That's all right. Mate of Archie's, aren't you?" She added another obscenely large shovelful to the greaseproof paper, doused the chip mountain in salt and vinegar as though treating a particularly virulent slug infestation, wrapped up the parcel and thrust it at him. "Here you go. Enjoy." Her tone subtly suggested that by *enjoy* she meant *choke on it*.

"Thanks." Robin grabbed the chips—he needed both hands—and deposited them on his storage box. Then he hefted his load, muttered, "*Bye*," and left. What had he ever done to Mrs. Archie? Apart from fancy her probable husband, that was, but she didn't know that, did she?

Oh God, did she?

CHAPTER  15

Robin slept uneasily after his overlarge supper, and woke up late, with barely enough time to pack his sleeping bag before haring off to work.

He bumped into Azrah on the way into Willoughbys. "Got all your stuff for tonight?"

"I'm all set." Azrah patted the surprisingly small roll she was holding under one arm, and eyed his bulging bin bag, unimpressed. "Looks like you've got a double duvet in there. And his-and-his pillows."

"We can't all afford the latest in microfiber technology for our camping gear."

She snorted. "You, camping? The last time you were in a tent was in my mum and dad's garden, and you thought my Mr. Bouncy was a rat and ran home screaming."

"Kangaroos and rats have many similarities," Robin said stiffly. He frowned. "Don't tell me you've got your pyjamas in there too. Or your, um, nightdress?" Having not had a sleepover with Azrah since they'd reached high school age, Robin was a little unclear what grown women wore in bed. He had a strong suspicion his mum's full-length button-to-the-neck winceyette nightie wasn't exactly the norm.

Robin realised Azrah was staring at him. "Um, sorry, did I miss something?"

"My *nightdress*? No, I haven't brought it. Think I'm letting all the pervs in this store cop an eyeful?"

"I thought you liked letting your inner slut out to play?"

"That's play. This is work. I've got a professional image to maintain."

Robin raised an eyebrow.

"Hey, I will have one day."

He patted her shoulder. "You just keep thinking positive like that. See you at lunch?"

"Can't—I'm having lunch with Gail. We're going to go over a few things for the Loyal Customers' Christmas Shopping Evening. See you tonight."

Damn it. Robin had wanted to talk to her about his encounter with Archie and his family in the chip shop. Get a female perspective on what it all meant—and in particular, the way Bridge had described him as a mate of Archie's. Had Robin misread everything? Was she just being nice last night, rather than trying to kill him with calories? Did that mean he'd got it all wrong about her and Archie?

Deprived of Azrah's advice, he resorted to asking his first female customer, an elderly lady buying novelty socks. "If a woman tries to feed you up, does it always mean she likes you? That'll be ten pounds, by the way."

"There you go, dear. Well, I'd say if she cooks for you, she's probably a keeper. Most of these modern girls seem to think that's all beneath them. You get a ring on her finger before she changes her mind."

A wedding ring! Why hadn't he thought to look for that? On either Bridge's *or* Archie's fingers? What an idiot. Robin slapped his forehead. "Ow. And thank you."

"You're welcome. And good luck with your young lady."

"Thanks."

She leaned over the counter, patted his hand, and lowered her voice. "Probably best not to go hitting yourself in front of her, though. She might think you're a little strange."

Usually, Robin liked the end-of-day ritual of cashing up and tidying the department. Not that he didn't enjoy serving customers, but it was always nice to be able to turn off the helpful smile, and let his resting bitch-face out to play.

But today, they had the photoshoot to get through. Robin half thought of trying to sneak off and hope he wouldn't be missed, but Gail was already bearing down on him like an iceberg to his Edwardian cruise liner.

"Have you brought your sleeping bag?" Gail sent him a piercing look.

Robin tried to make his nod enthusiastic. "Sleeping bag, jim-jams, the lot."

"Oh, excellent. I knew I could count on you to go above and beyond." Her expression softened minutely, then hardened again. "Well, don't just stand there. Go and get changed. The advert is due to run in tomorrow's *Hitchworth Echo*, so there can't be any slip-ups. Robin, *why aren't you getting changed*?"

Robin scurried to the loos with his bag.

Rudolph the Red-Nosed Reindeer stared apprehensively in the mirror at him as he rolled up his overlong pyjama sleeves and hoiked up the trousers as far as they'd go. At least he looked festive. Unfortunately, he also looked like a preschooler at a pyjama party. Robin sighed, and padded out to face his doom.

The shop staff congregated by the front doors, sleeping bags in hand or slung over a shoulder.

"Love the jim-jams, mate." Heath grinned down at him. *He* was dressed in work trousers and an improbably large cable-knit sweater.

Robin glanced around. He was the only one there in pyjamas— everyone else was still in their work clothes.

He was *definitely* the only one there clutching a teddy bear.

Worse, he realised as Gail shepherded them outside, there were some rough sleepers sitting bundled-up in doorways giving them curious looks. There was the large, friendly bloke Robin sometimes bought a sandwich for, and Sheppy's Mum who always told him she was fine, thanks, but Sheppy wouldn't mind a dog biscuit. Oh God, was Gail about to ask them to move on? Or worse, would she just pretend they weren't there and do the photoshoot around them?

Robin sprinted over to Gail as fast as his bunny slippers would let him. "I think we ought to ask them," he gasped out.

Gail turned, her harassed frown easing as she took in what he was wearing. "That's the spirit, Robin. Ask who, what?"

"The, um, the people in the doorways. We should ask if they mind being in the pictures. I mean, they might have reasons they don't want to be in the papers."

Gail's voice took on a mildly panicked tone. "If you think they're evading police, we certainly don't want them in our advert."

"No—I meant they might be, um, escaping a violent situation? Or they might not want their families to know they're homeless and worry about them? I'll deal with it," he added desperately.

She nodded, looking puzzled. Robin had always wondered what she thought about the homeless people of the town. He was starting to suspect she'd never actually noticed them—or had tuned them out, ignoring them like you'd ignore a litter of kebab wrappers, or an even less appetising memento of a really good night out.

Robin made his way over to Sheppy's Mum. He'd half expected her not to want to be photographed. She tended to hide her face a lot, showing only the locks of bright-orange hair that spilled out from her hood, so he wasn't surprised when she stood up. "I'll give Sheppy her walk, then. You keep the place warm for me, yeah?"

Robin nodded. "Thanks. And I'll buy you a bag of chips when we're done." It was a shame chips didn't keep, or he could've brought some of his mega-portion from last night.

"Oh, don't worry about that. But if you're passing Sainsbury's, Sheppy wouldn't mind a few biscuits, would you, girl?" She patted the dog's brown side with her tattooed hand and a heavy tail wagged, batting against Robin's pyjama leg.

"It's a deal."

The large, friendly bloke—his name turned out to be John, but he promised not to attack Robin with a quarterstaff on any local bridges—was happy enough to get his face in the papers. Or at least, he was after Robin promised him a cod and chips with mushy peas for his trouble. "And make sure you get the mushy ones. I'm not having those poncey garden peas. Roll all over the bloody place, they do, and you're finding them in your bedding for weeks afterwards."

"Mushy. Not garden. Got it," Robin assured him, and hurried back to Sheppy's Mum's sad little bundle of belongings.

Azrah was arranging her own sleeping bag not far away. "God, it makes you think, doesn't it? Here's us complaining about having to be out in the cold for half an hour while they take a photo, and these people have to live out in it."

"*I'm* not complaining about being out in the cold." Robin was undergoing a novel experience: feeling grateful that his mum had insisted on buying him thermal undies despite him never having been near a ski slope in his life.

"Well, I am. It's bloody perishing out here. And Mary-from-Haberdashery won't stop going on about how the cold's bad for her joints. That's why I moved down here to be with you."

"And here I was thinking it was because you love me so much."

"I might love you more if you moved a bit closer. Ditch the cuddly toy and cuddle me instead. And seriously, you brought your teddy? Did your mum make you bring him?"

"*Her*, actually." Robin sniffed and placed Teddina carefully on his lap. "And no. Mum doesn't even know I'm doing this. She'd probably pitch a fit if she knew I was hanging around with homeless people like John."

"Hah. Remind me to go round your house tomorrow when the *Echo* comes out with the ad in. That's gotta be better than watching *EastEnders* any day."

"Oh, God. She won't see it, will she? Mum doesn't think the *Hitchworth Echo* is a proper newspaper. She never looks in it. She only uses it for people to put their shoes on when they come into the house."

"Can you afford to take that chance? I can see her now, spreading out those pages on the carpet to stop any of that nasty dirt touching it—and oh, who's that in the picture?"

"Oh God. No." Robin grabbed Teddina, and held her firmly up in front of his face.

"Can we lose the teddy bear, please?" came a yell from the front, where the photographer was setting up.

"It's so it'll appeal to families," Robin yelled back in desperation.

"And furries," Azrah muttered, thankfully too low for anyone else to hear.

The photographer shrugged, and presumably decided either (a) the client was always right or more probably (b) it was too flippin' cold to stand out here arguing when there were warm pubs aplenty.

He spent the next ten minutes taking a couple of dozen shots from various angles, and Robin didn't come out from behind Teddina until Azrah had sworn on Mr. Bouncy's life it was all over. It was a relief to get changed back into proper clothes, duty finally done for the day. Well, all except buying the promised cod, chips, and Bonios for John and Sheppy. He bought a container of soup for himself—the smell of the chips was making him queasy—and "accidentally" picked one up for Sheppy's Mum as well. They all had a nice little natter over their food, with John explaining he'd been in the army until he got PTSD and Sheppy's Mum not saying anything about her past whatsoever. They both told him off for staying out in the cold with them.

Robin felt unusually contemplative as he caught the bus home.

CHAPTER  16

Tuesday evening was the monthly Hitchworth Steampunk Society pub social night, which for Archie meant a rare chance to be one of the least weirdly dressed people in the room. Bridge gave him a lift as she wasn't drinking—Archie was pretty sure it was down to the calories, but no way was he going to ask. Jerrick was being looked after by her mum and dad. Lyddie had offered to have him, but she'd also muttered something about taking the opportunity to tell Bridge off for doubting Archie, so he'd thought it best to decline. She'd forget about her anger soon enough. Lyddie was like that. Unfortunately, Bridge *wasn't*. She could turn grudge-bearing into an Olympic sport. Still, she seemed to be in a much better mood tonight, chatting away and cracking jokes.

Although the one about checking the coast was clear of Archie's so-called stalker hadn't struck him as all that funny.

Archie hadn't known what to think about his encounter with Robin on Monday evening. He half wished he'd made more of it at the time—he'd hardly spoken to the bloke—but it'd been awkward with Bridge there being all passive-aggressive with the chips. *She* clearly hadn't changed her views since Sunday lunchtime.

Robin had been dressed in a suit, presumably on his way home from work, so he was definitely older than school age. What did he do for a living that required him to stay so late—and maybe even take work home? Although that box could have held anything. It would have made a good conversation starter, if Archie had had half a brain cell about him. He felt a pang in his chest at the lost opportunity to get to know the guy better.

Then again, with Bridge in that mood, it might've ended in ketchup bottles at dawn, so perhaps it was just as well.

There was no parking at the Brick and Bottle, so they had to walk a short way through the centre of town, Bridge drawing more than a few glances in her heavy brocade coat and bustle skirt. She'd gone for a sort of Victorian mourning look tonight, and the ends of the gauzy black scarf tied around her top hat fluttered in the breeze. There were a couple of good-humoured catcalls from rough sleepers they passed on the way, and Archie's trouser pockets were soon lighter by a few pound coins. John, who dossed down on the square near Willoughbys, offered him a few leftover chips from the fish supper some Good Samaritan had bought him, but Archie turned him down when he saw Bridge's wistful look. "I think they'd gone cold anyway," he whispered to cheer her up once they were a safe distance away.

"You think that makes a difference? Worst thing about being on a diet. I keep getting cravings for stuff I don't even *like*, normally. I mean, I haven't fancied chips since the first week I got that job at the chippie, and now I *literally* want to grab them out of the hands of the starving."

"Want me to tighten your corset?" Archie grinned as they pushed open the door of the pub. "That'll stop you eating anything."

"Won't stop me wanting to. Oh look, the Doc's here," Bridge nodded at where the plague doctor was sitting at a table in their usual niche at the back, talking to Nikki. She was always the first one there. She said, what with all the faff of travelling in a wheelchair, she didn't want to have to worry about being late as well.

Archie reckoned the Doc liked to get there early to maximise his chances of creeping out the punters. The regulars at the Brick and Bottle didn't pay him much attention these days, being used to a six-foot-six apparition in a bird-shaped mask, wide-brimmed hat, and black duster leaning over the bar to order a pint with a straw, but there were always one or two newcomers for him to put the wind up.

Archie was pretty sure the Plague Doctor was a *him*. He certainly never corrected anyone's pronouns, and statistically speaking most people that tall with a voice that deep were guys. Archie was a bit short on any other physical clues, though, seeing as the Doc always kept in character and never took his mask off, at least not anywhere Archie had ever seen him.

Presumably he had a whole other life somewhere. Archie often wondered if he'd met the bloke in mufti, and had developed an embarrassing habit of peering suspiciously at anyone he encountered who was his height or taller. Although Bridge had pointed out the Doc's footwear had two-inch heels, and could have lifts in to—hah—boot.

Archie waved at him, and the Doc raised his nearly full pint glass and took a sip through the straw. "Right, they're sorted, so what are you having?" Bridge asked.

"G&T if they've got the Lincoln Gin back in. If not, I'll have a rum and Coke."

"Rum and Coke? That's not very steampunk."

"Hey, pirates drank rum. And they're sort of steampunk."

"Yeah, but they didn't drink *Coke*. On account of it not having been invented until, like, the 1900s or something."

"Time-travelling pirates might, and they'd be even more steampunk. And anyway, Coke was invented in 1886 which makes it totally steampunk."

"You do realise what knowing the exact date Coke was invented says about you, don't you?"

"That I'm an educated, well-informed gentleman?" And that it helped to be able to give younger visitors to the museum some information they could relate to.

"You keep telling yourself that. Nerd." She turned away to the bar, probably so she'd have the last word.

Archie went to join the Doc. "How are you keeping?"

"Good, good. The pestilence has not ensnared me with its fatal miasma. Although I think I might be coming down with a cold."

"Yeah, there's a lot of it about." Still, with that mask on there was no danger of the Doc spreading his germs to anyone else. Archie would rather not catch anything he might pass on to Jerrick while the kid was so little, thanks.

Soon after Bridge got back with the drinks, Lord Peregrine and Lady Edith Bressingham-Steam arrived in state, the crowds around the bar parting with the ease of long practice to allow room for

Perry's cane and Edith's impressively wide leg-of-mutton sleeves. There were very few doorways she could have got through without turning sideways, so it was just as well she wasn't wearing one of her equally impressive bustles or she'd have been doing the sand-dance just to get around. She hand-made all her and her husband's outfits, and her ball gowns were amazing. Tonight she was channelling Queen Victoria herself in a Black Watch tartan skirt-and-jacket combo, with a matching waistcoat for Perry under his frock coat.

Bridge nudged him. "I love those two. They're like a real-life romance novel."

"If you're talking about *Fifty Shades*, I don't want to know."

"I was thinking of one of Mum's doctor-nurse romances, actually, so get your mind out of the gutter. You know that's how they met, right? Perry was a dashing young doctor just arrived from Jamaica, and Edith was a midwife. They fell in love over an emergency caesarian."

"Sounds unhygienic."

Bridge tsked. "You've got no romance in your soul."

"If your idea of romance involves blood, gore, and danger of death, then no, I haven't. And were you aware the Herts vampire society is looking for new members?"

"Stop making stuff up. There's no vampire societies in Hertfordshire. You have to go into London."

"I am so not asking how you know that."

"I am so not volunteering that information. But seriously, don't you think they're romantic? Still together after all these years. I mean, come on, they're like *ancient*. Older than my gran. And they'd have had the whole racial-divide thing to worry about back then. It was a much bigger thing in them days."

A couple more members turned up in normal clothes, pulling hats out of bags and putting them on as they reached the group. Not everyone could get away with as much as steam casual for their day jobs.

Archie was one of the lucky ones with his job at the workhouse museum, where they actively encouraged him to dress in Victorian gear—although he had to leave his steampunk goggles at home. It was fair enough, as even his proper vintage welding goggles were at least twenty years too young to be in period, and it wasn't like anyone had ever welded in a workhouse anyway. They'd have been too busy picking oakum and looking forward to Sunday, when they might actually get to see their spouse for an hour or two. Much as he loved the Victorian era for its style, inventiveness, and insistence on good manners, Archie had to admit their idea of social welfare had been a bit crap.

Perry's grizzled curls glistened in the lamplight as he tapped on his glass with one be-ringed finger. Pomade, Archie guessed. "Ladies, gentlemen, and other esteemed members, welcome to our humble gathering."

If you listened really hard, you could just make out the warmth of Jamaica in Perry's tones. But you had to listen *really* hard. Maybe accents had been a lot more important when Perry came to Britain too.

Perry went on, "First on the agenda tonight—"

"Since when do we have an agenda?" Bridge yelled with a grin.

Perry raised his glass to her. "My dear lady, the agenda may not have been visible at previous meetings, but I assure you, it was always present in spirit. Now, *if* I may continue"—he fixed Bridge with a twinkling dark eye and she toasted him with a wink—"our first order of business is the proposed change to the name of our splendid society. As many members know, it has been brought to our attention that Hitchworth Steampunk Society, or HiSS, causes potential confusion with the Historic and Interesting Surrey Steampunk Society, or HISSS. Therefore, we invite alternative suggestions from the floor."

"Splendid Hitchworth Eccentrics and Explorers of the Paranormal?" the plague doctor suggested. "Although the acronym is perhaps somewhat lacking."

Yeah, Archie didn't reckon SHEEP really cut it, either. "Maybe if we added "Electric" at the start, to give us Electric SHEEP? No, hang on, that'd be cyberpunk. Ignore me."

"How about Steampunks of Hitchworth, Including Time-travellers?" Bridge called out.

"I like that one!" That was River, who tonight was dressed down as David Tennant's Doctor Who. They looked good in the sharp suit and overcoat, but Archie's fave was their TARDIS outfit. It was epic, complete with flashing light on the top hat and woop-woop noises.

Somebody laughed, and River frowned. "Wait a minute . . ."

Perry had to call for order after the rest of them worked out *that* acronym and choked on their drinks.

"Sorry," Bridge said, cheerfully unrepentant.

River rolled their eyes like a teenager. Fair enough; they *were* a teenager.

"We have a suggestion: Steampunk, Historically Eccentric and Retro-futurist Paranormal Alliance, or SHERPA." That was Pearl, of Roger-and-Pearl, a fun couple in their forties who always turned up in matching pith helmets. Pearl was wearing her dinosaur-print bustle tonight.

"Isn't that a bit, well, imperialist?" Archie couldn't help thinking of Victorian explorers getting all the credit while native guides and bearers did all the work.

"In fact, it's a subtle tribute to the *real* hero of the first successful Everest ascent, Tenzing Norgay," Pearl corrected in her school governor voice.

Archie had often thought she'd have made an excellent *actual* female Victorian explorer, never mind just dressing as one. He could see her taking no nonsense from any men who tried to tell her a woman's place was in the home.

"Commendable, and well overdue." Perry's voice was warm and approving.

Archie wasn't *totally* convinced it might not be taken the wrong way, but he wasn't about to accuse a black bloke of not knowing racism when he saw it. "Okay, fair enough."

"Votes, then?" Lady Edith quavered.

"Hang on a mo." Bridge had been frantically scribbling on a beermat. "What about Alternative, Eccentric Time-travellers of Hitchworth and Esteemed Retropunks? *AETHER*."

There was a general, impressed *ooh*. If there was one thing steampunks agreed on, it was the excellent qualities of aether. Aether was like steampunk vibranium. You could claim any properties for it you wanted, use it to fuel your imaginary airship or run your hypothetical communication device, and there were no pesky real-life limitations to get in the way. Just like goggles on top hats, octopodes on outfits, and cogs on everything under the sun were a hefty visual signpost that steampunk was being perpetrated here, aether was a sort of verbal clue to expect steam-powered servants and clockwork spaceships.

"It doesn't include the word 'steampunk,'" Pearl complained.

Bridge raised an eyebrow in a way that managed to subtly suggest the girding of loins and polishing of knives and other bladey things. "Does it have to?"

Pearl sniffed. "We *are* a steampunk society."

"Yeah, but some of us are into dieselpunk too. Retropunk's like an umbrella term. It's more inclusive." She folded her arms.

Archie fought the urge to applaud. *Way to take the moral high ground, Bridge.*

"We'll have a show of hands," Perry said firmly. "Who's for SHERPA?"

AETHER won by a stiffly waxed whisker. Bridge beamed. Pearl looked disgruntled but shook Bridge's hand with polite resignation.

"Now, plans for the festive season," Perry announced with an expression of profound relief. "Who will join us for a group visit to the Victorian Market?"

River raised a hand. "Would we need to be proper Victorian, or can we dress steampunk?"

"Good question, young River. I've spoken to the organisers, and they and I—and my dear Lady Edith, of course—feel it would be more appropriate for us to come as a visibly steampunk group."

"Cos they don't trust us to get Victorian right," Bridge muttered to Archie.

"What if we're trading at the market?" Nikki's clear voice carried across the hubbub, and the feathers on her hat bobbed as she spoke. "I know Dora's got a stall."

"Dora's not here tonight, is she?" Perry's gaze searched the room.

"Probably frantically crocheting stock for the market," Bridge whispered in Archie's ear. "That or panicking about it on social media." She pulled out her phone and, after a moment, cackled as she showed Archie a post from DoraLadyExplorer that started *Dammit dammit dammit I will NEVER book a stall again . . .*

Perry coughed. "I'm sure traders will have been given the market guidelines."

"Dora's always in full Victorian anyway," Archie pointed out. Dora was a fully paid-up member of the Steamstress Squadron and stitched her own historically accurate outfits, corsets worn under the clothes and, according to Bridge, traditional split-crotch bloomers too.

He hadn't asked Bridge when she'd got to see Dora's bloomers. There were some things no man was meant to know.

"Yeah, but there might be someone else trading?" Nikki looked around the group. "What, no one?"

River made a face. "You have to be over eighteen."

"Ah, that's a shame."

Archie agreed. River made jewellery and badges, which would have been a hit with the Christmas shoppers.

They finally got down to the business of agreeing on a date for the group visit—in just over a fortnight, the Thursday after the town Christmas lights-up—and the meeting moved onto the drinking-and-nattering bit.

Archie found his attention drifting. Wouldn't it be weird if Robin happened to walk into the pub? Given how much they'd been bumping into each other lately, it wasn't *totally* impossible. Lyddie reckoned all these chance meetings meant they were fated to be together. Archie wasn't sure if he believed in fate, but if there *was* some kind of higher force out there, it definitely seemed to want to guide his footsteps Robin-wards. Or the other way around.

And if Robin *did* happen to come in for a pint, that'd mean he wasn't too young for Archie, wouldn't it? They were pretty hot on checking your ID here if you looked under twenty-five. All the underage drinkers went down the other end of town to the Dog and Ferret, where the bar staff didn't give a toss how old drinkers were as long as they had money.

Then again, Robin already thought he was weird. Archie gazed around at his companions, clad in an eclectic mix of neo-Victorian and science-fiction styles with the odd whimsical nod to *Alice in Wonderland* or *Doctor Who*, and tried to see them with new eyes. He swallowed. If Robin walked in now wearing his fashionable yet conservative work suit, would he come and sit down with the group, maybe compliment the odd outfit or hat—or run a mile?

CHAPTER  17

A rchie had barely set foot in the house on Wednesday night when Lyddie waved a newspaper in his face. He blinked. "Huh, the *Echo*'s on time for once. Must be audit week."

Lyddie made an incoherent noise. "Have you seen this load of arsewipe? 'Bag your place in the Willoughbys sale queue now' it says. Har, har, I *don't* bloody think."

Archie frowned. "What's supposed to be funny about it?" The paper had been gone before he could tell what she was looking at.

"Cos they've bunged in a picture of people making like they're dossing in shop doorways. In sleeping bags, get it?" Her tone was savage. "Are they seriously taking the piss out of the homeless, at this time of year?"

Archie grabbed the paper from her and held it still so he could actually focus on the page. His grip grew tighter as he realised what he was reading. "Exploiting the homeless, more like. Oh, bloody hell, it gets worse. 'With prices like these, there's no need to go without at Christmas.'" One of the pretend rough sleepers—presumably shop staff, as actors would have wanted to be paid—was hiding his face with a teddy bear, so at least one person had some shame. Or maybe not—that was Sheppy's Mum's patch the bastard was squatting on, wasn't it? Most likely she and Sheppy had been told to bugger off while they all posed and pretended.

He threw the paper down in disgust. "What the hell were they even thinking? It's a total kick in the teeth to anyone who's struggling. How do they think it's going to go over with anyone who's out there in the cold, wondering where their next meal's coming from?" Archie stamped down hard on the memories that threatened to bubble over, but somehow a shiver still escaped him. He shot a guilty glance over at Lyddie, but luckily she didn't seem to have noticed.

"I've got a good mind to go and complain," she was saying. "Know what? I reckon I should. Everyone should. We ought to get a march going, or a demonstration, maybe. You'd come with me, wouldn't you, love? And Bridge would. We could get all the real rough sleepers to come along too. I bet they'd love that at Willoughbys, a load of down-and-outs turning up at their posh store. Serve 'em bloody right. Bastards."

"Okay, hold on a mo. I don't like it any more than you do, but I'm not sure we want to *start* with the civil unrest. How are you going to escalate after that? What about writing to the shop management first—or the local paper?"

Lyddie nodded. "Yeah, that'd work for a start. You can't let people get away with things, you know? It'll just keep on getting worse." She stared at the wall, obviously lost in thought.

Archie decided it was probably safe to leave her to it and make a start on dinner.

Work was pretty busy on Thursday. They had a school party visiting the museum, which meant Archie got to break out all his most gruesome tales of life below the poverty line before social security had been invented. He loved this part of his job. The kids ate up all the gory details of how harsh life had been back then, but it also got them thinking about how different life could be for other people.

He always ended it with asking the kids if they reckoned the workhouse paupers had deserved what happened to them. Nobody ever seriously suggested they had, although there was always the odd joker in the class who tried to play devil's advocate.

After they'd been through that, Archie decided to take it a bit further. "And what about people you see sleeping rough these days? Do you think it's their fault?"

Their teacher, a pretty young white woman with a middle-class accent, frowned but let him run with it.

One girl put her hand up. "Well, yeah, cos we've got benefits and council houses and stuff these days."

"What if their benefits don't come in time, or aren't enough to cover their rent? Or if they've been on the council's list for months to get a flat they can afford, but the housing just isn't there and because they're not elderly and don't have kids, they keep getting passed over?"

"My dad says they're all alkies," a lad near the back shouted out.

Archie looked him in the eye. "Some rough sleepers are. And some of them have a drug problem, or mental health issues. You really think that means they deserve to sleep out in the cold and the rain, rather than getting the help they need to get their lives back on track?"

Nobody seemed to want to speak up this time. Archie went on, "And once you're homeless, it can be very hard to break out of it again even if you haven't got health or addiction issues to deal with. You can't get a job because you haven't got an address—and let's face it, you probably wouldn't get past the interview anyway, because it's so hard to keep yourself and your clothes clean living on the street."

There were a fair few frowns as the kids tried to reconcile this with the limited world view they'd absorbed from their elders.

The teacher stepped forward. "I think that's all we've got time for. Thank you for that highly interesting and thought-provoking talk, Mr. Levine, was it?"

"Archie," he said, giving in with good grace.

"Archie." There was a hint of a blush on her cheek. "Children, if we could all show our appreciation for the talk?"

She clapped and was joined by the kids in dutiful applause.

As they filed out, one of the kids hung back. "Homeless people *aren't* all alkies," she said defiantly.

Archie guessed she'd wanted to say it to the boy earlier, but hadn't had the nerve. "No, they aren't. But they all deserve our help."

She nodded and headed for the door, where her teacher was waiting with a complicated expression on her face.

He wondered what the girl's story was, but it wasn't his place to ask.

Archie found Lyddie in the kitchen when he got in from work that night. "Did you have a good day?" he asked, giving her a hug and a peck on the cheek.

"Yeah. Got lots done." Lyddie hummed a happy tune and went back to pulling cans out of the cupboard. "Thought we could have curry for tea, but I can't find the chickpeas. Do we need chickpeas? Will kidney beans work instead? What do you think, love?"

"I think we'll never know until we try." There were used teacups and plates with cake crumbs on them stacked by the sink, so Lyddie must have had someone round while he was at work. Archie was glad. Her downward spirals always seemed to start with her isolating herself from everyone but him.

She didn't say anything more about Willoughbys during the evening, so perhaps that bee in her bonnet had flown off to find another hive. Probably just as well, although Archie wasn't planning to let the issue slide. Maybe he'd write to the *Echo* himself over the weekend. There wouldn't be another edition out until next Wednesday, so it wasn't as though there was any hurry.

Jerrick was grizzly tonight. His red little cheeks suggested it was teething, but he also chucked up his milk, so it could be colic. Or something else entirely. With zero evidence to go on, Lyddie blamed it on him picking up a bad atmosphere at Bridge's mum and dad's. In any case, there wasn't a lot Archie could do for the poor mite, apart from spend the evening walking around the house with his son in his arms.

"You need a sling for him," Lyddie suggested. "Save your arms. Or we could make one out of those long strips of cloth like all the yoga mums do."

Archie smiled down at the tearful little face. "No, he's fine. You're not heavy, are you, mate? Bantam weight champion of the world."

"Bantam. Like the chickens. Is that the lowest one?"

"What, weight category in boxing? Not sure. It's definitely lower than featherweight."

"Well, that's just stupid. Shows how bad boxing is for your brain. Why would a feather weigh more than the whole chicken?"

Archie chuckled. "Don't ask me. My mum never let me take part in combat sports."

"That's cos I didn't want you around a load of thugs. Violence doesn't solve anything."

Maybe not, but knowing which end of a fist was which might have come in handy during a certain part of his life. Knowing how to throw a punch—and more importantly, how to dodge one—could have saved him a lot of aggro. Archie didn't say it, though. It wasn't her fault things had turned out how they had, and anyway, that was all in the past now.

Next morning, Archie had his breakfast as usual and got ready to go to work. He was about to step out the door when Lyddie called him back.

"Wait a minute, Archie, love. I've got a letter."

Archie frowned. "It's too early for the post."

"No, I mean I've *written* a letter. To Willoughbys. You can take it in on your way to the museum. I'm not wasting the price of a stamp on them." She held out a sealed envelope to him. It was addressed to *The Manager, Willoughbys*.

"Uh, what exactly have you written?" Archie's misgivings flitted in his stomach like the butterflies of foreboding. "Maybe I should give it a read-through?"

"Don't trust me to write a letter, now?" Her tone was sharp.

"Of course I do. Just . . . sometimes these things are better with a second opinion."

"Well, hah to you, cos it's had one. I wrote it with Shirley from down the road, cos she volunteers with Crisis, so she knows what she's talking about. She thinks it's a crime and all. We've set up a group, and we're going to do placards today and write to all the papers."

"Wait, what? You didn't say anything about this last night."

She shrugged. "I was tired, wasn't I? Had a busy day. Now go, all right? You're going to be late for work. And I want that manager to see that letter as soon as they get into work. Let 'em know people care about this sort of thing, and we're not going to roll over and let them screw us for a profit. And don't worry, it's all anonymous, so no one's going to be knocking on our door."

Archie winced. "Lyddie . . ."

"Go!" She flapped at him with her hands.

The butterflies mutated into pterodactyls as Archie let himself be shooed out of the house.

He seriously considered just not delivering the letter, but . . . he couldn't do that. It'd be a total betrayal of trust, and if there was one thing he could never do, it was betray Lyddie. She'd had too much of that in her life already. He'd have to hope Shirley-from-down-the-road was a more stabilising influence than she'd seemed in his vague memory of a tall, middle-aged woman with a sharp nose and softly flowing hippy skirts.

CHAPTER 18

Friday morning, Gail was looking even more stressed. Deep lines had etched themselves at the corners of her mouth, which was so tight-lipped Robin imagined her having to drink her morning coffee through a straw. It gave him inappropriate giggles as she walked by.

"Is something *funny*, Robin?" she snapped.

"Uh, just remembered a joke on the telly last night. Sorry." Robin's conscience twinged. She didn't need him to make her life harder.

"Well go on, then, share with the class," Heath said from Gail's side. He seemed to be aiming to make that his permanent position lately, which Robin could only put down to Gail's warning about redundancies. "Think we could all do with a laugh this morning."

"Er . . . You had to see it. So, um, you're not having a good day, Gail?"

"No, I am *not*." An elderly gentleman came up at that point with a pair of socks, took one glance at Gail's face, and backed away hurriedly. Hopefully to find another till, rather than to abandon his purchase in fear. "I received a very unpleasant letter this morning. As though I haven't been doing my best to save this store for the community. Don't people *care* about keeping one of the last few independent department stores afloat?"

Robin peered closer, and was horrified to see she seemed close to tears. "What did it say?"

Heath gave him a shifty look. "Later, salesdude. You just keep ringing up the moolah for now." He put his hand in the small of Gail's back, and to Robin's astonishment she allowed Heath to shepherd her through the store and towards her office.

Heath caught up with Robin and Azrah in the cafeteria at lunchtime. "I sent Gail home to recover," he said, sitting down with his plate. He'd gone for the healthy option today—only one doughnut, and an apple.

Robin looked up from his quiche and salad. "You sent— Remind me who works for who around here?"

"I think you'll find that's '*whom* works for who.' And hey, so she's my boss, so what? Sometimes even the top dog needs permission to be human."

"Did you just call Gail a dog?" Azrah asked.

"Did you just call Gail human?" Robin put in.

Heath shook his head, tutting. "Walk a mile, my friends, walk a mile."

"Is that you telling us to piss off?" Azrah frowned. "And anyway, what's it all *about*? Gail's letter, I mean."

"So, The Letter." Heath paused to give them both a portentous look. "Delivered by hand this morning at some time before Gail arrived to open up."

He paused again. Robin wished he'd just get on with it.

"It's from an organisation calling themselves Community Over Consumerism. Or COC."

Azrah sniggered. "Cock?"

"You'll be laughing on the other side of your face when they picket our Black Friday sale."

"What? Why would anyone do that?"

"Seems they've taken exception to our ad in the *Echo*." Heath shook his head sadly. "Some people don't understand art."

"What was there to object to?" Azrah demanded, aggression in every inch of her five foot two.

"'Belittling the plight of the homeless,' the letter said," Heath told her.

"Some people are always after something to get offended about," she snapped, sounding worryingly like Gail at that moment.

Robin wasn't so sure. "I guess it could be seen as a bit . . ." He trailed off in the face of their, well, faces. "Don't look at me like that. I'm just trying to see it from their point of view." He'd found it hard to forget about John and Sheppy's Mum, and he hated to think he'd taken part in something that'd . . . what was the phrase? Belittled their plight, that was it.

Except *they* hadn't seemed to mind. Did that make it okay?

"You can't go around seeing everyone's point of view all the time," Azrah said flatly. "Sometimes you've simply got to pick a side. And *my* side's the one my bread's buttered on, which is Willoughbys' side."

"That's a bit harsh, isn't it?"

Robin quailed at her glare.

"Is it? How many homeless people were actually harmed in the making of that advert? From what I heard, you ended up giving at least two of them a hot meal as a direct result, so I don't see what anyone's got to complain about. It was a bit of fun, that's all."

"Yeah, but whoever came up with the idea for that ad could've put a little more thought—"

Heath interrupted him with a loud, fake cough that sounded a lot like *Azrah*.

Robin stared at her. "Wait, what? The ad was *your* idea?"

"Well, yeah! You're always telling me I need to be professional and serious about my career, so when Gail called me in for that meeting about the Loyal Customers' Christmas Shopping Evening, I thought, now's my chance to show I'd been thinking about Black Friday too. So I suggested it to her. And she *liked* it. She got straight on the phone and set it all up there and then so it'd make it into this week's *Echo*." She folded her arms.

"Losing sight of the real issue here, people." Heath looked unusually serious. "Which is that we have a planet-sized PR disaster waiting to happen."

Oh God. Things had to be bad if they needed *Heath* to drag them back on track. "Are these . . . COC people . . . seriously planning to stage a demonstration on Black Friday?"

"Nobody knows. But what would you do, if you were COC? Heh. COC Robin."

"So what are we supposed to do about it?" Robin asked, ignoring the snickering. "How do we stop them? What do they even want?"

"Apart from a few hints on avoiding Freudian slips?" Heath shook his head. "That's the question, isn't it?"

"Don't they say? That's so bloody helpful, isn't it?" Robin clenched his hands into fists to stop them doing anything unfortunate like tearing his hair out. "So what *do* we do? Cancel the Black Friday sale?"

"Yeah, cos it'll be *so* great for the homeless if we lose all our profits, Willoughbys closes, and the local economy tanks." Azrah's tone was withering.

"Shh!" Robin glanced around furtively. "You'll have everyone panicking."

"Let's not count our apocalypses before they're hatched." Heath made *calm down* gestures. "It could all be a bluff."

"Yeah, but we don't know, do we? Is Gail going to write back to them?" Robin was *not* going to start biting his nails again.

"Can't. No address on the letter. No names, even. Just COC."

Azrah huffed. "That doesn't sound very professional. Was it scrawled in crayon? Or made from bits of cut-out newspaper?"

Heath shrugged. "Printed out from your average home computer, I'd say."

Robin found his hand approaching his mouth and snatched it back hurriedly. "Should we tell the police? Was it really threatening?"

"Eh, more on the vaguely disquieting side. 'The people will make their feelings known,' and all that." Heath sat back and picked up his doughnut.

"So it *might* all be a load of nothing? And how come you got to see the letter, anyway?"

"I'm her rock. Her rock against COC." Heath grinned and took a huge bite of doughnut.

Azrah groaned. "I know why Gail went home. She couldn't take Heath's puns any longer."

CHAPTER  19

Robin didn't *mean* to peer into Archie's house as he passed by that Saturday afternoon. It just sort of happened without any conscious decision on his part.

He'd needed a bit of retail therapy after the events of Friday—there was nothing like buying stuff you didn't need to ward off the horrors of potential future unemployment and penury. So he'd been into town to go to the shops he *didn't* work at. He'd come back with a really cool shirt and an amazing pair of shoes, classic yet individual, which he'd put on as soon as he'd got home so he could start walking them in. As it was a nice day for the time of year, i.e. not actually raining, he decided he might as well walk them in outdoors.

He ambled along the street, idly wondering what he was going to have for his tea, and letting his feet take him where they would. Apparently his feet really liked Verne Avenue, which just so happened to be Archie's road. They were taking him past Archie's house when, oh look, his shoelace started to come loose. Better stop and tie it a bit tighter before it came totally undone and tripped him up as he was crossing the road, sending him straight under the wheels of a double-decker bus. Which would be tragic, as nobody had seen him in his cool new shoes yet.

While he crouched down, it was only natural to cast a glance through the rusty wrought iron gate. After all, his fingers had been tying laces for twenty years now, give or take. They could probably manage perfectly well without any input from his eyes.

The garden was mostly overgrown shrubs, with some signs of recent—and ruthless—cutting back having gone on. The front door was painted heritage green, which Robin recognised from having spent many a Sunday teatime listening to his aunt Susan complain about the limited range of paint colours English Heritage allowed to use on her house, which was a listed building. The bay window was a sash type Robin hadn't thought existed any more outside of Peter Pan movies, but which went perfectly with the large, old-fashioned knocker on the door. Despite the cold—the sun hadn't actually gone down yet, but it was, metaphorically speaking, putting on its coat and checking it had its keys—the sash was thrown up, and a woman was sitting on the windowsill, gazing out.

More precisely, she was gazing straight at Robin with a strong hint of amusement in her raised eyebrow.

As Robin lurched to his feet and struggled to untangle them enough to sprint far, far away, she met his gaze and beamed as though he were her long-lost son. "All right?" she called out. "Are you looking for Archie? He's not in right now. He had to go into work, some kind of a thing . . . I know he told me, but what was it, now? Works too hard, he does. Still, what can you do? Not like anyone'd hire me." She gave a loud . . . well, Robin had been brought up properly, which was a euphemism for strictly, so he'd call it a laugh, but he had a strong suspicion that anyone else might have termed it a cackle.

She was a petite woman, with very white skin, big brown eyes, and a huge mop of floofy dark hair as if she'd gone back in time to an eighties hairdresser just after they'd had a fresh crate of mousse delivered.

Who on earth was she? A lodger, Robin decided. It must cost a lot to keep up an old house like that, and with Possibly-Mrs.-Archie only working nights in the chippie, and child care to worry about too, they could most likely do with the extra money. Maybe this lady babysat for Archie and his wife when they wanted a romantic night out . . . Robin swallowed, and tried not to think about that. "Um, I was just passing . . ." He took a step forward, trod on the end of a shoelace, grabbed hold of the gate to stay upright, and almost fell over again as it swung open.

The woman threw her legs over the windowsill and jumped out of the window with total disregard for a couple of sad little plantlings in the flowerbed underneath. Her clothes were a weird mix—a pair of wide-legged pinstripe trousers, coupled with a tight T-shirt and a grandad cardi that looked like it'd been lent her by an actual grandad. She didn't have any shoes on, but her thick woolly socks were probably proof against anything short of Biblical floods.

She walked towards Robin, her footsteps barely crunching in the gravel drive. "So you thought you'd drop in? Aw, that's lovely! Come on in and I'll make you a cuppa. I think we've got some tea. Or was it coffee? We've definitely got all kinds of herbal stuff. No, come on, I insist. Any mate of Archie's is a mate of mine. Gets a bit quiet round here when he's out. Maybe I should get a dog? Do you have a dog? Or a cat. Cats are good. Or a ferret. Nice shoes, those. Archie's always saying I should wear shoes."

Stupefied by the flood of words, Robin found himself being taken by the elbow and steered into Archie's house—thankfully, through the front door, rather than the window. Then it hit him. If Scary Chip Shop Girl only worked nights, she could very well be in the house right now. He swallowed. "Is the rest of Archie's family in?"

The woman stopped so suddenly that Robin almost fell on top of her. "Over my dead body." Her tone had flicked a switch from babbling brook to glacial meltwater.

What the hell had they done to her? Was she even talking about the same people? "I . . . uh . . . The baby? And the lady with the . . ." Temporarily unable to remember the technical term for the sort of poofed-out skirt Scary Chip Shop Girl had been wearing when he'd seen her last, Robin found himself tracing a voluptuous figure in the air with his hands.

Sunshine broke back over the woman's face. "Oh, *them*. Thought you were talking about *my* family. No, they're over on Shelley Street, Bridge and Jerrick, bless him. Where the chippie is, you know? It's just me and my Archie here. Except he's not."

"Your . . ."

"Oh, didn't I say? Forget my own head next. I'm Lyddie. Archie's mum."

Robin blinked. "You don't look nearly old enough." She didn't—there was a wide-eyed innocence about her that didn't gel with Robin's ideas of parents of adult children.

She laughed again, much more musically this time. "Oh, get away with your bollocks! You're a proper charmer, ain't you? I'm telling

Archie that one, he'll have a fit. No, he's all mine. Child bride, I was. Well, less of the bride. Never really believed in it myself. Come on in and I'll get that kettle on."

She padded down the hall, her socks leaving faint muddy traces on the floorboards. Robin struggled briefly: his mum had always been strict about him taking his shoes off when visiting someone's house, but she'd also been pretty forceful about not walking on dirty floors in his socks. He decided in the end that anyone who wore socks outside probably wouldn't care too much what he did with his shoes, and kept them on. She led him into a medium-size kitchen that must have been the height of modernity sometime in the seventies and had been resting on its laurels ever since.

"How do you know my Archie, then?" Lyddie yelled over the noise of the kettle filling.

"Er . . . we've bumped into each other a couple of times, that's all. I'm Robin, by the way." Did she know her son went out at night to do unspeakable things to vulnerable fridges? Robin felt very strongly that he shouldn't be the one to break it to her if not.

"Biscuits, biscuits, biscuits . . ." Having put the kettle on, Lyddie looked blankly around the kitchen. Then her eyes lit up. "Cake! We've got cake. Bridge brought it round. You go and sit down. Not there; those chairs aren't fit to be sat on until we get them painted. Living room is over the hall. You can't miss it. Not unless you end up in the loo. I'll bring it all through."

Robin retreated into the hall and struggled with a brief, unworthy impulse to take the opportunity to escape. He pushed it down firmly and opened the door to, as it turned out, the living room.

It was a large room but nonetheless cosy, with a squashy sofa and a comfortable clutter of newspapers, discarded woolly jumpers, and— *Oh good God, what's that?*

A sizeable portion of one wall was covered in newspaper clippings. There were placards on sticks propped against the wall, reading *People Not Profits* and *Willoughbys Will Not Win*. A bit of old board had what looked like an oddment of wallpaper pinned to it, with a list of objectives penned in scruffy Sharpie.

Robin was apparently standing in the campaign headquarters of the alarmingly real and not at all bluffing Community Over

Consumerism group. *Well, this is all a bit of a COC-up*, he thought hysterically.

"So what is it you do for a living, love?" Lyddie came out of the kitchen brandishing a slightly lopsided Victoria sponge cake. And a very large knife.

Robin panicked. "I, I work in a . . . in an office. As a . . . an accountant. Lots of numbers. Totally boring. I don't like to talk about it."

She put her head on one side. "Aw, bless. You ought to think about a different career if you hate it that much. Can't waste your life doing stuff you don't like. Course, what would I know? Done bugger all in my life." Her shoulders slumped, the cake listing on its plate and the knife hanging limp by her side.

All at once she seemed fragile rather than frightening. Robin's stomach twisted. "Can I help you with that cake? Let's put it down here, and I'll go and get some plates. Wouldn't want to get crumbs on your carpet."

She didn't say anything, but her eyes held a hint of *Blimey, aren't you posh?* Robin was as quick as he could be fetching the plates—it helped that the kitchen was surprisingly well organised—and when he returned, cut her a large slice.

Lyddie, who'd ignored the sofa to sit cross-legged on the floor, gave him a brave smile. "You're a treasure, you are. And you're not even all that young, are you? How old are you?"

"Uh, twenty-four." Why was she so interested in his age?

"That's plenty old enough in anyone's book. Why aren't you with my Archie? He could do with someone like you."

"Um, because he's married to a woman? With a kid?" With a sort of when-in-Rome spirit, Robin hitched up his trouser legs and sat awkwardly on the floor in front of the sofa.

Her peal of laughter was high and delighted. "Archie? Married? Where did you get that one from? Oh, he's going to piss himself when I tell him. Married! Not that she's not a lovely girl, but them, married? It'd never work. Tell you the truth, I've always reckoned he'd go for a bloke in the end. Too like his old mum, he is."

"But . . . it is his kid, isn't it? The baby?"

"Oh yeah. He's a darling, isn't he? Spitting image of his dad. But they split up well before Jerrick was born, him and Bridge did."

"So . . . they're not together anymore? At all?" Okay, she'd pretty much *said* that, but Robin was feeling too elated to trust his own senses and would rather like some additional confirmation.

Lyddie leaned forward, her elbows on her knees. "They look after Jerrick together. He's a great dad, Archie is. I won't have no one saying he's not. None of this buggering off and leaving her to it like his own dad did. Well, I say his dad. Who really knows, right? But he could have been. If he'd wanted to. Archie has him evenings, after work, while Bridge does her shift at the chippie. Always has." She cocked her head and gave the now thoroughly confused Robin a curiously shrewd glance. "You like him, don't you?"

Robin inhaled a mouthful of cake. And not in the ate-it-quickly way.

Lyddie laughed her head off at his choking fit, her earlier sadness apparently forgotten. At least she thumped him on the back while she did so. It didn't seem to help much, and Robin had a feeling he'd be bruised in the morning, but the sympathy was welcome.

The coughing finally subsided, leaving him red-faced and still spluttering slightly, so of course, that was the perfect moment for Archie to walk in, debonair as always—for about a nanosecond. Then his eyes (which, even in his mortified state, Robin noticed were the same rich shade of brown as his mum's) widened comically as they took in Robin sitting down with his mum like the stalker who came to tea.

There was only one thing, Robin thought in a detached way, that could possibly make this more embarrassing, and that was if he'd blurted out "You're not married!" to the unwitting object of his affections.

And then Archie's jaw dropped, Lyddie burst out laughing again, and Robin realised that the reason he'd had such an oddly specific thought was that he had, in fact, done just that.

CHAPTER  20

A rchie had walked in on any number of strange or embarrassing scenes involving his mother, but somehow none of them had prepared him for this. He felt uncomfortably hot, and absurdly self-conscious. "Robin?" he said weakly. "And no, no, I'm not. Married. Never have been. Uh, who told you I was?"

Robin's face seemed to get even redder, which Archie would have bet a crate of Dapper Devil Moustache Wax wasn't actually possible. "I just . . . thought? You know, with the cog-thing—"

"Cogling?"

"Right, and Scary Chip Shop Girl—"

Lyddie shrieked with laughter.

"—and the whole family out for Sunday lunch and all. And, um, I think I'd like to go home now. And never go out anywhere ever again." He tugged at the collar of his flannel shirt, clearly miserable.

"You think Bridge is scary?" Archie asked, because of course that was the most important issue.

"You don't?"

"Um, no?" Archie glanced at Lyddie, but she was still having fits and was no help. "And anyway, you were out for Sunday lunch with the family too. Are you married?"

He meant it in the sense of *See how ridiculous your assumption was?* but had a nasty feeling it came out sounding more like *Please be single.*

"What, to Azrah? Oh God, no. *No.* She's like my oldest friend. Or frenemy. Sometimes it's hard to tell. And she doesn't want to get married. To anyone, not just me. Not that I would, because I'm gay. Did I mention I really ought to be going?"

"You want cake, Archie? We've got cake. And tea." Lyddie looked around, and frowned. "We were going to have tea, I'm sure we were."

"Sorry, my fault." Robin stumbled to his feet. "Forgot to bring it in. I'll get it now."

Archie watched him go, trying not to be ridiculously happy at the knowledge Robin was into blokes. It got easier when he turned to Lyddie and saw the state of her socks. "Where did you find him? And you know you shouldn't keep going outside without your shoes on. It's not the middle of summer anymore."

Lyddie did her usual note-perfect imitation of a teenage eye roll. "I only hopped out the window to say hi. Robin came to see you, didn't he? So I was making him feel at home."

Robin had come to see him? Archie couldn't imagine why. Unless . . . No, that was just wishful thinking. And hadn't he decided Robin was too young for him? In the event Archie was in the market for a boyfriend, which he certainly wasn't.

Except that Robin seemed a lot more mature today, in a pair of casual trousers and a much less objectionable sweater over his checked shirt. He looked older, and sharper, and not to put too fine a point on it, exactly like the bloke Archie had been dreaming about ever since they'd first met over the fridge. And he'd been sitting on the floor with Lyddie, which was all kinds of endearing.

No, no, it wasn't. Or it shouldn't be, at any rate. Archie had responsibilities. He couldn't go around finding people adorable. He took a deep breath. "Right. I'll go help him in the kitchen, and see what he wants."

"Oh, I know what he wants," Lyddie sang out, and laughed again.

Trying not to read too much into it—Lyddie was notorious for seeing things that weren't there—Archie left the room before she could start quizzing him on what *he* wanted. He found Robin searching the kitchen cupboards. "What have you lost?"

Robin jumped and banged his head on a cupboard door. "Um, mugs. And tea. And milk. And possibly sugar if your mum or you take it." He turned, rubbing his head, a lopsided expression on his face that in no way made Archie want to kiss him.

Get a grip. "Mugs are top left. Milk's in the cellar, but don't worry about it cos we're out of proper tea. Herbal okay? That's in with the mugs."

"You have a cellar? That sounds really cool. Um, literally and figuratively, I'd imagine." Robin retrieved two mugs and set them on the counter, then pulled out a couple of boxes of teabags. "Sorry, by the way. Didn't mean to, you know, intrude. I was just passing by, and then your mum invited me in . . ."

"Yeah, she does that. We're going to need another mug, by the way. You only got two out and my maths may not be that great but I'm pretty sure there's three of us."

"Oh, I didn't think you'd want me to stay."

"So you were going to make your hosts some tea, and then leave? I like to think we're a bit more hospitable than that." Archie gave a rueful smile.

Robin's answering expression was tentative but hopeful. The tension was leaving his eyes, and they shone bluer than ever. He really was adorable . . . Then he shook himself minutely. "Right. Tea. You've got, um, blackcurrant, or . . . I don't know how to pronounce this one."

"Rooibos," Archie supplied, his voice coming out a bit croaky. He cleared his throat. "And yeah, I'll have that one. Lyddie too. She says the blackcurrant one tastes like watery Ribena."

"Oh?" Robin raised an eyebrow, and opened the box of blackcurrant to give it a sniff. "Huh. It's like being a kid again." He put a blackcurrant teabag into one of the mugs, fetched down another from the cupboard and, in short order, had made two rooibos teas and the blackcurrant for himself. "My mum's never agreed with sugary drinks for kids, so when I had tonsillitis and the doctor told her to give me Ribena for my sore throat, she made it with about seventeen parts water. This smells just like it, only stronger."

"Fond memories?" Archie asked with a grin.

"Hey, days off school, staying in my pyjamas, and getting to watch cartoons all day—what's not to like?"

Archie tried not to wince. That sounded pretty much like a regular day in his childhood, and you could definitely have too much of a good thing.

"You know, you're a lot more normal than I thought you were," Robin said as they carried the teas to the living room. "Um, that came out sounding wrong."

Archie laughed and put on a posh voice. "How dare you, sir! Accusing me of normality—the very idea! This means teacups at dawn."

"It does?"

"Er, that works better if you've actually heard of tea duelling."

"People duel with tea?" Robin's eyes widened. "I suppose a fresh pot could give you a nasty scalding."

"No, nothing that painful. It's like competitive biscuit dunking," Archie explained, lingering by the door to the living room. "It's a steampunk thing."

"Is that what you are? A . . . steampunker?"

Archie did wince this time. "Steampunk. No *er*. You'd be amazed how uptight people can get about that."

"So that's why you dress up, um . . ."

"Like an extra from a Charles Dickens movie? Yeah. Well, and my job. I'm a guide at the workhouse museum, so they actively encourage this sort of thing. Most steampunks can't be splendid 24/7. Uh, that's what we tend to call going full-on steampunk. It's *being splendid*, not *dressing up*. We should probably take these drinks in before they get completely cold. After you. Nice shoes, by the way." Archie followed Robin into the living room, telling himself firmly to stop lecturing the poor bloke.

Robin stopped and looked around. "Where did your mum go?"

"Who knows?" Archie had a pretty good idea that this was her being subtle and trying to matchmake, but he wasn't going to come out and say it. "Don't worry about the tea. I'll make her a fresh cup later."

They sat down on the sofa, and silence fell for a moment. Archie almost wished Lyddie had stayed—except if she had, subtlety would probably have gone right out the window. In its socks, metaphorically speaking.

Some of the tension was back in Robin's eyes when he cleared his throat. "So, you and your mum are pretty into this COC thing, are you?" His eyes widened. "I mean, Communities Over Consumerism. I wasn't trying to imply you were both into, um . . ."

"Cock?" Archie laughed, then grimaced. "It's . . . complicated. Lyddie's always had a thing about Willoughbys—she'd most likely disown me if I ever even went in there for a browse—and if you ask me, they really have gone too far this time."

"They have?" Robin looked properly concerned about it, bless him.

"I take it you haven't seen their ad in the local paper, then? It came out last week. It basically makes a mockery of homeless people."

"Um, I'm sure they didn't mean to . . ."

Archie grabbed the paper, which was on their old-fashioned sideboard still folded to the offending page, and showed it to Robin. "See that? I bet they had to clear out half a dozen actual rough sleepers so they could put their poncey sleeping bags down." He could hear the bitterness in his own tone.

"There . . . probably weren't that many. And maybe they, um, made some recompense?"

"Doubt it. People like that don't care about anything other than profit."

"People like what? You mean retail workers?" Robin's tone was sharp.

Archie ran a hand through his hair, and tried to calm down. Robin didn't deserve his anger. "No. Sorry. Not expressing myself well. Don't suppose they had much choice in taking part, and I'm not suggesting anyone should have put their jobs on the line by refusing. It's management I blame—or whoever comes up with their marketing ploys."

Robin was studying the picture. "You know, it's a pretty harsh climate in retail at the moment. Maybe they're just trying to survive?"

Archie barked a laugh. "Trust me, I know who owns that store. They're *trying to survive* in a million-quid house, and if the store goes under, they'll make a fortune selling the premises anyway, in a prime site like that."

"That's— I mean, that must be worrying for the people who work there."

"Yeah." Christ, this was ruining the mood good and proper. Archie tried to lighten his tone. "Hey, you haven't said what you do for a living."

Robin was staring at Lyddie's campaign stuff again. "I'm, um, an accountant?" It came out sounding like a question, as if he was worried Archie might not know what one was.

Or maybe he was just worried how Archie would take it. Accountants didn't exactly have a reputation for being the life and soul of the party. Archie tried not to be charmed that Robin so obviously cared what he thought of him. "What's that like?"

"Really boring. I don't like to talk about it." It came out in a rush. "So tell me about your biscuit duels?"

Archie grinned, relieved at the change of subject. "Tea duelling. Well, basically, the idea is you get two people going head-to-head, and each has a biscuit and a cup of tea. They dunk for a count of three seconds—more if the tea's getting cold—and then hold the biscuit up. The winner is the one who eats it last—but you lose if it falls to pieces. The goal is to get a clean nom. Wanna try?" Archie crossed mental fingers. Like a well-dunked biscuit, this could go one of two ways. Either Robin was about to say, *No, thanks, it sounds a bit silly to me*, or—

Robin's eyes brightened. "Go on, then."

Delighted, Archie jumped up. "I'll grab the biscuits—you hold on to what's left of your tea."

He brought in a couple of tea towels too. "Put this over your lap—you don't want to ruin your clothes. Of course, in an actual competition we'd both have cups of English breakfast or Earl Grey, and the same amount of milk for fairness, but this'll do for you to get the idea."

"Are you just assuming I'm going to be rubbish at this? I could be the next world champion tea dueller." Robin gave him a sidelong look. "You're going to tell me there *is* a world champion, now, aren't you?"

"Not a *world* champ, at least not as far as I know, but they do have national finals at the Asylum."

Robin's look now had so much side it was a wonder he didn't sprain an eyeball. "At the *asylum*. Entertainment for the inmates?"

Archie laughed. "The Asylum's the UK's biggest steampunk festival. It's held in Lincoln on the site of a former asylum, which is—"

"Where they got the name?" Robin grinned. "I'm starting to get the feeling steampunks *like* people to think they're a bit weird."

Archie hadn't had this much fun in ages. "Yeah, now you're getting it! So are we going to dunk these biscuits or what?"

Robin took hold of a biscuit and adopted a fierce glare. "Bring it on."

CHAPTER

After three goes, Robin was forced to face the painful truth: he was utter pants at tea duelling. They'd had to stop at three as there was now more soggy biscuit in his tea than tea.

"I can't believe I just failed at biscuit dunking. Never ask me to do this in public."

Archie stopped laughing long enough to give him a sympathetic smile. "You need to work on your technique, that's all. Hold the biscuit more vertically. And away from the steam."

"Nope. I'm never doing this again. There's only so much humiliation I can stand. Aren't there any other steampunk games that might be more suited to my skill set?" Assuming he had one, which he was beginning to doubt.

"Teapot racing? How are you with a remote control? Or there's *Are You There, Moriarty?* Which basically involves hitting someone over the head with a rolled-up newspaper."

"I could probably manage that," Robin said cautiously.

"Blindfolded? And you have to hold hands." The gleam in Archie's eye hinted he was about to suggest they give it a go there and then.

Oh God. Holding hands with Archie. Blindfolded. Robin's nerve broke. "Um, maybe some other time? Oh, is it really that late?" He looked around desperately—and fruitlessly—for a clock. Who didn't have a clock in their living room? Then again, Lyddie didn't seem like the sort of mum who needed to know to the second exactly how late her son got back after a night out so she could guilt-trip him about it for the rest of the week. "I ought to be going."

Archie ducked his head. "Sorry. I forget normal people aren't into all this kind of stuff."

Robin felt oddly as though he *had* whacked Archie on the head with a rolled-up newspaper. The Sunday edition, with all the supplements, and a free audiobook of *War and Peace* stuck to the cover. "No, no, it's fine, it's great. I just . . ." All he could think of was some awful crack about not getting into the kinky stuff on a first date, so he shut his mouth tight before it could escape. Because this *wasn't* a date. This was Archie being friendly, that was all. It wasn't *his* fault Robin's mind kept going to unsuitable places. "Seriously, it's been fun, and I'm sure that would be fun too, but I just . . ."

"Yeah, no worries." Archie stood up. "Cheers for coming round. Lyddie enjoyed meeting you."

Robin had ruined it. He'd ruined it all. Archie was visibly retreating into polite-acquaintance mode. "Maybe I should say goodbye to her?" Robin was suddenly desperate not to leave until he'd fixed things at least a little bit.

"Uh, yeah, I could give her a shout?"

"I mean, I don't want to disturb her, if she's, um, in the bath or on the loo or something." *Great, Robin. So smooth.*

Archie gave him an unreadable look. "How about I tell her you said goodbye? And, uh, I'm sure she'd like to see you again. Anytime you're passing. I take it you live pretty close?"

Was he imagining it, or did Archie not want him to go either? "Yes. Wells Street. Not quite as nice as this place. I guess museum guiding pays better than, um, accountancy." Robin gave a nervous laugh.

Archie snorted. "I doubt that, big-time. No, Lyddie was left the house by a mate in his will."

Robin's eyes widened. "I wish I had mates like that!"

"Careful what you wish for. I used to call him Uncle Charlie, but he wasn't a relation." Archie shook his head briefly, and Robin got the impression there was more to the story than he was saying. "Lyddie hung around with an arty set when she was younger. Used to model for them."

"Have you got any of the paintings of her? I don't know anyone who's had an actual painting done of them. Well, not a proper one, you know, where they pose, instead of just doing it from a photograph."

Archie snorted. "You should have seen the attic when we moved in. Wall to wall nudes, most of them of my mum aged around fifteen."

Robin's eyes widened. In his (it was now clear, very limited) experience, the words *mum* and *nude* didn't belong in the same sentence. They didn't belong in the same *language*. "Uh, wasn't that a bit weird? Seeing your mum in the, um, altogether?"

And at age *fifteen*?

Archie shrugged. "She had a big nudist phase when I was a kid. Used to walk around the house naked all the time."

Robin swallowed. "Um, does she still do that?"

"Nah, don't worry. She reckons this place is way too draughty."

"Didn't her mum and dad mind her posing nude at that age for a load of—" Robin stopped himself in the nick of time from saying *dirty old men*—after all, some of them might have been dirty old women "—artists?" Had it even been legal, for that matter?

"Oh, they minded." Archie's tone was grim.

"I mean," Robin went on, trying not to trip over his tongue, "most parents would get a bit overprotective about stuff like that."

"Oh yeah. They got so fucking protective they kicked her out of the house and told her never to come home."

Robin wasn't usually shocked by people swearing. But coming from Archie, in that tone . . . "Sorry," he said quickly. "I didn't mean to bring up bad stuff. Families, eh?" His laugh sounded horribly fake.

"Wouldn't know. Lyddie's all I've ever had." Archie grimaced. "Uh, and Jerrick, now, obviously. And Bridge, and her mum and dad. Huh."

He seemed genuinely surprised, as if he'd somehow failed to twig that he now had a family and it'd all happened without his conscious input.

"So, no brothers or sisters, then?"

Archie shook his head. "You?"

"No. Mum and Dad were in their forties when they had me. Bit of a late decision. Dad's always said Mum was never that keen on kids before." *Or since*, he didn't add.

"Lyddie loves kids. Of course, she's a lot younger."

Robin didn't quite dare to ask how old she'd been when Archie was born. If she'd been fending for herself since age fifteen . . . "Is Archie short for something?" he asked instead. Robin hoped it wasn't

Archibald. Archie was a great name, but Archibald? That always made Robin think of hair loss. He had trouble coming up with anything else it might be short for, though. What other names even started with *Arch*? Archaeopteryx? Archenemy? Archipelago?

Archie shoved his hands in his pockets and stared at his feet. Oh God, it was Archibald, wasn't it?

"Mars," he said in the end.

Robin blinked. "Uh?" It might not be the most articulate comment, but it pretty much summed up his feelings.

"That's my given name. Mars."

"So . . . your mum was into astronomy? Or did she just really like gooey chocolate bars?"

Archie laughed. "Roman gods, actually. Or one of them, at any rate. Lyddie liked the story of how Juno had him, what with being a single mum and all. You know there's this version of the myth where Mars the god doesn't have a dad at all, just his mum and a magic flower?"

"Uh, Hitchworth Comprehensive wasn't all that hot on a classical education, so I'll take your word for it." Magic flower? That's what Juno told *her* mum and dad, was it? "So is Archie your middle name or something?"

"It's a nickname."

Robin was acutely jealous. His one and only nickname, which thankfully hadn't survived the transition from primary school to high school, had for a period of years been *Pooh*. "How do you get a nickname like Archie?"

"Railway arches. Dossed in one for a while. Back when I was in my teens."

"You mean you were, um . . ." Robin swallowed. Suddenly COC made a lot more sense.

"Homeless. Yeah." Archie gave a jerky shrug that made Robin want very much to put an arm around his shoulders.

"Sorry."

"Why? It wasn't your fault. It wasn't Lyddie's either," Archie added fiercely. "She was ill, so she couldn't look after me for a while, and then people she ought to have been able to trust just swept in and took advantage. Made it a lot harder for her to get me back. I didn't much fancy the options I was given by social services, so . . ."

"No, but . . . So that's why you're . . ." Robin gestured at the placards in the corner.

"Yeah. I wasn't happy when I saw the ad, and Lyddie's really got herself fired up about it. She's not wrong, either . . ." Archie sighed. "She hates thinking about that time in my life. She feels she failed me, you know? Even though none of it was her fault."

Robin *literally* couldn't imagine what it must be like. Mum had strong views on people who slept rough, especially if they begged for money. Back when he'd still lived at home, he'd had to hide the copies of *The Big Issue* he bought. She'd found one once, and had not only chucked it in the bin, she'd also made a production of disinfecting all the surfaces it might conceivably have touched. If *he'd* ever slept on the streets, she'd probably have refused to let him in the house ever again.

Either that or she'd have dragged him home by the ear, scrubbed him with Dettol, and never let him *out* of the house again. It wasn't always easy to tell with Mum, although maybe that was just him.

"So, um, are you going to take part in the demonstration?" Oh shit, would an accountant know about the demo? Robin had a brief yet intense moment of panic before reminding himself that there probably weren't a lot of other reasons to prepare placards. He crossed his toes inside his shoes nonetheless.

Archie shook his head. "Not sure. I've got a big school visit due that day."

So there was a day set already? Well, duh. Black Friday. It had to be. Just like they'd said in the letter.

"But even if I didn't," Archie went on, "me being there might not be a good thing. A bit too much of a painful reminder for Lyddie. She gets protective. I think she forgets I'm not that kid anymore."

Robin wasn't certain how Archie staying away from the demo was supposed to make Lyddie think about him *less*, but he guessed the guy knew his own mum best. And to be honest, she did seem a bit . . . distractible. His heart lurched. Maybe it hadn't been a *physical* illness that'd stopped her looking after Archie when he was a teenager.

"Bridge has offered to go along and make sure she's okay," Archie said, sounding like he was worried Robin would think he didn't take enough care of his mum. Or like he was trying to convince himself.

"Scary—I mean, Jerrick's mum, right?"

Archie grinned. "That's right. The one I'm *not* married to."

That wasn't good. Not that Archie wasn't married, no, that was entirely good and wonderful and altogether fantastic. But if Bridge or, God forbid, Archie was at the demonstration, and if he or she happened to see Robin working at Willoughbys . . .

Then again, would they? The demo would presumably be outside the store—or at least, Robin fervently hoped that was where it'd stay. In the unlikely event the shop was stormed, Robin couldn't see the protesters bothering to march all the way through Perfumes and Cosmetics, past Haberdashery, Kitchen and Home, and on into Menswear. And if they did, he could always hide behind the counter until they went away again. Which would probably be the safest thing to do in any case.

Speaking of safety . . . "Wasn't it really dangerous living on the street when you were a kid? How did you even live if you were too young to claim benefits?" Oh God, he hadn't had to sell sex to buy food, had he?

Archie shrugged. "It was all right, actually. You get to know people, and you look out for each other. And I was six foot tall by the time I was fourteen, with a punk haircut—not a soft target. It was only for six months, anyway."

Robin thought back to the photo shoot and tried to imagine himself lasting six *hours* sleeping rough. He failed. "But what did you do for money?"

"Oh, you get by."

It was annoyingly vague, and could have encompassed anything from begging for change to dealing in crack cocaine. Still, it didn't seem polite to push it, pun not intended.

And it wouldn't be polite to outstay his welcome, either. Robin could have kicked himself. They'd been having a great time, and then he'd had to go and ruin it by turning the conversation from fun and games onto all these heavy topics like homelessness, protest rallies, and naked mothers.

"I probably ought to be going," he said, the words dragged out of him like drawn teeth, although thankfully with less bloodshed. The pain was about the same, though.

Archie started. "What? Uh, tell you what, how about another cup of tea for the road? No duelling involved, I promise."

"Um . . ."

"Come on. You hardly got to drink any of the last cup. I'll go put the kettle on." Archie leapt up and headed for the kitchen without waiting for an answer.

Robin's heart flipped. And then it flopped. Archie was just being hospitable.

Wasn't he?

CHAPTER 22

rchie filled the kettle feeling like he had that time he'd been working on his outfits all night before the first day of Asylum, adding finishing touches to gadgets and the last coat of Rub 'n Buff to his Nerf gun, and downing Red Bull by the bucketload to stay awake. Hyperaware, but light-headed all the same. As though he'd been chugging gin and taken a dare to try walking a tightrope.

Robin was here, in his house. And he was *adorable*. Archie could totally see why he'd thought him so much younger than he really was— there was an air of innocence, of naivety about him. But underneath it there was a deeply caring heart, and a sly sense of humour that only dared to poke its head over the parapet every now and again, as if worried it'd get shot down if it got too obtrusive.

He'd forgotten to bring their used mugs out with him, so Archie grabbed a couple of clean ones from the cupboard. Had it been those parents of his that'd made Robin so wary of showing his true self? There hadn't been a lot of smiles over at their table in the Ploughman, had there? Robin's mum had had a sour look on her face every time he'd seen her, while his dad had mostly seemed to ignore the rest of them altogether. It made Archie wonder why they'd even bothered to go out for a family meal. Maybe they had different ways of showing they cared?

Or maybe they didn't, given how Robin had blossomed under Archie's attention this afternoon.

He still couldn't work Robin out. He'd seemed really into the tea duelling, and it'd been beyond awesome to find he was willing to give the steampunk stuff a go. Archie hoped he hadn't overdone it. Robin had backed right off when he'd suggested a second game, so did that mean he'd just played along for politeness, earlier?

The kettle boiled, and he hastily grabbed a couple of teabags and slung them into the mugs. Hopefully Robin would be okay with blackcurrant again. Of course, he probably wouldn't say even if he wasn't. Archie could see that mum of his being a stickler for manners. She was that generation.

He gave the teabags a good stir and a squeeze in the hot water. Robin had heard what Archie hadn't said about his and Lyddie's past, he was pretty sure. Funny—it'd been ages since Archie had talked about that stuff. He wasn't ashamed of any of it, but other people always seemed to get embarrassed if it ever came up, so he'd mostly kept quiet.

Robin hadn't been embarrassed. He'd been interested—had seemed to really care about what Archie had gone through. Enough that Archie had found himself glossing over the details, because that part of his life was over and he'd survived it, so there was no sense anyone else getting worked up about it now.

Biscuits. Robin might fancy another biscuit—one that hadn't gone all soggy, and that he actually got to eat. Or more cake, maybe? That was still in the living room with Robin—if he hadn't got fed up waiting and snuck out already. Time to get a move on. Archie carried the mugs back into the living room.

Robin—still there—looked up from his phone and smiled.

His heart doing weird things inside his chest, Archie opened his mouth to offer him some cake, but was interrupted by a knock at the door.

Damn it, was it that late already? Archie glanced out of the window at the pitch-dark. Yes, it probably was. Where had the time gone? "That'll be Bridge, with Jerrick," he said with an apologetic grimace in Robin's direction.

Was she going to react badly to seeing Robin here? Even though it was all totally innocent? *Yeah, you just keep telling yourself that.*

He told himself not to look guilty as he opened the door. "Hey, Bridge. How's my little lad today?"

"Pukey." Bridge's tone was flat.

Archie gave her a closer inspection as he took the car seat from her. Jerrick was sleeping and didn't stir. "Bad night last night?"

"Yeah. Gave him the world's smallest bit of cabbage yesterday, cos we were having bubble and squeak. Won't be trying that again till he's

old enough to wipe his own bum. And you wouldn't believe the farts."
She snorted. "Course, some of them were Dad."

"Something to look forward to tonight, then? From Jerrick, that
is. Unless you're so sick of it you'll be sending your dad over as well?"

"Should be okay tonight. Little man had carrots for his tea, so
it's just the orange puke to watch out for. The rest of us are supposed
to be having toad in the hole when I get back." She rolled her eyes at
Archie's grimace. "Mum thought it'd be fun to try out all these old-
fashioned British meals. She says since I'm into retro fashion, I ought
to be into retro food. All I can say is, if women in the forties and fifties
were scoffing down sausages in batter every other night, there's no
way they'd have fitted into those dresses. Is your mum in? I thought
I'd say hi."

"Er, yeah. Think so. Come in." Archie led the way with Jerrick
into the living room, where Robin was examining the campaign stuff.
He seemed to be really interested in it. Archie hoped he wouldn't
want to join in, though. For Lyddie's sake, he reckoned it'd be better if
it stayed fairly low-key, maybe even fizzled out before the Black Friday
demo got a chance to take place.

"Oh," came from behind him. This time, Bridge's tone could have
been used as a spirit level. In more ways than one. "I didn't realise you
had company."

"Er, yeah. Robin just popped round for a friendly visit. Robin,
you remember Bridge, Jerrick's mum, right?" Archie put Jerrick's car
seat carefully down on the floor, so as not to wake him.

Robin had jumped up when they'd entered. He wiped his hands
on his trousers, and Archie could see him climbing back into his
polite-yet-reserved shell. "Oh—hi. Nice to, um, see you again." He
gave an awkward wave.

"Nice to see you too, Robin," Bridge said with a saccharine smile,
and then turned to Archie. "Better give you this, hadn't I?"

Archie winced as she thrust Jerrick's rucksack into his stomach.

"You, er, like working at the chip shop, Bridge?" Robin persevered,
and Archie kind of loved him a bit for it.

"It's a job. Don't recall seeing you in there much. Until recently."

"I was trying to eat a bit more healthily," Robin said with a nervous
laugh. "Um, not that chips are *bad*. I mean, I love them, really."

She gave him a very obvious once-over. "Yeah? You don't look like it. There's nothing of you."

"I'm, um, I'm on my feet a lot at work." An odd expression crossed Robin's face. "That is, we're, er, we're trialling standing desks."

"Robin's an accountant," Archie explained.

"*Someone* worked hard at school, then." Was Bridge making a subtle dig at Archie's lack of qualifications there, or was he just imagining it? "Bet you've got a degree and all."

Robin had the wide-eyed stare of a rabbit facing down a tank regiment, which seemed a bit over the top seeing as she was being perfectly nice to *him*. "Er, yes. Music. From Reading. You?" His voice cracked on the last word.

"Never was all that academic. One thing me and Archie have in common." She sent Archie a mulish glare.

No, he hadn't been imagining things. "I'll give Lyddie a shout, okay?" he said, fed up with this.

"Actually, I really should be going." Robin made a beeline for the door. "It's been great. Tell your mum thanks for inviting me in, please? I'll see you. Bye."

He was gone so quickly, Archie had only just opened his mouth to say goodbye when the front door closed.

Their untouched cups of tea sat forlornly on the floor by the sofa where Archie had left them.

"You didn't say it was your mum who invited him." Bridge still looked mulish, but like a mule that was starting to realise it might not actually have its hooves on the moral high ground here.

"Yeah. I think they got talking or something. I wasn't even in at the time."

"Oh."

"Yeah, *oh*. So no, I haven't been lying to you about going out with the bloke, okay? Because I could tell that was what you were thinking." Archie folded his arms just as she unfolded hers, as though they were doing some kind of improv comedy skit.

Bridge sat down heavily on the sofa. "Well, what was I supposed to think? I walk in here, and there he is, looking ten times fitter than he did last Sunday."

Archie's heart skipped. "You think he's fit?"

"*Er.* I said fit*ter.*" She gave a weak smile. "At least he wasn't looking like his mum dressed him today. But he seems a bit . . ."

"Too intelligent for me? You made that pretty clear, thanks."

"Oi, it's not like I've got more than a couple of GCSEs to rub together, either. That's not intelligence, though, getting degrees and stuff. That's book learning."

"I read books."

"Yeah. You do, don't you?" She gave an unhappy little laugh. "S'pose you'd never have been with me at all if your life had gone different. Do you really like him?"

Yes. "I hardly know him," Archie said instead, because it was more tactful and also, as he needed to remind himself, true. "And don't do yourself down, okay?" He gave her a hug.

"Lyddie obviously likes him," Bridge persisted.

"Yeah, but you know what Lyddie's like."

"What am I like?" Lyddie asked, padding into the room on bare feet.

Archie smiled. "Friendly." He wondered how long she'd been standing out in the hall.

"Oh, yeah, can't argue with that. You've gotta get on with people, haven't you? Live and let live. Unless they're a bastard. Oh, hello, Bridge, love. You all right?"

Bridge jumped up to give her a hug. "I'm fine. Knackered, though. Don't know how I'm going to manage this exercise class tonight. Which, speaking of, it's high time I buggered off. We'll have a chat when I get back, yeah?"

"Love us and leave us," Lyddie said vaguely, looking around.

"I'll see you in a couple of hours, maybe a bit less, okay?"

"Have fun," Archie told her.

"Like *that's* gonna happen."

Archie grinned at her sour expression. "You never know, you might enjoy it."

She made a rude gesture, glanced over at Jerrick, who was luckily still sleeping soundly, and left.

"She's a lovely girl, bless her," Lyddie said. "Where's Robin got to? I was going to ask him to stay to dinner."

"He had to leave," Archie said. "Look, be careful what you say about him to Bridge."

"Why?"

"She's got the idea I want to go out with him."

"But you do." Lyddie said it as if it was a simple, incontrovertible fact. Archie's gut twisted. He did . . . Oh, God, he did.

Then she frowned, and her tone sharpened. "What's it got to do with her who you go out with now, anyway? Archie, love, is there something you're not telling me? Are you and Bridge—"

"No! That's not it. She's not jealous. She's just feeling a bit down right now. Vulnerable. And protective of Jerrick. Don't be hard on her." The last thing they needed was Lyddie turning against Bridge. He hesitated. "When you had me, did you start feeling different about your life?"

"Oh, everything. Makes you grow up, doesn't it? Having kids. There's this tiny person and you're their whole world, and they're yours." Lyddie was smiling. "I fell in love with you the first time I saw you, did I ever tell you that? You with your wrinkled-up face and your little starfish hands. I couldn't believe you'd come out of me. You changed my life."

"You're the best mum ever, you know that?" Archie gave her a fierce hug. "So how long was it before you started thinking about blokes again after I was born?"

"I don't know. Months. Years? Course, just cos I wasn't thinking about them didn't mean they weren't thinking about me. That's blokes for you."

"So how old was I when you started going out with them again?"

"You were the most gorgeous baby. Always smiling, you were. Everyone loved you. They all said it was like you'd got everything from me and nothing from your father. Shouldn't we be getting some dinner on? It must be dinnertime by now."

Archie fought down the familiar sharp ache in his chest he always got when Lyddie was evasive about her past, and smiled at her. "Yeah, let's see what's in the fridge. Did you have something for lunch while I was out?"

"Oh, I 'spect so. I think I'd be hungrier now if I hadn't. Oh—I never asked you how it went. Your thing today."

"It wasn't a thing. I was just covering for Steve. He had a family wedding to go to. Yeah, I know, a bit late in the year."

"I always wanted a winter wedding. Lots of lush velvet in the snow."

"Snow, in Hertfordshire? You could be waiting years for that. And I thought you didn't want to get married."

"Doesn't have to be my wedding, does it? Could be yours." She giggled. "You and little Robin Redbreast. Getting hitched in Hitchworth in the snow. I could wear one of Charlie's old fur coats."

Archie laughed. "You would too, wouldn't you? Looking like you'd been eaten by a bear, and smelling like a taxidermist's dustbin. Sorry to break it to you, but I'm not marrying Robin. We're not even going out together."

"Course not, love. So when are you seeing him again?"

"I'm not. I . . ." Realisation made his heart sink. "Christ, I never got his number."

"Archie, love." Lyddie's tone was reproachful. "What were you doing all that time, then?"

"Tea duelling." Archie knew he was flushing. "He'd never done it before."

"Hm. Not going to get a lot of chance to do it again, either, is he? If you're not seeing him again. Which you said you weren't."

No. No, he wasn't, and the thought made Archie sadder than he could have imagined. "Maybe I'll bump into him sometime," he said, mostly to comfort himself. "He only lives over in Wells Street."

Lyddie seemed to perk up at that. "Oh, in those flats? Poor love. Still, he's young. You can live anywhere when you're young."

Archie huffed under his breath, feeling a weird mix of amusement and remembered pain. Yeah, you really could.

CHAPTER 23

Robin wasn't sure what to think. He racked his brain to work it out as he walked home from Archie's house, but all that happened was that he nearly got run over twice when crossing the road without due care and attention.

They'd been getting on so well. And then *she'd* turned up, like the ex from Hell. *Exactly* like, because she *was* the ex from Hell. Robin hadn't missed those barbs she'd kept sending in Archie's direction. She probably kept a forked tail under all those poofy skirts. And a trident in Jerrick's nappy bag. Or was it Neptune who had one of those? Hitchworth Comprehensive, he couldn't help thinking, had let him down badly on this sort of stuff.

Except . . . did anyone actually *enjoy* bumping into their ex with the new boyfriend? Robin was pretty sure he'd find it hard to be nice to Ethan and whoever he was currently banging, should he ever have the misfortune to encounter them. Having a baby together . . . Well, Robin didn't have any relevant experience to draw on, but he had a fair idea it was unlikely to make things better. It couldn't be easy, the prospect of someone you didn't know from Adam spending time around your little baby just because he and your ex fancied each other, could it? If he was rubbish with kids, you'd worry about the baby hating him. And if he was fantastic with kids, you'd worry about the baby loving him too much and getting hurt if that relationship broke up too.

And if Robin dug deep down inside himself, he'd have to admit he was . . . not jealous, exactly, but possibly a little bit *threatened* by Bridge. She was good-looking, confident, and the mother of Archie's son. What did Robin have to offer in comparison to that?

Not, of course, that he was in a position to be offering Archie anything right now. Archie had made that pretty clear with his *friendly visit*.

There were obviously some complicated emotions going on in Archie and Bridge's relationship, even if it was a platonic one these days. Baggage. Most likely all kinds of subtle—or not so subtle—pressure from family or friends for them to get back together. Well, perhaps not from Lyddie, but from everyone else, probably.

He was better off out of that. In any case, Archie was a man with a baby, and what did Robin know about kids? He'd end up giving the poor boy a neurosis. After all, he had so many of his own to choose from.

Robin sighed, and climbed the weary stairs to his flat.

Probably the last thing Robin expected to see Sunday morning when heading down to the corner shop was Lyddie, sitting on a wall. She was bundled up in an old man's overcoat that was comically too big for her, but at least she had shoes on today. Well, boots. They'd quite possibly had the same original owner as the coat, and she'd teamed them with thick woolly socks that looked like they'd been made from an actual sheep. The whole sheep.

She greeted Robin cheerily. "All right there?"

"Hi. Um, yes, I'm good. How are you? Are you waiting for Archie?" Robin cast a glance at the shop, but couldn't see a thing through the window, filled as it was with a hopeful display of money-off offers.

"No, he's off at a vintage market today. Went with a few of his steampunk mates." Lyddie hopped off the wall and slipped her arm into Robin's. "Are you going to the shop? You're not wearing your nice shoes today. Not that those ones aren't nice," she added after a moment.

Robin looked down at his worn-out trainers, and thanked God he'd put them on instead of coming out in his bunny slippers, as he'd been tempted. Then again, Lyddie was the last person in the world who'd have judged him for that. "Er, yeah. Forgot to get stuff in for breakfast."

"You've not et yet? Oh, you poor lamb. Tell you what, why don't you come round mine? I'll make you something. We've definitely got bacon in, cos it fell off the shelf when I got the butter out. Bacon butty? My Archie's always loved those." She started to pull him along.

It was either go with her or *literally* dig in his heels and cause a scene. "That's really kind, but I couldn't possibly—"

Lyddie dragged him on a few paces—then stopped dead, and Robin almost fell over her. She swung around to face him, her chin up. "You think I can't cook, don't you? You're worried I'm going to give you food poisoning, or burn the house down, or—"

"No! I mean, I'm sure you're a great cook. Archie's turned out all right, hasn't he? Not a hint of malnutrition. But I wouldn't want to, um . . ."

"Don't be daft, you wouldn't be," she said firmly, and started dragging him off again.

Robin gave in. After all, she was probably lonely with Archie out, and it wasn't like he'd had anything in particular planned for his day.

And, well. Bacon.

She *could* cook, Robin realised in surprise twenty minutes later, as he bit into fresh white bread, thickly sliced bacon crisped to perfection, and an egg with a gloriously runny yolk. At the very least, she could make a mean breakfast butty. "This is great," he said enthusiastically if indistinctly around his mouthful of heaven.

"Told you. Better than your mum used to make?" Lyddie was sitting cross-legged on the floor with her plate on her lap, gazing up at where Robin perched on the sofa with his.

Robin swallowed. "My mum doesn't believe in bacon butties." She didn't believe in having meals on the sofa, either, and what she'd say about sitting on the floor to eat he didn't like to think.

"Well, that's just daft. I mean, here they are, right on our plates. You can get them in McDonald's, even, although I'm not sure I *would*. Not while I've got a kitchen of my own. Do you cook?" She took an enormous bite of her bacon butty.

"Er, sort of." That was actually a pretty accurate description of Robin's culinary capabilities.

"Everyone should cook," Lyddie said vaguely, her gaze wandering around the room. Then she seemed to recapture her train of thought, and sat up straighter to look him in the eye. "I was thinking, seeing as you seemed so interested in the COC stuff, maybe you'd like to join us?"

Robin didn't choke on his mouthful, but it was a close-run thing. "I really don't think—"

"You'd be perfect! You work in an office, right? So you could photocopy some flyers for us. And you could be treasurer too—I'm just daft with numbers, me. Mind, we haven't actually got any funds yet, but we will have. Once people get to know about us."

"But—" Robin could imagine the faces of everyone he worked with if they caught him churning out flyers reading *Willoughbys: Shame on You* on the store's ancient printer.

"*And* it'd be a perfect opportunity to spend more time with my Archie."

Oh. Yes, it would, wouldn't it? Robin wavered. But— "Isn't Bridge part of it too? I don't think she likes me."

"Oh, she's a lovely girl. Course she'll like you. She hasn't even met you yet, has she? When did you meet her?"

"Um, yesterday. Properly. But I've seen her around before that. At the chippie, and places."

"She'll warm to you. And anyway, she's not involved with COC. Not yet. I haven't decided whether to ask her. Don't want to put too much on her plate. I know how hard it can be, on your own with a baby. Not that she's on her own. She's got her mum and dad and Archie does his bit—he's a great dad, my Archie is—but it's not the same as having someone to talk to at the end of the day, someone to give you a kiss and a cuddle. Someone who's always got your back." She sighed.

Robin knew how she felt. "Yeah," he said, and cleared his throat after it came out sounding a bit rough.

Lyddie gazed into his eyes. "My Archie needs someone like that too."

Robin found himself nodding, and coughed again to hide his embarrassment.

"So anyhow," Lyddie said brightly. "You eat up and get on with your day, and then you can come back tonight. We're having a meeting for COC."

Robin choked. Did she realise how that sounded? "Um . . ."

"Go on. Try it? You might like it." She gave him a winning smile. Robin had a sudden mental image of a younger Lyddie getting baby Archie (dressed in Jerrick's monocle onesie) to eat his veggies.

"Can I think about it?" he said desperately.

"Course you can. No problem. And no need to let me know. You just turn up. Archie's going to be here. Oh, and you'd better give me your phone. I'll put my number in for you, all right?" She held out her hand.

"Er . . ." Robin failed utterly to think of a single reason to refuse that wouldn't sound rude. And anyway, she hadn't asked for *his* number, had she? So she probably wasn't planning to spam him with calls and texts about COC. He unlocked his phone and handed it over, and she thumbed in the number with a look of concentration.

"There you go. All done." She handed it back.

"Me too," Robin said, having cleaned his plate. He made to get up, but then realised she hadn't finished. In fact, she didn't seem to have eaten more than that first bite. "Sorry—you're still eating."

"Oh, don't worry about me. I'll have it later. Or feed it to the birds. Birds like bacon, and it's not like they're going to catch their own pigs, is it? Unless they're eagles. I think an eagle could carry a piglet." Lyddie frowned, then beamed. "Archie would know. He's a bright lad."

Funny how it always seemed to come back to Archie.

Robin walked home with a happy stomach and a mind in turmoil. *Should* he go to the COC meeting? Okay, so he was diametrically opposed to all they stood for— Well, not all, he totally thought people should look after vulnerable members of the community; he just didn't think closing down his place of employment was the way to go about it.

But it'd make Lyddie happy if he went. And he'd see Archie . . .

Then again, he'd *also* get to meet all the other COC members, any or all of whom might be regular shoppers in Willoughbys' menswear department and would therefore recognise him as a traitor in their midst. Robin winced, visualising something akin to a scene from *Invasion of the Body Snatchers* with everyone pointing and screaming at *him*. And he was never letting Azrah talk him into watching old horror films at Halloween again despite her *"Come on, don't be a wuss, they're rated like UU for Utterly Unscary."*

Of course, the COC members might not recognise him. Robin was used to customers who regularly stopped for a friendly chat in the store, only to blank him completely if they saw him out of context. But could he chance that?

No, there was no way he could go to the meeting. The risk was too great. They'd probably string him up from the nearest lamp post if they recognised him. Or burn him at the stake, and invite the homeless community to come and toast marshmallows. Would Sheppy's Mum shed a tear for him?

But he'd better give Lyddie a ring and let her know, despite what she'd said. It was only polite. He'd give it a few hours, though. Just to make it vaguely plausible that something might have come up.

When Robin finally rang Lyddie's number late that afternoon, he found himself saying, "This is Robin," before the voice that had picked up with "Hello?" had fully filtered into his brain.

The *male* voice.

"Um, have I got a wrong number?" he said quickly. "I thought this was Lyddie's phone."

"No, this is my phone," the warm, oddly familiar voice answered. "And I'm not at home now, so I'm sorry, I can't hand you over. But I can give you her number if you like."

Ice-cold water washed over Robin. "Archie?" he squeaked.

"Yes. It's Robin, isn't it? Is everything okay? Only you sound a bit—"

"I'm fine! Only Lyddie said she'd put *her* number in my phone, and I wanted to let her know about this evening, and—"

"What about this evening?"

"That I can't come. To the meeting. For COC." Robin winced. "I mean, Community Over Consumerism. Not . . . cock."

Archie chuckled, the warmth of it not only thawing the ice that had enveloped Robin, but threatening to heat it up to dangerous levels. "Uh, you do realise Lyddie knew exactly what she was doing when she came up with that name, right? And this is the first I've heard about the meeting. I suppose she must have organised it today while I've been out."

Robin supposed she must have. Although it was odd—after all, it'd seemed to be already a thing when he'd seen her this morning. Maybe all the members of COC were early risers?

"Didn't know you were that into, uh, COC," Archie went on.

At least, Robin was fairly sure he was talking about the campaign group. After all, he *had* already told Archie he was gay. "Um, yes?" he hedged.

"Don't let Lyddie dragoon you into doing stuff you don't want to."

"Well, that's easier said than done," Robin said without thinking.

Archie laughed. "So is there anything else I can do for you?"

Yes. Yes, there was. Quite a lot of things, actually. Many of them X-rated, but also a significant number that would be suitable viewing for tots, open-minded elderly folk, and fluffy bunnies of all ages.

Oh God, he had it bad. Robin took a deep breath. "Um, I was wondering . . . if you, you know, would like to, um, go out for a drink?"

There was a pause. "I . . . should probably tell you I'm not really looking for a relationship at the moment. Sorry."

The ice water was back, and it had brought along an Arctic wind to keep things extra nippy. "Oh, no problem." Robin made a wretched attempt at a laugh. "Me neither. I just thought . . . I was planning to go to the pub anyway, after work one day this week. With some friends, I mean. My friends. From work. So if you wanted to join us. After work. When you've finished your . . . work."

"Oh—I . . . Sorry. Shouldn't have assumed. Hah. You'll be thinking the size of my ego is compensating for something. In that case, yeah, why not? Did you have a date in mind?"

"Tuesday?" That gave Robin two days to persuade Azrah and Heath to back him up. Or find some other friends. That would be enough, wouldn't it? "At the Millstone? Around six?"

"Yeah, Tuesday's good. I'll look forward to it. Listen, I've got to go—I was in the middle of haggling for a table."

"See you Tuesday, then." Robin hung up, feeling warm in parts and shivery in others. So Archie was only in the market for tables, not blokes? That was bad. Beyond bad, particularly after they'd got on so well yesterday. Then again, just because you weren't looking for something, didn't mean you wouldn't find it, did it? And a friendly drink was a good start. They could get to know each other better with no pressure.

It was only later that he remembered he still hadn't got Lyddie's actual phone number, and hadn't told her he wouldn't be at the meeting tonight.

Maybe he should wander over to her house to tell her he couldn't make it?

No. No, he really shouldn't.

CHAPTER 24

Archie got back from the vintage fair pretty pleased with his day. He'd managed to get hold of a table for the kitchen at a pretty decent price, and it wouldn't even need repainting. And he'd found a sweet set of vintage Swiss army snow goggles in their original tin—handy for getting them to and from events.

Not to mention, that phone call from Robin.

It'd been great to hear from him. All the better for it being so unexpected. If she hadn't been so staunchly anti-establishment, Lyddie could have had a great career with MI5.

Of course, there was a significant danger Archie was going to end up in trouble, at least if Bridge heard about him going out for a drink with the bloke. But . . . she couldn't really expect him to never have another relationship, could she? Just because she was worried someone new in his life would mean he'd be a rubbish dad to Jerrick?

Archie had had a good, long think about it, and he'd decided he wasn't going to feel selfish, or like he was neglecting Jerrick, for not closing the door on romance until the kid was eighteen. Bridge and he were in different places right now, emotionally speaking, but that didn't make either of them wrong. He had to do what was right for him.

Then again, Bridge probably *could* expect him not to start going out with Robin, because he'd expressly told her he wasn't going to, hadn't he? And the thing was, he'd meant it when he'd said it. But that had been before he'd got to know the bloke. Now . . . although he'd told Robin he wasn't looking for anything—had felt he *had* to, at the time, because of what he'd said to Bridge—he'd known while he'd been speaking that it was totally not true.

But Robin had rolled with it like a star, and they were still going to see each other in a couple of days. So yeah, good day. And anything could happen in a couple of days. Bridge might start feeling better about herself and stop being all doom and gloom about the future. She might meet the love of her life over the counter at the chip shop.

Archie grinned to himself. He might even man up and tell her what he'd decided.

It was just as well they'd be meeting in the Millstone, though. Archie had never known Bridge to drink there. She reckoned it was always full of shop workers hogging the seats because they'd been on their feet all day.

Archie wasn't planning to keep secrets from her. He simply wanted to choose his time to tell her about him and Robin. If and when there was actually a *him and Robin* to tell her about.

He told his conscience to shut up, and walked into the living room. Lyddie had his laptop out on the floor in front of her, which was unusual.

"Had a good day?" he asked. "You'd better not be getting me flagged by MI5."

She grinned. "They've had your number since you were in nappies. Good time at the vintage wotsit?"

"Not bad at all. I've got us a table to go in the kitchen with those chairs. The guy's going to deliver it on Wednesday. And talking of numbers, I got a call from Robin today, but he seemed to think he was ringing you." Archie gave her a pointed look.

"Oh, did he really? I must have put the wrong number in his phone. You know what I'm like. Forget my own head if it wasn't sewn on. When are you seeing him?"

"Tuesday. And when did *you* see him?"

"This morning. He likes bacon sarnies—did I tell you we're eating meat again? I was in the supermarket and I just thought, 'Sod it, farmers are people too'—but he calls them butties. Like a Northerner. I blame television. We'll all be talking the same, soon. Won't be any dialects left by the time Jerrick grows up." Her smile twisted. "I miss my little lad. You should tell Bridge we'll have him for a weekend."

"Thought you were busy with the campaign?"

"You mean COC?" Her eyes were wide and innocent.

Archie wasn't fooled. "You know exactly what I mean. Robin said you'd invited him to a meeting tonight. I'd better get dinner on quick. How long have we got until people get here?"

"No, there's no meeting tonight. He must have got the wrong end of the stick, bless him."

"Only because you handed it to him." Archie pulled up his trouser legs and squatted down beside her. "You know it could cause problems with Bridge if I go out with Robin. That's not gonna help you see more of Jerrick."

Lyddie pouted. "Oh, she doesn't have to know. What's it to do with her? Anyway, you are going out with him." Her smile was sudden and eager.

"I'm going out *for a drink* with him. And his mates from work. I'm not *going out* with him."

Lyddie gave the sort of shrug that seemed to say, *Details.*

"What are you looking up, anyway?"

"Oh, stuff. Demonstrations and the law."

"Uh-*huh*." Archie let his tone do the talking.

"You always get upset if I get arrested," she said distractedly, scrolling down.

"Funny, that."

"Ooh, here's a good web page. *Keeping the* Civil *in Civil Disobedience*—I like it."

Archie wasn't sure he did. "Remember there's laws on trespass, right?"

"Do they count for a shop? I mean, it's not like they don't want people going in."

"They don't want people going in *with placards*." Archie sighed. "You do realise it's—" He stopped himself from saying *never* "—unlikely to make a difference to how the place operates, don't you? People like that don't change."

"Nothing ever changes if nobody tries to change it. Maybe they won't change, but I'm still not sitting on my backside letting them think no one gives a toss."

No, that wouldn't be like her, would it? Archie gave her shoulder a squeeze, and stood up. "I'll go make a start on dinner."

CHAPTER  25

On Monday, Azrah had another lunchtime meeting with Gail, and Heath was nowhere to be found, so Robin went to lunch on his own. He quite enjoyed the peace and quiet, and ended up getting a cup of tea and a biccy to string it out a bit longer.

"What on *earth* are you doing?" Azrah's voice was a discordant note in his happy reverie. She stood beside his table with a plate full of pasta and an incredulous expression.

Robin started, and his well-dunked biscuit reached the point of catastrophic failure, landing with a *splat* in his cup of tea. "Now look what you've done. And I thought you were with Gail?"

She pulled out the chair opposite him and sat. "I was. We finished. Because women are efficient. And if you ask me, that soggy biscuit needed warming up anyway. You were staring at it for at least as long as it took me to walk over with my lunch. *And* I stopped to say hi to Mary-from-Haberdashery. She's fine, by the way. Her knee's giving her gyp, whatever that's supposed to mean, and the customers haven't been putting the lace trim away properly so now the ivory's all mixed up with the white. It's basically lace anarchy there. So *why* were you staring at that biscuit?"

Robin flushed. "I was practising."

"Practising what? Looking like you've discovered the secrets of the universe in a soggy digestive?" She forked up some pasta with a derisory air.

Okay, possibly Robin was feeling a little oversensitive. "Tea duelling. It's a steampunk thing. You wouldn't understand."

"Would I want to? And anyway, *what*?"

"So . . . I might have gone to Archie's house at the weekend." If that didn't make her stop grilling him about biscuit dunking, nothing would.

Azrah bit. "What, just walked up to the front door, rung the bell, and asked if Archie could come out to play?"

"Not exactly. Um, I had to stop to tie my shoelace—"

"Pull the other one, it plays the Johnny English theme tune."

"—and his mum saw me out there and invited me in."

She raised a sardonic eyebrow. "Because she's got a soft spot for saddo stalker types?"

"I think she was lonely," Robin said honestly. "Archie wasn't back from work yet."

"Oh. *Oh*." Azrah drew in a deep breath. "She wasn't wearing leopard print, was she? Or something inappropriately tight and revealing?"

"What? No. Just . . . normal clothes." Robin somehow didn't want to mention the jumping-out-of-the-window-in-her-socks part.

"Uh-huh? But when you went in, did she sit down on the sofa and pat the seat next to her?"

Robin was beginning to view the soggy biscuit conversation in the rosy hues of nostalgia. "No! Nothing like that. She was just really friendly. In a *very innocent* way. Not everything's about sex, you know."

"Eh. Sometimes it's about money. Did she offer you money for sex?"

"I'm not even going to dignify that with an answer." Robin took an absentminded gulp of his tea and gagged on a mouthful of biscuit slurry.

Azrah gave his spluttering an unsympathetic look. "Is that a *yes*, then?"

"No!" Robin made up his mind there and then that he was never, ever going to tell her about Lyddie inviting him in the next day as well. She'd only misunderstand—and honestly, it was laughable. Lyddie didn't fancy him.

Did she?

No. No, that couldn't be it. She wanted him to go out with Archie, not her.

Didn't she?

Azrah smirked. "You're thinking about it, aren't you?"

"Nothing further from my mind." Shit, she'd ask what he had been thinking about, now. Robin had a flash of inspiration. "I was thinking about Heath, actually."

"Why? Fancy him, do you?"

"*No*, but I think he fancies you. Think about it. He's worked at Willoughbys over a year and he's never taken any notice of me, but the minute you get a job here, he starts hanging around all the time."

"I've been working here two months. That's not exactly *the minute*."

"So it took him that long to notice your finer qualities. Or to get up the nerve."

"Just as likely it took him a year to notice *yours*. I've known you most of my life and I'm still looking for them."

"You wouldn't know a finer quality if it bit you on the bum. So anyway, what do you think? Snog, marry, or avoid?"

"What, out of Heath, Heath, and Heath?" She made a face. "Avoid. You know what I think about marriage. And snog? Not if he was the last bloke on earth and he came wrapped in tinsel with a bow tied in his ginger—"

"Oh, hello, Heath." Robin sent a welcoming smile over Azrah's shoulder.

She froze.

Robin smirked. "Oh, sorry, not him after all. Just a shadow on the wall."

"Arsehole." Azrah glared at him.

"Ah, but I'm *your* arsehole. Okay, that came out sounding wrong."

"Too right." Azrah looked queasy. "Moving on . . ."

"Moving on . . ." Was now a good time to ask? Probably not. But then again, probably no worse than usual. "I sort of need you to do something for me. And no, it's not about sex."

"That's a bit of a letdown," Heath said, appearing from nowhere—did he have a stealth mode? Had he been there all along?—and sitting at their table with his tray. Today he'd gone for Pasta of the Day and a jacket potato, which was at least technically a vegetable.

"Is it about Archie?" Azrah asked, effortlessly ignoring Heath's lanky, overelbowed presence, although Robin was *almost* sure there was a faint flush on her cheek.

"Maybe."

"Then it's about sex."

"No! I just want a chance to get to know him better, that's all." Did she *have* to do this in front of everyone? Meaning, obviously, Heath.

"Don't mind me." Heath blithely picked up his jacket potato in his fingers and took a bite, which was all kinds of wrong.

Azrah snorted, and turned a few degrees further away from him. "Where 'get to know him better' is a euphemism for 'have lots of steamy, hot, naked sex.'"

"Not . . . exactly. I mean, not yet. But . . . we were getting on so *well*, Az. And then his ex came in with the baby and it got all awkward. I think he felt bad about, you know, moving on from her so soon." Robin turned on the puppy eyes at both of them, figuring if he could only get one of them on side, the other might topple like the world's shortest domino run. "I just need you to come out for a drink, that's all. If I'd asked him to go out with me on my own, like on a date, he'd probably have said no." More like *definitely*. "So I told him it's with mates, just a pint after work, so he'd say yes. I'll look like a liar or a total saddo if I turn up on my own, won't I? *Please*? This is my only hope. I can't keep hanging around his house."

Heath nodded. "Restraining orders can be a proper bastard. And what if he goes and gets himself murdered? No one would ever believe it wasn't you."

"Nobody's getting murdered, Heath. We're simply going for a drink. And, um . . ." Robin squirmed in his seat, which all at once was too small and too hot for him. "We need to pretend we don't work here."

Azrah and Heath turned eerily identical narrow-eyed expressions on him.

"Look, it . . . Hah, funny story, but, guess what, it turns out his mum's a founder member of the Community Over Consumerism group."

"*What*?" Azrah's tone could have cut steel.

Heath shook his head sadly. "Fraternising with the enemy. Not cool, man. That's like feeding the hand that bites."

"Feeding the— That doesn't even make sense. How can a hand bite? Or eat, for that matter? Where are the teeth, for God's sake?"

"I knew a girl once with wicked sharp fingernails," Heath said dreamily, forking up some pasta. "Course, the tetanus shots were less fun."

"Last I heard," Azrah's voice dripped acid, "it wasn't his mum's pants you wanted to get into. So what's all this about?"

"Because I told his mum I'm an accountant, and then obviously I had to keep up the pretence with *him*."

"Why would you even—"

"I panicked, okay? She had a knife. Um, it was a cake knife, but still. I saw all the campaign stuff at her house, she came in with a knife and asked me where I worked, and I panicked."

"You're an idiot," Azrah said flatly.

"No, on second thoughts I like it." Heath tapped his nose. "You could get him to spill all their secrets in bed."

Azrah's lip curled. "It's not *secrets* he wants this bloke to spill in bed."

Robin looked briefly up in the direction of heaven, but the cafeteria ceiling appeared to be currently out of divine inspiration. "This isn't *The Spy Who Loved Me*. So his mum and me have different opinions on certain issues—so what? *My* mum and me have different opinions on nearly *all* the issues."

"Yeah, but . . ." Azrah put down her fork. "*This* issue might cost us all our jobs. And what's going to happen when he finds out you lied to his mum?"

"Which is why I want you to pretend we're all accountants. Look, it's fine, Archie and his mum never come in Willoughbys. He said so. His mum hates the place, remember? So there's no chance we'll be recognised."

"We could don disguises just in case," Heath suggested. "Azrah could wear a headscarf—"

"*You* wear a bloody headscarf. You're the one with hair you could spot a mile off on a foggy day."

Heath nodded sagely. "It's true some of us stand out in a crowd more than others."

Robin could feel the conversation, not to mention his lunch break, slipping away from him, possibly never to return. "All I want you to do is have a drink with the bloke and pretend you're accountants. Is that really too much to ask?"

Azrah folded her arms and sat back. "You're buying the first round. *And* the second. And probably all the rounds until the apocalypse, which for some of us can't come soon enough."

"And a packet of pork scratchings," Heath added.

"You're the best mates ever," Robin said with heartfelt relief.

On Tuesday night, Robin went through things one more time with Heath and Azrah before they got to the pub.

"Right, who do we work for?"

Azrah rolled her eyes. "A firm of accountants, it's very boring, we don't like to talk about it," she parroted.

Robin glared at Heath, who was busy putting on a pair of owlish spectacles he'd acquired from somewhere. "And the name of the firm is?"

"Smith and Wesson?" Heath said airily, as if none of this really *mattered*. He pulled out a comb and a small mirror, and started giving himself a side parting.

"*Jones and Gunn.* Three syllables, Heath. How hard can it be to remember?"

"Yeah, but why that one?" Azrah put in. "Why not Hewitts & Co., or Wilson Freemantle?"

Robin took a deep breath and counted to five. "Because those are *real* firms, so there's a chance he might know someone who *actually* works there."

Heath pursed his lips. "I'm not convinced about that name. Seriously. Who do you know with an "and" in their name anymore? That's totally last century, man."

"Jones and Gunn were established in 1989," Robin ground out from between clenched teeth.

"Which means they're well overdue for a rebranding. And old Jones, well, since the stroke he's only been a silent partner, so I'm thinking Gunn Jones." Heath nodded to himself, looking smug.

"*Old Jones* doesn't exist! I made it all up!"

"He's got a point," Azrah said. "I'd be much more likely to take my accounts to Gunn Jones than to Jones and Gunn. You don't want the firm to go down the pan just cos you're fuddy-duddy about names."

"There is no firm! No firm, and no flippin' pan!"

Heath tutted. "Mate, you're getting nowhere with that attitude."

Azrah fixed Robin with a steely glare. "The way *I* see it, for the three of us to be employed at a similar level at one and the same time, this nonexistent firm's got to be doing pretty bloody well for itself—not doddering along with one foot in the grave. Of course, if you don't *want* this story to be believable . . ."

"Fine." Robin's shoulders slumped. "We work for Gunn Jones."

Heath, who'd been scribbling on a napkin, held it up for inspection. He'd done a surprisingly succinct, stylised illustration of a handgun and a calculator. "Quick rough-up of the logo. What do you think?"

"I think it makes us look like contract killers," Azrah said flatly.

"Hey, at least it'll get the fees paid on time. Tell you what, after I get home tonight I'll pull out the old graphics tablet, do a proper job of it, and knock up some letterhead."

"We don't need letterhead! Or a logo." What Robin *really* needed right now was a lie-down. "It's just a story. A cover. In case you get asked point-blank."

Heath shrugged. "Got a mate who can do you a website on the cheap."

Robin hid his face in his hands. He had the worst mates *ever*.

CHAPTER 26

Archie headed to the pub after work, anticipation and, despite his best efforts, a touch of guilt fluttering in his stomach as he walked down the lamp-lit streets. He'd half thought of calling Robin earlier and saying he wouldn't be able to make it after all. Coming here tonight meant he'd be late back to look after Jerrick. Maybe Bridge was right, and he really should concentrate on the lad while he was so young.

But he'd already agreed it all with Bridge: she was fine with Lyddie minding Jerrick for an hour until he got home. And an hour was all it would be. A quick drink after work. It couldn't hurt, just going out for a drink with Robin and his workmates, could it? It wasn't like it'd be a date. Just a friendly drink. With friends.

But if it was all so innocent, why hadn't he mentioned to Bridge that Robin would be there? Archie sighed. He *wasn't* doing anything wrong, for God's sake. So why did it feel like he was?

Sheppy's Mum was bundled up against the wind with her dog in their usual doorway. Archie stopped to say hi. Actually, he'd intended to make sure she had something warm to eat, but she was already clutching a cup of hot soup. Apparently a young man who worked in Willoughbys had bought it for her. Archie made a mental note to mention that to Lyddie. She ought to know that not everyone who worked at Willoughbys was totally lacking a social conscience.

As Archie walked into the Millstone, Robin glanced up by some sixth sense from where he was sitting with his mates and broke into a smile. Somehow all Archie's doubts seemed to melt away. He'd have been crazy to let a few worries stop him coming along tonight. He waved a hand and made his way over to their table.

Robin stood up, still beaming, made an abortive move as if he was about to give Archie a hug, then sat down again, pulling out a stool next to him. Archie *wasn't* disappointed. "Glad you could make it. Guys, this is Archie. And, um, that's Heath, and that's Azrah. Azrah's my oldest friend, and Heath . . . works with us." An adorably confused expression crossed Robin's face for a moment.

No. Not adorable. Cute? No, that was just as bad.

The tall, bony redhead saluted Archie with a raised pint glass and an "All right, mate?"

The petite girl in the trouser suit looked him over as if sizing him up for a shallow grave in the woods. "So give: what's with the Dick Dastardly moustache and the grandad gear? And what do you *really* do with looted fridge innards?"

Robin groaned. "At least let him get a drink in before the interrogation starts!"

The redhead stood up. "My shout. G&T, mate? They've got Lincoln in here, or there's Tanqueray."

Archie guessed Heath must have encountered steampunks before. "I'll have the Lincoln, cheers." He shrugged off his jacket—it was warm in the pub—and folded it neatly before putting it on the shelf under the table.

"No worries. Same again, fellow wage slaves?"

Robin and Azrah nodded. As Heath sauntered off, Azrah turned very deliberately to Archie and rested her chin on her hand. "You were saying?"

Archie had to laugh. "Okay. I'm a steampunk."

She raised an eyebrow. "If you think that's an explanation, I've got news for you."

"We're . . . sort of retro-futurists. It's like dressing for science fiction, but the science is based on that of a bygone age? Typically, it's the Victorian era, so, well, steam."

"So where does the 'punk' come in? Because no offence, but I really don't think Sid Vicious would recognise you as a kindred spirit."

Thank God. Archie had nothing against the music, but getting drugged off your head and stabbing your girlfriend was taking rebellion a step too far in his opinion. "It's a counterculture. Rejecting both current social norms and those of history. And honestly, anything goes. Most people base their outfits around Victorian clothes, but you get Edwardian gear, steampunk Vikings, postapocalyptic stuff—you name it. If someone tries to tell you that your flintlock pistol or your Nerf gun's from the wrong century, you just tell them you picked it up on your travels with your time machine." Archie paused. Had he forgotten anything essential? "Oh, and goggles are a bit of a thing too." And cogs, and clocks, and the colour brown, but he didn't want to completely overload her with information right at the start.

"And there's tea duelling. And teapot racing. And Moriarty," Robin added helpfully if not particularly comprehensibly.

"So Sherlock Holmes is steampunk?" Azrah asked, presumably latching on to the one bit she recognised.

"Well, he's definitely steam. And the Robert Downey Jr. movies played up the punk."

"And the gay," Robin put in. "Not that I was watching them for that."

Archie couldn't help a smile. "But actually *Are You There, Moriarty?* is a Victorian parlour game."

"You have to hit each other with a rolled-up newspaper," Robin explained.

"I'll be sitting here thanking God I live in the age of Netflix, ta very much." Azrah took a long drink of her Coke. "So . . . you all dress up like Victorian science-fiction characters? And play silly games?"

"Pretty much," Archie agreed with a shrug. "Nothing wrong with a bit of daft fun. And there's gadget makers, and bands, and loads of festivals up and down the country."

"Uh-huh." Apparently Azrah wasn't finished with the interrogation. "But you dress like that every day? Don't you get funny looks at work? Where *do* you work?"

"The workhouse." Archie grinned. "Museum, I mean."

"Remember we had that school trip there in primary school?" Robin said, turning to Azrah. "And we all had to dress up as workhouse kids?"

Azrah snorted. "And George Billings tried to tell me I couldn't be in a Victorian workhouse because brown people hadn't been invented yet, or something."

"And the museum lady told him to stop talking nonsense as there were plenty of ethnic minorities in Victorian Britain," Robin continued. "I still think it was totally unfair Miss tried to give you detention. You hardly hit him hard at all."

"Yeah, but his nose bled *everywhere*." Azrah cackled.

Archie laughed. "I wondered where those bloodstains on the schoolroom floor had come from. So I guess you two really have known each other a long time."

Robin nodded. "Since playgroup. Azrah got me into trouble on my first day for picking Michaelmas daisies outside the church hall."

"*You* were the one who came up with the idea of wearing them in our hair."

"Yeah, but I wouldn't have actually done it if you hadn't dared me."

"Truth or dare, is it?" Heath had returned with the drinks, all four of them held precariously in his large hands.

"Nah," Azrah told him. "Just reminiscing about our old schooldays."

"Growing weed in the greenhouses, and knocking up incendiary devices in the science department?"

Azrah's eyes widened. "What kind of school did *you* go to?"

"Small public school outside Stevenage."

"Yeah? Why aren't you posh, then?"

"Oh, they tried, they tried. It didn't stick." Heath grinned. "Good times, those were. The food was crap, but the masters didn't give a shit about anything so long as the police didn't get called and you passed an exam or two at the end of the day."

"Did you go to school in Hitchworth, Archie?" Robin asked.

Archie grimaced. "Uh, kinda? There were a few. Not my fondest memories." He'd been forever getting into trouble for falling asleep in class, or turning up late, unprepared, or not in uniform.

It hadn't been Lyddie's fault. She'd done her best. And it wasn't like things had got better when she'd had to go away and he'd been taken into care. "So where is it you all work?" he asked, keen to change the subject.

"Jones and Gunn," Robin said, just as Azrah chipped in with "Gunn Jones."

They exchanged looks that were lost on Archie.

"Rebranding," Azrah said quickly. "Robin keeps forgetting."

Heath nodded. "Some people can't handle change."

"I can handle change! I moved out of Mum and Dad's house, didn't I?"

"*Finally*," Azrah muttered.

Robin frowned. "You can talk. You're still living at home."

"That's because I know which side my bread's buttered. When you were living at home, your bread wasn't buttered *either* side. And there wasn't any bread, for that matter."

"Too proud to go to the food bank?" Heath asked sympathetically.

Azrah let out an exasperated squeal, like an old-fashioned kettle boiling. "It's a metaphor!"

Archie sent Robin a quizzical glance.

"Um, they're not particularly supportive of me being gay," Robin explained. "My parents, I mean."

"Or of you being *you*." Azrah glowered. "Or of me being me, for that matter. I bet if they met Archie, they'd hate him too."

Everyone looked at Archie. He tried not to twiddle his moustache self-consciously.

"I dunno," Robin said. "I mean, there's the gay thing—"

"I'm bi, actually," Archie put in.

"Yeah, I don't think that's an *improvement* in Robin's mum's eyes," Azrah said.

"—but you do dress smartly. Mum likes that. And working in a museum would impress her. She thinks history's very important."

Azrah snorted. "You mean she wants Britain to go back to the 1950s, when men wore the trousers and women lived on Valium, gin, and diet pills."

"That's three of your basic food groups," Heath said.

Robin frowned. "Seriously, diet pills?"

"Well, yeah." Heath shrugged. "Nineteen-fifties diet pills were mostly amphetamines."

"And that's why women in those days had such stupidly small waists." Azrah rolled her eyes. "Have you *seen* actual vintage clothes from the fifties? People go on about Marilyn Monroe being a size 16, but that was in old money. She'd be like a busty size 10 these days." She shot Heath a sharp look. "What, no comment about her being a *real* woman, or anything?"

Heath held up his hands. "Ah, but was she? How much of the woman we think of now is the studio-created fantasy? And if that's all we remember, does that make the fantasy Marilyn the real one?"

"No. It doesn't," she said flatly.

Archie grinned. "You'd probably enjoy steampunk," he said to Heath, then turned to Azrah. "And you'd hate it."

"What about our boy wonder?" Heath asked, leaning forward to stare at Robin.

Robin flushed. "Don't call me that. And I think it's great," he added, smiling at Archie in a way that made his stomach flip over.

"So what would you dress him in, steampunk-style?" Azrah asked.

Everyone turned to Robin, who went even redder under their examination.

Archie shrugged. "Steampunk's all about the individual. So it's not for me to say. But you'd look great in a waistcoat," he added.

"He does, in fact," Azrah said. "Except he never wears one."

"That's because when I did, you laughed at me and my *three-piece suite*."

Heath shook his head. "Fashion shaming. Not cool."

Azrah glared at him. Archie spoke up hastily before hostilities could kick off. "There's loads to choose from. A lot of people like to build up a persona, you know? Like, an inventor, or an explorer. Or there's military outfits. Or occult-based stuff. Anything, really. Some people do steampunk versions of famous characters."

"Like Batman?" Azrah's eyes lit up.

"No," Robin said firmly.

Archie blinked. "Actually, I've seen that done—"

"Yeah, but what *she* means is, can she use steampunk as an excuse to get me into a pair of tights as Robin the Boy Wonder. So *no*."

"You're so boring," Azrah grumped. Then she yelped and glared at Heath again. "Oi, watch what you're doing with your size-I-don't-even-want-to-knows."

Heath gave her a significant look.

The penny visibly dropped. Azrah froze. "Ah, when I say boring? That's just sour grapes. I mean come on, who *wouldn't* want to see Robin in tights?"

Archie tried not to laugh. They weren't the *worst* wingmen he'd ever encountered. But they were quite possibly the most obvious. And the fact they were acting this way . . . it had to mean that Robin *did* still want to be more than friends, didn't it? Warmth spread through Archie's chest. "Anything take your fancy? Uh, outfits, I mean?"

Robin made a cute little thinky-face. "Not military, I think. Inventor sounds cool. Or explorer. Although I'm not sure about the pith helmets. I, um, may have done an internet search on steampunk," he added. "Just to get a few ideas."

Even better. "We need to get you to a market and you can try on some hats, see what suits you."

"And remember: pics or it didn't happen," Azrah put in. Then she yawned loudly and stretched her arms out wide. "I am *sooo* tired. Aren't you tired, Heath?"

Heath shrugged. "Nah, I'm— Oh. Yeah. Dead knackered, me." He winced and rubbed the lower part of his leg where, Archie was fairly sure, Azrah had just kicked him.

Yep, the wingman act *definitely* needed work. Then again, Robin was doing a pretty good job without them. Archie glanced at his watch. Damn. "Sorry. It's later than I thought. I'm going to have to get going. Can't leave Lyddie on her own with Jerrick all night."

"Catching the bus?" Robin asked hopefully.

"Yeah—number 37. You too?" Okay, maybe the evening didn't have to end right now.

Robin nodded.

CHAPTER 27

R obin felt a bit like someone had spiked his drink with 1950s diet pills as he and Archie walked along the street to the bus stop, having said their goodbyes to Azrah and Heath. His senses were hyperalert, his skin tingled with possibly overoptimistic anticipation, and his stomach was faintly queasy. It was a mild night, but with a deceptively strong breeze that ruffled Robin's hair and even made Archie's moustache quiver like a startled bird. Was it weird to want to smooth its contours with his fingers?

Was he getting ahead of himself? Archie probably had firm rules on moustache fondling on a first date. Not that this was a date. Obviously.

Except that it was starting to feel like one. Their shoulders brushed as they walked, leaving Robin flushed hot and cold all over. "Thanks for coming tonight," he said as a distraction—both for himself and in case Archie had noticed their proximity. "Hope you didn't mind Azrah and Heath too much."

"No, not at all. They seem like good mates. To you, I mean. I'm still trying to work out what they are to each other. And hey, I'm a steampunk. I'm used to spending time with all kinds of oddballs. Not that your friends are odd," Archie added hastily.

"No, I wouldn't go with *odd*. Heath, maybe. Actually, Heath, *definitely*. But Azrah's, um . . ."

"She reminds me a bit of Bridge, to be honest."

"Really?" Alarm pierced the warm glow that had been pervading Robin's chest. Did this mean Archie fancied Azrah?

"Yeah. Well, seeing her with you. You've got that brother/sister relationship with her, just like me and Bridge."

Robin nodded, relieved. "Except you had a baby with *your* sister."

Archie winced. "Now it sounds creepy."

"Er, sorry. Didn't think that one through."

"No, pretty sure that's on me. But yeah, me and Bridge were never meant to be more than friends."

Robin gave a mental fist-pump. Yes! That meant Archie *didn't* fancy Azrah. Almost certainly.

There was a moment's silence, then Archie spoke again. "I wondered—seeing as you were on board with the tea duelling—if you'd like to come to a convivial at the weekend?"

Robin swallowed. "A convivial?" he asked, stalling for time. He was chuffed to death that Archie had asked, and of *course* he wanted to see Archie again, but it wasn't as simple as that.

"It's a sort of organised gathering? There'll be tea duelling—and no, you don't have to do it if you don't want to—and other games, and a small market with traders selling jewellery and hats and stuff. And some bands, and maybe some other acts? It's going to be in a pub," he added persuasively, as if he thought the prospect of alcohol might tip the balance for Robin.

Not that it hurt, but it wasn't anything like that which was making Robin hesitate. He really, really wanted to go—but what if someone there recognised him from Willoughbys and said something about it? "Is it in Hitchworth?"

"No. It's in Ely. About an hour and a quarter on the train—I'm guessing you don't drive? Normally I'd get a lift up with Bridge, but she's not going to this one. She's got an old school friend coming to stay who's not into steampunk."

So no Bridge, and probably not that many people from Hitchworth, either. It was still a risk, though.

"I can lend you a hat and some goggles so you'll feel like you fit in."

That did it for Robin. How could he *not* go when Archie wanted him to so much?

Also, the hat and goggles would be a handy disguise. "Okay," he said, his mouth dry. Then his heart sank. "Oh. Is it on Saturday or Sunday?"

"Both days, actually. Which one works best for you?"

"Sunday," Robin said with relief. He was down to work Saturday this week, which would have been awkward to explain, given that he was supposed to be an accountant. His conscience twinged at this timely reminder that he hadn't been entirely honest with Archie.

He promptly forgot all about it as Archie's moustache twitched and his face split in a huge, happy smile that had Robin wondering if he even *had* knees anymore. "Fantastic!"

Going via Archie's house wasn't *precisely* the quickest way home from the bus stop for Robin. But it was definitely the way that got him more time with Archie. It was funny, though, how Verne Avenue, which Robin normally considered to be quite a lengthy street as they went around Hitchworth, seemed to have shrunk to little longer than your average garden path. Robin found his steps slowing to compensate the closer they got to Archie's house. If Archie noticed that they'd decelerated so much they were in danger of going backwards, he was too polite to mention it.

Eventually, though, all the dawdling in the world couldn't stop them arriving at their destination. Well, Archie's destination. Could it be Robin's as well?

"I'd ask you in, but you probably don't want to spend your evening babysitting my kid," Archie said in a perhaps worrying display of telepathy.

Given the sort of lines Robin's mind had been running along since they'd got off the bus, there was no *perhaps* about it.

"That's not a problem," Robin said quickly and maybe just a little too eagerly. "And I'd like to say hi to Lyddie again."

As he'd hoped, those seemed to be the magic words. "Well, if you really don't mind . . ." Archie gestured in invitation. "I'm not sure she'll have cooked, though. We'll have to rustle something up ourselves."

"That's fine. I like rustling." Okay, this time it was *definitely* too eager.

Archie laughed. "Cows, sheep, or paper bags?"

"All of the above. But food, for preference, right now. Um, if you don't mind me inviting myself round for tea."

"That's okay. I'm pretty sure I invited you. And if I didn't, Lyddie will. She was very upset you got away without her feeding you on Saturday."

"That's supposed to be a mum thing, isn't it?" Robin's shoulders slumped. "My mum pesters me about eating properly, but she never seems all that keen to actually feed me."

Archie laughed. "Okay, this has to be the first time I've ever known Lyddie to come out top in a stereotypical mum competition."

"She's great, you know. You're really lucky."

"I know. But it hasn't all been plain sailing."

"No, I guess it can't have been. But . . . at least she accepts you for you." Robin hoped he didn't sound too bitter.

"Yeah. Can't argue with that one." Archie's tone was warm. "If you don't mind my asking, what's your mum got against people being bi, particularly?"

Robin sighed. "You don't want to know."

"Go on, try me. I can take it. I'm a big boy."

"She says she can understand how, for some people, being gay isn't a choice. But if you *can* choose, why not choose to be *normal*?"

"Ouch."

"Told you. She's still praying I'll find a nice girl. Or even a not particularly nice one. The important word is *girl*."

"You ever tried dating women?"

Robin shook his head. "It'd be weird, you know? Because there's nothing there. Which is not a rude Shakespearian joke, by the way. I like being friends with girls, but I just can't imagine wanting to kiss one." He stopped, the k-word having totally derailed his train of thought. They were still standing under the lamppost outside Archie's house, in their own little oasis of light. He couldn't help glancing at Archie's lips, which looked plump and soft, surrounded by his beard and that truly splendid moustache. Would it tickle if Robin kissed him? Or would the wax make it scratchy? They were standing very close together. Almost touching. All he'd have to do would be to lean forward—

Archie coughed and moved back half a step. "We should probably go inside. I told Lyddie I'd only be an hour later than usual."

"Oh. Yes, of course." As he plodded into the house after Archie, Robin tried to console himself that this wasn't good night. He'd get another chance to kiss Archie—wouldn't he?

As Archie hung their coats on the stair rail, Robin cast his gaze around in search of Lyddie—and then stared. The door from the hall through to the kitchen was wide open in front of them, and the kitchen looked like it'd been flour-bombed. Jerrick was sitting in his high chair, covered in the stuff, banging a wooden spoon on the tray and laughing his little head off.

Lyddie didn't just have flour in her hair; there were what had to be lumps of raw pastry dotted about in there too. She beamed at them. "Archie, love! And Robin, bless you. Lovely to see you again. We've made pie, haven't we, Jerrick? It's in the oven right now."

"What kind?" was all Archie asked as he walked over to give his mum a hug and a kiss on the cheek, getting flour on his waistcoat in the process. Then he picked up Jerrick from his high chair, wooden spoon and all, and swung him around. "Have you made dinner for your daddy?"

"It's steak and kidney on one side, and ratatouille on the other, cos we only had one can of each. So if you have a bit from each side, that's your meat *and* your veg." Lyddie looked proud.

Could you even do that? Have a pie with two different fillings? It sounded dangerously subversive to Robin. He wanted some. "Can I do anything to help?"

Lyddie glanced around the kitchen. "Maybe we should clean up?" She didn't sound all that decided.

"Probably a good idea," Archie said. "We can't ask you to do that, though, Robin. You're a guest."

"I don't mind," Robin said quickly, all too aware that if he wasn't cleaning, he'd undoubtedly end up holding the baby, which had far more potential to go rapidly sideways. "Just point me at the cleaning stuff. You'll want to have some quality time with your son."

"Bless him, isn't he a darling?" Lyddie said vaguely. "You go and play with Jerrick, love. Me and Robin will sort the kitchen out."

"If you're sure . . ." Archie hesitated, then headed towards the living room, Jerrick in his arms.

There was a wail. Then another.

Archie came back, frowning. "Think he wants you," he said to Lyddie.

She beamed and held out her arms, and sure enough, the howling stopped as soon as Jerrick was back in her embrace. Archie shrugged and turned to Robin. "Looks like it's you and me on cleaning duty, then."

He had a slightly lost quality about him, as if he'd found Jerrick's blatant favouritism a little wounding. Robin pasted on a cheery smile and opened the cupboard under the sink, because what else would you keep there but cleaning stuff? "Not to worry. We'll be finished in no time, then we can all go and play."

Amongst other things, the cupboard held a new packet of J-cloths, three bottles of washing-up liquid of varying degrees of fullness, and what appeared to be a pair of Lyddie's shoes. Did she ever wear stilettos? They were definitely too small for Archie. Robin blinked, and pulled out the J-cloths and one of the bottles. "Have you got a mop?"

"Right. Yeah." Archie seemed to snap out of himself, and grabbed a mop and bucket from behind the door. "Just let me fill this, and I'll do the floor and you can clean the surfaces, if that's okay?"

"No problem. Oh, do you think we should take a look at that pie first? Wouldn't want to burn it."

"Good plan." Archie opened up the oven and peered inside. "No, I'd say we're good for at least another ten minutes. Maybe longer."

If Robin had ever been asked his opinion on cleaning as a date activity, he'd probably have turned his nose up at the idea, but in fact it was weirdly companionable. He and Archie worked around each other with quiet efficiency, smiles, and a lot of *Watch that bit, I've just cleaned it.* Robin was always a bit uncomfortable being a guest in someone's house—shades of his mother's disapproval of his behaviour when visiting her friends as a child hovered in his subconscious at all times. But it was impossible to be awkward while wiping their kitchen worktops and trying not to step in the wet patch.

By the time they'd finished, a rich meaty-cum-tomatoey smell filled the air, cutting nicely through the aroma of lemon-scented cleaning products.

"Are we done?" Robin asked. "I think the pie may be."

Archie smiled and parked the mop. "Yeah, we're done." He'd rolled up his sleeves, and a pair of strong, tattooed forearms were on display. Robin tried not to stare too overtly. One arm had a vaguely mythic, floral design, while the other, which was Robin's favourite, showed the cogs and gears of a mechanical arm. Steampunk down to the bone, almost.

They ate the pie sitting at the freshly cleaned kitchen table, Jerrick in his high chair once more as he chewed on a piece of cooled-down pie crust. The pastry was excellent—okay, it was kind of soggy on the bottom, but Robin actually liked that in pies—and even the weird mix of fillings was surprisingly tasty.

"He's not really hungry, bless him," Lyddie said. "I fed him before we started cooking."

"He's lucky to have a granny to do baking with," Robin said, giving him a fond look. "I never knew mine. Either one. All my grandparents died before I was born. Mum and Dad had me in their forties, and their parents had them late as well, so . . ."

"Archie never had any grandparents either," Lyddie said. Her mouth turned down, and she drew in a breath. "At least—"

"I didn't need them," Archie said fiercely, putting his hand on hers.

Robin felt spare-partish for the first time that night. Then the moment passed, and they talked about something that'd happened at Archie's museum that day.

They moved into the living room after they'd eaten and washed up. Lyddie's COC placards were still neatly stacked against the wall.

Robin wasn't sure what to do. It'd probably be *polite* to ask her how it was going—but it'd also make him feel like a traitor, pretending to sympathise with her cause. Then again, did he owe it to all his fellow employees to get over his personal scruples and do what he could to stop their jobs being endangered?

In the end, he decided it was entirely too complicated a moral dilemma to solve while full of pie, and settled for pretending that corner of the room didn't exist.

After playing for a while, Jerrick went grizzly for five minutes, then conked out, asleep. Lyddie did her disappearing act again, which Robin felt guiltily glad about. He and Archie sat on the sofa and mostly ignored the telly, chatting about all kinds of stuff—Robin's years at uni, Archie's stint on the streets, and nothing in particular.

It felt like no time at all had passed when Archie glanced at his watch. It was a strange one, with a cutaway face that showed all the little gears whirring and oscillating inside. How on earth did he manage to tell the time from it? The hands didn't show up at all. But apparently he did, because he gave a sigh and said, "Bridge'll be here soon to pick up Jerrick."

"I should get going," Robin said quickly. "Work tomorrow, and all that. But thanks for dinner. It was really . . . interesting."

Archie laughed. "I'll pass on your compliments to the chef."

"You should get him a little hat. And an apron that says *Kiss the Cook*." Robin could feel his face heating up. Should he have mentioned the k-word again?

Archie's eyes seemed to darken, and Robin wondered if he was thinking about kisses too. His breath hitched—but then Archie turned away and the moment was lost.

Robin swallowed. "So, are we still on for Sunday?"

"Yeah! Absolutely. If you come round here about nine, say? Then we can travel up together."

"Looking forward to it." Robin forced himself to make a move. For the door, unfortunately, rather than for Archie. "Bye, Jerrick," he added in a whisper, giving the sleeping child a wave.

Then he dragged himself out of the front door and into the night.

CHAPTER  28

Archie closed the front door softly, so as not to wake Jerrick. Should he have kissed Robin good night? Archie wished he'd held his nerve and gone for it—but he'd been worried how bad it would look to Bridge if she ambled in and found them mid-snog. Or even mid-peck-on-the-cheek.

Lyddie came downstairs while he was still debating with himself. "Oh, has Robin gone, then?"

"As if you weren't listening for the front door. Yeah, he's gone."

"So you're seeing him now?"

"Not . . . exactly. But he's coming to the convivial on Sunday."

"Then you're seeing him. That's good. He's a sweet boy."

"Yeah. Yeah, he is."

Bridge turned up not long after Robin had left—in fact, if he'd stayed any later, he'd have bumped into her on the way out.

"How's he been?" She sounded tired, but not fed up.

"Asleep for most of the evening." Archie was pretty sure it was Jerrick she was asking about, not Robin. "I think Lyddie wore him out with all the baking."

"Yeah?" Bridge shot Lyddie a look that was equal parts admiring and incredulous. "Rather you than me. I get enough messes to wipe up without letting him loose on the contents of the kitchen cupboards."

"He was a little angel. Hardly made any mess at all."

Archie didn't bother to suppress a snort. "Selective memory, much?"

Bridge laughed. "Right, next time they need cakes for the toddler group I'll get you and him on the job. S'pose I'd better get him back home now." Despite her words, she dropped onto the sofa with an *Oof* and did a spot-on impersonation of someone who wasn't planning on moving for a good long while.

"Cup of tea first?" Archie offered.

"Shouldn't." Bridge grabbed a cushion, punched it into submission and stuck it behind her back with a wriggle and a sigh.

"I'll put the kettle on," Lyddie said, and disappeared into the kitchen.

Archie sent Bridge a speculative glance. She had her eyes closed, and there was a half smile on her face. Would now be an opportune moment to tell her about him and Robin? Not that there *was* a him and Robin, not yet at any rate. It was definitely starting to look like there would be, though. Archie couldn't help smiling at the thought. And Bridge seemed in a good mood tonight, if a bit weary. There must have been a friendly crowd of customers at the chippie.

Yes. No time like the present. Archie opened his mouth to begin—and was interrupted by a gentle snore.

Okay. Maybe not *quite* the time to tell her, then.

CHAPTER 29

Robin spent an uneasy night after leaving Archie's house. His conscience was pricking him not only about the continued deception, but also about the whole homelessness issue.

The more time he spent with Archie and his mum, the more he could see Lyddie's point about that advert. Or at least, could see it wasn't *entirely* nonproblematic. And while he didn't agree with her methods—the ad was a done deal, and damaging Willoughbys wasn't going to help anyone—he *did* think that perhaps some amends ought to be made.

He'd have to admit there was a smidge of self-interest in there too. Well, maybe more like a splodge. No, not that much. A smodge? But if Willoughbys redeemed itself, hopefully Lyddie would call off the Black Friday demonstration, and what was better for the store's image would definitely be better for Robin and his friends' long-term employment prospects. And it'd make it much, much easier for Robin to own up to working there.

But how, exactly, could Willoughbys redeem itself? What did homeless people actually *want* from the store? Archie would probably have a good idea, but that might lead to awkward questions.

He tried to sound Sheppy's Mum out over a cup of soup after work the next day, but she was having a bad day and wasn't all that chatty. "Where's John?" he asked finally, as the large, friendly bloke was nowhere to be seen.

"He managed to get into the emergency shelter on Queen Street. Nick of time, too. He's not very well at the moment. Bad cough."

The shelter! Why hadn't Robin thought of that? The shelter was bound to need donations, and they'd be able to take stuff like food from the café and get it to people who needed it. "Do you ever go there?"

She shook her head, lank orange hair escaping from her hood. "Can't leave Sheppy."

"Oh. I suppose they don't take pets? That's a shame. Are you okay, though, out here on your own?"

She nodded and didn't say anything else. Conversation over, Robin guessed. He gave Sheppy a pat and headed home, his mind working.

The shelter was probably pretty busy right now, with people turning up for a meal and a bed. If that was how it worked? From what Sheppy's Mum had said, it sounded like it was a bit more complicated than just rolling up at the door. Anyway, he could go over there one lunchtime and speak to someone. If they were open. Did homeless shelters open during the day? Or were they like bed and breakfasts, and kicked you out to fend for yourself during daylight hours? The longer Robin thought about it, the more he realised he was utterly clueless.

He made a mental note to read up on it all online. When he got home, though, the first thing he saw was this week's *Echo* on his doormat. Robin picked it up with nervous fingers, and turned to Letters to the Editor.

As he'd feared, there was one complaining about the Willoughbys advert in last week's edition, although if it'd been written by Lyddie she'd used an assumed name. It was signed Ms. Shirley Gatsby. Robin winced as he skimmed it, his eyes catching on words like *outrage* and *rampant capitalism*.

Then he read the editor's response, and physically cringed. The editor, apparently, was either best mates with Willoughbys' owners or had received a hefty kickback. The phrase *bleeding heart liberals* actually appeared in print. As did the suggestion that the author of the complaint should attempt to purchase herself a sense of humour. Possibly at Willoughbys, which was *a fine local store steeped in tradition*.

In his mind's eye, Robin could see the battle lines being drawn up, with Archie, Lyddie, and their friends on one side, and Willoughbys plus various other establishment figures on the other.

And Robin caught, like a bunny in the headlights, in the kill zone between them.

He turned the page, hoping for something to stop the churning in his stomach—a heartwarming story of a local man winning a tenner on the lottery, say, or a report on a school nativity play. Instead, he found a rerun of the sleeping bag advert, complete with Robin, his colleagues, and his teddy bear.

Robin felt a strong urge to go to bed, cuddle Teddina very tightly, and never get up again.

Robin soon realised he couldn't do the hostel visit in his lunch hour. By the time he got there, and factoring in time to walk back, he'd have around twenty minutes to spare. Not nearly long enough for an in-depth discussion on how Willoughbys might best help them, including the tricky bit where he'd have to explain his lack of authority and how this was all pie in the sky for now, when what the hostel really wanted was pie in the dining room. No, it'd be better to go in on a day off, which as he had the steampunk convivial on Sunday meant not before Monday.

Robin felt guiltily glad to be able to put off worrying about the hostel visit until next week. It meant he had more time to worry about the convivial. What if he made Archie look bad in front of his fellow steampunks? Called them steampunkers by mistake, or made some other hideous gaffe Archie hadn't got around to warning him about? Archie had promised to lend him a few things, so not all his clothes would be an embarrassment, but what if he wore them wrong?

What if he just didn't *suit* steampunk? Archie had assured him facial hair wasn't obligatory, which was good, because the only time Robin had tried to grow a moustache he'd been mortified to find nobody even noticed. But actors and actresses were often described as having "the look" for period drama—maybe Robin had a particularly modern face, one that'd be totally ridiculous in steampunk stuff?

What if—and Robin would have had to admit under torture that this was what he was *really* stressing about—Archie took one glance at Robin next to all his wacky, crazy steampunk mates and wondered what the hell he was doing with someone so normal and boring. Robin could see him now, confessing to his mates he didn't know what he'd been thinking, his face twisted up in a sneer that was uncannily like Ethan's . . .

Oh God. Robin shuddered. *Get a grip.* Archie hadn't found him boring when they'd spent all that time together in his house, had he? And he'd asked him to the convivial, so there was a good chance he wanted him there. Wanted him to meet his mates, even. Although as it was out of Hitchworth, of course, there might not be many of them there . . .

Stop it. Archie thought he was interesting. At least enough to turn up for drinks at the Millstone and *still* invite him out again. It would be fine on Sunday.

Right.

CHAPTER 30

The rest of Robin's week seemed to pass at the speed of a geriatric snail that'd just had a hip replacement, probably because, despite his best efforts, he didn't *once* manage to bump into Archie or even Lyddie. Of course, he could have called or popped round, but if his relationship with Ethan had taught him anything, it was that most blokes didn't find neediness an attractive quality.

They had a date for Sunday that Robin was almost certain might actually *be* a date. That would have to do. At least he was kept busy at work, what with preparations for the Loyal Customers' Christmas Shopping Evening and a number of increasingly desperate attempts to get Heath to tell him what, precisely, his *pivotal role* was supposed to be.

Robin barely slept Saturday night. He'd dug out his waistcoat that evening, but as Sunday dawned he still wasn't sure whether to wear it or not. Did it look too modern? Too pinstripey? All the steampunks he'd seen online wore fabulous waistcoats in a variety of eye-catching colours and designs. There were jewel-coloured paisley waistcoats, airship waistcoats, dinosaur waistcoats, and—Robin's mouth had *literally* watered—Van Gogh-style exploding-Tardis waistcoats. Some of the designs were more prosaic, true, but they were generally paired with jet packs, mechanical arms, or splendidly coggy ray guns, none of which Robin felt able to knock up on short notice. Or long notice, for that matter.

All Robin had was a *boring* waistcoat. Although it did have the advantage of making him look decidedly accountant-esque.

No. No, he wouldn't wear it, he decided, feeling a sudden, inexplicable aversion to the thing. Archie had said jeans and a plainish shirt—grandad collar if possible—would be fine for Robin's first event.

Robin riffled through the shirts in his wardrobe dispiritedly. Why didn't he have any grandad neck shirts? Okay, so maybe they hadn't been in fashion in his lifetime, but surely they were a style classic? Robin briefly considered cutting the collar off an ordinary shirt, but the trouble was, he *liked* all his shirts. All the unflattering ones Mum had bought him had ended up at the charity shop when he'd moved. He couldn't quite bring himself to commit acts of sartorial vandalism on any of the shirts that remained, so settled for the least modern looking of the bunch.

Jeans he could do; Robin pulled on his favourite washed black pair, and topped them off with a thick leather belt with a plain buckle. He grabbed his biker boots from the back of the wardrobe—Mum had put her foot down about him getting a moped, but he'd fallen in love with the boots. They were so wonderfully strappy and buckle-y. Robin checked his reflection in the full-length mirror, and nodded. Okay, the shirt wasn't great but he looked good from the waist down, even if he did jingle a bit when he walked.

At least he didn't have to leave the house before it was light, which was one of the most depressing parts of going to work in a British winter. Steampunks were apparently not noted for their early rising. Robin felt an affinity with them already.

It was, however, chilly, so he reluctantly pulled on a coat on his way out. It kind of ruined the almost-steampunk vibe he had going on, but he could take it off when they got to the convivial.

It was really only a hop, skip, and a jingle from Wells Street to Verne Avenue. Robin knocked on Archie's door ten minutes early, since hanging around in the front garden until nine on the dot would be weird and stalkerish.

Lyddie opened the door wearing an enormous man's plaid woollen dressing gown with the sleeves rolled up and the hem trailing on the floor. Her hair was so wild it might easily have actual birds nesting in it, although they probably had plans to move somewhere with a nicer postcode when they could afford it. She beamed at him. "Come on in, love. Aren't you looking good today? You should wear jeans more often. And I *love* those boots."

"Thanks." Robin stepped inside and was grabbed for a hug and a kiss, which was nice but embarrassing. "Is Archie ready?"

"I'm sure he'll be down in a minute. He was getting out hats, I think, or was it goggles? Maybe it was both. Or a pocket watch? I've always loved pocket watches. Nobody seems to wear watches these days."

"Well, apart from Archie. Do you ever go to steampunk events?" Robin asked.

"Me? No. It's his thing, isn't it? He spends enough time here with me, I wouldn't go cramping his style. Oh, here he comes."

The sight of Archie ambling down the stairs, tightly waistcoated and—yes—with a watch chain attached, made Robin's own chest feel oddly constricted. Archie's shoulders appeared even broader than usual, his waist trimmer and his hips . . . But now was *not* the time to be thinking about Archie's hips. At least, not the sort of thoughts he'd been having. "You look amazing," he said a little hoarsely.

Archie smiled. "Hey, you too. Love the boots. Listen, this is in no way a requirement but I thought, you and me are about the same size, right? Do you want to borrow some of my stuff? A waistcoat, maybe a jacket?"

"Um, yeah, thanks. That'd be great." He'd be wearing Archie's clothes. Robin felt warm at the thought. Should he casually suggest his shirt was too modern looking too? Maybe his underpants . . .?

No. That would definitely be pushing it. Especially in front of Lyddie.

"Okay, come on up and I'll show you what I've got."

With an offer like that, how could Robin refuse? He followed Archie up the stairs, which creaked and clattered a welcome as he trod. They were bare of carpet, and showed the wear of countless feet, but the polished wood handrail felt good in his hand.

Archie's room was large, with a bay window that would overlook the street if they ever decided to cut the top two-thirds off the trees out front. It was probably cool in summer, but must need the lights on most days in winter. The furniture was an eclectic mix of styles, with the common themes of *real wood* and *old*. Robin felt a twinge of embarrassment as he compared it to his own furniture, which was literally cheap as chipboard.

Archie had a nice big bed, Robin couldn't help but notice. Currently, on top of the usual duvet and pillows, it appeared to be wearing enough vintage clothes to stock a reasonably sized gentlemen's outfitter's. "Wow, you have a *lot* of steampunk stuff."

"Uh, yeah. It kind of accumulates." Archie rubbed the back of his neck. "And to be fair, that's all I ever wear."

"Hey, that wasn't a criticism. I think it's great." Robin picked up a tweed jacket. "Oh, this is *nice*. Can I try it on?"

"Hang on a mo." Archie rummaged through the clothing, coming up with a red woollen waistcoat that toned beautifully with the tweed. Robin made grabby hands.

The waistcoat needed cinching in at the back—Robin revelling in the light touches as Archie adjusted it—but the jacket fit as though it'd been tailored especially for him. Robin gazed at his reflection in Archie's standing full-length mirror, and preened. "Okay, you've sold me on this. I look like I'm just off for a day's huntin', shootin', and fishin'. Except for the hair. Um, I probably shouldn't have styled it as normal." Yep, vanity would get him every time.

"Not to worry. That's what hats were invented for." Archie tossed over not the expected top hat, but a brown felt bowler.

Robin took it with misgivings. "Is this a reference to accountancy?"

Archie laughed. "No, but I thought the style would suit you. Go on, put it on."

Dubiously, Robin did so. When he checked his reflection, he was pleasantly surprised. "Huh. That's actually pretty cool."

Archie nodded. "You've got to remember, for most of the Victorian era, the bowler was the working man's hat of choice. It was popular for a reason, and not just because it's practical. Tall hats aren't for everyone. Right—time to add the finishing touch." He came over with a pair of vintage welding goggles, and fitted them carefully onto the brim of Robin's bowler. "Oh yes. Much more steampunk."

Robin grinned at himself in the mirror. "I love it. Now I look like I'm off for a day of inventin', tinkerin', and airship piratin'."

"You've been reading up on the subject again, haven't you?" Archie's smile was warm. He strapped on some sort of one-shoulder leather armour and slung a small box sporting weird dials and a strangely familiar bit of copper wire around his neck. Then he took a tall top hat from a shelf, gave it a brush off with his sleeve, and popped it on his head. Instead of the welding goggles, there was a single, brass-rimmed lens on its brim—a monoggle?—with a couple of extra, moveable lenses on little arms. To finish, he shrugged on an overcoat.

"*Wow.*" With the long coat, the leather, the hat . . . Archie looked about six million feet tall and very, very cool. Robin had never had fantasies about steampunks before. He was starting to suspect he was never going to fantasise about anyone else ever again. "I have *got* to take a photo of you. Hold still." He took a couple of quick snaps with his phone, which Archie posed for in epic fashion, serious expression and all.

When he'd finished, Archie pulled out his own phone. "Let me take some of you too."

Robin did his best to strike a pose that was both dignified and implied he dressed like this every day.

The journey to Ely passed without incident, unless you counted the group of beer-drinking lads on the train who made up a song about Archie's and Robin's hats. And the three times they were stopped and asked where the fancy dress party was. Plus the number of people who snapped surreptitious pictures of them on their phones. And the group of Japanese tourists outside the cathedral, each of whom asked them politely if they'd mind posing for photos.

"Do you think they're planning to troll their friends and family with stories of how this is the way English people dress all the time?" Robin whispered through his best smile. "Oh, wait—this *is* how you dress all the time."

"To be fair, the goggles and gadgets are only for proper steampunk days," Archie murmured back. "Right, I think they're done. Come on. The pub's not far."

CHAPTER 31

Archie had had a few last-minute misgivings about taking Robin to his first-ever steampunk event via public transport—it wasn't always easy to be visibly counterculture when surrounded by normal people—but Robin dealt with the public reactions like a total star. It'd never fazed Archie to have people taking such an interest, but he knew other steampunks sometimes felt like they'd been attacked by paparazzi.

Robin took it all in stride, happily posing for photos and seeming to get more confident all the time. And he'd been asking Archie about gadgets and accessories, mentioning stuff he'd seen online, and just generally seeming *into* it all. Archie was on a total high. Not that it'd *necessarily* have been a deal breaker if Robin hadn't wanted anything to do with steampunk, but . . . yeah, okay, it would've made it all a whole lot harder. And less fun.

The Rabbit's Revenge, where the convivial was held twice a year, was a traditional old English pub with high ceilings and horse brasses on the walls. Robin glanced up at the painted sign outside, which showed a rabbit with a shotgun. "Was this place named before or after the hunting ban came in?"

"Not a clue, but they do a great range of vegetarian food." Archie pushed open the door.

"Nobody ever thinks about the poor, orphaned baby carrots," Robin said sadly, and stepped inside. Then he stopped dead, leaving Archie holding the door. "Uh . . . there's a *lot* of people in here. And by people I mean steampunks."

Archie put a reassuring hand on his shoulder. "Yeah, they're pretty well attended, these events. Think we'd better move on in, though. We're blocking the doorway."

"Oh—sorry." Robin made his way further inside, dodging around a cluster of chatting convivialists and a table where an earnest game of Jenga was in progress.

Archie followed him, giving a smile and a nod to people he knew as they passed. "Drink? Or do you want to have a look around first? There's a function room upstairs where the rest of the traders will be, and the bands and other acts."

"Let's look around," Robin said almost before Archie had finished speaking, then he flushed faintly. "Um, unless you're desperate for a drink?"

Archie shook his head. "I'm good. Let's see who's here." He spotted Dora almost immediately; her stall was in prime position, in between the bar and the stairs to the function room. "Come and say hi to Dora. She's another Hitchworth steampunk. If you can imagine it, she can crochet it."

He led the way over to Dora's stall, which was well-stocked with Lovecraftian Elder Gods, Krakens, and three-headed dogs, plus a few wearable items like shawls. "Hey, Dora. How's it going?"

She looked up from whatever she was currently crocheting—a spider? There weren't enough legs yet to be certain—and smiled only slightly manically. "I'm calm, I'm calm. I got here on time, I didn't bring the wrong stock, and I've sold two pairs of spats already today. They said crocheted spats couldn't be done, but I've proved them wrong, hah! How are you? Is this a new member of AETHER?"

"This is Robin," Archie said. "Not sure if he'll be joining AETHER, but he's from Hitchworth."

Robin beamed. "I love your outfit. Where on earth did you get it?" Dora had on a beautiful deep-green velvet ensemble today and could have stepped straight out of *A Christmas Carol*.

"Made it. Used to be a pair of curtains. Found 'em in a charity shop."

"That's amazing! And you make all these too?" Robin gestured, wide-eyed, at the crocheted what-nots.

Dora preened. "All my own work. Can I interest you in a familiar?"

"A . . . what?" Robin was clearly baffled.

Archie laughed. "It's his first convivial, Dora. I haven't told him about familiars yet. We'll come back, okay? Once we've had a look around."

"Ah, I see. Steampunk virgin. Don't let him spend all his money on plastic tat."

"As if." Archie took Robin's arm and led him towards the stairs.

"Come to the Christmas market!" Dora called after them. "I'll be trading there too! With all new stock!"

"Sorry about the aggressive sales tactics," Archie murmured as they made their way up the stairs. "Dora's . . . well, *Dora*."

"That's okay. I'm used to all that kind of thing. Er, what's a familiar? Has she got a basket of kittens under that table for sale to witches?"

"Similar concept, as it happens. But steampunk familiars are generally stuffed toys. You'll see a lot of people carrying around plush octopuses, maybe the odd dinosaur or raven . . . I've even seen a rat. It's a good icebreaker, actually. You'll often see people who get chatting about their familiars. Well, you can't talk about outfits *all* the time. Although that is a popular topic. Top marks for admiring Dora's seamstressing."

"It really is amazing. I wish I could sew. Mum and Dad were never that keen on me learning." Robin's mouth turned down. "They made me go to football instead."

They'd reached the top of the stairs and could hear the music coming from the function room, but Archie lingered on the landing, wanting to finish the conversation. Wanting to know everything there was to know about Robin, and where he'd come from. "Big on the old gender stereotyping, were they?"

Robin nodded. "Although to be fair, I think they were also pretty keen on getting me out of the house." He stepped aside to let a lady in a crinoline past.

Archie winced. The more he heard about Robin's mum and dad . . . "You could always take an evening class. There are bound to be some starting up in January."

Robin brightened. "That's true. And now I'm not living at home anymore . . ."

He didn't have to add, *I won't get stick about it from my parents.* Archie had it on the tip of his tongue to ask Robin why he bothered with them, but he bit it back. Not his family; not his business.

He wouldn't mind it becoming his business, though.

Robin leaned a little towards the doorway, as if trying to hear better what was going on inside. "I was thinking of looking for a ukulele group too."

"You play?" Archie's eyebrows shot up and he completely forgot to move, even as a couple of guys in full military parade uniform marched past, one of them grazing his shoulder with an epaulette.

"Yeah." Robin shuffled his feet on the carpet. "I mean, I know it's not a classical instrument, but—"

"Are you kidding me? It may not be classical, but it's classic steampunk. It'd probably be quicker to name the acts that *don't* have a ukulele in there somewhere." Archie couldn't believe it. This guy was *perfect*. "Hey, do you sing at all? Preferably about tea?"

Robin gave him a long look. "I can do 'I'm a Little Teapot,' but I'm not sure anyone would pay to hear it. I'm not big on the singing. I just like to play the music."

That struck a chord. "Wait a minute. Do you play . . . ah, what's it called? I was down your street a while back and heard someone playing this song." Archie hummed a few bars.

Robin turned bright red. "'Mr. Lonely.' Yes. Um, shall we go in?"

Christ, he was adorable. "Yeah. Sorry. Let's go. But I really liked your playing. I'd love to hear it again." Robin muttered something incomprehensible and if anything, turned even redder. Charmed, Archie resisted the urge to take his arm as they walked into the room. They weren't like that, were they?

Yet, his inner devil whispered, and twiddled its moustache.

Inside the function room, they were setting up for the first act, so the music was recorded for now. The seating area in the centre of the room was almost empty, most of the steampunks milling around the stalls at the edges of the room, or standing around in groups chatting and comparing their finery. Archie snuck a glance at Robin and had to suppress a laugh at the wideness of his eyes.

"Where do they even *get* cogs that huge? And how did they get them up there? Oh my God, I *love* the inflatable airship."

Huh. After all the convivials Archie had been to here, he barely noticed the décor these days. It *was* pretty impressive, actually. "Dan made the cogs. He's the DJ. They're polystyrene, I think. And yeah, the dirigible's cool. Fell on my head one time and knocked my goggles off, but mostly they're good about tying it securely."

Robin stopped so suddenly Archie nearly walked into him. "Can you see a plague doctor over there?" he asked in a strained voice. "In a long, black robe thing, with a mask like a bird's head?"

"Oh— Yeah. Didn't know he was coming today. I'll introduce you. Better warn you though, he never breaks character."

Robin still didn't move. "So he's not, um, a ghost?"

Archie cracked up. "Sorry. Shouldn't laugh. But no."

"What does he look like under all that stuff?" Robin seemed fascinated.

"Not a clue—he never takes off his mask. Come on, let's go and say hi. Unless you're scared?" Archie added with a grin.

"Of course not!" Robin marched towards the plague doctor, who was leaning on the wall, customary pint-with-straw in hand.

Archie caught up with him as he reached the Doc. "All right, mate? This is Robin." He had a momentary qualm as to how to introduce Robin, and decided in the end to leave it at that.

The plague doctor pointed his massive beak at Robin. "Lepers, sir, are required to utilise a bell at all times to warn the populace of their approach."

"Er, sorry?"

The Doc turned to Archie, and asked in a sympathetic voice, "Is the poor creature afflicted also with deafness, or merely idiocy?"

"Just suffering from a bit of culture shock, I think," Archie said over Robin's spluttering.

"Ah. An innocent. We shall treat him kindly. But I must leave you, good sir. I spy a soul in need of succour." He swept off in a flurry of swirling robes.

"Wow," Robin said breathlessly.

Archie frowned. "Oi, do I need to be jealous?" Then he wondered if that was going a bit far. They hadn't *said* this was a date, had they?

"No. Really not. No jealousy required." Robin gazed into Archie's eyes with such an open, heartfelt expression that Archie's heart melted.

"Good," he said, giddy and off-balance in the best possible way. "That's good. To know. Um. Shall we go and do the bits we haven't seen yet?"

"I'd like to," Robin said, and maybe Archie was simply hearing what he wanted to hear, but he didn't seem to be talking about just the convivial.

"Okay," he said. "Let's do that."

Of course, five seconds later Robin was off again. "Is that a whole steampunk family? Oh my God, they've got mini-me outfits for the kids! That is just so *adorable*."

It totally was—and not just the kids. Archie's heart swelled as he smiled at Robin. "Yeah, they come here a lot. Oh, hey, here's some more people from AETHER. Robin, this is Lord Peregrine and Lady Edith Bressingham-Steam."

Robin turned to the stately couple approaching them, his eyes now as wide as his goggles. "Oh, wow, your outfits are incredible. Should I curtsey? I feel like I should curtsey."

Lady Edith inclined her head graciously. "No need, dear, but if you want to, feel free. You must be Archie's new . . ."

"Friend," Robin said quickly, with a glance in Archie's direction. "I live near him, and we bumped into each other one day."

Everything seemed to dim a little—but he'd said *friend* for Archie's benefit, right? Because Archie had been an idiot and said he wasn't after a relationship.

Yes. Definitely for Archie's benefit. He hoped.

"Oh, so you're from Hitchworth, then? I thought you seemed a little familiar," Perry said.

Robin's gaze darted wildly. "I, um, yes. I'm about the town a lot. On the streets. That's where you've probably seen me. On a street."

"I expect that's so. Well, we'll leave you to have fun. My dear lady wife tells me she's in need of a new hat, and who am I to stand in the way of millinery?"

"Um, yes. Hats. Very important." Robin nodded repeatedly as the Bressingham-Steams promenaded away.

Archie managed not to laugh at Robin's obvious awe. Despite how sweet it all was. "They're not actually a real lord and lady, you know. It's just their steampunk personas. Personae?"

"I knew that," Robin protested. "Oh, look, there's a stall with leather . . . things."

"Yeah, that's Ruthless. He makes some wicked cool stuff."

"Ruthless?" Robin gave Archie a sidelong glance as they made their way over.

"Well, his mum calls him Rufus, but he drives a hard bargain." Archie raised his voice. "Hi, mate. How are you? I see you've restocked the gauntlets. Nice." He picked one up, more to feel the heavy, quality leather than to examine it by eye, although it was definitely worth a closer inspection. "Hey, you've changed the design. Upped the rivet count."

Ruthless nodded. He was a big man, and didn't try to dress like a Victorian gentleman, even one with science-fiction tendencies. He was clad like the artisan he was, in a thick apron and rolled-up sleeves. "Tried them out at Asylum and they practically flew off the stall. Ran out the first day. So if you want a pair, get in quick."

Archie shook his head, smiling. "I'm good. Still got my old pair. Course, you might get lucky with Robin here."

Ruthless raised a sardonic eyebrow. "Looks like someone might," he said with a smirk.

Okay, so that hadn't been *quite* the best phrasing Archie could have used. Fortunately Robin didn't appear to have heard. He'd picked up a pair of brown leather bracers with an intricate embossed design and was staring at them like a starving man presented with a pork pie and pickle supper.

"Try them on," Archie suggested.

Robin startled. "Oh, I'm not sure—"

He was cut off by a hearty laugh from Ruthless. "Now, with a name like Robin, why am I not surprised it's the bracers you go for? Go on, try 'em for size. That's your best quality veg-tanned leather, all hand-made. They're softer than a lot of bracers you can buy. Feel that suede inside? Makes 'em more comfortable for when you're hanging round Sherwood Forest aiming your arrows at all them rich bastards."

"Maybe if I shot a few rich bastards, I could afford them." Robin laid the bracers reverently back down on the stall. "They're great, though. Amazing. How did you learn to make them?"

"Well, it wasn't watching videos on YouTube, I can tell you. I've been leather-working twenty years now. Sure I can't tempt you?"

"When I win the lottery, I'll be back to see you first thing," Robin promised.

"Better take a card, then. So you'll know how to find me."

"I will." Robin picked up a business card and put it carefully in his wallet.

Archie made a mental note to nip back and ask Ruthless to put them aside. He could probably afford them, and, well, Christmas was coming, wasn't it? This was shaping up to be a fabulous day.

They wandered around a few more traders' stalls, then decided to go down to grab a drink before the first act started. "What can I get you?" Archie asked as they stepped up to the bar.

"Hey, I thought steampunks only drank tea?"

"*So* not true. But if you want a steampunk drink, you could always try the Kraken rum. Or the Lincoln gin. Bit early for me, so I was going to stick with a lime and—" Archie broke off with a gasp.

Bridge was walking towards them, her eyes narrowed.

Oops. He never had got around to telling her about him and Robin, had he? It just hadn't ever seemed to be the right moment—even with the best part of a week to do it in.

Archie was beginning to regret that.

CHAPTER 32

Archie's voice stopped dead, and the rest of him did as well. Robin nearly cricked his neck darting a concerned look in Archie's direction. "What's up?"

Archie took a deep breath. "Nothing. Nothing at all. Hi, Bridge. You made it after all?"

This time, Robin *did* crick his neck turning to follow Archie's gaze, which meant he winced directly in Bridge's face. It probably didn't improve her impression of him.

She looked *totally* different to the last time he'd seen her, which was most likely why he hadn't realised the voluptuous young lady steampunk heading their way was her. Her waist was cinched in unbelievably tightly with a corset, making her boobs roughly the size of twin dirigibles. Instead of a top hat with goggles, she was wearing a full, black wig and a pair of devil horns. The outfit was finished with a burlesque-style skirt, high in the front and floofy in the back, and boots designed to march on boldly where Hells Angels feared to tread. Jerrick, clad this time in an adorable little T-shirt printed with a waistcoat and fob watch, perched on one well-defined hip.

"Nat's come down with a cold. Didn't want to give it to Jerrick." Her tone was curiously flat, and her gaze never left Robin. "See you've got company."

"Yes." Archie sounded wary. "You remember Robin?"

"Oh, yes."

Robin gave her a tentative smile. "Er, hi. Nice to meet you again. You look *amazing*, by the way. I love the wig. Are the horns attached, or are they separate? And oh my God, that corset! That brocade is just gorgeous. Is it really uncomfortable all the time, or do you get used to it? Hey, Jerrick, you look great too. Very dapper." Robin gave a little wave, and Jerrick hid his face in his mother's wig.

Was Robin talking too much? He was talking too much, wasn't he?

Bridge blinked, and shook her head slightly, but her mouth had turned up at the corners. "God, you make it hard not to like you. How are you doing, then? I see Archie's got you into his pants."

Robin flushed. "Just the jacket and waistcoat, actually. Oh, and the hat. The jeans are mine. And the, um, pants." He tugged at his collar, realised what he was doing and snatched his hand away.

Bridge rolled her eyes. "Right, if I'm going to be seeing you all the time, you can make yourself useful. Look after Jerrick while me and his dad have a little chat."

She unceremoniously handed over her baby. Robin took him with a great deal of trepidation. He *had* held babies before, of course he had, but that was generally while their parent was fumbling for a purse or wallet, and only lasted as long as it took to make a purchase. "Um, what does he like to do?" He hoped desperately the answer wasn't going to be *Howl the place down when his mum leaves him.*

"Chew stuff. He's a baby." Bridge's tone was matter-of-fact. "Don't let him have anything small enough to choke him, and he'll be fine."

"You're okay with this, aren't you?" Archie asked, giving him a worried look.

"Fine," Robin lied through his fake smile. "No problem. Do this all the time."

Archie was still frowning. "If he cries, just walk him up and down a bit."

"Right. Got it. Chewing, no choking, and walking." He could handle this.

"And here's his nappy bag." Bridge handed over a familiar rucksack, which meant Robin had to clutch Jerrick awkwardly to his chest with one hand so he could take the bag with the other. He couldn't help feeling hips like Bridge's must come in handy at times like this.

"Try not to totally squish him," Bridge said, not unkindly, and then she and Archie were gone.

Robin slung the nappy bag onto one shoulder, relieved to be able to devote both hands to holding the baby once more. "It's just you and me, then," he said to Jerrick, who stared at him solemnly. He'd clenched one tiny fist tightly around the lapel of Robin's waistcoat, so clearly he wasn't confident in Robin's ability not to drop him either.

"Ooh, isn't he adorable?" the lady behind the bar cooed at him. "How old is he? About six months?"

"Something like that." Robin couldn't remember off-hand, and was fairly sure she was a better guesser than he was.

"Aren't you a sweetie?" she carried on, reaching out a finger for Jerrick to hold. He took it in one tiny hand, then his little face screwed up as though in deep concentration, and turned brilliant crimson with impressive speed. Were babies supposed to go that colour? What did it mean? Oh God, was Robin holding him too tightly? Had he squished him after all?

What it *actually* meant became swiftly, and pungently, apparent.

"Um, I think he needs a change?" Robin said to the barmaid, hoping against hope that her feminine nurturing instincts would kick in and she'd take Jerrick off his hands out of pity. If not for him, for the poor kid.

"Ooh, he does, doesn't he? Who's Mr. Stinky, then! There's no changing table in the gents' here, but you'll be fine to take him in the ladies," the barmaid said helpfully, flapping her hand in front of her nose to ward off the evil odour. "If anyone gives you a hard time, just tell them I said so."

Robin swallowed. "Thanks," he managed. Should he try to find Archie and Bridge, and hand over the problem? After all, they were the experts. But that would mean interrupting their talk, and he'd had a strong impression of air needing to be cleared there as well as in Jerrick's immediate vicinity. Plus, he could imagine Bridge's withering look, and he really didn't want to disappoint Archie. How hard could it be anyway, changing a nappy? Robin had been wiping his *own* arse for over two decades now. He squared his shoulders and headed for the ladies'.

At least his dad wasn't here to witness it.

Neither, it seemed, was anyone else. When Robin pushed the door open and walked in he found the place empty. The changing table, instead of being in the main bit of the ladies' toilets as he'd vaguely expected, was in one of the cubicles, thoughtfully marked with an explanatory hieroglyphic illustrating a gender-free adult bending over a be-nappied baby.

Robin had mixed feelings about this. Although locking himself in the cubicle would shield his ineptitude from any actual ladies who happened to wander in, it'd also nix any possibility of them offering to help. While Robin was firmly of the belief that men were as able to look after children as people of any other gender *in general*, he was painfully aware that this didn't also hold true in the specific, i.e. him. How on earth did new parents cope? Did the hospital hand them an instruction manual on the way out from the delivery ward?

Not without difficulty, Robin manoeuvred himself, Jerrick, and Jerrick's rucksack into the cubicle, and somehow managed to shut the door. The changing table folded out from the wall, and on the second attempt Robin even managed to get it to *stay* folded out.

Right. Changing table. Clearly the baby was supposed to lie on it, but which way? Robin had a vague idea you weren't supposed to put babies on their stomachs—or was that only for sleeping?—so down on his back Jerrick went, Robin holding carefully onto his little head so as not to bang it on the hard plastic.

He didn't howl in outrage, so presumably Robin was doing okay so far. He bent over Jerrick, and his hat dipped alarmingly. "Right. Hat off, then. Your mum would smother me with her wig if you got brained by falling goggles." There was a windowsill just wide enough for the bowler hat and the nappy bag to perch on precariously.

Okay, now to get to the nappy. Luckily, instead of a onesie consisting mostly of poppers, Jerrick was wearing a pair of tiny trousers today. "We know what to do with trousers, don't we? Yes we *do*," Robin cooed. "Off they come." He eased the elasticated waist over the nappy and off the kicking legs, Jerrick giggling all the way.

"You can laugh, but you're the one who's pooped his pants, and I don't see you changing them without my help," Robin told him with mock severity. "Let's get this nappy undone. Must be these sticky tabs, yes, that's the tic— Oh dear *God*, what are they feeding you?"

Robin gagged and decided breathing was definitely overrated. Asking to borrow the plague doctor's mask might have been a good move. Weren't their beaks usually stuffed with herbs and stuff to ward off smells? This wasn't just poop; this was industrial toxic waste.

It looked like a pre-digested late-night chicken korma and smelled like a chemical weapon. One hand on Jerrick's tummy so he wouldn't do a lemming-leap off the side of the changing table, Robin rooted around frantically in the nappy bag with the other, trying not to dislodge it or his hat from the windowsill. Wipes, wipes . . . surely there must be wipes in here *somewhere*? There— No, that was nappy sacks. Still, a useful find. And a fresh nappy, also likely to come in handy, and—yes!—baby wipes. With a triumphant grin, Robin turned back to the squirming Jerrick.

Who promptly peed in his face.

CHAPTER 33

Archie and Bridget had found a quiet table near the door to the beer garden—at this time of year, braved only by die-hard smokers. Bridge swept her skirts out of the way and sat, her corset ensuring correct posture at all times. Archie felt like a small boy about to get a stern ticking off from his governess, and did his best not to slouch as he sat down.

"Right," she said. "What's the *real* story with you and that Robin?"

"We're not going out together," Archie said cautiously.

She raised a beautifully contoured eyebrow so far her left horn twitched.

"But . . . we may be kind of working up to that?" Archie sighed. "Look, I never meant to keep it a secret. And I didn't want to hurt you. But I can't live my life as if we're, I don't know, married or something. You and me . . . it was only ever a bit of fun, and it ended with no hard feelings either side—or am I wrong, there?"

Bridge shook her head. "No. You're not wrong. But—"

"Just let me say it, yeah? Let me have my say, and then you can tell me why you don't agree. *If* you don't agree."

She rolled her eyes but nodded. It wasn't until she added a mime of zipping her lips and throwing away the key that Archie felt safe to carry on.

"We both went into this parenthood thing knowing that, well . . . we've got obligations to Jerrick, yeah? But not to each other. Not romantically. You know I'll always be there for you, Bridge—I *will*," he stressed at her look. "But in other areas . . . change is gonna happen. It's bound to. Jobs change. Family circumstances change. One day, and I don't reckon it'll be too far off either, you're gonna find someone you want to be with. And maybe you'll move in with them, you and Jerrick, and I'll have to deal with him having another parental figure in his life. That's just . . . That's just *life*. We can't stop living simply because we've had a kid. We're gonna have to trust each other to keep on putting Jerrick first, that's all. And I swear to you, that's all I want to do. But I need my own life too, and so do you."

"Can I speak now?"

Archie risked a grin. "Depends. Let me know in writing first what you're planning to say?"

"Bugger that. Look, I *know*, all right? I know. And *you* should know better than to listen to my bollocks when I've had a hard day."

Archie stared at her. "I should? Uh, so you didn't mean it about feeling betrayed by me wanting to go out with someone else so soon?"

"Well, I meant it a *bit*. But that was then. It's hard sometimes, that's all. You know what Dad's like, and I've had to listen to him a lot more than you have. He worries about me. About Jerrick." She huffed. "And it knocks your confidence, having a kid. At least, it's knocked mine. I don't even *look* the same—and you can shut your mouth. I'm not after compliments."

"Truth, then. You're gorgeous."

"Up yours." She said it with a smile, though. "Oh, sod it. You go on about change happening, and I know it does—life'd be dead boring otherwise—but it's scary, innit?"

Archie gave a rueful nod. "Believe me, you're not the only one who feels that way."

"It's like, there's times when I want to be taken care of and told nothing has to change. Sad thing is, they're usually the times I need someone to tell me to pull up my big girl's knickers and get on with my life. You know why me and you didn't work out?"

"Uh . . ." Archie decided discretion was the better part of not getting his top hat knocked off with his head still inside it.

"It's cos you wanted to look after me, and yeah, that's great, but I don't *need* looking after all the time. Not even most of the time." She sighed. "We never really had any rows, did we?"

"You're saying that like it's a bad thing."

"Yeah, well, that's just it, innit? For you, it isn't. But for me, it kinda is." She shook her head, black curls flying. "Why are we still talking about this anyway? Talk about flogging a dead horse. This one's a bloody fossil. So go on, tell me about this bloke of yours. You really like him, don't you? Your Christopher Robin?"

"That's Robin Christopher. And . . . yeah. Yeah, I really do."

"Poor sod. Name like that, his parents must hate him."

"You have no idea."

"Shame. He seems . . . nice."

"You're saying *that* like it's a bad thing too."

"Yeah, well, I think we've established that *nice* is not exactly top of my list of things to look for in a partner." Bridge huffed. "And they say opposites attract. Load of bollocks, if you ask me."

Archie smiled. "You can be nice. Sometimes. I'm sure I've seen it happen at least once. Or heard about it. Unless I dreamed it."

Bridge held up an eloquent finger, and stood. "Come on. We'd better rescue your nice, not-quite-boyfriend from Jerrick before he gets him hooked on beer and cigarettes."

Archie followed her back the way they'd come. "I hope Robin knows enough about babies not to give Jerrick either of those."

"Did I say it'd be *Jerrick* getting hooked? Huh." Bridge frowned. They'd reached the bar, and Robin and Jerrick were nowhere in sight. "Where do you think he's gone off to?"

"Maybe he took Jerrick for a wander?" Archie leaned over the bar to talk to the barmaid. "Have you seen a young lad with a baby?"

She smiled. "Blond hair, worried expression?"

"That's the one."

"You're in luck. Here he comes now." She nodded, and Archie turned to see Robin approaching, baby in one arm, hat in his hand, and profound relief on his face the moment he saw them. "Here you go," he said, handing Jerrick back to Bridge.

She gave him a kiss. "How's my little man, then? Uncle Robin been taking good care of you?"

Robin flushed. "I've changed his nappy."

"Aw, you didn't have to do that." Bridge slung Jerrick expertly on her hip, while Archie grabbed the changing bag from Robin's shoulder.

Robin's face was a picture. "Trust me, I did."

"Bit of a stinker, was it?" Archie said with sympathy.

"Oh, you know. Birds dropping from the skies, local towns preparing to evacuate . . ."

Archie laughed. "And do I want to know why your hair's wet?"

"Not in the least," Robin said fervently. "Just be thankful I didn't put your hat back on afterwards."

Bridge cackled. "We've all been there. Gotta watch out for little boys and their pee-pees. Although honestly, I'd have thought you blokes'd be more on your guard. It's not like you haven't got one of your own to keep under control."

"To be fair, mine hardly ever goes off without warning like that," Robin said.

"And I'm happy to say *yours* is Archie's problem, not mine. Right. I'm going to go and catch up with Dora. See you later." She grabbed back the rucksack from Archie and walked off, her skirts swaying as she went.

Robin goggled after her. "Did she just say . . ." He swallowed. "Never mind."

Archie gave a relieved smile. Yep, probably a *little* early in the relationship for a formal statement on Robin's penis being Archie's responsibility.

And how great was it that he could think about them having a relationship without feeling he'd let Bridge down? He wanted to kiss Robin this instant, pee-soaked hair and all, and had to remind himself to take things a little slower. And preferably a little less public, for a first kiss at least.

"So . . . everything's all right, is it?" Robin asked. If tones could tiptoe, his would be very much *en pointe*. "I mean, between you and her?"

Archie nodded, his heart light and the immediate future getting brighter all the time. "Yeah, everything's all right."

CHAPTER

Robin felt like he hadn't just dodged a bullet with Bridge, he'd side-stepped an entire nuclear arsenal. "I'm glad things are okay there," he said fervently.

Archie was wearing the sweetest smile *ever*. "You know, even if they hadn't been, I think you'd have won her over with that nappy change. Have you done that a lot?"

"Actually that was my first. I'm just hoping it doesn't fall off or turn out to be inside out."

"Seriously? You'd never changed one before? That was definitely going above and beyond, then. And sorry about the, er, shower."

"Not the finest moment of my life, no. Can you give me five minutes? It'd be kind of good to clean up a bit, now I've got my hands free." Robin handed Archie his bowler hat, and legged it for the loos. Almost walking into the ladies' again, he caught himself in time and headed for the gents'. He couldn't help thinking that gender-free loos would make life a *lot* simpler.

He gave his face a quick rinse in the sink. Thankfully only the front of his hair had been, um, affected. The hot air hand dryers were the sort where you could twiddle the nozzley thing to blow the air upwards, so he was able to dry his hair too.

It left him looking a little more like Tintin than he was comfortable with, not helped by the product he'd put in his hair this morning, but then wasn't that what hats were invented for? Emerging from the gents', he found Archie hadn't moved, although he had picked up a companion who seemed vaguely familiar, and was wearing the most amazing Tardis suit. Four eyes widened as Robin approached, but he didn't care. "That is so cool! I just love the light on the top hat. Did you make it yourself?"

"Thanks. Yeah. Had a bit of help from my dad." They—Robin couldn't work out if the person was a boy or a girl, and suspected that might be the point—seemed chuffed to bits over the compliments, although their gaze mostly stayed on the floor, only occasionally darting to Robin's epic quiffage.

"Robin, this is River, who's another member of AETHER. Uh, are you happy re-enacting that scene from *There's Something About Mary*, or would you like your hat back?" Archie seemed to be struggling to contain laughter.

"So much yes. Thanks." Robin took the bowler and jammed it firmly on his head. "Did you make the suit too, like from scratch? Or did you manage to find a suit the right shade of blue and just add the details?"

"Tailored it myself." River shifted minutely—was there a button hidden in a pocket?—and the suit began to make actual Tardis-dematerialising noises.

Robin almost had a nerdgasm. "Okay, I've run out of superlatives now. But I am seriously in awe."

"Thanks. Um, I'll catch you later, Archie?"

Archie nodded, and River scurried off.

Robin groaned. "Did I chase them away with my overenthusiastic fanboying? I did, didn't I?"

"Don't worry. River was pleased, believe me. They're kind of an introvert, though? And they're only seventeen. Still finding their feet, socially."

"Me too, honestly. Um, not the seventeen part, in case you were worried. Not that you'd have any reason to worry about that . . . Shall we go and look at some more stalls?"

They left the convivial early, soon after five o'clock, because of having work the next day. Well, Archie had work, and it was obvious he assumed Robin did too. Robin guiltily didn't correct him. It felt later than it was as they took the train back in the dark, which was weird because the day had seemed to pass in a flash of outlandish hats, customised goggles, and voluminous skirts. Also boobage.

Robin supposed it was only natural that what was squished *in* at the waist by a corset had to go somewhere, and *up* was one of the only two possible directions, but how on earth did people who were into that kind of thing know where to look? Even he'd found it a little distracting, although more from the *Are those things loaded, and if so please stop pointing them at me* perspective than because of any sexual connotations.

"Penny for them?" Archie asked, smiling.

"What?" Boobs? Robin hoped not.

"Your thoughts. Although that'd probably be around £1.50 in new money."

"Seriously not worth it." Which fortunately could be taken either way. It'd take a much larger sum than £1.50 to get Robin to admit he'd been thinking about breasts of the female persuasion. "Just . . . looking back on the day. It was great—really great. I can't believe there's been all this going on for years and I never even knew about it. And River, with that Tardis outfit—that was so amazingly cool. It blows me away how you can make *anything* you love be steampunk."

Archie's smile had grown broader, and somehow softer. "So you think you might come again?"

"Hey, I've got my own goggles now." He had, too—a customised set in aviator style that looked fabulous with the hat Archie had lent him and which he was hoping to forget to return. "Just try and stop me. When's the next event?"

"It slows down a bit this time of year, but we're having a group visit to the Victorian Market on Thursday. AETHER, that is. In full splendid. Do you fancy coming along?"

Robin's heart sank, pausing only to give his conscience a hefty kick en route. That was the date of the Loyal Customers' Christmas Shopping Evening, which to Robin's annoyance *everyone* now seemed to be calling Customas. He might not be organising it anymore, but there was no way he'd be able to get out of working that night. "I, um. Sorry. I mean, I'd love to, I really would, but I've got to, um, go round to Mum and Dad's."

"That's okay. I guess family comes first."

"Er, yes. Sorry." Robin coughed and crossed his fingers. "Is the group just going to the market, or will they be doing general shopping as well? In shops that are open late?"

Archie shrugged. "People can do what they want. We'll be meeting up for photos first and maybe a drink after, but we won't be going around in a group all the time. I'd think most people would stay in the market. I've heard there's a record number of gin stalls this year so yeah, not a lot of incentive to pop into the normal shops. You can do those any time. And sober." His lopsided, roguish grin made Robin want to tell Willoughbys where to go, and spend Thursday night drinking gin in goggles, but common sense prevailed. Gin wasn't cheap, so continued employment was pretty much a necessity.

"Wish I could go. Have a pint of gin for me, yeah?" Robin would still have to keep an eye out for anyone from AETHER who might happen to walk into Willoughbys and recognise him, but steampunks in full splendid would at least be easy to spot.

They got lucky with the bus after getting off the train—this time on a Sunday evening if you just missed one, it was probably quicker to walk than wait for the next—and were almost home by seven. Well, almost at Archie's home. Robin's was a little further away. He dawdled as they neared Verne Avenue, the five-minute walk from there to his own flat looming ahead of him, cold, dark, and dreary. And, more importantly, *alone*.

Except . . . did it? "Do you want to have dinner at my place?" Robin asked in a rush, just as Archie came out with, "You're coming in to say hi to Lyddie, aren't you?"

They stopped and stared at each other, faces lit dimly by a flickering streetlamp. Archie seemed to have a hopeful glint in his eye, but maybe it was only a reflection. "How about—"

"I say hi to Lyddie and then you come round to mine?" Robin's heart was thumping, probably because the words had once again come out at world-record speed.

"Yeah. Sounds great." Archie paused. "Cheers for understanding. She'll be fine but . . . I just need to check."

Robin's heart went all melty. Maybe he couldn't exactly relate—his mum always seemed to be aggressively all right—but, well, seeing Archie being so caring was making it very, very difficult not to jump on him right this instant. "No problem."

The house, when they entered it, was noisier than Robin had expected. A *lot* noisier.

"Is Lyddie having a party?" he whispered as they stepped into the hall, although the chances of anyone in the living room hearing him through the closed door *and* over the sound of their own voices seemed pretty minimal.

Archie grimaced. "I hope not. She can be a bit free with the invitations." He opened the living room door with an air of once bitten, twice shy.

Inside, there were around half a dozen people of varying age and gender, seated variously on the sofa and on the floor with Lyddie. A tall, vaguely boho lady on the sofa was holding forth about how something shouldn't be allowed, with emphatic hand gestures. Robin's heart sank. Of course, it *could* be just a particularly opinionated book group . . . No. His money was on COC.

The tall lady fell silent as they entered, and a dozen or so eyes turned their way. Lyddie beamed at Archie and Robin. "Hello, love. You're home early. Everyone, you know my Archie, don't you? This is his boyfriend, Robin."

Robin flushed, derailed by being described as Archie's boyfriend. Cart before horse, much? Not that he minded. He could get *entirely* behind this new sort of carriage-drawn horse.

"Uh . . . campaign meeting, right?" Archie said. "We'll leave you to it, then. I'm going over to Robin's for dinner. Have you eaten?"

"Pizza," boomed the tall lady from the sofa. "On the way. Plenty to share if you want to stay and get involved."

"We're good," Robin said quickly, worried that might prove too tempting for Archie. "But thank you." He backed out of the room, immensely relieved that Archie followed. "Although now I really fancy pizza," he added.

"Have you got anything in at home? We could pick up something on the way."

Robin liked how Archie didn't assume he had a well-stocked fridge, or indeed, any idea what to do with the contents if he'd had them. "Actually, the shop round the corner will still be open. We could get some basic pizza and chuck a load of stuff on top? Uh, unless that's going to lead to World War Three over the pineapple question?"

"Sounds good. And no, while pineapple on pizza wouldn't be my first choice or even my ninety-ninth, I respect everyone's right to choose."

"Oh, thank God." It came out so heartfelt that Archie laughed. Robin liked his laugh. It was totally worth the prickling embarrassment and the reminder of Ethan. "Um, I had an ex who used to say it made him gag to look at it, which kind of ruined the mood at dinnertime."

Archie's smile was soft. "Yeah, I can see that. Come on then, let's see what this shop can do us."

They ended up with a margherita each, which, once back in Robin's flat, they piled high with a selection of extra toppings and a shedload of grated cheese before bunging them in the oven. Archie was bigger on the vegetables than on the meat, whereas Robin would've been tempted to pile on the entire pack of pepperoni if there hadn't been any witnesses. Or such a thing as heart disease.

Having been in Archie's house and met Lyddie, Robin didn't feel the slightest bit self-conscious about eating on the sofa in front of the telly. Once he'd divested it of his ukulele and a scribbled note of the chords to "Eleanor Rigby," that was. Not that they actually watched the . . . crime drama? Soap opera? It was just background noise to the conversation.

"Hey, isn't that the box you had in the chippie the other day?" Archie asked idly as they finished off the last slices of pizza. "I was wondering what was inside."

"Oh . . . it's just stuff I haven't unpacked yet." Still smarting from Mum's dismissal of his toys, Robin didn't like to be more specific.

Then he remembered this was Archie, who dressed up in top hats with goggles and played Victorian parlour games. "Actually, it's my *Doctor Who* figure collection."

Archie sat up straight. "Yeah? Cool. Can I take a peek?"

"Go ahead. And don't worry about the socks. They're clean."

Archie gave him a sidelong look, and visibly decided not to ask. He knelt by the storage box, opened it up, and pulled out a bright-red Totes Toastie, from which he carefully extracted Rose Tyler. He smiled, the sight doing strange things to Robin's insides that weren't all that compatible with a large helping of pizza. "I love Rose. She had a great character arc."

"*And* she ended up with the Doctor. Well, his sort of defective clone. But still good going." Robin would be happy to go on record that he wouldn't kick *any* version of David Tennant out of bed.

"Not wrong there." Archie put Rose carefully down on the floor, and pulled one of Robin's old school football socks out of the box. "What are the chances of me getting the Doctor this time?"

It suddenly struck Robin that Archie could quite easily fancy both the Doctor *and* Rose, which was somehow hotter than it ought to be. "Pretty low, actually. I'm fairly sure he's in blue. You know, like the Tardis."

Archie laughed and pulled out a Weeping Angel figure. "Sorry, Rose. I'll try and get your bloke next time. Are you planning to display them?"

Instead of delving further, he turned to Robin, who nodded.

"When I get around to buying some shelves. And working out how to get them home on the bus."

"Could give you a hand there. I've got a mate with a van. Do you want to buy new, or secondhand?"

"I . . . honestly hadn't thought that far ahead." It wasn't entirely true, but it had only just occurred to him that his mother's views on *secondhand tat* no longer needed to be taken into account.

"I'll keep an eye out for you." Archie's gaze roamed the room. "I can see you're going for . . . uh, an eclectic look here."

"That's a very polite way of putting it. Actually, most of this stuff came with the flat." The essentials, like the sofa and his bed, had. The rest, such as the scratched and wobbly nested side tables and the saggy pouffe, had been bits and bobs his mum and her friends no longer wanted. Apparently this didn't count as secondhand tat because she knew where it'd been.

There was a pause, and then Archie spoke, his voice hesitant but somehow resolute. "Listen, about Lyddie describing you as my boyfriend . . ."

Robin waited, his heart inconveniently lodged in his throat, but Archie didn't continue. "Um, yes?" It might have been a squeak.

Archie laughed. "Okay, so confession time: I was totally hoping you were going to jump in and say that's fine."

Had he said that? He had, hadn't he? "It is? I mean, yes. It is. Fine." Robin attempted to wrestle his wayward tongue under control. "With me. If it is with you? Which you seemed to be saying?

So assuming that's a yes, if you could kiss me now and stop the babbling, I'd appreciate it quite a lot."

Archie was still laughing as he leaned over and closed the short distance between them.

His lips were every bit as soft as they looked, and seemed somehow charged with electricity as they met Robin's. *Probably a steampunk thing*, Robin thought crazily, drowning in heady sensation. Archie's beard tickled gently, while his moustache, although stiff, gave off a pleasing aroma of cinnamon.

Robin hoped he didn't taste too strongly of pepperoni. Or pineapple. Even if he did, Archie didn't seem to care, deepening the kiss and—yes—slipping in a bit of tongue.

Oh God. This was really happening. Robin could feel the kiss throughout his entire body, his skin tingling and yearning for more. He pressed closer to Archie. Why were they wearing so many clothes? The flat was *definitely* overheated. Robin scrabbled one-handed at his tweed jacket and managed to get it halfway off his shoulders, where it stuck. Bugger.

Archie saved him from his predicament by pushing it the rest of the way off, which was good, but there were still at least four layers of cloth between them. Steampunk, Robin realised, definitely had its downside. "We should . . ." he breathed.

"Yeah," Archie agreed, and pulled back.

Robin could have cried. "I meant—"

"Me too," Archie said, and unbuckled his shoulder harness.

Robin had a sudden, fervent wish to see Archie wearing that *and nothing else*, but it was probably a little soon to ask for that kind of thing. Instead, he fumbled at the buttons of his waistcoat—*Archie's* waistcoat—and managed to get it undone.

"Oh, yeah," Archie said, and undid his own waistcoat with far greater dexterity. Well, he *had* had more practice. Robin couldn't wait any longer, and fell upon Archie's shirt buttons. Every one that he undid revealed another tantalising few inches of a firm, muscular, tattooed chest. Had it hurt, when he'd had them done? Robin wanted to kiss every single inky boo-boo better.

"*Honi soit qui mal y pense,*" he read around Archie's neck, and raised an eyebrow. "Does this mean you're wearing a garter?"

"Wanna find out?" Archie's mischievous grin, combined with the moustache, made him look like, if not the devil incarnate, definitely a close relation.

Robin shivered and dived back in.

"Wait," Archie gasped.

Robin froze.

"Want to see you too."

He unfroze. That? Not a problem. Robin slipped the waistcoat off his shoulders and pulled his shirt over his head.

"Oh, yeah," Archie said again, and closed the distance between them as their mouths found each other once more.

It was incredible. Robin couldn't remember *ever* feeling this good, pressed tight against Archie, skin to hot skin. Breathing the same air. "Do you want to . . ." he gasped, not even knowing how to end the sentence, but that was okay, because *anything* Archie wanted was okay. More than okay. Absolutely perfect and utterly essential.

"Can I . . .?"

Robin could only nod. "There's . . . in my bedroom."

"Right." Archie looked momentarily nonplussed, as if the thought of relocating was a little too complex right now. "We could . . .?"

"Yes." Robin nodded and scrambled to his feet, pulling Archie after him. "This way."

Robin felt rather proud of himself for making it into the bedroom without tripping over his own feet, given how much of his blood supply had rushed south, leaving his brain high, dry, and incapable of any but the most basic thought processes. Such as trousers: off.

Well done, brain.

Archie got with the programme with impressive speed, and then they were there, on Robin's bed, with only their underpants between them. Any minute now they'd both be naked, just as Robin had been dreaming of ever since he'd first seen Archie disembowelling a fridge.

It was . . . For a moment, Robin couldn't believe it was happening. He flung out a hand to search his bedside drawer, coming out with a packet of sticking plasters, a weird massage gadget Azrah had given him one Christmas, and then, *finally*, condoms and lube.

Archie drew in a shaky breath. "You're sure?"

"Oh God, yes." Robin stripped off his boxer briefs to emphasise the point.

Above him, Archie still had his open shirt on, framing that incredible chest. It was heaving with ragged breaths. "You're so fucking gorgeous," he said, and Robin glowed in every fibre of his being. It was almost too much. Except it wasn't; it was very much not enough, because he needed Archie in him, preferably right now.

He opened his mouth to say so and without meaning to let out a needy, wordless whine.

Luckily, Archie seemed to be fluent in incoherence. He fell upon Robin, kissing him everywhere, touching him everywhere, until Robin was a senseless, writhing mass of pure *want*.

"Need you," he managed, shoving his hand into Archie's pants to tug on his cock just in case it wasn't clear precisely *what* Robin needed.

"Going to take such good care of you," Archie breathed, and it was so *him* Robin melted.

Archie grabbed the lube and slithered down the bed, farther than he needed to unless— Oh God, yes. Robin moaned as warm lips engulfed him while a finger teased his entrance. Archie sucked him as he prepped him, until Robin had to push him away because no way was he coming until Archie was inside him.

As Robin squirmed out from underneath, Archie scrambled back up the bed to kiss him. The salty taste of himself on Archie's lips made Robin hunger for more, and he pulled down Archie's boxers with shaking hands. When Archie's cock sprang free, Robin wanted to punch the air, to high-five the world, because he'd wanted this for so, so long. Somehow he managed to fumble the condom onto Archie, forgetting what he was doing half the time because this was *his* hands on Archie's *cock*. Long, thick . . . and oh Christ, Robin was going to come if he didn't distract himself.

Archie was making that very, very hard. Pun not intended. He kissed his way down Robin's chest, taking his gorgeous cock out of Robin's reach again, but that was okay, because he pushed Robin onto his back and eased his legs up and—oh God—Archie was going to be inside him any minute now. Robin gave a manly whimper at the thought.

Archie froze. "Okay?"

"Yes, God, don't stop. I mean, carry on." Robin hooked his hands under his thighs as a visual aid, because communication didn't seem to be his strong point at this present moment.

Chuckling, Archie lubed himself up—why hadn't Robin done that? He should totally have done that.

Apparently thinking wasn't his strong point right now either.

"Ready?" Archie breathed, and lined himself up.

He pushed in, so gently Robin could have cried. It felt as though this wasn't for Archie, it was all for Robin, and he wanted to say, *No, it's for you,* but his tongue couldn't form the words. Archie was filling him, inch by inch, and it was so much better than anything Robin had imagined. He felt cared for, treasured.

Loved.

It was too much, so he moved before he was ready, snapping his hips up to meet Archie's. Archie gasped, then started to thrust in and out. The burn eased and Robin was lost, submerged in a sea of ecstasy. Was he holding on to Archie's hips, urging him deeper? He couldn't have said. All he knew was Archie, in him, driving him closer and closer to the brink.

Robin tried to hold it off, but it was no good. His orgasm rushed upon him like a tide, and he bucked helplessly, out of control and loving it. Hot come spurted between them, coating both their bellies.

Archie thrust once, twice, until Robin almost couldn't take it anymore—and then he groaned, low and heartfelt, and collapsed, panting, on Robin's chest. "God, you're incredible."

"Same," Robin breathed, because there were no words for how he felt right now. He relaxed into Archie's arms, basking in the warmth and the love.

CHAPTER 35

Archie lay there, on top of Robin, breathing heavily. That had been *amazing*. Was sex usually this good? Archie couldn't remember it *ever* being this good.

He'd desperately wanted to kiss Robin all day. To touch him. It almost felt unreal, now, that he'd been granted his wish. The bliss was bone-deep, his skin still fizzing where they touched, and he never wanted to leave this bed.

Why the hell couldn't it be a Saturday night? Then they could sleep late, waking up to make love once more.

Did he say *once*? Make that several times. Hell, they could go for the record.

If it'd been a Saturday night. He sighed.

"Y'okay?" Robin asked drowsily.

Archie sat up reluctantly. "I'd better go. Work tomorrow."

"Oh—yeah. Forgot about that." Robin's lips formed an adorably childish pout.

"I'll take that as a compliment. But I'll see you soon, yeah?" His heart full, he bent down to kiss Robin one last time.

Walking the short distance back home, Archie could've danced. Christ, if he'd had an umbrella and a handy thunderstorm, he could have reenacted the whole iconic sequence from *Singin' in the Rain*. He and Robin were together, and everything was right in the world. He was whistling the tune as he opened the front door, but cut himself off so he could listen for any signs COC was still in session.

Lyddie's voice rang out in the silence. "It's all right, love, they've buggered off now. Want some cold pizza?"

Archie grinned, kicked off his shoes, and went to join her. "No, thanks. Had pizza round at Robin's."

Lyddie was sitting on the floor again, this time surrounded by photos from a shoebox by her side, and she looked up to give him a sly smile. "Bet that wasn't all you had."

"Nope. Had a glass of water too. And that's all I'm going to tell you." Archie lowered himself down to sit cross-legged beside her, and picked up a photo of himself as a toddler covered in chocolate. "I hope you're not getting these out to embarrass me in front of my new bloke."

She squealed and hugged him. "I'm so happy for you, love. He's a lovely boy, your Robin. You need to bring him round more often. Anytime he wants to stay over for breakfast is fine by me. He needs feeding up a bit, and he likes my cooking. You sure you don't want any pizza?"

"Sure. So what are all the photos out for, if it's not embarrassing me?"

"I wanted one of you when you were Jerrick's age. To show Bridge. What do you think about this one?" She held out a picture of a round-faced baby Archie, clutched precariously in a teenaged Lyddie's arms. Just as in the photo, she was beaming fit to burst as she handed it to him.

Archie's heart clenched as he took it. It wasn't one he remembered seeing before. It was rare to find Lyddie in a nostalgic mood, and it could easily have been years since she'd had this particular shoebox of photos out. There weren't that many pictures of her from when he'd been a kid. She'd always been the one taking the photos. He'd known all his life she'd been young when she'd had him, but seeing that picture really brought it home. He'd had schoolkids visiting the museum who looked older than that. Who *were* older than that.

"Isn't he just like you? Jerrick, I mean, cos that little one *is* you. Duh." Lyddie laughed.

It was infectious. "Yeah, I assumed if you'd had any other kids, I'd have found out about it by now."

"Bit hard to keep a kid a secret. Especially if you're crap at it, like me." Lyddie frowned. "I meant at keeping secrets, but love, was I crap at having kids? I never—"

Archie cut her off with a hug. "You're the best mum a kid could ask for. And Bridge is going to love that photo. Now, do you want a cup of tea?"

She glanced around vaguely. "Gonna head up to bed. Now you're home. Bit knackered from earlier. Some of those women can't half talk. I'll just pack these up first. Oh, and the pizza boxes. Can't leave them out all night. We'll get mice. Archie, love, do you think we should get a cat?"

Archie gave her a squeeze. "I think I'll tidy things away. You head on up."

It didn't take long to wrap up the leftovers. Archie put the photos away, promising himself a proper look at them another time, and then headed to bed himself. As he slipped between the sheets, he couldn't help remembering Robin's bed, and the gorgeous, warm man he'd left inside it. Yeah, he was definitely going to have Robin stay the night soon. Archie wanted to go to sleep with him, and wake up with him in the morning.

He wondered if Robin had stayed there, or if he'd got up for a bit after Archie had left. Maybe made a cup of tea, sorted his clothes out for the morning, that kind of stuff. Alone in the darkness, Archie smiled to think about it. Then he turned over. Time to go to sleep. His dreams should be pretty sweet tonight, anyway. Robin was his, and everything was good.

No more helpless longing, and no more secrets.

CHAPTER 36

The next morning, Robin woke up late, luxuriating in his nice, warm bed that still smelled faintly of Archie. The only thing that could've improved on the perfection of last night would have been if Archie had stayed.

Except, if he'd stayed, he probably couldn't have failed to notice Robin *not* getting up for work. Which would have meant more lies... Suddenly the bed didn't feel so comfortable anymore. Robin groaned aloud, because who was there to hear him?

He was sick of all this. Well, no, he actually very much liked *most* of this, but he was sick of the deception. He needed to come clean and admit to Archie that he worked at Willoughbys. Archie could then break it to Lyddie, preferably while Robin was far, far away and she didn't have a knife in her hand.

His stomach roiled uneasily as he thought about telling Archie he'd lied about his job. Maybe he could make a joke about it? Would Archie find it funny?

No. No, he really wouldn't.

Oh God. Robin needed to pull his finger out and talk to Gail. Try to get something done for the homeless. Then, if Archie was mad at him for working for the enemy, Robin would be able to point at how he'd made things *better* by working there.

Yes. That was a plan. A *good* plan. And today, he'd go and visit that shelter.

Ten minutes later he was sitting at his laptop with a slice of toast in hand, trying mostly without success not to get crumbs in his keyboard. There was a lot of information online about the Queen Street shelter, which in defiance of the whole county's landlocked state was known as the Anchorage. Robin had had a vague idea that hostels for the homeless provided a bed for the night and presumably a meal or two, but in fact the Anchorage offered laundry services, counselling, and a computer suite as well, to name but a few of the amenities. And they were definitely open in the daytime, as they served lunch.

You couldn't, however, just roll up there and expect a bed, which was fair enough as space was limited. You had to be referred by someone official like a doctor or a social worker or probation officer. The website seemed to be saying that the hostel was there to cater for people who didn't fall under the local authority's duty of care, which was kind of horrifying. Shouldn't the local authority have a duty to care for *everyone*? But then, probably they had limited space too, and had to prioritise the most vulnerable people.

So . . . if you were an able-bodied adult without children, the hostel, or another like it, was your only hope. It was a frightening thought, in a there-but-for-the-grace-of-God way. And even if you did qualify for help, you could still slip through the cracks, couldn't you? Archie had.

Robin considered carefully what he was going to wear to the shelter. Should he put on a suit, so as to be taken seriously? But it wasn't as though he was actually going as a representative of Willoughbys, and he didn't want to raise false expectations. Or look like he thought he was better than the residents and wanted everyone to know it.

In the end he pulled on an old, comfortable pair of jeans and Mum's sweater, and gave himself a critical once-over in the mirror. Yep, that would do. No one could accuse him of thinking too much of himself in *that*.

Weird to think that this time yesterday he'd been staring at a very different image: bowler hat, waistcoat, goggles . . . Robin missed them already. They'd been quirky, and different, and more to the point, they'd been *Archie's*. Warmth flooded through him at the memory. It'd been a fantastic day, every second of it. Well, not *every* second. The ten or so he'd spent getting peed on by little Jerrick wouldn't exactly count as the best of his life. Still, it'd definitely been an experience. Robin huffed a quiet laugh at the thought of telling Azrah about it. She'd probably pee herself too.

Right. Time to focus. Robin gave his reflection a confident smile, and set off for the bus stop.

There was no one on reception when Robin got to the shelter, and while there was a bell to attract attention, he always felt it was impolite to actually use those things. A stint on customer service at Willoughbys had left him with a Pavlovian response of bracing for verbal evisceration every time he heard a bell ring, and he didn't want to spread the misery. So he dawdled in the narrow hallway, reading notices about claiming housing benefit and getting off drugs. You never knew when a bit of knowledge might come in handy.

"All right there?" A bearded figure had appeared and was peering at him with friendly concern.

"Oh—hi. I'm, um, Robin."

The man was casually dressed in a sweater, and unlike Archie's, his facial hair was less the dapper and debonair sort, and more of the oops-I'm-going-bald-better-grow-a-beard variety. "Good to meet you, Robin. I'm Dave. I'm afraid we're full at the moment, but I can put you onto youth services?"

Robin coloured. "Um, thanks, but I'm not a customer. A client? I mean I'm not homeless. I just wanted to ask about things local businesses can do to help."

"Oh, school project, is it?"

On reflection, perhaps putting on Mum's sweater hadn't been the *best* idea Robin had had this morning. "No—I'm, um, I work at a local shop? With a café?" He couldn't seem to stop it all coming out with a questioning tone, as if he were in dire need of reassurance. "I wondered if you accepted donations of food at the end of the day?"

"Oh yes. Obviously food safety standards have to be adhered to, and certain things we wouldn't be able to take, but we'd be very grateful, if it's on a regular basis and we can rely on it. Can you give me an idea of the sort of items and quantities that'd be involved?"

"Er . . . this is really just a fact-finding mission? I— Well, I had an idea it'd be good if we could help, but I'm going to need to run it by my boss. I wanted to find out a bit more so I could know what to say to her."

Dave's eyes lit up. "Okay, no problem. Do you want to have a look around the shelter?" He took a step, and made follow-me gestures.

"I don't want to be a bother . . ."

"Not at all. The more people who know about the work we do, the better."

"Then thanks, that'd be great."

It was . . . mostly as Robin had expected: slightly dingy, with the décor not being top of their priorities, and smelling faintly of cleaning fluids. But it was warm, and had a kitchen that was busy with preparations for the midday meal, and there was a room where you could go and watch the telly. The beds were in dormitories, but Dave explained there was a newer hostel in the next town that had single rooms "so they can help people with more complex issues."

"You mean, um, mental health issues?"

"That, or alcohol or drug dependencies." He was very matter-of-fact about it. As though there was absolutely no question in his mind that addicts deserved help too.

The computer suite turned out to be a small room with several clunky but clearly serviceable computers in it. Of the three men sitting there, two of them were wearing business suits. Mum's sweater became uncomfortably hot and itchy, and Robin fought the urge to scratch.

Then he realised he knew the man in casual wear. "John! How's it going?"

John glanced up from his screen. He'd shaved, and there was more colour in his face than Robin was used to seeing. "All right, mate—what are you doing here?"

"Just visiting."

"Thinking of volunteering?"

"Um, yes, actually." Robin realised that at some point he *had* started to think seriously about it. "But how are you? Sheppy's Mum said you had a bad cough."

"Been a lot better since I've been in the warm, thank God. Just updating my CV—going to try to get a job."

"That's great!" Robin darted a glance at Dave, who was waiting patiently while he chatted. "Um, I'd better leave you to it, but it's great to see you looking so well."

Dave's running commentary throughout the visit included a shedload of ways Willoughbys could help that Robin had never even thought about, including sponsorship and payroll-giving schemes, and donations of toiletries and kitchen goods for those who'd been helped to find permanent accommodation. By the end of the visit, his head was feeling like it was about to explode and spatter the walls with all the information.

When he got home, skull miraculously still intact, Robin glanced in the mirror. Huh. Mum's sweater *did* make him look a lot like an earnest sixth-former. He pulled it off. Yep, back to midtwenties Robin, although with a suspicion of backwards passage through hedges. He put the sweater on again, and was immediately troubled with a sense of maths homework not satisfactorily completed.

Uncanny.

Robin shook his head and got down to the serious business of working out what to say to Gail in the morning.

Halfway through, Robin's phone *bloop*ed with a text alert.

Archie: *Hi, good day?*

His heart doing surprisingly energetic backflips, Robin texted back quickly, *Yes. Busy,* he added, because he had been, and still was.

Archie: *OK. Come over for dinner?*

Robin *wanted* to. God, he wanted to. But Lyddie would be there, with her placards and maybe with her coconspirators as well. He couldn't face it—not without at least having tried to get Gail to agree to his ideas. *Another time?* he texted back in the end, hoping it didn't look too unenthusiastic.

Archie replied with *No probs,* so he guessed it was okay.

Robin was about to text again, but then he remembered Ethan moaning about him always carrying conversations on too long like a teenage girl who couldn't bear to hang up, so he left it at that.

He didn't want to chase Archie off just when he'd finally got him.

When Robin got into work on Tuesday morning, he marched straight into Gail's office. Gail glanced up from her computer screen with a worryingly haggard look. "Yes?"

When was the last time *she'd* had a day off? Robin cleared his throat and focused on what he was there for. "I've been looking up ways businesses can help the homeless, and I think there's several things Willoughbys could do. We could start by donating unused food from the café to local hostels." Robin paused. Gail didn't seem *un*receptive. She also didn't say anything, so he carried on. "Maybe ex–display bedding and towels and kitchen goods as well. All stuff we can't use anymore, but they can. It wouldn't even cost the store a thing."

"That . . . sounds reasonable. But I'm not sure, with all we've got on at the moment, that now is the time—"

"It's exactly the time!" Robin leaned on her desk to fix her in the eye, desperate to grab her attention. "That ad for Black Friday—bit of a PR disaster, yeah? So this is how we can redeem ourselves. Establish Willoughbys as a force for good in the community."

Gail's whole posture appeared to lift. "That's actually not a bad idea," she said, her tone growing more optimistic with every word.

"And there's plenty of other things we can do." Robin paused. The next bit was probably going to be a harder sell. "Employment initiatives. Helping former homeless people get back on their feet. And making it easier for Willoughbys staff to volunteer with community programs—flexible working, time off, that sort of thing."

She took a deep breath. "Robin, I know you mean well, but in the current economic climate—"

"Okay, forget the stuff that costs money for now. What about starting with food donation?" Robin leaned forward conspiratorially. "We could get the *Echo* to do a report on it. It might even stop that campaign group from demonstrating on Black Friday."

"They're holding a demonstration? What have you heard?" Gail's tone was sharp and shrill.

"Uh . . . I just thought it was something they might do?" Robin lied guiltily. "Possibly. Maybe. Not that I know anything about it really."

"Oh. I see. Yes, I suppose it's a reasonable fear. All credit to you for thinking ahead, and coming up with a means of deflecting it. A demonstration would be very bad publicity for Willoughbys, but your plan sounds like it might work. The directors have always been resistant to charity outreach—they can be a little old-fashioned in their attitudes—but if we stress the PR benefits of it . . ." She stared into space, lost in thought.

Robin was about to politely leave her to it when she suddenly snapped to attention.

"I want you to prepare a presentation."

"Me?"

"Yes. You've been looking into it, so clearly you're the best man for the job. And as you're no longer involved in the planning for Customas—"

Et tu, Gail? Robin thought sourly.

"—you'll have plenty of time."

"Um, will I have to *give* this presentation?"

"It'll be an excellent opportunity for you to make an impression with the directors. I won't be your manager forever, Robin." She stared at nothing again, and her face sagged momentarily.

"Um, are you planning to move on?" Robin asked, because he didn't quite dare to ask her if she was all right. Where on earth was Heath when Robin needed him?

"Who knows what the future will bring?" Gail's tone turned brisk. "Now, I'm sure you have plenty to be getting on with. Come and see me first thing tomorrow with your presentation, and I'll look it over before the lunchtime meeting with the directors."

"Tomorrow?" Robin definitely didn't squeak. "But, um, are you sure they'll be free at such short notice?"

"The meeting's already booked to discuss the worrying situation re Black Friday. Your idea could be exactly what we need." She closed her eyes for a moment, smiled, and opened them again. "I knew I could count on you, Robin. Now, don't let me down."

As votes of confidence went, it wasn't entirely unambiguous.

There was a text from Archie on Robin's phone when he got back to his flat: *See you tonight?*

Huh. In Robin's dreams. He groaned, and texted back quickly, *Soz, got to work*. Accountants did overtime, didn't they? And anyway, he was going to explain it all the next time he saw Archie, so even if it didn't sound quite right, that'd all be cleared up soon.

For now, it was time to grab whatever he could find in his cupboards to stave off the hunger pangs, and get this presentation sorted.

CHAPTER 37

Leaning against the wall just inside his front door, Archie read the text from Robin, and reread it. It didn't look any better the second time. Was Robin avoiding him? That was twice now he'd turned down an invitation, and both times in four words or less. Had one night been enough for him?

Robin hadn't struck him as the type to cut and run, but had Archie read him all wrong? He'd seemed so keen to spend time together, and enthusiastic about steampunk—he'd even changed Jerrick's nappy, for Christ's sake. And Archie could have sworn Robin genuinely liked Lyddie.

But maybe he'd decided it was all too much hassle—the family, the steampunk, whatever. Or maybe it'd been like trying some local speciality or unusual activity on holiday: good enough at the time, but not something you wanted to repeat.

"Everything all right, love?" Lyddie asked. "Did you ask Robin if he's coming over?"

"Uh, yeah. And no. He can't make it. Work." Was it a busy time of year for accountants?

She frowned. "He shouldn't work so hard. He'll waste away. Do you think he's eating properly? I thought we should have proper food tonight too, after all that leftover pizza last night."

Archie forced himself to think about other things than Robin. "Yeah. We should cook. Did you go shopping?"

Lyddie nodded happily. "If there's a vegetable we haven't got now, it's cos the local shops haven't heard of it. Oh, and bacon was on special offer, so I got that too."

"I'll take a look in the fridge, but I'm thinking pasta. That okay?" About to head to the kitchen, Archie was stopped by a knock on the door and a shout of, "Oi, let us in."

He turned to see the fuzzy outline of Bridge's face through the glass in the door, and opened it wide. "Come on in. How's everyone?"

Bridge hefted Jerrick's car seat inside, and Archie took it from her. "Buggered if I know. But I'm fine, and little man's had a good day. Ate all his parsnips tonight, didn't you, darling?" She handed over the nappy bag.

"Got time for a cup of tea, love?" Lyddie asked.

"I wish. Maybe later, yeah? See you after work." She gave Jerrick a wave, and left.

Lyddie hadn't been kidding about buying all the vegetables. Archie was probably going to have to give some of those away. He pulled out mushrooms, leeks, broccoli, and peppers for a quick pasta dish. It was a shame Robin wasn't here to help eat them . . .

Nope. Not going to think about that now. Archie chopped and cooked, adding fresh garlic, passata, and a few herbs.

Robin must just be busy. Right?

CHAPTER 38

Robin was *not* panicking as he walked into the store on Wednesday morning with his laptop under his arm. He had all the information he needed, with statistics to back it up, and his PowerPoint slides were a masterpiece of elegance and readability. Who needed sleep, anyway? Caffeine was a wonderful substitute. Yes, yes, it was.

"Morning!" Heath's obnoxiously hearty voice in his ear made him jump and almost drop his laptop. "Bright-eyed and bushy-tailed, ready for another day of retail servitude?"

"Fine!" Robin coughed and repeated it two octaves lower. "I'm fine."

Azrah elbowed her way around Heath. "Why are you so twitchy? You look like a cat in a haunted house full of cucumbers." Her eyes narrowed. "Or something the cat dragged in. Your Fridge Bloke been keeping you up all night?"

"His name's Archie. And I wish." He'd suffered a pang of regret on seeing Archie's missed call from last night when he'd switched his phone on this morning. Still, there would be plenty of time for that kind of thing once the Willoughbys issues were sorted. "No. I had to work on a presentation for Gail. About helping the homeless."

Azrah's eyes doubled in size. "Gail wants to help the homeless?"

"Hey, she's a very caring lady," Heath put in.

"Actually it was my idea. But she agreed it's got good PR potential."

Azrah humphed. "You kept all this quiet. Normally you'd be all over me begging for help."

"Sometimes a man has to stand on his own two feet," Heath said wisely. "Or use the disability aids of his choosing."

"I, um . . . I thought you had enough on your plate what with Customas." Robin cursed under his breath. Now they'd got *him* saying it. "I didn't want to bother you."

In fact, he'd felt an overwhelming need to put in all the work himself. He wasn't sure why. Maybe this was his penance for not being entirely honest with Archie and Lyddie?

"Never stopped you before," Azrah muttered sourly.

"People change. Mature."

"Like investment bonds." Heath nodded and made an abortive gesture as if to stroke the long white beard he didn't, in fact, have. "And like them, you don't always get back what you put in."

Robin and Azrah shared a look of mutual *WTF?* which seemed to break the tension between them nicely.

"Anyway, I've got to go." Robin patted his laptop. "I'm supposed to get this to Gail first thing." He decided not to mention the meeting with the directors, having a feeling that might upset the apple cart all over again.

His morning was spent in the sort of counter-intuitive time loop he chiefly remembered from school report days, when the hours seemed to flash past with dizzying speed while the minutes managed to crawl along with agonising slowness. It wasn't helped by the caffeine having mostly worked its way out of his system by lunchtime. He'd briefly considered sneaking over to ask Azrah for a can of Coke from her secret stash in the kitchenware storeroom, but if he did that, he might accidentally blab about the meeting. That way madness lay. And the total losing of nerve.

At twelve on the dot, he trotted upstairs to the boardroom, a seldom-used and rather dusty space on the top floor. It seemed to act as a heat-sink for the rest of the store; at least, Robin was sweating into his shirt within five seconds of setting foot inside. Gail was already there, and introduced him to the directors with a nervous air.

The directors weren't just directors. They were the actual store owners, real life descendants of the first Mr. Willoughby. Okay, maybe not the *first* Mr. Willoughby, but the first one to have a store in Hitchworth under his name. Mr. Willoughby and Miss Willoughby, first names apparently redacted. *Mrs.* Willoughby, also a director, wasn't there, but maybe she didn't count, having only married into the family.

They seemed rather dusty too. Both of them were tall and thin. Robin wasn't sure of their ages, but they were definitely older than his parents. Mr. Willoughby had a shock of unexpectedly unruly, wiry grey hair, while Miss Willoughby kept hers ruthlessly subdued in a rocklike chignon. With a jolt Robin realised they were quite good-looking in a way that seemed strangely familiar. They must both have been really striking in their younger years. Assuming they hadn't yet taken on the sour, pinched expressions they sported now.

Gail seemed as twitchy as Robin, which didn't bode well. She'd collared him midmorning to hand back his laptop and tell him in no uncertain terms that he was to stress the benefits of his plan to the *store*, not to the homeless.

Mr. Willoughby looked down his nose at Robin as he was introduced, although it *could* have been because he was wearing bifocals. "So this is the young man with the ideas?" he asked Gail, as if she were a supplier and Robin a line of goods he was considering doing the honour of stocking.

"Yes. Robin was responsible for coming up with the Customas event too."

Finally, recognition! Robin preened.

"*Don't* use that detestable contraction," Miss Willoughby snapped.

Yes, Robin muttered under his breath, although not so deeply under that he didn't get sharp glances from the other three. He cleared his throat and gave his shoes a thorough examination.

"I'm sorry. The Loyal Customers' Christmas Shopping Evening," Gail said appeasingly.

"And now he's come up with a plan to stop the store being dragged through the mud by that ridiculous campaign group?"

"Hopefully, yes." Robin spared a pang for Lyddie on hearing COC described that way. Then again, she *had* named the group.

He ran through his presentation, doing his best to grit his teeth and gloss over the helping-people bit while laying it on thicker than a drag queen's makeup about the PR benefits. The Willoughbys listened quietly, expressions unreadable, while they munched away at a platter of sandwiches as thin and white as they were. Too busy talking to eat, Robin tried to avoid staring at the food and prayed his stomach wouldn't rumble too audibly. By the time he'd finished, he felt as though the layer of grime that filmed the room had detached itself from the walls and adhered to his soul. *It's for a good cause*, he reminded himself, and tried not to think about what the road to hell was paved with.

When he'd finished, the Willoughbys quizzed him on figures, logistics, and actual connections with local homeless shelters. Most of these he was well able to satisfy them on, but when he couldn't, he pulled out his secret weapon: name-dropping all the major and not-so-major, but still highly regarded, businesses that were already doing just what he proposed for Willoughbys.

At the end of it all, Mr. Willoughby sat back in his chair. "It's a good plan. It could well work. And more importantly, it won't cost us anything."

Miss Willoughby huffed. "I do hope this will put paid to that campaign. Have you discovered the identity of the ringleader?"

Robin's heart tried to simultaneously plummet into the basement and leap out through his throat. Did they know about Lyddie? Could they cause trouble for her if they did?

"I'm afraid we've still no idea who it is, or even how seriously we should take this threat of a demonstration," Gail said.

Robin's heart settled back down in his chest and slowed its beat to merely stratospheric speed. "I think we have to take it very seriously," he felt duty bound to say.

"Thank you, Robin," Gail said with a touch of impatience.

"Yes, thank you, Robin," Mr. Willoughby said in a much more flattering tone.

"You don't think it could be . . .?" Miss Willoughby gave her brother a significant look.

His face hardened. "I hope not. Not after all these years."

"But—"

"We'll cross that bridge when we come to it." The silent *And that's the end of the matter* was clearly audible.

Robin had a moment's panic—had he meant bridge or Bridge?—but told himself firmly to stop hearing things that hadn't actually been said. It was probably one of the signs of madness. Did he have hairy palms? No, no, he was fine; they were only sweaty.

"Robin?" Gail said sharply.

"Oh." He cleared his throat. "Sorry. Did I miss something?"

"Mr. Willoughby asked you a question." There was a clear, unspoken, *And your answer had better be good.*

Oh, God, he was doing it again.

"I asked you for your full name."

Okay, he could answer that one. In fact, Gail could have answered that one for him, which might have been helpful in the circumstances. "Robin Christopher."

"Robin . . . Christopher. Oh, dear me." There was a wheezing sound that, Robin realised after a horrified moment, was the old man laughing. At his name.

It was no worse than he'd experienced at school. "If you don't need me anymore, I should probably get back to my department," he said, trying not to let the hurt show.

"Yes, yes. That will be all." Robin was dismissed with a wave of one crepey hand. "Now, we need to get an announcement about this initiative into the paper as soon as possible . . ."

Mr. Willoughby's voice cut off as Robin closed the door behind him.

Great. He'd worked all night, he'd been laughed at, and he'd missed his lunch as well. The elation he knew he should be feeling at having his idea approved seemed to have got lost en route.

At least Gail had been looking happier at the end there.

The adrenaline crash after the meeting with the directors was truly epic. Robin was little more than a zombie with a name tag for the rest of the day. Going home, he nodded off repeatedly on the bus. Luckily his route had plenty of potholes to jolt him awake again, so he didn't miss his stop. He staggered back to his flat in a daze.

But it was done, now. He'd pitched his idea to help the homeless, and it'd been approved. *Finally*, he felt free to get back in touch with Archie. Robin collapsed down on his sofa. He'd have a brief rest, get some food inside him somehow, and text Archie.

Robin closed his eyes and didn't wake up until 6 a.m.

CHAPTER

Archie was glad it was the AETHER visit to the Victorian Market on Thursday evening. He was beginning to worry he was getting the brush-off, and he seriously needed a distraction.

Maybe Robin was snowed under at work? Tax returns were due in soon, so maybe that was it. Yeah, Archie was probably worrying about nothing. Of course, he didn't know if Robin even worked in tax. A lot of accountants just did auditing and accounts and stuff, didn't they? But Robin had said he didn't like talking about his job, so Archie had respected that. He was kind of wishing he knew *something*, though. Apart from the name of his firm, which Archie was *not* going to be all stalkerish and search out online.

Archie was starting to wonder if the benefits of staying off social media really outweighed the disadvantages. If he'd been on one of the popular platforms, he and Robin could have friended each other, and then it wouldn't have been weird Archie checking out what was going on in his life. It didn't seem right, trying to look him up when Robin couldn't do the same to him.

If Robin was on social media. Archie had assumed he was, because wasn't everyone, apart from him? But then wouldn't Robin have asked Archie for his details? Most people did.

He sighed. He'd just have to be happy with what Robin told him. If he ever saw him again . . . So yeah. Steampunk as a distraction. Yay!

The meeting point was at the corner of the market square nearest to the pub. Bridge had suggested they meet *in* the pub, but Perry had politely reminded her how difficult it was to get steampunks *out* of the pub once they'd made themselves comfortable. It also made it easier for people with mobility issues, meaning Nikki, if they didn't have to get themselves into a building only to have to get out of it five minutes later.

Luckily, although it was a cold night, there was no sign of rain and not even much of a breeze. Archie was one of the first to get there, finding Perry and Edith well wrapped up in thick woollen capes. A few others were there as well.

"No plague doctor?" Archie asked when he'd greeted them. "It's not like him to miss an opportunity to go out and alarm the general public."

"He said he had a prior engagement," Perry told him.

"Actually, he *said* he had to lance the boils of some poor dying souls over Leeside way," Edith put in. "But we took that to mean he had a prior engagement."

Archie laughed. "Yeah, let's hope so. Oh, hey, Nikki's here." A taxi had pulled up and Nikki, and her wheelchair, were emerging from it.

It took some time before Nikki had got herself sorted and rolled over to them, bundled up as she was in an immense woolly shawl over her jacket. "I just can't get warm," she said cheerfully, arranging a thick tartan blanket over her legs. "The heating broke down while I was out at the shops, and the house was like the North Pole when I got back. I kept expecting to get mauled by polar bears."

"Anything I can do?" Archie asked, concerned. "I don't know much about boilers, but I could take a look. And I know Bridge's family have a couple of electric heaters you could borrow, because they lent them to us one time."

"Aw, thanks, but no, it's fine. I've got the engineer coming tomorrow, and the neighbours came round with like half a dozen fan heaters to keep me from freezing overnight."

"Okay, but if there's anything, you just let me know, okay?"

"Will do. Thanks. Ooh, here's some more coming." Nikki waved vigorously at several members of AETHER who'd arrived together.

Bridge was next to get there, wrapped up in a long, hooded cloak and the usual wide petticoats, so she looked roughly conical. Archie grinned at her. "Is there going to be room for anyone else in that market with you and your skirts?"

"Oi, there's women in there wearing full crinolines, so don't get judgy on *my* clothing choices."

"Yeah, but I bet they're mostly *behind* the stalls, not walking around between them."

She shrugged. "Eh. Actually these petticoats are a good way of enforcing your personal space. You should try it sometime. Your boy not here? He seemed pretty into the steampunk lifestyle on Sunday."

Archie's smile faded. "He seemed pretty into a lot of things on Sunday."

She stepped closer. "What's happened? You two haven't broken up already, have you? When I saw you Monday night you said it was all going well."

Archie wished he hadn't said anything. "He's just been a bit distant since then. Come on, time to get your smile on." The last stragglers had arrived, and Perry was mustering them for a group photo.

"Fine. But if I find out he's been messing you around, I'll be shopping for a set of antique nutcrackers in there."

After the group photos were done, they trooped into the market en masse, gathering stares that ranged from appreciative to bemused. Willoughbys, Archie couldn't help noticing as they walked past, was all lit up for Christmas, and seemed to be busy with some kind of special event. Taking advantage of the Victorian Market to pull in a few punters, no doubt.

"Ooh, gin!" Bridge cooed, and dragged Archie to the first stall. "Are you doing tastings?"

"I thought you were off the alcohol?" he muttered as the stallholder, dressed in bow tie and boater, poured them a couple of tots of sloe gin.

"Eh. Life's too short. So's my patience. Bottoms up!"

They tasted a total of four gins and gin liqueurs at that stall, and then moved on, Bridge with a bottle of the really sweet stuff for her mum. There was a good crowd at the market, and Archie and Bridge got separated early on. It wasn't easy to keep track of someone when you kept getting distracted by more stuff to look at.

There was a lady Archie recognised as having done a talk at the museum a while back, strolling around in full Dickensian carol-singer getup. She had a basket of bonnets over her arm, and was merrily accosting men, women, and children alike and getting them to try on her wares—often over their own hats, which led to some pretty bizarre selfies.

Archie lifted his top hat to her, and she curtseyed. "Try a bonnet, fine sir?"

"Thank you, but I believe I'm well served in the millinery department." He ended up lending his hat to a lad of about ten, so his dad could get a photo of him in a top hat and his little sister in a bonnet. And then, of course, they had to get a picture of Archie in full splendid.

When he looked around after that, he couldn't see a single member of AETHER, so, feeling a bit lost, he headed to the next gin stall for another tasting.

Archie eventually caught up with Nikki at yet another artisan distiller's, where she was sampling their green tea gin. "Any good?" he asked.

Nikki made a face. "Not really my cuppa. And I swear, if one more person warns me about getting caught drunk in charge of this thing . . ." She slapped the side of her wheelchair.

"It's a classic for a reason. And that reason is that most people don't think before they speak." Archie basked for a moment in the warm glow of the gin he'd drunk. They only gave tiny tots, but once you'd had a few, they added up. "Want to come and help me find a Christmas present for Lyddie? She likes unusual stuff."

Nikki laughed. "Are you suggesting I know all about unusual? Because if so, good."

They made their way through the market—not so easy, when it was this crowded—and stopped at a few stalls. There was one with some witchy crocheted gloves Archie thought Lyddie might like, but he decided to wait until he'd seen all the stalls before buying. And it would've felt disloyal to buy anything crocheted without at least checking if Dora had similar stock in trade.

"Just how many of these stalls are selling gin?" he wondered as they passed yet another distiller's. "No wonder you had to be eighteen to trade here."

"Poor River. D'you think they've managed to convince anyone they're old enough to drink?"

"In a word, no. Although to be fair we don't know if they even *want* to drink."

Nikki shrugged. "True. Oh, let's go and look at the wooden toys. Did I tell you I've got a new nephew?"

They wandered around the market together, dropping in at Dora's to say hi and then dropping back out quickly to leave more room for paying customers. Nikki bought a few things here and there, stashing them in the bag hung on the back of her chair. Archie ended up with a bottle of gin, and started thinking about getting back to that stall at the start before they sold out of the crocheted gloves.

"While we're this end of the market, I really need to pee. It's all that gin." Nikki giggled. "Still, it's been keeping me warm."

"I'll come with you." The public toilets were down a long, dark side street, and he wasn't about to leave her to go on her own.

"You're a proper gentleman, Archie Levine." She rolled herself down the street, progress much faster than it'd been in the market.

When they got there, though, the accessible toilet, in defiance of its name, was locked. A notice helpfully gave instructions for getting hold of the key during working hours.

Nikki's cheerful façade showed the first cracks. "Well, bugger. So outside working hours we're just supposed to cross our legs, are we? Or maybe disabled people are just supposed to stay home in the evenings. Couldn't have us going out. We might enjoy ourselves, and that'd never do."

"This is rubbish." Archie suppressed the urge to give the door a good, hard kick. "It never used to be locked, did it?"

"No. There's progress for you. Looks like it's Willoughbys, then. Good thing it's Thursday. Sorry, Arch, I know you hate that store, but they're the closest place I know around here with an accessible loo."

"Hey, if you've got to pee somewhere, it might as well be on Willoughbys. Think I'll join you, in fact." He wasn't just being gentlemanly. By now he really did need to go, and there was no way he was going to ask Nikki to wait here while he nipped in the gents'.

Nikki laughed and turned her chair around.

CHAPTER 40

As the store was staying open throughout the day and into the evening, Robin didn't have a lot of time to get ready for Customas. There was often a lull after six, but tonight the customers kept on coming, leaving Robin feeling frazzled and rushed by the time he managed to get away from his counter. It was probably down to the Victorian Market giving people another reason to stay in town. Which was good, of course, but exhausting.

Azrah had told him to meet her at the stockroom at half past six. She hadn't been very clear on what for, except that it was to do with setting things up. He still wasn't entirely sure what he was supposed to be doing after that either, but he had a vague idea it involved meeting and greeting, so it couldn't be all that taxing, could it? When asked, Heath had kept tapping his nose in a gesture that got steadily more annoying until Robin had been seriously tempted to borrow a knife from kitchenware and remove either nose or finger or both.

At least, since he hadn't been asked to bring either guitar or ukulele, it couldn't involve him out the front playing jolly Christmas tunes, which had been a bit of a worry, since he didn't know how to play any.

Mind you, having been stopped three times on the way to the stockroom by shoppers wanting help to find clearly signposted departments—once while the customer was actually *standing* in the department they were looking for—Robin was beginning to doubt his ability to keep his customer-service smile intact until the *start* of Customas, let alone the end.

"Finally," Azrah seethed as he rounded the corner into the stockroom at a run. "Customas starts in *fifteen minutes*. Pull your finger out of your whatsit and get this costume on."

Robin skidded to a halt. "This what?"

"Costume." She gave an evil smile. "Surprise! You're going to be *literally* Sales Assistant Robin."

She stepped aside, and Robin's gaze fell on a costume, wrapped in a clear plastic sack, that he'd taken for a bizarre item of stock.

It was worse than Robin's worst nightmares, and he'd had some spectacularly bad dreams in his time. It was *enormous*. And spherical. Whoever had designed it seemed to be under the impression that *E. rubecula*, robin redbreast, was basically a ball with a beak. Covered with fake fur, and with a ridiculous tuft of feathers masquerading as a tail.

"That's not a robin! It looks more like a turkey."

Azrah cackled. "Let's hope no one tries to give you a good stuffing. Nah, from the back, maybe, but from the front you're okay. Turkeys have that long, red neck and the droopy nose thing. This bird's got no neck at all."

"How am I supposed to move in it? How am I even supposed to see out?"

"I don't know, do I? Put it on and have a go." Azrah folded her arms. "But you're never going to get that into one of the changing room cubicles. You'll have to get into it out here."

At least she hadn't suggested he change on the shop floor. "Couldn't I just stay in my normal clothes?"

"If you want to be a total Scrooge, maybe. I'm sure Gail will understand your vanity trumps loyalty to the store, and it won't impact your career in any way, shape, or form."

Robin's shoulders slumped. "How do I get into it?"

"What am I, world expert on costumes? Like a dress, I s'pose. You know. Pull it over your head."

"No, I *don't* know, because I don't make a habit of wearing dresses."

"Well, it's not rocket science." She grinned. "Go on, just stick your head up its bum."

"Oh, come on. There's got to be a zip up the back or something."

"And how's that supposed to work with the tail? Come on, whip it out and we'll have a look, all right?"

Not without difficulty, Robin pulled the monstrous thing out of the plastic sack and turned it over, exposing a large hole in the base.

Great. He really was going to have to stick his head up its bum.

Robin gritted his teeth, took off his jacket, and got down on his knees.

Once he'd clambered inside the robin, he had to be helped to stand. He could barely see out of the eyeholes in the beak, and could only walk with a lumbering waddle.

His arms were of no use to him whatsoever, being wholly contained inside the costume, while his legs, the mirror told him, stuck out the hole in the bottom like spindles in slacks.

Azrah frowned. "Hm. How many birds do you know that wear trousers? They're going to have to go."

"What? I'm not walking around with bare legs!"

"Too right you're not. I can see the headlines now: 'Festive bird arrested for indecent exposure.' No, you're going to need tights."

"You planned this, didn't you? Anything to get me in a pair of tights."

She ignored him. "They'll need to be thick ones—unless you're willing to shave your legs? Or we could get some wax from Cosmetics?"

"Thick tights are fine!"

"Okay, I'll head over to hosiery. Do you want matt or sheer? And are you bothered about fibre content? Cotton rich would be best for comfort and health—you don't want to end up with thrush—"

Someone sniggered, and Robin realised Heath was now in here with them, witnessing his humiliation. With relish. "Sorry, mate. It's just the thought of a robin with thrush. That's like a lobster getting crabs."

"Yeah, intimate health problems are a laugh a minute." Azrah's sarcasm was so thick you could use it to grout tiles. "Look after Robin and I'll be back in a mo."

Robin watched her go, close to despair—and made it all the way there when a subtle *click* alerted him to Heath taking pictures on his mobile phone. "Oi! Stop that. And don't even think about putting it on Instagram."

"Oops." Heath grinned.

Robin sagged against a wall. Or at least, the costume did. No part of Robin was any closer than three feet away, and it was hideously uncomfortable. He straightened again.

"Oi, you've missed a bit," Heath said, helpfully pulling something out of the bag. "Here you go."

It was a pair of red leggings with massive felt flippers on the end. Presumably they were supposed to look like birds' feet. "Oh God."

He'd be lucky if he could walk at all in those. Then again, they weren't actually women's hosiery, so there was that. Robin sighed. "Help me off with this, then? There's no way I can change my trousers with this on."

An uncomfortable, sweaty ten minutes later, Robin was ready to rock and roll. Come to think of it, if he tripped over, rolling would be all he could do.

"Oh. So I ran all the way to hosiery for nothing?" Azrah stood there, her hands on her hips. "And hang about, how's he supposed to hand out mince pies in that? He's got no hands!"

"You'll have to come with me." Robin was going to need her. "I can hardly see where I'm going anyway."

"Great. So now I have to babysit you all evening."

"Well, if you'd rather be *in the costume* . . ."

"Sorry, couldn't hear that. It came out all muffled." She huffed. "Fine. I'll hand out the mince pies; you just stand around, I dunno, radiating good cheer or whatever."

"What's Heath doing?" Given that this humiliating costume was apparently Heath's idea, Robin hoped *he* was doing something, if not equally ridiculous, at least fairly onerous.

"Me? I'm in charge of mulled wine distribution. And general overseeing, of course. Very responsible position. I'd better get back on the shop floor before it all falls apart." Heath loped off.

Robin would've *killed* to be in charge of mulled wine. He'd probably have maimed just to be handing out mince pies in his normal clothes.

"Right, you, stop griping and get a move on. It's showtime."

"Why's Angry Bird here?" a piercing, childish voice whined ten minutes later, as Azrah handed out mince pies with a sugary smile.

Robin tried to angle himself to see where it'd come from, but was worried if he leaned any farther, he'd topple down arse over beak.

"This is Robin Redbreast," Azrah said brightly.

"Why?"

"Because it's Christmas, and Robins are Christmassy." Azrah's tone had dimmed by quite a few lumens.

"Why?"

"Because . . . red. And . . . I don't know." There was a thump on the costume roughly where Robin's left wing should have been. "Robin? Help me out here. Why are robins Christmassy?"

"I think it looks like a turkey," the child said loudly. "Gobble gobble!"

Another joined in. "Gobble gobble! Gobble gobble!" There was a surge of laughter, not all of it childish.

Just as Robin was about to expire from the heat and the humiliation, a woman's voice said firmly, "Come on, kids, we haven't got all night. Don't you want to get to the Victorian Market?"

"Well, *that* was a good start," Azrah muttered sourly.

It didn't get any better. Several children burst into tears at the sight of Robin, for which he couldn't blame them. His back and shoulders began to ache with the force of a thousand fiery suns from the weight of the costume, and his throat was sore from putting on his Jolly Robin Redbreast voice, which was similar to a Santa voice only much, much tweetier. At least it seemed to make him less scary to tots. Also funnier.

Getting laughed at appeared to be his new role in life. Could anything make this evening any worse? Right now fire, floods, and acts of God would have been a distinct improvement.

Robin should have known not to tempt fate like that. He glanced up from a particularly giggly toddler who kept kicking his legs from her pushchair—and looked straight at Archie.

Robin's stomach plummeted so fast he glanced down automatically to check it wasn't lying, egg-like, at his feet, only to realise once again that, in this monstrosity of a costume, he couldn't actually *see* his feet.

Then again, *in this costume*, nobody could see him, could they? Heady relief made him feel, for a moment, as if the transformation into avian form were complete and he was flying. He was safe—safe from the utter disaster of being recognised.

But what if Archie recognised Azrah? Robin prayed that (a) Archie would prove to have some form of face-blindness and (b) she wouldn't give the game away. Archie'd only met her once, for an hour in the pub over a week ago—she wasn't *that* memorable, was she?

No, no, Robin was safe, just as long as Azrah thought to pretend she was a customer they'd be fine.

But what was Archie doing here? He'd said he never came into the store. Robin was starting to feel rather hard done by; if you couldn't trust what your boyfriend told you . . .

"Heath, why are you making faces at me?" Azrah said. Heath was there? Oh God. Robin turned his beak to locate him. Yes, yes, he was. Archie was going to recognise them, wasn't he? Even if you were the worst person in the world at recognising faces, the combo of Heath and Azrah was bound to ring a bell or two. "Is there something behind— Oh shit."

There was a pregnant pause.

"Um, hi, Archie. Fancy seeing you here. Nice top hat, by the way. Makes you look very Artful Todger. I mean Dodger." Azrah was clearly shooting for bright and breezy. She missed it by a couple of light-years.

Then Heath's voice rang in his ears like a portent of doom. "All right, mate? Hey, get a load of our Robin, here. That was my idea, that was. Geddit? Robin, dressed as a robin?" He cackled.

Archie's eyes widened.

Somewhere in the infinity of parallel universes, there must be a version of Robin who, having made a variety of different choices, hadn't ended up in this position, and was even now being fatally mown down by a double-decker bus.

Some bastards had all the luck.

CHAPTER  41

Archie stared. He'd finished in the gents' and had been hanging around near the entrance, waiting for Nikki, when he'd seen the giant robin, accompanied by a petite female figure wearing a familiar trouser suit and a slightly less familiar pair of reindeer antlers.

Azrah? She'd had her back turned, but Archie was pretty sure it was her. He wandered over to say hi. Just as he got there and was able to confirm that yes, it was Robin's mate Azrah, Robin's other mate Heath—and there was no mistaking him—popped up bearing a steaming jug and a stack of disposable cups. His eyes widened when he saw Archie.

Archie knew, even before Heath spoke, who the robin must be. This was *his* Robin. Robin, who'd said he was an accountant. Dressed as a giant festive bird and handing out mince pies to shoppers.

In *Willoughbys*.

No wonder he hadn't wanted to talk about his work.

"I thought you were accountants, not shop workers," Archie said slowly. The buzz from the gin had faded, leaving him unpleasantly sober.

Heath gave him an assessing look. "Would you buy that we're moonlighting here for some extra Christmas cash?"

"*Are* you?" Archie glared the giant bird right in the beak. He could just see part of Robin's face in there, his eyes wide and guilty.

Robin seemed to shrink further into his costume, like a tortoise pulling in its limbs in the face of a threat. "Not . . . as such."

"You lied to me. You lied to *Lyddie*."

"I'm sorry! I panicked, okay, and then it all kind of snowballed. I didn't mean—"

"You lied, and you kept on lying. Were you ever going to tell us the truth?"

"I'm sorry," Robin said again, hanging his beak.

"Sorry doesn't cut it," Archie said harshly. When was he ever going to learn? Men were bastards. They'd been bastards to Lyddie, and now he was carrying on the fine old family tradition of getting shafted by someone he lo— someone he'd trusted.

Robin squawked something unintelligible and waddled off, his beak down low and his ridiculous tuft of tail feathers waggling sadly behind him.

Archie closed his eyes for a long moment, but when he opened them again, Azrah was still there. "You *all* work here?"

She put her hands on her hips. "Well, yeah. We're colleagues, like we said."

"Totally," Heath put in. "We didn't lie about *everything*."

Archie winced. "And that's supposed to make me feel better?"

Azrah cocked her head. "Kinda?"

"Sorta?" was Heath's contribution.

"Not doing a great job right now, I can tell you." Archie folded his arms.

Azrah looked shiftily away, then rallied. "Anyway, *you* told Robin you never shop here, so where's your bloody moral high ground now, huh?"

"I'm not shopping. I'm in here because one of my friends needed a wheelchair-accessible loo, and the public one's locked."

"Oh." Azrah seemed to struggle with herself. "I could get you a mince pie?"

"Mulled wine?" Heath offered.

"No, thanks. I'll be leaving as soon as my friend's back." He turned away, then spun back to face her. "Did you *know* about COC?"

"About— Oh, your campaign." A steely glint entered Azrah's eye. "Yes, about that. Cheers for doing your best to lose us all our jobs. Especially at Christmas. Really appreciate that."

It was Lyddie's campaign, not Archie's, but he didn't want to talk to Azrah anymore. All he wanted was to get far, far away. "Maybe you should pay more attention to the kind of employer you're working for," was all he said before walking off.

Luckily Nikki was rolling towards him. Her eyes widened as she met his gaze. Archie wondered what she saw. Tight-lipped and silent, he held the door open for her and followed her outside.

"What's up, Arch?" she said urgently once it'd closed behind them. "Are you banned from there, is that it?"

It startled him out of his anger. "What? No."

"Then what is it? You've never said why you hate that place."

It wasn't quite true—he'd only mentioned that Lyddie disliked the store—but, well, there was no reason for her to remember everything he said, was there? "I . . . It's turned out someone's not who I thought they were, that's all."

"Shall I get Bridge?"

Archie gazed over the crowds, tempted to say yes. Not the done thing, though; crying on your ex's shoulder over your latest love. "Think I'm heading home. Are you going to be all right?"

"Course. I didn't have *that* much gin. I can see Perry and Edith over there, anyway. You won't be leaving me on my own." She clasped his arm for a moment. "I'm sorry about your person, whoever it was."

"Yeah," Archie said, his voice harsh. "I'm sorry too."

CHAPTER

Robin was getting on quite nicely with his nervous breakdown, thank you very much, when Azrah found him slumped in the stockroom in his work shirt and bird leggings. The body of his festive costume rolled listlessly at his feet like the Ghost of Christmas Utterly Fucked.

"Well, that went a bit tits up," she said by way of comfort. "I did *say* you shouldn't have lied about your job."

"No, you didn't."

"Okay, so I should have. Hindsight's a bitch."

Robin hid his face in his arms. "He hates me now, doesn't he?"

"He didn't actually *say* so. But he did bugger off pretty quickly. Then again, you'd already beaten the land speed record on buggering off. You know your fight-or-flight reflex? I'm fairly sure it's not supposed to be stuck on flight *all* the time."

"Would you *rather* we'd fought? That'd really put Willoughbys on the map, that would. I can see the headlines: 'Steampunk and Robin in Festive Fisticuffs.'"

"Yeah, probably not what Gail was hoping for." Azrah crouched beside him. "Want me to make Heath wear the costume for the rest of the evening?"

Robin shook his head. "No. It's fine. Just . . . give me a moment, okay?"

She nodded and stood. "I'll be back in five minutes to give you a hand. If anyone asks, you're on a pee break."

"Cheers, Azrah," Robin said hollowly.

"Only an hour to go, then we can get paralytic on what's left of the mulled wine," she said, and left.

There wasn't, as it turned out, anything left of the mulled wine, but the Millstone was mercifully close and there was still an hour until closing time. The barmaid, whose T-shirt tonight said, *Todger Dodger*, gave Robin a sympathetic smile and a free packet of ready salted, so he was guessing he looked almost as bad as he felt.

"Do you think I should call him?" he asked his friends for the ninety-fifth time. Probably. He kept hoping for an answer that would miraculously mend his shattered relationship, and so what if the previous ninety-four tries hadn't worked? It wasn't like there was anything else he could bear to talk about.

"No," said Azrah, her patience audibly wearing thin. It was probably the lack of alcohol, Robin decided muzzily.

"Give it some time, mate," Heath's voice was enviably calm, and *he'd* had almost as much to drink as Robin had. "Let him cool down a bit."

"But he hates me now. I can't have him hating me." It *hurt*, a physical pain like a hot, lead weight in the pit of Robin's stomach. "I can't believe you told him it was me," he whinged to Heath for the seventy-eighth time.

"Told you, mate. He knew. The game wasn't just up, it was menacing satellites. The pitch was queer as a new fifty pound note. Your festive bird, my friend, had been roasted, carved, and served up on an artisanal chopping board with a dollop of homemade chutney."

Azrah threw her head down on her arms with a groan. "Do you even *speak* English?"

"Your only hope," Heath went on, ignoring her to jab a bony finger in Robin's face, "was to plead guilty as charged and throw yourself on the mercy of the court."

"Yeah." Azrah snorted. "Shame you bottled it and did a runner."

"I was going to tell him everything," Robin said plaintively.

"You were? When?" Azrah didn't sound convinced.

"I was! Last night. But I fell asleep."

"Well, what did you do that for, you numpty?"

"I was tired! I stayed up all night working before my meeting with the directors."

There was a long silence.

"What meeting?" Azrah snapped.

"What directors?" Heath asked, leaning forward to fix Robin with a tipsy eye.

"It's . . . complicated."

"No worries." Heath pulled out a pen from his breast pocket, and grabbed a beer mat. "You can draw us a diagram."

"It's not *that* complicated. Look, it was just a . . . a thing, okay? The directors were coming in anyway to talk about COC—" Robin glared at Azrah until she'd stopped snickering "—so when I went to Gail with my suggestion, she told me to present it to them."

"Huh. So when you told us you were brown-nosing Gail, you were *actually* brown-nosing the Willoughbys themselves?"

"There was no brown-nosing! It wasn't about me, or them, or anything. It was about helping the homeless. And about stopping Willoughbys—the store, not the people—from becoming a byword for 'socially irresponsible.' You know, looking after all our jobs?"

Heath nodded and raised an unsteady glass. "Hero of the hour. Man of the match."

Robin flushed with a sort of prickly pleasure. Then he sighed, and slumped back down in his seat. "Not according to Archie, I'm not."

When he got home, Robin poured himself a pint glass of water, had a brief internal debate over whether he *deserved* to avoid a hangover tomorrow, told himself he owed it to the customers, and drank it. Then he collapsed into bed and closed his eyes.

Three seconds later he opened them again, and checked his phone. Just in case he'd missed a text from Archie. He didn't care if it was an angry text—Archie had every right to be angry with him. But at least . . . at least it'd mean Archie hadn't cut Robin out of his life completely.

But there was nothing.

CHAPTER  43

A rchie made his way home. There was a hollow ache in his chest, worse than that time when he'd been sleeping rough and he'd got back to his patch to find the council had cleared away his stuff and taken it to the tip. And now he was going to have to tell Lyddie what Robin had done. There she was in the living room, happily filling in a crossword in the paper—she never looked at the clues, she reckoned it was more fun to put any old words in and try to get them to fit—and he had to go in and ruin her night.

And he had to tell her tonight, because otherwise she'd be bumping into Robin accidentally-on-purpose and inviting him round the house again, and Archie . . . just couldn't.

"Love?" was all she said when he walked in the room. His face must have tipped her off he wasn't bringing good news.

"Hey." His voice came out rough. "Come and sit with me on the sofa?"

Lyddie nodded and scrambled to her feet, but instead of moving to the sofa, she came to wrap her arms around him where he stood.

Archie's eyes pricked. It was stupid—he was twenty-eight years old and a father himself, and he still wanted his mum to make it all better. He let her hold him for a few more moments, then pulled away. Best to get this over with. "Uh, I found out something about Robin tonight."

She made a face. "Not gonna like it, am I? What's he done?"

"Lied. To me and to you." Archie drew in a shaky breath. "He works for Willoughbys."

"Oh, love." She held him tight again and muttered, "Bastard," into his chest.

"I went in the store this evening—Nikki needed the loo. And there he was. With his mates, who'd gone along with it. Made up a load of . . . of rubbish about the place they worked."

"Why would they even do that? You don't think it was all a . . . a ruse, do you? Robin making nice with both of us. You don't think *they* sent him, do you? To keep an eye on us, find out what we were up to?" Lyddie looked more scared than he'd seen her in years.

If Robin had walked in the door right now, Archie would've been hard put not to punch him in his lying mouth. But . . . "No. No, I can't believe that of him."

He couldn't.

Could he?

Later that evening, Archie was numbly drinking a cup of cocoa Lyddie had made him, when she spoke up, her voice small. "Archie, love? I've been thinking, and . . . maybe it was my fault Robin lied?"

"How could it possibly have been your fault?"

"No, listen—I mean, he walks in our living room, and there's my placards and stuff staring him in the face. He probably didn't want to cause a fuss. And then he had to stick with it, didn't he? Couldn't change his story after that." She gave him a long look. "Don't tell me you've never been there, cos I certainly have."

"He still shouldn't have lied to us and kept on lying."

"Sometimes you've gotta lie. When the world shits all over you—"

"You hadn't done anything to him! You invited him in and offered him cake."

Her shoulders hunched up. "Yeah, but he didn't know me, did he? I could have been any weird old bat."

"Oi, no calling yourself that. And . . . Robin's not like us. He's never had to worry about a roof over his head, about social services . . ."

"Maybe, but from what you've told me about his mum and dad, it's not been all beer and skittles there. Bet you he's had times when he was too scared to tell the truth to them."

"I guess, but . . ." Archie screwed up his face. "He's a grown man now. Living on his own. Free to make his own choices."

She gave a bitter laugh. "Never goes away, though, does it?"

Archie took a deep breath. "No. No, it doesn't."

"So maybe he's not as bad as you think he is. Maybe he'll call you. Or pop round. Apologise. Tell you why he did it, and . . ." Lyddie looked around blankly.

"Maybe." Archie couldn't help remembering how Robin had basically just walked off and left him.

"If he does, will you listen? Archie, love, I know he did what he did. But maybe you're taking it a little too hard? You were so *happy* with him. He's a good lad at heart, I know he is. And we've all done stuff we wish we hadn't, that we wouldn't want anyone to find out about. Especially not people we love."

Archie hugged her. He'd always known she'd made a few bad choices in her time. But trust her to think about other people before herself. "Look, I'll listen, if it'll make you happy. *If* he comes to me with an apology."

Archie wasn't going to make any promises about how he'd act after he'd listened, though. Robin had lied and kept on lying—and he'd known full well how Archie and Lyddie felt about Willoughbys. Christ, no wonder he'd kept trying to make excuses for the place when they'd talked about that ad. Archie had even admired him for it—thinking he was simply trying to see the good in everyone.

When he'd just been trying to cover up the bad in himself.

CHAPTER 44

Robin was glad of his work, in the next few days, even though everyone was busy and on edge about the upcoming Black Friday sale. It gave him something to take his mind off the grey, leaden feeling in his soul. There had been no word from Archie, and Robin hadn't quite dared to get in touch. Heath was still urging him to give it time—Robin was beginning to suspect he was thinking along geological timescales—and Azrah vacillated between telling him he'd blown it and going on about how he and Archie were clearly incompatible anyway.

Which they *weren't*. They'd been like gin and tonic. Goggles and hats. Cogs and . . . well, anything a steampunk happened to have about their person, really.

He wished he knew what Archie was *really* upset about. Okay, he knew only too well, but . . . was it that he'd lied, or that he'd turned out to be working for the enemy? If it was that he'd lied, all he could do would be to grovel abjectly and promise never to do it again. And hope that Archie would be able to begin to trust him once more.

If it was his job, Robin didn't see how he could make it any better while continuing to work there. And if he *stopped* working there, little things like rent and food would rapidly become an issue. No way was he moving back to Mum and Dad's. Maybe Heath had a sofa he could kip on for a bit?

Robin was beginning to get a glimmer of just how ordinary people might end up homeless.

The thing was, Robin didn't want to give up his job. Okay, there were things about it he wasn't so keen on, but he *liked* serving people, most of the time. He liked chatting with customers, helping them find what they were looking for, and making suggestions when they didn't have a clue. And . . . Archie couldn't *really* expect him to give that up, could he?

So the only thing was to make Willoughbys not be the enemy anymore. Hopefully the helping-the-homeless initiative would be a good start in that direction. Maybe Archie would read about it in the paper and realise Robin wasn't so bad after all?

If Robin got mentioned in the article, which might not even happen. They might just announce the plans and not give him any credit at all. In fact, that was the most likely outcome. Mr. Willoughby hadn't seemed like the sort to give credit to underlings. Especially underlings whose name he found ridiculous. Which was fair enough. Robin had always thought it was pretty ridiculous. When he'd been young, Mum had sent him to Sunday School to get him out of the house—somehow she'd swung it, despite her and Dad never going to services—and he'd daydreamed of being named Steven, which was a perfectly sensible name that would never have got people thinking he was a girl. Plus it had the added advantage that he could have abbreviated it as St. Christopher, who'd always been depicted as a very manly sort in their bibles and workbooks.

Robin had torn one of those pictures carefully out of his workbook and stuck it on the wall by his bed, but it'd mysteriously disappeared the next day. With hindsight, Mum had probably had a fair idea he was gay long before Robin himself had.

But *anyway*, the point was, whether or not Robin got any credit, at least Willoughbys would look better, so Robin would hopefully look . . . less worse?

Heath's advice to give it time and wait until the news got out about Robin's plan for Willoughbys to help the homeless became harder and harder to follow as the week dragged on. Robin's flat, which despite its grotty location and cheap furnishings, he'd come to love as a symbol of independence and a haven from pressure, seemed now bare and depressing. It needed an Archie in it.

Robin ended up volunteering to go into work on Saturday *and* Sunday just to get out of the place. Fortunately the extra seasonal staff hired had proved as unreliable as usual. Robin honestly didn't know how Willoughbys picked them.

Every time he got off the bus from town, he felt the urge to turn down Verne Avenue, go to Archie's house, and say he was so, so sorry. But he couldn't face Archie looking at him like that again. As if he'd stomped on his dog and kicked his hopes and dreams in the teeth. As if he'd promised him roses, and given him chlamydia.

And he couldn't face Lyddie looking at him like that either.

He'd failed them both.

At least Gail seemed happier now. She'd actually smiled at Robin when he'd bumped into her the other day, which was all kinds of unnerving. And the customers helped cheer Robin up. Many of them were elderly retired people who had plenty of time for a chat, and it was hard to wallow in despair while being flirted with shamelessly by an octogenarian.

Robin spent a lot of time rearranging his stock in preparation for the Black Friday sale. Willoughbys' own brand cotton Y-fronts were going to be half price on Friday, although Robin couldn't help thinking it was a waste of time. Who was ever tempted in the door of a shop by the prospect of a pound or two off their skivvies? It was big-ticket items that got the punters in. No, if *he'd* been in charge of pricing for the sale, he'd have gone for designer label goods exclusively. And no knickers. Well, maybe boxer briefs at a pinch. Modern, flattering, *and* supportive. You couldn't go wrong with a pair of boxer briefs.

Except he probably could. He could go wrong with *anything*. Robin let out another heartfelt groan.

"Are you all right, dear?" an old lady asked. "You don't sound very well."

Robin pasted on the ghastly smile he'd been wearing since Customas. "I'm fine, thank you! How can I help you?"

"I'm looking for Y-fronts for my Ted. The store's own brand ones. Everything seems to have been moved around."

Ted was presumably the husband. Although Robin brightened a few moments by imagining Y-fronts on a teddy bear. "Er, yes, we're getting ready for the Black Friday sale."

She shook her head. "It's a funny old business, this, having sales before Christmas. You don't know where you are."

Robin found himself nodding along.

"Will there be any savings in this department, then, or are they all going to be on tellies and electricals? Where we're both on our pensions, we have to be careful. I suppose I could just go down to the market—people tell me things are ever so cheap there—but we've been shopping at Willoughbys for years, and it doesn't do to let your standards drop, does it?"

"Can't argue with that." Robin lowered his voice—they'd been told to keep quiet about sale items until the double-page ad appeared in this week's *Echo*, so as not to put people off shopping before then. "I shouldn't say, but those Y-fronts are going to be half price on Friday. Do you think your Ted can hold out to the end of the week?"

"Oh, I should say so." She beamed up at him. "He won't be getting them until Christmas anyway."

Lucky Ted, Robin thought, having received a fair few similarly disappointing presents in his time. Then he mentally slapped his own wrists. Maybe Ted wanted nothing more than a few pairs of spanking new undies for Christmas. He lowered his voice even further, bending close to the lady to compensate. "I could put some by for you if you like. Just in case there's a rush on them. What size is Ted?"

"XXL," she said. "It's all the telly. Would six pairs be too many? Only he does go through them."

"Not in the least," Robin said quickly, in case she decided to elaborate. "Enjoy the rest of your day, and I'll see you on Friday."

Thursday morning, Robin's copy of the *Echo* still hadn't come, so he popped into a newsagent on the way to work to buy a copy. He wasn't sure he'd quite believe in Willoughbys going through with the plan to help out homeless people until he'd seen it in black-and-white. Plus, until the paper came out, there was no chance *Archie* would see it in black-and-white.

Trouble was, he couldn't see the *Echo* on any of the shelves.

"Have you got the *Hitchworth Echo*, please?" he asked the lady behind the counter, who was humming along happily to the Bhangra music playing in the shop.

"No, dear. They have a problem with the printing this week. They think maybe Friday they will be out."

"That's too late!" Robin blurted and clapped a hand over his mouth, horrified. This was going to ruin *everything*.

If the paper wasn't out, Archie and Lyddie wouldn't see the announcement about Willoughbys helping the homeless, so there would be no reason for the COC demonstration to be called off. Which would be bad for Willoughbys and therefore for the continued employment prospects of the staff.

Plus, Archie would still hate him. If the article came out *after* the protest, it'd look like damage limitation, wouldn't it? Robin winced at the thought. He hadn't realised how much he'd been pinning his hopes on Archie seeing the article and deciding Robin wasn't so bad after all.

No one ever un-dumped their boyfriend over a PR stunt, did they?

But at the end of the day, the homeless shelters were still going to get their help. Assuming the Willoughbys hadn't backed out of the deal, in which case . . .

No. Robin had enough to worry about without hypotheticals. Right. What was certain?

What was certain was that he needed to make sure Gail knew about the *Echo*'s nonappearance. She probably wouldn't shoot the messenger, given how weirdly good-moody she'd been lately. Yes. First thing today, he'd—

Robin's train of thought was derailed by a loud throat-clearing behind him.

"Are you all right, dear?" the lady behind the counter asked. "Only you've been standing there for ages. If you don't want anything, I'd like to serve the customers behind you."

Robin flushed. "Sorry," he said, and scuttled out.

Gail was in her office, sipping at a travel cup of what smelled like coffee. It had pictures of fluffy llamas on it. Robin had never seen her as a fluffy llama person, but apparently he'd been wrong.

He broke the news about the *Echo* to her very, very gently, and then braced for impact.

She shrugged and put down the llamas. "These things happen."

Robin stared at her. "Uh . . . aren't you worried that no one will have seen the double-page ad for the sale?"

"It's a shame they won't know about the bargains, but it isn't the only advert we've run for the sale, as you well know."

"And what about hoping to stop the demonstration?"

She stood up. "Really, Robin, I understand your concern for the store and it does you credit, believe me. But there's no point getting stressed about issues we can't do anything to change. Now, if you'll excuse me, I need to go down to Electronics. Just to check they're all ready for tomorrow. I'm sure you've got your department well in hand." She smiled, picked up the llamas once more, and sauntered off.

Robin realised his mouth was hanging open, and shut it with a snap.

Maybe she'd taken up meditation? Or smoking weed?

He walked slowly back to Menswear, the message *404: Error: Reality not found* ringing through his baffled brain.

On his way back from the bus stop that night, Robin agonised over whether he should knock on Archie's door and tell him and Lyddie what they should have read in the paper, if it'd managed to get printed. It might still stop the demonstration tomorrow . . .

Except, without the report in the *Echo*, what reason would they have to believe him?

Robin certainly hadn't given them any reason to.

He trudged on back to his lonely flat and barely mustered up the energy to pour a bowl of cornflakes for his tea.

CHAPTER  45

Lyddie was up early on Black Friday morning—COC members were planning to get into position with their placards well before Willoughbys opened for business.

"Are you sure you want to do this?" Archie couldn't help worrying. "I don't want you getting in trouble with the police."

Lyddie rolled her eyes. "We're not going to be breaking any laws. There's freedom of speech in this country, or hadn't you noticed?"

"Yeah, but laws can be twisted. You know that. And you know what *they're* capable of too."

"Oh, love. You're a grown man now. No one's going to take you away from me."

No, but they might try and take you away from me. Archie couldn't say it. And . . . it'd be okay, wouldn't it? Lyddie was in a much better place than she'd been ten or fifteen years ago. Not vulnerable, like she'd been back then. And it was only going to be a peaceful demonstration. "You'll make sure you don't do anything they could get you for, won't you? Stay outside the shop, and don't get in people's way."

"I have been on demonstrations before, you know."

"You've been arrested before too." Released without charge, thank God, but it'd been a worrying time.

"So I've learned my lesson. We're just going to stand there with our placards and hand out flyers. Maybe have a chant or two to keep it interesting. No breach of the peace, no blocking the public highway, and no harassment. No, sir!" She saluted him.

Archie laughed. "But do you honestly think one little protest is going to make a difference to the way they do things?"

Lyddie squeezed his arm. "I want to make a statement, that's all. Let them know they can't keep on doing what they want and not caring for anyone but themselves. Not without consequences."

"And you won't try and stop the staff going into work?"

"No. Although there's one of them I might have to give a piece of my mind if I see him. You've not heard from him, have you?"

Archie shook his head. "I really thought—" He broke off at the sound of a car horn from outside. "Is that your ride?"

"'Spect so. Do you want to come in with us? We could drop you off in town," Lyddie called over her shoulder as she ran to open the door. "Course, we're picking up two more on the way."

Archie took a look outside. Lyddie's ride was a Mini Cooper that already had one passenger, without Lyddie and her placards. "Thanks, but as I'd have to sit on the roof, I think I'll get the bus as usual."

He helped her get the placards into the car, then she gave him a quick kiss, slid into her seat, and they were off. Archie checked his watch as he went back into the house. Still the best part of an hour before he had to leave. Time for a cup of tea.

On his way out again, Archie almost trod on a newspaper that'd come through the door sometime after Lyddie left. Huh. The *Hitchworth Echo* was back to its usual schedule—only two days late. He'd never known it to be delivered this early in the morning, though. He picked it up. He might as well have something to read on the bus—or to hide behind, if Robin got on the same one.

So far, they'd managed to avoid bumping into each other, but it had to happen eventually.

Turned out he was spared the pain of an encounter this morning as well. Of course, it was Black Friday, wasn't it? Robin had probably gone into work early to prepare. Maybe he was even now putting on some other daft costume, although what was appropriate for Black Friday, Archie wasn't sure. A turkey? They could just reuse the robin for that.

His gut twisted. That'd been the worst night of Archie's life, at least since he'd been back living with Lyddie and her bloody parents had agreed to leave them alone. They'd both had nightmares for ages about her being dragged off again.

Maybe he should swing by Willoughbys on the way to work. Make sure there wasn't any trouble brewing. The school visit wasn't until ten, after all. And okay, so he'd been planning to use the time until then to prepare his talk, but he'd simply have to wing it. It'd be okay.

Lyddie might not be.

As he flicked through the *Echo* to distract himself, a headline caught his eye: *WILLOUGHBYS TO HELP THE HOMELESS.* Incredulous, he read on.

Independent department store Willoughbys, a much-loved fixture in Hitchworth since 1863, has announced a major initiative to help the homeless of the town. The store plans to donate food and bedding to local shelters. According to Gail Winters, the store manager, "The plan will not only help more vulnerable members of the community, it'll reduce waste and help the environment. Far too much good food is thrown away, when it could go to those in need. From now on, all surplus food from our café will be donated to local shelters." According to Ms. Winters, the idea is the brainchild of Robin Christopher (sic), a member of staff on a graduate fast-track. "Robin's always been keen to bring positive benefits to the community, and Willoughbys is delighted to be part of this endeavour. We've always felt our status as an independent department store means a greater connection to the people we serve than can be the case with a centrally run chain store."

Dave Endicott from The Anchorage, a homeless shelter on Queen Street, welcomes the initiative. "When Robin came to us with his idea, I was immediately on board with it. It's great to see a young person, one who's never experienced the hardship of homelessness, engaging with those less fortunate and wanting to do some good for them."

Robin himself was unfortunately unavailable for comment, but a colleague assured us he's "over the moon and away with the stars" that Willoughbys will be implementing his idea.

Archie stared at the paper, unseeing and scarcely believing what he'd read. Could this really be the same guy who'd lied to him and Lyddie? Who was literally working for the enemy? Archie hadn't even truly expected to get an apology—much less what looked like an attempt to make amends.

But why hadn't Robin *said* something to him? What was the point of making a big gesture like this and then keeping quiet about it? If it'd been Bridge in Robin's shoes, she'd have marched into Archie's house with a *So what? Actions speak louder than words* and rubbed his nose right in it, and basically told him to take her back, if that was what she wanted.

Robin wasn't like that, though, was he? He didn't throw things in your face. He just left them where you might pass by, and let you look at them or not as you chose.

Archie closed his eyes. He missed Robin fiercely, painfully. For days, he'd been telling himself Robin wasn't who he'd thought he was—and now to find out he might not have been totally wrong about him after all . . . He wanted to go and find Robin right this instant. Have it all out with him, in the middle of Willoughbys' Black Friday sale—

Oh God. The sale. The protest. He had to stop Lyddie. He couldn't let her go ahead with the demo without knowing all the facts. What if she came face-to-face with Robin, and gave him that piece of her mind? She'd feel terrible about it when she found out what he'd done. Lyddie hated it when people were attacked undeservedly. And by then, it might be too late for them ever to get back on good terms again.

How would Robin react, having made a mistake—okay, more than a mistake, but still—and tried to fix things, only to get a kick in the teeth for his trouble? He'd probably decide being with Archie wasn't worth the pain, that was how. Archie swallowed. He still wasn't sure how he felt about Robin—but to slam the door on any chance of reconciliation? He couldn't let that happen. For Robin's sake, for Lyddie's sake—and Christ, for his own.

Maybe one of the other campaign members would've seen the paper? But if everyone had had their copy delivered this morning, chances were they'd all left before it'd arrived. Archie pulled out his phone to call Lyddie, but it went to voice mail, so he sent off a quick text, hoping against hope she hadn't left her phone at home again. If only he had a number for anyone else in the group.

He'd stayed out of it, trying not to encourage Lyddie, figuring that the more people who got involved the more enthusiastic she'd get—and the greater the crash when it all came to nothing. Because people like that didn't change.

And now, it seemed, they had. Because of Robin.

CHAPTER 46

Black Friday morning, Robin snagged a copy of the paper from the shop on the corner of his street, relieved it'd gone to press at last. It went against the grain, paying for the *Echo* when there would be, in all likelihood, a free copy waiting on his doormat when he got back home, but he just couldn't wait that long.

He flicked through until he found the article on Willoughbys' plans to help the homeless. It was on page four, just before the double-page advert for the sale, which Robin really hoped people got to see this morning, or the Black Friday sale was going to be the dampest of all squibs. He read the article, then read it again. And again for good measure.

Warmth flooded through him. It was far more than he'd hoped for, name-checking him several times and making it clear that the plans were Robin's idea. If Gail had been there right then, Robin might have been tempted to kiss her, so it was probably just as well she wasn't.

But would it be enough? Would *Archie* think he'd done enough? Robin crossed his fingers, bought another copy of the *Echo*, and heart in mouth lest he be seen, made his way to Verne Avenue and stealthily slipped it through Archie and Lyddie's letterbox. Then he ran for the bus.

He needn't have worried—he got in so early, he was actually at Willoughbys before Gail and had to hang around for her to come along and open up. Luckily Sheppy's Mum was huddled in a doorway across the square from the store, so he had someone to chat to. "Thought you were heading somewhere quieter for a bit?" he asked, giving Sheppy a pat.

"Was going to. Thought I'd stick around and see the fun." She gave a rare smile.

Robin bit his tongue on a comment that *fun* wasn't exactly how he'd describe it. "Want anything from the shop? Either of you?"

She shook her head. "We're okay. John came round and gave me some food for Sheppy last night. Told me what you done for the hostel too. You're a good lad."

Robin flushed. "Depends who you ask. Right, I'm just going to get a sandwich. Skipped breakfast to get in early. Sure you don't want anything?"

He couldn't help noticing, as he made his way to the shop, that Gail's envisioned queues of people in sleeping bags hadn't materialised.

By the time Robin return ed with his sausage, egg, and bacon butty, he wasn't surprised to see that Gail had finally appeared outside Willoughbys. "Oops—boss is here. Looks like I'm not going to have time to eat this. Do you think you could use it?"

"Aw, cheers, love." Sheppy's Mum smiled as she held out a tattooed hand.

Not without a pang—he really hadn't had breakfast—Robin handed over his sandwich and headed across the square. Gail looked . . . strangely relaxed. And Heath was with her.

Had Robin been right about the weed? Had Heath been going back to his old-school gardening habits? Having lived, in many ways, a sheltered life, even at uni, Robin wasn't entirely sure what weed smelled like, but he still gave a surreptitious sniff when he reached them.

"Good morning, Robin." Gail peered at him closely. "I hope you're not coming down with a cold?"

Apparently not *that* surreptitious. "Er, no, I'm fine. Probably early hay fever."

"In November?"

"Pine allergy," Heath said sagely. "Makes people allergic to Christmas. Terrible affliction. You should eat more honey."

"I . . . will," Robin said instead of asking for an explanation. It was unlikely to make him any less confused. "Um, shame about the paper being late this week."

"Oh, well. These things happen." Gail smiled and turned to go, Heath still eerily by her side.

Robin stared, then scrambled after her. "Gail, can I have a minute? I wanted to thank you for the newspaper article. For naming me in it, I mean. Or, um, do I need to thank Mr. Willoughby? He did make a point of finding out my full name."

Gail snorted. Robin wasn't sure he'd ever known her do that before. "I wouldn't bother Mr. Willoughby with your thanks. I doubt he'd know what you were talking about. No, in fact, Heath was very persuasive on your behalf," she added, a pink tinge colouring her cheek.

Heath winked at him.

Robin blinked, but decided that if there was something going on there, he *really* didn't want to know about it. Not least for plausible deniability if Azrah asked. He didn't *think* she had romantic designs on Heath, but then again, as recent events had proved, Robin was a total moron when it came to romance and shouldn't aspire to have an opinion on anything ever again.

"Um, well, thank you." He tried to address them equally, leaving them to share the gratitude among themselves as appropriate.

"Anytime, my friend, anytime. Virtue should be rewarded. Credit where credit's due. Names changed only to protect the innocent."

Gail turned to Heath with what looked very nearly like a laugh on her lips.

Robin shook his head. The day had barely started, and already it was *totally* surreal.

CHAPTER  47

When Archie got to Willoughbys, there was no protest group in sight. There was, however, a small queue of customers standing in a patient line, waiting for the store to open. Archie checked the time. The doors should be opening any minute now.

But where was Lyddie? Where was the rest of her group? He checked his phone. Yes—he'd missed a text from her: *wat a turnup gon 2 caff.*

She didn't specify *which* café they'd gone to, but it wasn't hard to spot the neat stack of upside-down placards outside Has Beans, the vegan place on the other side of the market square.

Passing Sheppy's Mum on the way, Archie stopped to say hi. "Hey, did you see what happened with the demonstration?"

She pointed in the direction of the café. "Think the revolution's been cancelled."

"Huh." It wasn't very informative, but he could get the story from Lyddie. "Thanks. You need anything?"

"I'm good. Robin got me this." She held up a still-wrapped breakfast sandwich.

Archie stared. "Robin?"

"From Willoughbys. He's always been good to me and Sheppy. John likes him. And he's come up with this scheme to help the hostel. 'S in the paper." She paused. "Nice lad. Think you'd like him."

"I . . . think you might be right. Uh, I've got to go. You stay safe, yeah?" Archie gave her a wave, and headed for Has Beans, his head spinning.

Robin knew Sheppy's Mum and John? Had always been good to them?

That meant this scheme he'd come up with to help the homeless wasn't just a flash in the pan.

Robin *cared*. Had always cared, even when he'd been lying about his job.

Lyddie had been right. The lies hadn't been cynical, they'd been self-preservation. Robin hadn't been riding roughshod over Archie's ideals. He'd embraced them.

Archie suddenly wanted very much to embrace Robin in turn.

As he walked through the café door, Archie could see Lyddie sitting in the corner, with about half of COC. He guessed the rest of them either hadn't turned up or had already gone back to their normal daily routine. Lyddie caught his eye and beamed. "Archie, love! Have you seen the *Echo*? Your boy done good."

Your boy. Archie's chest felt oddly tight at the thought. "Yeah, that's why I'm here, to make sure you saw it."

"We were just setting up when this tall ginge from the shop brought over a copy to show us. Didn't I tell you he's a sweet boy?"

Archie assumed the last bit was about Robin, not Heath. It had to be Heath who'd brought the paper over, right? He must have realised who they were, and set out to check they'd heard the news.

"It's definitely a victory for the campaign," Shirley-from-down-the-road boomed. "We had them running scared."

"That we did, love, that we did." Lyddie stood up. "So I was thinking, Archie, maybe it's time we went shopping?"

"You mean . . . I thought you'd taken a solemn vow not to set foot inside that store?"

"Oh, vows are made to be broken. And when did I ever do anything solemn in my life? Well, come on, then." She grabbed his arm. "Cheers for taking care of those placards, Shirl. I'll see you all later, yeah?"

As they neared Willoughbys, a taxi stopped outside and an elderly man got out. Archie didn't pay him any attention at first, but then Lyddie's grip on his arm tightened painfully.

She was staring straight at the man, who was frowning down at her—and all at once Archie realised who it was. Even before the old guy took in a sharp breath, and let it out with a censorious, "Lydia."

"Hello, Daddy," Lyddie said, her chin up and a tremble in her voice Archie was pretty sure nobody could hear but him.

Christ. Archie hadn't seen his grandfather in well over a decade, and then for no longer than he could avoid. He found himself standing up straighter without consciously deciding to.

Those hooded eyes flashed to him. "Mars."

"It's Archie, now." Not that Archie wanted to be on familiar terms with the git, but if anyone got to use the name Lyddie had given him, it wasn't going to be the bastard who'd left her to fend for herself as a pregnant teen—and then had her locked up when she had trouble coping. "Or you can call me Mr. Levine."

"At least *you're* looking more respectable these days." His grandfather's gaze flickered over Archie for an instant, who experienced a brief but intense urge to go home, shave off his moustache, and spike his hair up like he'd used to.

The cold eyes returned to Lyddie. "I might have known you'd turn up on an important day like this. I suppose you were behind those letters, were you? Empty threats. I knew it."

There had been more than one letter? Archie wondered who'd delivered the others. One of the other members of COC, most likely. Unless dear old Grandad was exaggerating to make Lyddie look worse, which Archie wouldn't put past him in the least.

"Empty threats?" Lyddie stepped forward. "Oh, no. We came ready to cause a scene. I can show you a placard if you like. I can tell you where to shove it and all."

He stiffened and opened his mouth, but she hadn't finished.

"Lucky for you, not everyone who works for you is a cold-hearted bastard. And I'm not one to make a fuss when people are trying their best to help. You'd better make sure you keep your promises, though. That's all I'm saying. Wouldn't look good for the store if I went to those journalists from the *Echo* with all the stories I could tell, now would it?"

"Lyddie . . ." Archie tugged at her arm. She could get into trouble for making threats.

"It's all right, love. I think I'd like to go and peruse the wares in this fine emporium. If you don't mind?" She gave her father a fierce glare, and he backed off a pace. "Come along, Archie."

She put her arm through his, and they marched past her father and into the store, heads held high.

Archie wanted to punch the air, but he restrained himself, and just whispered, "You were fantastic," in Lyddie's ear.

She burst out in a peal of laughter. "Oh my God, did you see his face? Stuffy old git. I hope Robin's plan costs him lots of money."

"We're not *actually* shopping here, are we?" Archie asked in a low tone.

"I should bloody think not. I wouldn't give him a penny."

"So what are we—"

"Going to find Robin, of course! Do you know which department he works in? Oh, well, we can ask someone. Everyone's going to know your Robin, aren't they? Him being in the papers and all. 'Scuse me," she yelled to a woman behind the perfume counter who was already besieged by customers. Archie winced at the sudden increase in volume. "We're looking for Robin? Lovely lad, wears nice shoes. He's my Archie's boyfriend."

The perfume woman stared and clearly decided giving Lyddie what she wanted would be the best way to get her to move on and stop shouting. "Menswear," she said, and pointed to the back of the store.

"Thank you! Ooh, don't get that one, love," Lyddie added to a middle-aged man waiting in line with a box of top-brand perfume whose name Archie vaguely recognised. "My grannie used to wear it. Made her smell like a horse's arse. After it'd been eating flowers, mind, but still. Horse's arse. Try the one in the shocking pink wrap, that's much nicer."

"Er . . . thanks?" The man hopped from foot to foot, clearly caught between the twin evils of staying to talk to Lyddie and losing his place in the queue.

"*Lyddie*," Archie chided with a grin and swept her onwards. "Let people make their own mistakes."

"There's a woman in his life who'll be thanking me, come Christmas."

"He might have been buying it for a man. Or himself."

"If it's for him, *everyone* in his life will be thanking me. Ooh, we're here, aren't we? Menswear. Can you see him?"

Archie stopped. Now he was here, about to see Robin again, his palms were feeling uncomfortably moist. What was he going to say?

What would *Robin* say? It had better include an apology to Lyddie. She hadn't deserved to be lied to. He looked around until he spotted Robin's blond head, the rest of him hidden by a crowd of customers. "Okay, so I'm thinking, coming to see the guy at work on the busiest day of the year might not have been the *best* plan."

Robin seemed to be even more snowed-under than the perfume lady. His customers were a lot older than hers, and mostly female. They were all clutching packets of . . . Y-fronts? Huh. Well, you couldn't beat an old lady for an eye for a bargain. And underwear was a traditional Christmas gift for a man, or so he'd heard. Lyddie had never bought him underpants for Christmas—she said they were way too boring—but she had once bought him six pairs of rainbow-coloured toe socks.

"Oh, they won't mind. Go on and give him a kiss!" Lyddie seemed to have forgotten the lies already. "They'll love it."

Archie gave her a sidelong look. "Because old folk *never* have old-fashioned views about same-sex relationships."

"If they do, they're wrong, so who gives a toss?"

"Robin, maybe?" Archie would have laid money on Robin being unable to hear them over the hubbub, but at the very moment he said his name, Robin glanced up from his customer and their eyes met.

Archie's heart clenched at the raw, naked *hope* he saw in Robin's gaze. Without even thinking, he took a step forward, then another. "Excuse me, ladies," he said to the grannies in his way. "I need to talk to Robin."

Miraculously, they melted out of his way. He barely registered mutterings of *There's a proper young gentleman* and *Did you see his moustache?* as he stepped up to the counter, and tried to tune out the lady who said something like *I wonder if it's the only thing that's long and stiff?* and then cackled loudly. "Hey," he said, when he got to the counter, his heart pounding.

"Hey." Robin swallowed.

There was a heavy pause. Even the old ladies seemed to be holding their breath. The lone man started to say, "Excuse me, but—" and was roundly shushed.

"So, I, uh, I saw the paper," Archie managed to get out.

"Me too. Um, I mean—" Robin's face was a little pink, and he was twisting a packet of Y-fronts in his hands. "I'm sorry!" he blurted. "For . . . you know."

There was an *Oooh* from the ladies, overshadowed by a loud, "What did he say? What's he sorry for?" that was shushed as ruthlessly as the guy had been.

The counter between them ought to vanish, Archie thought vaguely. It ought to shimmer into nothing, and then he'd be able to take Robin in his arms. "It's . . . it's okay," he said instead. "I mean, I'm still not happy about . . . But what you did was, well." *Great, Archie. Really eloquent.*

"Nobody speaks clearly anymore," the old lady from before grumbled, and was shushed again.

Lyddie was saying in a proud stage whisper, "That's my son, Archie. Him and his bloke had a bit of a spat, but they're all right now." Then she shouted, "Go on, give him a kiss!"

Robin looked briefly scandalised. Then his face firmed, and he hopped up to sit on the counter. "Can I?" he asked Archie breathlessly. "I mean, are we . . .?"

Yes. Yes, they totally were. Somehow all the rottenness that had cankered Archie's soul for the past week crumbled away, leaving his heart fresh, clean, and fit to burst. He took Robin's face in his hands, and kissed him. Robin's mouth was soft and yielding, and tasted sweeter than Archie could ever have imagined.

There was a general *Awww*, marred only by a loud, "Well, I think it's rather exhibitionist if you ask me, but then nobody ever does these days. And we never *did* find out what he was sorry for." It sounded like the last bit was what had really got her goat.

"Excuse me," the man from before said in a long-suffering tone. "But can I pay for those pants before you turn them into dishrags?"

Robin froze and broke from the kiss to look down at his left hand which, yes, was still clutching a now extremely crumpled pack of Y-fronts. Archie couldn't help it. He burst out laughing, and was swiftly joined by an adorably dishevelled Robin.

"I'm so sorry," Robin gasped, as he slipped back off the counter to stand behind it once again. "I'll get you another pack."

The man shook his head. "Don't worry, it'll all come out in the wash."

Robin rang up the sale, smiling like it was Christmas already. Archie was pretty sure they made a matched pair.

"I'll see you after work?" Archie said, because he couldn't stand here all day grinning at his boyfriend. No matter how much he might like to.

"Meet in the Millstone and then go to yours?" Robin gave him a sheepish glance. "Can't promise not to fall asleep if it carries on like this."

"Sounds good. Uh, not the falling asleep bit. Although that'd be good too."

The nearest old lady elbowed past Archie. "Stop being spoony and sell me these pants, will you? He'll keep, but the rest of us may not."

Archie feasted his eyes on Robin a moment longer, and left to a chorus of *Speak for yourself* and at least one *I'll keep him for you*.

Lyddie was waiting for him, chatting with the male customer who looked worryingly smitten. Archie took her arm. Best get her out of there before she offered to iron the guy's undies. "Come on, we need to get you on a bus. Unless your lift's hung around? And then I need to get to work."

"If you need a ride, I'm parked in the car park," the man said hopefully. He was a bit older than Lyddie, and soft around the edges with a hint of middle-aged spread. His collar was turned up on one side, and he'd missed a bit shaving.

Lyddie gave him a smile. "That's lovely of you, but my Archie's always told me not to get into cars with strange men."

"Oh—right. Better give you my card, then." The man rummaged in a pocket and pulled out a card case. Opening it, he dropped several on the shop floor.

Lyddie squatted down to pick them up. "All right, Colin Cotton, Freelance IT services. Maybe I'll give you a call."

He flushed bright red. "That'd . . . that'd be lovely."

She linked her arm in Archie's once more, and swept him out of the department in aristocratic fashion. Halfway through perfumes, she giggled. "Cotton. Like his Y-fronts."

"And that is the last time you're seeing them," Archie said sternly.

"That's what you think. I'll make my own mind up whose knickers I'm going to see."

Archie groaned. "I can't believe you're seriously considering dating a man who wears Y-fronts." Time for some intensive internet stalking of Mr. Cotton. But the guy looked like a decent sort.

Or maybe Archie was just in a mood to believe the best of everyone. Yeah, that could be it.

CHAPTER 48

The rest of Black Friday passed in a blur of customers, cash, and credit cards. The menswear department sold completely out of store-brand Y-fronts, and Robin had to resort to all his most cunning sales tactics to persuade disappointed customers to buy the more expensive boxer briefs. He resolutely didn't feel guilty. He was doing them and their loved ones a service, wasn't he?

Lunch was a wolfed-down sandwich, and he barely got to speak to Azrah or find out how the other departments had been doing. Heath wandered past during the afternoon and told him there had been a run on stockings and aviator shades were flying out of the store, but Robin was fairly sure that was just a windup.

Gail wasn't much in evidence, which was surprising. Robin had thought she'd be keeping a stern eye on proceedings. Or at least, a serene, drugged-up eye. Still, if *he'd* had a nice little office to escape to from all the mayhem, he'd probably have been tempted to use it too.

It was a weary crew of Robin, Heath, and Azrah who trooped down to the Millstone after closing time. Robin wasn't entirely certain why the other two were there—he'd made a point of telling them he was going to meet Archie—but in the end he was glad they'd tagged along, as Archie wasn't there.

Robin ruthlessly squished any worries that dared to raise their heads above the parapet of his heart. Archie would *not* have had second thoughts during the day. Nevertheless, he pulled out his phone.

They all slumped against the bar. "So where's this bloke of yours?" Azrah asked as Robin checked his messages. "Hasn't had second thoughts, has he?"

Robin hoped this telepathy of hers wasn't going to be an ongoing thing. It could be all kinds of embarrassing. "No. He's texted. He's going to be a bit late. Something about 'unrly kidz'?"

"Ah, well," Heath nodded gnomically. "It's an ill wind that gathers no moss. Got a couple of things to get off my chest."

Robin gave him a tired look. "Oh?"

Azrah narrowed her eyes. "I knew it. You're shagging the boss, aren't you?"

Robin winced. "*Please* tell me you mean Gail and not Mr. Willoughby."

"One rum and Coke, one Diet Coke, and a pint of Old Peculier, cheers," Heath said to the barmaid, who turned to get the drinks before Robin's eyes could focus on tonight's T-shirt. "And no, I wasn't about to tell you I'm shagging the boss. It's about Archie."

Azrah's eyes were like saucers. "You're shagging *Archie*?"

"Oi!" Robin didn't feel that was a subject that should be joked about.

She had been joking, right?

"Shagging? No. Strictly a ladies' man here. But me and Archie are . . . kinda closer than I've let on. Friends, you might say."

Robin frowned. "But how come he didn't tell me that?"

"Because he—oh salty winter's child—didn't know. Cheers." The barmaid had returned with their drinks, and accepted Heath's twenty-pound note with a smile. "Bottoms up and the last one to drink is a bargain-bin reject."

"Hang on." Robin clutched his drink like the only sure thing in an uncertain world. "How could he not know you're friends?"

"Because I . . ." Heath drew himself up to his full height, and there was a long pause, presumably for dramatic effect. It might have worked if Robin had been anything other than too exhausted to care. ". . . am the plague doctor."

Robin blinked. Okay, he hadn't expected *that*. "Hang on, what about 'I've seen him lots of times'?" And they'd met at the convivial, and Heath hadn't let on. That was deception, that was. Almost like lying, and . . . and Robin didn't have a leg to stand on there, so he wisely shut up.

"Well, I have, ain't I?" Heath winked and took a sip of his pint.

"Yeah, but you didn't mention it was *in the mirror*." Robin gulped down half his rum and Coke in one.

Azrah glared. "So how come Archie didn't recognise you?"

Heath gave her a pitying look. Robin pitied her too, but in his case it was because she had to deal with all this without benefit of alcohol. He gave her a withering look instead. "Have you *seen* what a plague doctor wears? You wouldn't recognise your own mother under that getup."

"What about the way you speak, then? Or did you only communicate in mime or interpretive dance or something?"

Heath smirked and perched on a barstool before declaiming in a voice several tones lower and umpteen social classes higher than his usual, "This pestilence, sir, is sent upon us by God, a judgement for your wicked ways." He slumped back down into his usual hunchbacked prawn shape. "Wodger think?"

Robin shook his head. "I think if you talk like that all the time when you're being steampunk you must get a terrible sore throat. And why is it *my* wicked ways that have brought down the wrath of God? Sounds a bit homophobic if you ask me."

"I was thinking more of you lying to your boyfriend's mum, but who knows with the big dude in the sky? Or dudess, naturally. I was reading how they've proved angels don't have gender, but the jury's still out on the boss."

"How can anyone *prove* angels don't have . . . never mind. Archie's here." Robin beamed.

Nothing else was of any importance whatsoever.

CHAPTER

Robin looked tired, but his face lit up when their eyes met. Archie found himself grinning back as he joined them at the bar, sliding his arms around Robin from behind and craning his neck so they could kiss. The barmaid gave them a wink.

"Busy day?" Archie murmured.

"Don't even ask. How was yours? With the *unrly kidz*?"

Archie laughed. "It was . . . a day. And this particular school only visits once a year, thank God. It's the teachers I feel sorry for."

"Hear you caused quite a scene in Menswear this morning," Azrah said archly.

Robin grinned. "You're just mad cos you missed it."

"And this," Heath put in, "is why the good Lord gave us CCTV."

"We don't have CCTV *inside* the store, do we? Do we?" Robin sounded genuinely worried.

"Never mind that, what's *she* doing here?" Azrah hissed.

Archie turned to see a slim, white woman in her midthirties making her way over to the bar. She was wearing a businesslike skirt suit, but she'd swapped the heels for a pair of bright Converse.

"Gail!" Robin hopped off his barstool and out of Archie's arms as though he felt the need to stand to attention. "Um, this is my boyfriend, Archie? Er, Gail's our manager."

"But not for much longer." She smiled and slipped an arm around Heath.

Robin and Azrah goggled.

Archie wondered if it was what she'd said that'd stunned them, or what she'd done.

"I'll be making an announcement on Monday, but I've handed in my notice. I'll be leaving in the New Year. So there will be a vacancy for manager." Gail gave a pointed look at Robin, then smiled up at Heath, who gave her a peck on the nose.

"That's, um . . . We'll be sorry to see you go?" The questioning tone was all too clear in Robin's voice, and he winced as though he knew it.

Heath jumped in. "Gail's officially free of cancer as of yesterday, so me and her, we're off around the world to celebrate."

"You've had cancer?" Robin stared at her. "I'm so sorry— I should have realised— I mean, I thought you were just stressed . . ."

Trust him to feel it was a personal failing he hadn't known. Archie moved to get his arms around him once more.

Gail patted her hair. "I must admit, I thought everyone knew. What with the wig . . ."

"That's a wig?" If Azrah's eyebrows flew any higher, they could have a nifty sideline delivering Amazon packages.

"Oh, ye of little observational skills." Heath shook his head sadly. "Although it's true she rocks it. You *go*, girl. Rrr."

"Shall we go and grab that table?" Gail said, slipping coyly out from Heath's arms and striding over to where a group of women were leaving.

Azrah grabbed Heath's arm as he made to follow. "You said you weren't shagging the boss!" she snapped in a low voice.

"No, I said I wasn't about to *tell* you I was shagging the boss. Thought I'd wait until Her Magnificent Authoritativeness got here." Heath cocked his head. "And making assumptions, much? How do you know she's not shagging me?" With that, he loped off to join Gail.

"Too much information," Robin blurted out, grabbing Archie's hand. "Um, I think we need to go? To be back on time for Bridge and Jerrick?"

"Oh, fine," Azrah snarled. "Just leave me to be all green and hairy, why don't you?"

Robin froze. "Uh . . . you're not upset about Heath and Gail, are you?"

She rolled her eyes. "What did I tell you about him?"

"I thought maybe you were protesting too much?"

"No, I was protesting exactly the right amount. Because that's what people *do*." Her face turned speculative. "I s'pose if nothing else I should be able to get the goss on how they got together. *And* what they've been up to in Gail's office. Go on, sod off then, you two."

Robin let go of Archie's hand and gave her a hug. "I'm glad you're okay with it."

She mock-shuddered. "Ugh. Go maul your boyfriend, will you?"

Smiling, Archie grabbed Robin's hand back and let his boyfriend lead him out of the pub.

Half an hour later they were walking back from the bus stop hand in hand, cocooned in darkness, the evening air cold but still around them. There were few people on the street. Everyone else was at home getting their tea ready, Archie reckoned.

It was the first time he and Robin had been alone together since the morning. No, since the night after the convivial. Crazy. They'd been broken up, and now they were back together, all without a single conversation in private.

Was it possible to sort out relationship issues properly with the eyes of the world upon them? If Archie knew one thing, it was that they needed to be honest with each other. Could anyone be totally honest with an audience?

Maybe Robin's thoughts were running along the same lines. "I really am sorry I lied to you," he said, squeezing Archie's hand almost painfully. "I just . . . Look, I know *now* your mum's totally not scary, but there were all these placards everywhere, and she had a knife—for the cake, but I didn't know that—and I panicked? And then it kind of snowballed."

"Yeah, Lyddie reckoned that was what had happened. It's okay. I . . ." Archie took a deep breath. "All the bad stuff that happened to her years ago, I never got to make anyone pay for that, you know? So I think maybe sometimes I overreact to anyone who doesn't do right by her now."

"Yeah. I get that. I mean, I don't blame you. She . . . she's very quick to forgive, isn't she?"

Archie nodded. "Yeah. Way quicker than me. But it's not always a good thing."

"No . . . I get that too."

"Although I'm pretty glad she's not holding a grudge against you." Archie gave Robin's hand a final squeeze, then let go so he could put his arm around him. "Or it'd be awkward taking you round for dinner tonight."

Robin melted into the hug, an arm slipping around Archie's waist. "I feel so bad about the whole Jones and Gunn thing."

"Gunn Jones," Archie reminded him with a laugh.

"Oh God. I'm not making excuses, but it was Heath who came up with the whole backstory, you know? He was scarily into it. I guess it's not surprising. Did *you* know he was the plague doctor? Or do I mean the plague doctor was Heath, from your point of view?"

"Huh." Archie almost missed a step. It was lucky he had Robin's arm around his waist to hold him steady. "He is? I definitely feel like I *should* have known."

Robin sighed. "That's pretty much my default state of mind these days."

Archie ran a finger around his collar. "Uh . . . there's probably a couple of things I ought to tell you, now I know who you're really working for. And that's not a dig, by the way."

"Is it to do with shagging? Because I don't think I can cope with any more shagging-related revelations tonight."

Archie tightened his grip on Robin's shoulder. "All the shagging happened a long, long time ago, don't worry. It's about Lyddie. Her mum and dad, who she cut ties with after they treated her badly? They're actually your ultimate bosses. The Willoughbys."

"Oh. *Ohhh.* So *that's* why she was so quick to get angry with them over the ad?" Robin frowned. "But your name's Levine."

"Yeah, Lyddie changed her name legally once she was eighteen. *Levine* came from an old great-aunt who'd been nice to her. And yeah, I'm pretty sure it was a factor in COC."

"No wonder you were so mad with me when you found out. Um. I'm probably going to have to start looking for another job, aren't I?" Robin eyed the pavement with a fatalistic air, as though a trip was inevitable.

"Don't be daft. Just when you've got a shot at manager? Not gonna lie, it's a weird situation, you working for my . . . Lyddie's mum and dad, but I'm not about to let you shoot your career in the foot over it. And who knows? Maybe you'll be able to get the old git to behave even more like an actual human being in the future."

"Yeah . . . I'm sure there's something about not going into relationships with unrealistic expectations." Robin huffed a laugh. "So maybe it's just as well you've already seen the worst of me."

Archie wasn't about to let that one go. He stopped walking and pulled Robin around to face him. "Maybe, but I've seen the best of you too. I'm really proud of you for getting Willoughbys to do something for the wider community at last." He pulled Robin into his arms and held him tight.

Robin smiled, his blond hair glowing in the lamplight. His eyes turned coy. "If I get a cuddle for that, what do I get for telling you I've signed up to do some volunteering?"

"This," Archie said, his heart swelling, and kissed him. Robin kissed back eagerly, and they pressed together in the dim light. God, it was good to finally have Robin to himself again. Archie could almost wish it was Robin's flat they were heading to, instead of an evening with Jerrick and Lyddie—but only almost. They'd have plenty of time for the other stuff later.

He was fully prepared for catcalls and comments—he wasn't naïve, and he knew what this neighbourhood could be like—but wonder of wonders, if anyone passed by while they were kissing, they kept their opinions to themselves.

When they broke apart again, Robin's eyes were shining. "I can't believe I've got you back. Um, I have got you back, haven't I?"

Archie laughed. "Well, if you want any more proof, I think we'd better get off the street before we're had up for public indecency. Come on. Lyddie and Jerrick will be looking forward to seeing you."

"You know, it's funny," Robin said as they walked on, hand in hand once more. "Heath and Gail. He always acts like he wants a woman to take charge, but I get the feeling he just wants someone to care for."

"Yeah. It's a common problem, needing to take care of someone." Archie squeezed Robin's hand as they walked the last few yards home.

Bridge's little car was parked up outside the house—as was a car Archie hadn't seen before. "Hey, looks like they're here early. Wonder whose the Volvo is?"

"If it's your granddad, I may be searching for a new job after all," Robin said darkly.

"You think he'd fire you for going out with me?" He might, at that, but Archie hoped not.

"No, I think he'd fire me for what I'd say to him if I found him upsetting Lyddie."

Archie pulled Robin in close. He couldn't seem to stop doing that tonight. "You're a keeper, Robin Christopher, you know that?"

"Always thought of myself as more of a Seeker, but who knows?" Robin smiled at him, then turned more serious. "I've been thinking about Lyddie, and her mum and dad, and how she cut them right out of her life for what they did to her. It's . . . Okay, my parents are, well . . ."

Archie could think of a few choice words to say about them from the effect they'd clearly had on their son, but it was up to Robin, not him. "Go on."

"Look, I'm not saying I'm thinking of doing that with my mum and dad. Not seeing them anymore, I mean. I'm not saying I even *want* to do that. It's just . . . knowing the option's there makes it easier, you know? So, um, thanks."

"What, for being Lyddie's son?" Archie stroked his hair. It was softer than it looked. "Not sure I deserve the credit, but I'll take it anyway. I'm glad it helps."

"Yeah. It does. Um, we seem to be at the door, so . . ."

"Time for a quick snog before we face the family?"

"Oh God, yes." Robin's lips found his, and they kissed deeply. *Now* Archie felt like he was home. Hands roamed places they probably shouldn't, and heat was rising between them.

They broke the kiss and rested their foreheads together for a moment, breathing hard.

"I'm looking forward to getting you on your own again," Archie said, in the understatement of the millennium.

"So much. Oops—sorry." Robin reached up to smooth Archie's moustache. "Don't want Lyddie thinking I'm too rough with you."

Archie grinned. "You're fine with Lyddie. She loves you."

"Really?"

"Yep. It's Bridge you've got to worry about."

He laughed at Robin's panic-stricken expression, and unlocked the door.

They walked in to find Bridge in the kitchen, putting the kettle on. She groaned when she saw them. "I suppose you're going to want tea too? I do have a shift to work in ten minutes, you know."

"You're a star," Archie said, and meant it. "Any chance of a biccy?" he added, because he was a git.

Bridge turned to Robin with a long-suffering sigh. "You might want to get your boyfriend out of here before I get creative with a teaspoon and a kettle full of boiling water."

"Actually, it's kind of tempting to stay here and watch . . ." Robin grinned as Archie dragged him off towards the living room.

Inside, Lyddie was sitting on the floor playing peek-a-boo with Jerrick, who was giggling fit to burst. And on the sofa with Archie's laptop on his lap was Mr. Cotton Y-fronts, frowning at the screen.

"Archie, love! And Robin, bless you. Come on in. More the merrier. Say hi to Colin— Oh, you know him already, don't you, Archie? He's come round to fix that problem with your laptop. Wasn't that good of him?"

Colin glanced up, his face pink and cheerful. His collar was still turned up on one side, and now he was sitting down, Archie could see he had odd socks on. "Soon get it sorted, not to worry."

"That's . . . very good of you. Sorting out *that problem*." Which, as it existed only in Lyddie's imagination, would probably take him quite a while to locate. Archie sent her a mock glare.

She giggled, and Jerrick joined in.

"She's . . . really not shy about inviting people round, is she?" Robin whispered. His tone was admiring, not censorious.

Archie put an arm around his waist and pulled him close, his heart full. Even if he hadn't felt the way he did about Robin, he'd have had to love him for how he was with Lyddie.

"Yeah, she gets all sorts coming round, but you know what? Sometimes it turns out for the best."

Dear Reader,

Thank you for reading JL Merrow's *Counter Culture*!

We know your time is precious and you have many, many entertainment options, so it means a lot that you've chosen to spend your time reading. We really hope you enjoyed it.

We'd be honored if you'd consider posting a review—good or bad—on sites like **Amazon, Barnes & Noble, Kobo, Goodreads, Twitter, Facebook, Tumblr,** and your blog or website. We'd also be honored if you told your friends and family about this book. Word of mouth is a book's lifeblood!

For more information on upcoming releases, author interviews, blog tours, contests, giveaways, and more, please sign up for our weekly, spam-free newsletter and visit us around the web:

Newsletter: riptidepublishing.com/newsletter
Twitter: twitter.com/RiptideBooks
Facebook: facebook.com/RiptidePublishing
Goodreads: tinyurl.com/RiptideOnGoodreads
Tumblr: riptidepublishing.tumblr.com

Thank you so much for Reading the Rainbow!

RiptidePublishing.com

ACKNOWLEDGEMENTS

With thanks to Lillian Francis, Elin Gregory, Kristin Matherly, and all the many splendid steampunks I've been privileged to encounter over the last couple of years.

No familiars were harmed in the making of this story, although some might have been flung.

ALSO BY
JL MERROW

ABOUT THE AUTHOR

JL Merrow is that rare beast, an English person who refuses to drink tea. She read Natural Sciences at Cambridge, where she learned many things, chief amongst which was that she never wanted to see the inside of a lab ever again. Her one regret is that she never mastered the ability of punting one-handed whilst holding a glass of champagne.

She writes across genres, with a preference for contemporary gay romance and mysteries, and is frequently accused of humour. Her novel *Slam!* won the 2013 Rainbow Award for Best LGBT Romantic Comedy, and her novella *Muscling Through* and novel *Relief Valve* were both EPIC Awards finalists.

JL Merrow is a member of the Romantic Novelists' Association, Crime Writers Association, International Thriller Writers, Verulam Writers and the UK GLBTQ Fiction Meet organising team.

Find JL Merrow on Twitter as @jlmerrow, and on Facebook at facebook.com/jl.merrow

For a full list of books available, see: jlmerrow.com or JL Merrow's Amazon author page: viewauthor.at/JLMerrow

Enjoy more stories like
Counter Culture
at RiptidePublishing.com!

Apple Polisher	*Blank Spaces*
This straight-A student has a dirty little secret.	Absence is as crucial as presence.
ISBN: 978-1-62649-035-2	ISBN: 978-1-62649-484-8

CPSIA information can be obtained
at www.ICGtesting.com
Printed in the USA
LVHW031908221019
634989LV00004B/642/P